SMOKE AND LIGHT

SMOKE AND LIGHT

KRISTIN ARDIS

VALENCIA PRESS

Hardcover ISBN 979-8-9887333-1-7
Paperback ISBN 979-8-9887333-0-0
Ebook ISBN 979-8-9887333-2-4

Cover Design by Saint Jupiter Graphics.
Hardcover Case Design by Kristin Ardis.
Edited by Renee Dugan.
Map by Rachael Ward, Cartography Bird.

This book is typeset in EB Garamond 11pt.

First edition, March 2024.
10 9 8 7 6 5 4 3 2

VALENCIA PRESS
Indianapolis, Indiana, USA

www.kristinardisbooks.com

To anyone who's ever forgotten who they are,
and to the ones who help them find their way home.

And to the one who carried me home
in one of my hardest seasons.
It's you and me.

ELDORYN RIVER
ALASÉ
LAKE DHAMARLI
WHISTLEVEYN PRISON
NÉFELI
HAIZEA
OZRHYN
CORODEN
AURANDEN
MYRAGIN
AZMARYN MOUNTAINS
INNA RIVER
TESRYN

MONAVAO SEA
THE
DIAMOND
KINGDOMS
OF VEYHAAN
TOWNS
VILLAGES
PRISONS
GHALDALENE SEA
BRANTON
ISKRALEYN
LYRADNÉ
INNA RIVER
PRIMAVEY
ORVEYIN FOREST
FYRTH
THE WALLS
ISIRADEN FOREST
ANLUAN
INNARISA
THARHYNDE
LYARAN FOREST
CAMDEN
KILHELM PRISON
AMADHÉ RIVER
ONATÉ
MARSILAYNE
PANRA
LUSHANÉ SEA

1

One more step. All you have to do is take one more step.

It was a lie. This hallway alone seemed unending as I shuffled forward on bare feet, the chill of gleaming black tiles seeping through my skin with every step. I had no way of knowing how far I had left to go. I couldn't even tell if I was still in the medical wing. If I could feel so lost within the palace Annex, I couldn't imagine trying to wander through the palace itself. But one step seemed doable when everything else felt insurmountable, so lie or not, I kept repeating it: *one more step.*

I had to get away before anyone realized I was gone. I couldn't stand to go back to that stifling recovery room. They'd promised I would be released from medical last week. I refused to wait for permission anymore.

My legs swayed as pain flared in my head. Squinting against the harsh overhead light, I reached to brace myself against the wall as I pushed forward. I was tired of the limitations of my body and refused to let them hold me back anymore. But as I stumbled into the wall on my next step, I knew I wouldn't make it to my room. I didn't even know where it was. Its location was blank, like every other important memory I should have had, but didn't. Nineteen years old, and all I could remember was the past three months.

I gasped against another stab of pain. My knees buckled, and I slid down the wall, gripping my head through thick brown hair, though it would do nothing for the pain. As my fingers glanced across the shaved strip I kept covered, they brushed over the raised scar hidden there. I winced, unwilling to dwell on it or the circumstances that had made the surgery necessary. Not that I knew much about it anyway.

Pills. I had to take my pills.

My hands shook as I blindly searched my pockets. When I came up empty, I groaned, dropping my head back against the wall. Had I left them behind?

Dropped them along the way? This had to be the most disastrous escape attempt in Anluan's history.

A heavy sigh rang in my ears, followed by the familiar clink of pills against glass. "Looking for these?"

I squinted my eyes open, defeated.

My best friend stood before me as I'd expected her to—pill bottle in hand, brow arched, her angled bob barely brushing the shoulders of her red dress as she stared down at me with an unimpressed frown. Only the soft waves in her black hair surprised me. She usually wore it straight. I assumed I had the styling change to thank for my chance to escape. It must have been why she'd been late for her regular visit.

Rather than speak, I held out a trembling hand. Emila immediately dropped a pill into my palm. I grimaced and swallowed it dry.

"Thanks," I said as I slumped into the wall and waited for the medicine to bring relief. I closed my eyes, having no desire to watch Emila take in how awful I looked. I hadn't bothered to braid my hair back, let alone brush it, and I always seemed to wake with sunken eyes on the mornings I struggled to remember my dreams. Add in the sheen of sweat covering my skin thanks to this latest episode and I was sure Emila would be ready to bundle me back into bed at the first opportunity.

"You should've waited, Khara," she chided, carefully settling in front of me on her knees before tucking her hair behind her ear. "Doctor Jensen was going to release you today."

"She said she would last week and the week before that." I blinked back tears. Pain still lanced through my head ... or maybe these were tears born of frustration. It was hard to tell anymore. "I can't stay in medical anymore. Not one more day. It's been three months. I've recovered enough. I just want to go to my room. *Please.*"

Emila stared into my eyes, observing me in her quiet way. They all looked at me like this—too long to be polite, always searching my face for something I couldn't offer. I wasn't sure they'd ever find what they were looking for. With most of my memories lost since the attack, I couldn't give myself what I needed, let alone anyone else.

"I'll take you to your room."

My heart leapt, but before my smile could fully form, she held up a hand.

"But I'm calling Doctor Jensen there to look you over."

"Emila!" I groaned, covering my face. The only thing I wanted less than *that* was to return to the medical wing.

"She'll already know you're not where you should be. You just left! Did you think no one would notice?"

I shrugged, folding my arms. "I wasn't focused on that part."

I'd just wanted *out*.

Emila scoffed. "You mean you didn't think. Because if you had, you would've called me to help you break out of there. I would have at least brought you some shoes!"

She met my wide eyes with a smirk.

"That's what friends are for. Besides, I'm sick of spending all my time there too." She sniffed. "It smells terrible."

I laughed, warmth filling my chest. It faded fast. "I didn't want to bother anyone."

"Or maybe," she argued, "you're tired of needing help all the time, so you didn't reach out to any of the people you know would drop everything for you."

I shifted uncomfortably. She wasn't wrong. My skin itched with the need to take care of myself. How could I do that if no one ever left me alone long enough to try?

"Am I that transparent?"

"I just know you."

The words stung. I didn't know myself, let alone her, no matter how desperately I tried. All I had to go on was what I'd learned while stuck in my recovery room.

"It's okay to need help, Khara. All we want to do is help."

I breathed out slowly, not hiding the way my breath and body shook. Throat too tight to speak, I nodded. Emila relaxed, patting my leg. I hadn't realized she'd been so tense.

She stood, offering me her hand. "Then let's get you to your room."

I let her pull me to my feet and steady me as I swayed, blinking back the dizziness. She remained steadfast against my side, an unmovable wall of support holding me upright. Despite standing a few inches taller than her, I sank my weight into her warmth.

"You were going the wrong way, you know." Amusement lined her words. "As in, you were heading in the completely opposite direction."

I huffed a laugh. "Maybe I was taking the scenic route so I could see more of the Annex than the medical wing."

Emila's eyes flicked down the hall. I followed her gaze. The only thing I could see was a dark wooden door, a single camera glowing a soft green above it. Everything seemed quiet here, outside of us.

Her voice went as tight as her smile as she turned back to me. "Trust me. There's nothing scenic down there."

2

WE SHUFFLED THROUGH THE winding halls of the palace Annex side by side. I kept my head bent, focusing on putting one foot in front of the other as Emila led us forward. I ignored the people we passed, not feeling up to engaging with anyone new and hoping they'd overlook me too. But as the floors shifted from black tile to white marble, I forced my eyes up. The farther we ventured from medical, the more extravagant the halls became. I couldn't help but marvel.

Morning light poured in through tall windows trimmed in black, casting long, square shadows across the floor at regular intervals. While the soft rays were preferable to the artificial lights in medical, they still made me cringe. I had to look away without seeing much more than a glimpse of the ornate carvings in white stone through the windows. I barely registered the black lantern chandeliers dangling from the ceiling or the artwork decorating the white walls.

It didn't bother me as we pushed ahead. The pain had overshadowed my curiosity.

It took several more minutes to make our way to my quarters. I couldn't tell if that was due to how far removed my room was from the medical wing or if it was down to my slow pace. Either way, by the time we'd woven through the halls, entered and exited elevators, and stopped before an ornate wooden door, I was thoroughly exhausted. My head throbbed in time with my heartbeat, and while the dizziness had faded, nausea had taken its place. All I wanted to do was rest.

Emila gestured to the door. "Here we are."

I couldn't manage to do more than lift a corner of my mouth in response. Emila frowned and placed the back of her hand against my forehead. It was a useless gesture. I hadn't had a fever since the second week of my recovery. These migraine episodes just left me reeling. I batted her hand away.

"I'm fine." Sensing she was about to argue, I pulled away and slumped against the wall before motioning to the door. "Do you mind?"

Emila shot me an unimpressed look but moved to a small wooden keypad beside the door. "You have two methods of entry. The keypad requires a six-digit code. You have a separate one for guests. That's what I'm using."

A soft green light glowed from beneath the edges of the keypad before Emila pushed the door open. She left it cracked as she turned back to me.

"You can try the other way later. Just place your palm in the center of the door where the carving leads and the Isiraden magic imbued in the wood will release the lock for you."

I raised a brow as I studied the intricate maze of flowers swirling around a tree carved into the center of the door. A section in the middle left just enough space for my palm to fit inside. "Does everyone here use magic like this?"

"Of course not. We can't harvest too much from Isiraden Forest or no one would have its magic. You're a special case, Khara. You should know that by now."

"Because of Ramsey?" I asked, spinning the delicate gold band around my finger. The deep teal sapphire and surrounding diamonds gleamed as they caught the light. Three months of its weight on my finger and I still could hardly believe it was mine.

"In part," she allowed. "Being engaged to Anluan's Sovereign does have its perks. But Ramsey's not all you are. You've always been special." Her eyes took on a glossy sheen as she leaned toward me. "There's a reason they call you *Coryndé Isiraden*. I mean, you were the first in generations to be born in the sacred grove!"

I shook my head with a sigh. The name meant nothing to me, but Emila said it with admiration, even a trace of pride. It had to hold significance, even if I didn't know—couldn't remember—what it was.

She winced. "Right, sorry. It means *friend of Isiraden,* or *heart*, depending on who you ask. That connection to magic ... you'd have access to all of this on your own."

More information about myself to file away. I was too tired to dwell on it now. Still, it was nice to know my sense of self wasn't entirely wrapped up in my fiancé—even if he was the Sovereign of Anluan.

Fiancé. That hadn't settled in, even after months of Ramsey at my bedside during my recovery.

"Go on." Emila coaxed me from my thoughts, motioning to the room as she opened the door wide. "You should get settled in. You look like you could use the rest."

It was the best idea she'd had all day. All I wanted was to fall face-first into a soft bed and sleep away the effects of this latest episode.

I stepped over the threshold and froze. The term *room* paled in comparison to the space in front of me. It was more like a suite—one that had to take up at least half this floor.

Mouth agape, I stood in the entry and stared into the large, open space. The sitting area held a large sectional couch arranged around a wooden table. Tall, arched windows thinly trimmed in black made up most of the far wall, highlighting the two chairs seated opposite the sofa. I darted my eyes away from the bright light with a grimace. I'd have time to admire the view when my head wasn't pounding. Instead, I focused on a gray brick fireplace that lent a cozy feeling to the open, modern style that defined what I'd seen of the Annex so far.

I turned to Emila, who had entered behind me and closed the door. "*This* is my room?"

She grinned, squinting with happiness as she shrugged. "Your suite, yes. This is your living area. Through there"—she pointed down the hall—"is your private library and art studio. Ramsey made sure you had a dedicated space to sketch to your heart's content." She gestured toward another door. "Your bedroom is this way."

She walked farther into the suite and I dutifully followed. "And, of course, over there you have a small kitchen. We typically eat with the other officials in the commons. I'm sure Ramsey will come get you for breakfast tomorrow. But in case you get hungry and aren't feeling up to leaving your room, he made sure you'd have plenty here."

She opened the cold storage box to reveal an assortment of fruits, vegetables, cheeses, and meats. *Plenty* was an apt description. Everything looked incredibly fresh. If my nausea hadn't grown on the way to my room, I would have reached for something.

As it were, I turned away, my hand trailing across one of the throw blankets folded over the back of the couch as I passed. The deep olive fabric was remarkably soft, a far cry from the blankets in the medical wing, and even those weren't half bad.

My eyes caught on a large tapestry map hanging behind the dining table. A banner along the top read *The Diamond Kingdoms of Veyhaan.* Though my head continued to throb in time with my pulse, the quality of the craftsmanship piqued my interest. I shuffled closer, tilting my head as I scanned the map.

The land formed a peninsula, hemmed in by the Mardhraya Ocean. It reached across the northern edge, flowed to the east, and down across the southern border. On the other side, the expansive Azmaryn Mountains stretched from top to bottom in a winding trail, separating Veyhaan from the land beyond.

Anluan sat in the middle as if it were the heart of the Diamond Kingdoms. Boundary lines revealed the breadth of our kingdom and the spaces where it brushed against each of the other four. If the elaborate marker above the city was any indication, Anluan was the largest. I trailed a finger along the canvas from the city center to Anluan's eastern land, where the Isiraden Forest sat nestled between the Orveyin Forest to the north and the Lyaran Forest to the south.

"It's smaller than I thought it would be," I murmured, tracing the elaborately drawn tree beneath the *Isiraden Forest* script.

Emila stepped closer, the fluttering sleeve of her dress brushing against my arm as she settled beside me. "Isiraden is a small forest. The grove's even smaller. But we do our best to take care of it."

"Because it's sacred."

"All of it is, to a degree, but mostly the grove. That's where the original tree—the source of the most magic—grows." She tapped a finger against the Orveyin Forest marker to the north of Isiraden. "Most of our wood harvests come from Orveyin, less from Lyaran. We only harvest from Isiraden for specific magical needs—secure doors, medicines, technology. We can't take too much at once. There's only so much replanting we can do in a season and little to guarantee those trees will produce the same magic."

"Sounds like a gamble."

Emila straightened, her shoulders rolling back as she lifted her chin and cleared her throat. "Without risk, we make no gains."

My brow furrowed. "What?"

"Your fiancé says it all the time," she said, faux-seriousness slipping. "Part of his inspiring speeches as Sovereign. It reminds the people why harvesting from Isiraden is necessary."

"Not everyone approves?"

She snorted, a wry smile forming on her face. "Can we expect our people to collectively approve of anything? Ramsey's policies on harvesting from Isiraden are one of the reasons he's popular, but ..."

"It's also a reason some disapprove."

She shrugged. "Can't make everyone happy, Sovereign or not."

Politics were far too complicated to dwell on before sleeping away the pain in my skull. I let the conversation die and focused back on the map. My eyes drifted from the forests to the other Diamond Kingdoms.

I took in Fyrth, nestled along the eastern coast with small waves detailed above its name. Farther inland from the southern coastline sat Panra, decorated by a boulder wrapped in a vine. To the far west, Coroden was tucked at the edge of the Azmaryn Mountains, the kingdom's name accented by two lines that curled upward at the ends while a third curled down—a stylized depiction of wind that I couldn't help but admire. To the north, Branton was embellished with a single flickering flame.

Something about the details on the map called to me. The Inna River that flowed from the northern coast through Anluan's territory until it branched in two and emptied into the Lushané Sea. The dots that marked the towns surrounding Anluan with names like Myragin and Primavey, and smaller villages like Penvale, Camden, and Lerte.

Forests and farmland. The Azmaryn Mountains and Dhamarli Lake. I wanted to know the Diamond Kingdoms, wanted to study this land until it became more than a piece of art on my wall. I wanted to look at this map and sense familiarity—to not just know it was home, but feel it.

I wanted to remember.

My hand fell from the tapestry as I sighed and pinched the bridge of my nose against a fresh flare of pain. It always came back to remembering.

"Why doesn't anyone use *Veyhaan*?" I asked, my voice laced with an exhaustion I could no longer hide. "They always say 'the Diamond Kingdoms.'"

Emila frowned, her eyes brimming with concern. "It's more accurate. Each of the Diamond Kingdoms has a seat on the consul. Their collective rule and contributions are made for the good of all the kingdoms. Our ancestors bound us together, but each city-kingdom still has a ruling family with sovereignty over its own affairs. We use 'the Diamond Kingdoms' out of respect for the alliance our ancestors forged. Outsiders tend to call us Veyhaan. Maybe they find it easier, or they just don't understand us. I don't know. Either is correct, technically."

Worry lined Emila's face when I didn't answer. "There will be time for all of this later, you know," she said, rubbing a soothing circle against my back. Her voice took on a wry note as she added, "You'll need to rest if you're going to defend yourself to Doctor Jensen."

I groaned. That wouldn't be a pleasant conversation even if my head weren't throbbing. "You said the bedroom was where?"

"Come on." She nodded to an open doorway off the living room as she rubbed my arm. "You should get off your feet."

My bedroom was as extravagant and spacious as the living area. A large dresser stood along one wall and looked to be made of a similar wood to the front door. Floral designs had been carved into each drawer. A mirror hung above it, running the full width and brightening the space by reflecting the light from the arched windows on the opposite wall. While I'd be grateful for them one day, today they only served to worsen the throbbing in my head. I'd be making use of the thick curtains that hung at the sides of the windows sooner than later.

To the right stood another doorway. Through the partially-open door, I glimpsed a clawfoot tub and rain-style shower. Between the glint of gold trim along the glass walls and the white marble tiles, I could already tell the bathroom would be just as luxurious as the rest of the suite.

Gratitude warmed my chest. The showers in the medical wing had left much to be desired. I couldn't wait to rinse the remnants of that place from my skin.

A chaise sat in front of another fireplace featuring the same gray bricks as the one in the living room. I imagined myself settled in front of it with a blanket, a cup of tea, and a sketchbook, and couldn't help but smile.

I moved to the massive bed against the back wall, running my fingers over the rich, green comforter. It was soft and plush and much too inviting to ignore. I stretched out on top of it and sighed, rubbing my forehead as the light dimmed.

"Let's get you settled so you can rest," Emila said softly as she moved from the curtains she'd drawn shut. "I'll stall Doctor Jensen for half an hour, but I think that'll be the most I can manage."

I nodded, not bothering to open my eyes as I listened to her flit about the room. Water ran in the bathroom before she set something on the side table by my bed with a soft clink.

"Khara," she said, shaking my shoulder as softly as she spoke. "You can sleep soon, but first, I need to know. How bad is it?"

I had long moved past hating that question. It felt like someone asked me once an hour. After every episode, someone wanted to know how bad my pain was and if I needed another dose of medicine. As awful as the pain was, I hated the pills just as much. I always felt dulled around the edges when I took them. But they forced the pain to a tolerable level, at least for a while.

With a sigh, I admitted defeat.

"It's bad." I cracked my eyes open, grateful the only light remaining was what filtered in from the living room through the open door. "I should take another pill."

Emila nodded, doling one out of the bottle before setting it back on my side table. "Here," she said, helping me sit. "Take this last one and then you can sleep."

I accepted the medicine and some water, grimacing as the bitterness grew. With a shudder, I swallowed.

Emila gave me a moment to breathe before helping me relax back against the pillows. As my head sunk into them, I was already halfway to sleep.

"There we go," she whispered as she maneuvered the comforter from beneath me and pulled it up to my chest. I felt like a child being tucked in, but I was far too weary to care. That would be something for me to stew on after I'd slept off this thick exhaustion.

"Rest well, Khara. I'll wake you when the doctor gets here."

I made a humming noise of acknowledgment—all I had the energy for—and let the medicine carry me off to sleep.

3

Doctor Jensen didn't hide her disapproval when she strode into my suite, her crimson lips set in a frown as deep as her auburn hair. Sleep had dulled my pain, but I was still groggy as I leaned back against the arm of the couch with my legs covered by a blanket, wearily watching her approach. As Doctor Jensen stared down her nose at me with narrowed eyes that deepened the lines on her face, I tried not to shrink back like a child about to be scolded.

"What you did was foolish." Doctor Jensen set her leather bag on the floor and crossed her arms over her chest. The sleeves of her too-short lab coat inched up her arms with the movement. "I thought you were smarter than this, Khara. You're recovering from a major surgery. You can't just decide you've had enough and run off without telling anyone!"

"I left a note," I muttered, gathering my hair over my shoulder like a shield. I was careful to keep both the undercut strip and my surgical scar covered before pulling my knees closer to my chest. Now I *really* felt like a child.

"A note." The doctor scoffed. "Well, that makes it all better."

Heavy silence filled the room. Emila stood at my back, but facing Doctor Jensen's anger made me feel alone. I hadn't meant to upset everyone. I just wanted to feel normal again, more like myself. Whoever that was.

"I'm sorry." I risked a glance at her and tried not to grimace at her dour expression. "It wasn't well thought out. I just—I needed to get out of there. I couldn't handle another day where my release was pushed back."

She sighed, dropping her arms to her sides. "I can understand that, but I make these decisions in your best interest. If I tell you we need to keep you longer, there's a reason for it."

It wasn't that I didn't believe her. Doctor Jensen had years of experience and was very attentive. Ramsey thought highly of her. But I couldn't bring myself to trust her fully. It wasn't surprising, considering I couldn't even trust myself.

"Khara," she said, her clinical voice laced with concern, "are you spacing out again?"

I shook my head and mustered a tight smile. "No, nothing like that. Just thinking."

"Anything I can help with?" She knelt at my side, digging into her bag for supplies. My health had her full attention now—that was never a good sign. But it was better than facing her disappointment.

"I'm just frustrated." I sighed, my fingers playing with the edge of the blanket. "My memory ... when do you think I'll get it back?"

The doctor stared at me in concern, the exact opposite of what I wanted. I couldn't say or do anything to give her a reason to haul me back to medical. She shifted, her brown eyes boring into mine, and I forced myself to maintain eye contact, though the urge to hide was growing.

"We've discussed this," she said carefully, glancing at Emila before pinning me with her gaze again. "These things take time. With the severity of the injuries you sustained in the rebels' attack and the brain surgery you underwent, it could be months before you regain memories—"

"—if I regain them at all."

My words sounded bitter, but I could stand to hear myself say them. I couldn't stand to hear *her* say them again, not in the matter-of-fact tone she favored.

Her face took on a look of genuine sympathy. It might've been worse than the professional blankness she typically wore. "Yes, there's a chance you won't regain your memories. But I'm hopeful that given time—and by following my instructions—you'll make a full recovery."

A full recovery. I resisted the urge to scoff, but couldn't stop the growing tension. My shoulders rose, inciting a small twinge that had me reaching for my right shoulder with a grimace. The arrow wound had mostly healed by now, but some days I still felt a lingering pain.

"That will take time too." Doctor Jensen nodded to the hand I'd placed over it. She hesitated, then reached forward to lay her hand over mine. "You're progressing beautifully, Khara. Keep taking your medications. Continue doing your physical therapy exercises. And let me know if your migraine episodes change in any way, especially if the pain worsens or you begin to hallucinate."

"Does this mean you're releasing me?" I couldn't hide the longing in my tone.

"I believe you already released yourself." She arched an unimpressed brow. "But yes, I'm signing off on you staying here in your suite."

I turned to grin at Emila over the back of the couch. She smirked and gave me a wink. When I turned back to the doctor, she was holding out a blue glass bottle. My nose scrunched as I leaned forward to take it. More of the dreaded pills.

"I know you don't like them," she said with a knowing look, "but they're vital to your recovery. If you're going to stay here, I need to know you'll take them."

I straightened and held her gaze. "I will."

Doctor Jensen frowned. "I mean it. You need to take a pill as soon as you feel an episode coming on. We don't want you having any setbacks and ending up right back in medical."

The chastisement prickled against me, but I nodded. I would have agreed to just about anything to stay out of medical. "I'll take the pills, Doctor."

For a long moment, she searched my face for a lie. She wouldn't find one. I *would* take the pills. Even though I hated them, they were key to my recovery. I wanted to remember more than anything. I refused to jeopardize that.

Finally, she nodded and released the bottle to me. "Take one if it's a typical episode. Two if it's one of your bad ones. Any worse than that, you call me immediately. Understood?"

"Absolutely."

Doctor Jensen gathered her bag. "Then I'll leave you to it. Enjoy your freedom, Khara." She rose to her feet and paused, turning back to me. "And for all our sakes, behave yourself."

Emila snorted behind me, and I glared at her without any heat. Now that I'd finally have a shred of the independence I'd been craving, I planned to be a model patient.

As Emila saw Doctor Jensen to the door, I tuned out their conversation. Closing my eyes, I smiled and let myself sink deep into the cushions.

Freedom at last. I wouldn't take it for granted.

4

I BLINKED INTO THE dark, groggy and unsure of where I was or what had nudged me from sleep. The day came back to me slowly—from leaving medical to falling asleep in my suite after taking my medicine—and I relaxed back into my bed. As I scrubbed a hand over my face, paper crinkled.

I bolted upright. My notes!

Patting against my loose sweater, I sighed when paper brushed against the skin of my waist. The pages must have shifted down my camisole in my sleep. I couldn't believe I'd fallen asleep before hiding them. I was lucky Emila hadn't noticed.

I carefully smoothed my notes out on the bed, hoping I hadn't ruined them while I slept. It was too dark to see, so I stretched out my arm in search of a light. When that didn't yield results, I resigned myself to getting up and inched my way to the bathroom, papers clutched carefully in hand.

The hardwood floor was chilly beneath my bare feet. I'd worn thick socks every night in the medical wing to ward off the chill of the sterile tile floor. I'd have to see if I had any socks here.

Later. This was far more important.

When my hand grasped the frame of the bathroom door, I moved forward with my arm stretched out until my hand bumped into a raised knob. I pushed it up and a dim yellow light faded in. That was all I needed.

I stared at the pages, biting my lip. They were torn around the edges, scraps of paper more than anything else. Still, these messy scribbles were my most treasured possession—notes and quick sketches of everything I remembered from my dreams over the past month.

Good or bad, I wrote down whatever I remembered when I woke in a cold sweat with a pounding headache. Somewhere in the chaotic, nonsensical pieces of my dreams, I hoped my subconscious was working to help me remember something. Anything. Each night gave me more clues to collect, more possibilities to sift through.

No one knew. I couldn't chance them telling me to stop or taking my notes from me. I couldn't risk any of them believing I wasn't ready to be out of medical. Couldn't risk them knowing my nightmares had only grown worse the longer I'd been awake, that I woke with headaches more often than not.

No, they couldn't know about my attempts to piece together memories from my dreams.

Not yet.

I needed somewhere safe to store these pages until I could find common threads between them. So far, there hadn't been anything I could act on. Until there was, I would write my notes and keep them close. I had to do something to help myself remember. One way or another, I would find what I needed.

In the dim light, I could see into my bedroom enough to move around. I went to the chaise and considered lighting a fire, but a glance at the clock made me wince. I'd slept for several hours. It was past three in the morning, and Ramsey would come by in a few hours. I needed more sleep.

And yet, the idea of piecing something together tempted me to stay awake.

Near the chaise sat a small table with delicate golden legs and a white marble top that I hadn't noticed before. It evoked the same luxurious feeling as the rest of the suite. A brown leather book lay on it, a white envelope settled on top. My name was written in swooping handwriting across the front.

I brushed my fingers over the supple leather book as I picked up the envelope and tore it open. Inside was a single piece of thick stationery, full of the same elegant handwriting.

Khara,

I hope your bedroom is to your liking. I've made sure to prepare it for you in anticipation of your return. Seeing you persevere despite your pain has only made me love you more. Please accept this gift, one I hope will help you as you continue to heal.

All my love,
Ramsey

I gingerly set the note aside and picked up the book. A strap wound around the cover, tying it shut. I unwrapped it with care and opened the front to find it wasn't a book after all, but a journal full of blank pages. I would be able to write or sketch in it.

My eyes filled with tears that I blinked away as best I could. This wasn't the first time Ramsey's thoughtfulness had overwhelmed me, and I doubted it would be the last. He knew me so well, and yet I couldn't remember anything about him from before the attack. We'd been friends since we were young. It wasn't fair I'd lost so many memories—to him, most of all.

When I first woke up, disoriented and in pain, his was the first voice I heard. He was the first person I saw—slouched forward in a chair pushed as close to my bed as it could get, days-old black scruff lining his face and dark circles under brown eyes that lit with relief when they met mine.

He sat by my side that entire miserable first week, soothing me as best he could when the pain grew to be too much. He never left, not even to sleep in his own bed. Every time I woke, crying from pain and confusion, he hushed me softly while holding my hand or running his fingers through my hair as he placed a cool cloth on my forehead. He made sure I knew I was safe.

I wasn't sure I deserved a fiancé like Ramsey.

Weariness rose at the thought, and sleep suddenly sounded better than being left to my spiraling mind. I slid my scrap papers inside the journal, tied the cover shut, and shuffled back to my bed. For now, I'd keep the journal somewhere hidden. I moved the slew of pillows at the head of my bed and carefully wedged the book into the space between the back of my mattress and my headboard before moving each pillow back into place.

I turned off the bathroom light, then climbed into bed. With a sigh, I buried myself under the covers and tried not to think until I drifted off to sleep.

5

A MASSIVE TREE LOOMED before me, strong and old and full of an indescribable majesty that thickened the air. Its broad white trunk swirled with curls of gray and brown. The outer bark had peeled away in several places, revealing smooth planes and knots that made it even more captivating.

I stood at its base, craning my neck to take in as much of the twisted branches as I could. No matter how hard I tried, I couldn't see the top.

I moved forward, hand outstretched to touch it.

"Come home…"

The words were barely a whisper—delicate, yet heavy with meaning. I spun to find the speaker. The moment I looked away from the tree, it disappeared, leaving me alone in a dark void.

"Hello?" I called out, turning slowly as I searched the darkness.

Eyes blinked into existence all across the void, narrowing and widening in a multitude of expressions. I whirled, trying to take them all in. So many colors. So many emotions. Compassion, rage, pride, grief—all of it focused on me.

A pair of eyes flashed in front of me, inches from my face, and I froze, my heart in my throat. They stared like they were seeing through me, a piercing brown that stole my breath. The ghost of a hand caressed my cheek, and I flinched back in surprise.

Just as suddenly as the eyes appeared, they vanished, leaving me alone in the dark.

I tried to call out, but my voice was carried away by the wind.

6

I woke with a raging migraine. While the pulsating throb in my head wasn't surprising, I hated it all the same. Navigating pain had become the norm for me over the last few months. The breathing exercises, the medication, the waiting for my pain to shift into discomfort and hoping it faded entirely—it was all I knew. And still, the shock of it could steal my breath.

The dream had been strange, much like they all were, but already I could feel the details slipping away. *A tree, a message, eyes.* If I could at least remember the general idea, maybe I could do something with it.

Light had begun to pierce through the cracks beneath the bedroom curtains, and more filtered in from the wall of windows in the living room. I wished I'd closed the bedroom door before falling asleep. The light was driving knives behind my eyes.

Deciding the notes about my dream could wait—even if it meant I forgot the details entirely—I fumbled for my pills. I overshot my arm in my haste, swallowing back a curse as it sent the bottle flying off the side table. It clattered loudly to the floor, and I winced at the renewed pain.

I buried my head in my hands and took a steadying breath. I couldn't afford to lose it, not if I wanted to stay out of medical.

Slowly, I pulled myself off the bed and made my way to where the bottle of blue pills landed. Bending to grab them would have been a bad idea, so instead, I lowered myself to sit on the floor, quickly opened the bottle, and shook out two pills. The pain was merciless on the mornings I remembered pieces of a dream.

I couldn't help shuddering as I dry-swallowed the tablets. For the hundredth time, I wished I could see one of the healers who'd practiced in the city before the divide. But wishes didn't change anything. Too many of them had been loyal to the rebels. Most had fled or died in the war's outbreak two years ago. The ones who remained weren't people Ramsey trusted enough to let them use their healing powers on me.

I was stuck with the pills, whether I liked them or not. Doctor Jensen assured me they were my best option for a complete recovery. I couldn't help but wonder if she took some sort of sick pleasure in watching me grimace every time I took one. They were terrible. But I had to admit they dulled the pain—quickly, too.

After a few minutes of deep breathing, I felt well enough to move. The fuzziness I'd started to get used to after taking the pills settled in, leaving me feeling somewhat disconnected, but without pain.

I heaved myself from the floor and made my way back to bed. Moving my pillows out of the way, I searched for my journal. It hadn't moved at all in the night, though my tangled blankets were a sure sign of my restless sleep. Relieved, I pulled it out and took it with me to the living room.

The sun had risen over the city, the glowing morning light highlighting a spectacular view of Anluan. My windows didn't face the city center. They looked out toward the Eastern District, where a sprawling collection of homes and small shops sat. The varied heights of brick and stone buildings lining narrow roads formed beautiful layers from above.

I loved that I could see over the top of the wall to the trees beyond. I wasn't sure if I was staring at Isiraden Forest, but the vast treeline view made me feel closer to my roots. My lips quirked into a small smile. That was something, at least.

Setting the journal on the couch, I went in search of a pen. On a ledge near the kitchen, I found a cup filled with an assortment of pens, markers, and drawing pencils. It didn't look like it belonged there, and I was pretty sure Emila had moved it for me. Maybe from the art room she'd mentioned.

Rather than taking the whole assortment, I settled for a drawing pencil and a black ink pen. I pulled the throw blanket off the back of the couch and settled onto the corner cushion.

On the first page of the journal, my name was written in Ramsey's elegant script. On the next, I found a photograph of us slipped between the pages. I blinked at it, delight and grief warring in my chest.

The image was a few years old at most. My hair was a few inches shorter, the brown waves falling to the top of my chest rather than mid back. My face showed no signs of pain, and health shone through the glow of my olive skin. Ramsey's face lacked any stubble and his grin shone with youth. I sat tucked under his arm in the grass, my dress short enough to reveal bare legs from the knee down. He had one leg bent up, his other arm resting across the knee. Our eyes sparkled with laughter.

It stung that I couldn't remember this moment when we'd been so happy.

Turning to the next page, I shoved down my longing for lost memories. My focus needed to be on something else. I left my dream notes where they were, tucked toward the back of the journal. There would be time for that later. Right now, I needed to write what I could remember of last night's dream. It wasn't much—only three words—but I quickly scribbled them: *tree, message, eyes.*

I bit my lip. The eyes had already faded entirely from my mind. There was no use trying to draw them or make any notes. I couldn't remember the message either, just a haunting voice that seemed to fade in and out with the wind.

Frustrated, I closed my eyes and gripped the drawing pencil, letting it hover over the empty page as I tried to recall the tree. The details were fuzzy, but I did my best to let the vision linger in my mind as I began to sketch.

It took longer than I'd anticipated, but by the time I finished, the dream tree was full of detail. I couldn't be sure they were the *correct* details—or that they meant anything at all—but if nothing else, it was a nice drawing.

I jotted the date in the corner and gave it one last look. A tree that seemed to stretch to the heights of the sky. A wide trunk and twisting limbs, peeling bark and swirls of subtle variations on smooth planes. I felt more settled with it reflected on the page.

Shutting the book, I stretched my arms into the air before pulling my knees to my chest. My suite was quieter than the medical wing. While the lack of noise was a gift, I found it a little unsettling. Another thing for me to get used to.

The clock seated on the mantle above the fireplace read nine in the morning. I'd been drawing for over an hour. If Ramsey was coming by today, I needed to get ready. I picked up the journal to return it to its hiding place.

Before I tucked it away, I removed the photo of me and Ramsey and propped it against a small potted plant on my side table. The photograph shouldn't be hidden away, even if not knowing what had made us laugh pricked my heart.

I had just enough time to shower and slip into the simple sundress I'd found in my closet before a knock echoed from the front door. If Emila had access to my suite, Ramsey did too. It was reassuring he didn't use it to come in. How well he seemed to know me and what I needed from him was both a comfort and a source of pain. I didn't know enough about him to do the same.

"I'm coming!" I called, belting a loose cardigan around myself as I walked to the door.

When I pulled it open, I blinked. Ramsey looked remarkably put together, more so than while I'd been recovering in medical. While he'd sat at my bedside, letting me squeeze his hand through the worst of the pain, he'd worn simple clothing—short-sleeved shirts in neutral colors, sometimes a thin sweater to ward off the chill of my room.

Today, he sported a tailored suit in a blue so deep it was almost black. The light streaming in from the windows caught the sheen of the lapels and highlighted the warm orange-brown undertone of his skin. And his eyes—the depth of them was evident here in a way I'd never seen in medical. I stared, captivated.

"Hi," Ramsey said, jolting me from my gawking.

He grinned down at me from the doorway with a pleased spark in his eyes. Heat flooded my cheeks. He'd noticed my staring. How could he not, when I'd left him standing there for so long? But we were engaged. Surely it was okay to admire him.

My mind raced as I tried to figure out how to greet him. Maybe with a hug? But had I greeted him that way before the attack? Things like this hadn't crossed my mind while in medical. It felt like its own world there, and I was too distracted by my recovery to worry about normal interactions. But now the uncertainty made itself known in full force.

"Do you mind if I come in?"

I winced. In trying to think ahead, I'd missed the obvious. I should've let him in already. What was wrong with me?

Ramsey didn't comment on my blatant staring or lack of social graces. He'd been good about guiding me toward how things used to be. No matter how adrift I felt, at least I had his cues to follow.

I really didn't deserve this man.

"Of course you can." Shaking my head, I stepped out of the way. "I'm sorry, Ramsey. I've already taken my medicine this morning and I'm still feeling out of sorts."

His lips dipped into a frown as he stepped inside. "Another bad episode?"

I gave him a weak smile and shrugged as I shut the door. "Bad enough. I figured it would be better to take two so it wouldn't get any worse."

"I know how badly you want to be back in your own space, but maybe it would be better—"

"No. I'm fine." Taking in his pained expression, I softened. "I promise. I'll let you know if that changes."

He smiled sadly, bringing a hand to my cheek. My stomach fluttered as it had every time he touched me over the past few months.

"Please do. You're fiercely independent, which you proved, yet again, with your escape attempt yesterday."

He raised a brow at me. I shrugged and looked away, trying not to think about how much I must have scared him. He chuckled, the warm sound drawing my eyes back to his face.

"I love that about you. I just don't want to see you hurt. Not again."

I swallowed thickly. In the face of his concern for my well-being, I could do nothing but agree. "I promise I'll tell you."

Ramsey's tension eased as he let out a heavy breath. He trailed his hand to my shoulder before running it down my arm, a light touch that sent a shiver down my spine. When he found my hand, he squeezed it once before bringing the back of it to his lips. "Thank you."

Guilt tightened my throat at the hoarseness of his voice. All I could do was nod, but it seemed to be enough for him. His eyes were full of so much fondness, I had to look away.

He released my hand and cleared his throat. "Are you feeling up to breakfast? We can go to the commons and join the others."

I wasn't sure who *the others* would be, but the least I could do was join him.

"I think I can manage breakfast."

Ramsey's grin returned in full force. "Excellent. It shouldn't be too crowded today. Emila will probably meet us there later. She tends to sleep in whenever she can. A few of my advisors and guards will be in and out. Is that okay?"

I took a steadying breath. Since the attack, I hadn't been around many people. The medical wing had restricted access—my room more than most. I'd primarily been around Ramsey, Emila, Doctor Jensen, and her occasional assistant. My heart raced at the idea of being around new people, though there was no reason to be afraid. Nothing would happen to me—not in the middle of the Annex, and especially not with Ramsey by my side.

Ramsey had proven himself adept at sensing my anxiety over the past few months. He stepped closer, taking both of my hands in his. "If you're not ready, you don't have to do this. You've only just been released. I don't want you to push yourself."

"No, I'm ready." I couldn't quite manage to meet his eyes. "It just feels strange, to face all these people I've met before but can't remember. I've been so isolated since the attack."

He dropped his head. "I'm sorry. I didn't mean to make you feel that way. I was scared, and I couldn't let anything else happen to you. Seeing you like that—"

His words choked off, and he looked away, sniffing and running a hand over his face. The idea of him feeling like he needed to hide his emotions hurt. I hesitated before reaching up to draw his hand away, squeezing it gently.

"I understand. I didn't mean to make you feel ..." I sighed, then looked up at him with a wry smile. "Things are just a little overwhelming right now. I wasn't blaming you. You don't have to hide how you feel from me. I'm struggling to keep up, that's all."

"You're keeping up just fine."

I scoffed. "If you say so."

"I mean it. You're not as far removed from who you used to be as you think. Give yourself time to recover. Until then, I'll be right here, at your beck and call for as long as you need and then some."

"You might get sick of me," I challenged, even as my lips curved into a smile.

"I doubt that." He tapped the center stone of my engagement ring before letting go. "And even if I did, I made you a promise—one I fully intend to keep. Bonded for a lifetime."

My heart flipped in my chest. I'd read that phrase in a book Emila had given me to pass the time as I recovered. It was a vow from Anluan's covenant ceremony. *Bonded for a lifetime.* I couldn't imagine making that commitment right now.

But a past version of me had chosen Ramsey, loved him that deeply. Given time, I was sure this version of me, however broken, would be able to do the same.

Ramsey smirked as he stepped back. "Let's go before Argusten and Radnor take all the good food."

"Who?"

"Two of our guards. Bottomless pits, the both of them." He waved me off. "Do you need anything before we go? It's a bit of a walk."

I glanced around the room. My pills were the only thing I might need, in case of an episode. "Just my medicine."

Ramsey's eyes pinched. "You think you'll need more so soon?"

I massaged my forehead and gave a helpless shrug. It wasn't something I could plan out. The fierce migraines were unpredictable. We both knew that. The situation was frustrating for each of us in different ways.

"I hope not," I said as I moved into my bedroom to grab the bottle. "But Doctor Jensen wanted me to carry them with me whenever possible. Better safe than sorry, I guess."

Ramsey nodded, though concern lined his face when I turned back, pills in hand. "Better you have what you need when you need it."

"I seem to need a lot these days." I fiddled with the lid, the pills clinking lightly against the glass container.

Ramsey stilled my hand and tipped my chin up. I inhaled shakily as our eyes met and his intense gaze held me in place. "It's okay to need things, Khara. Everyone does."

"Some of us need more than others."

Warm amusement danced in his eyes. "Well, lucky for you, I tend to have an abundant supply to help meet them all."

I shook my head, but couldn't stop a smile from creeping up. Ramsey's grin widened and my heart skipped a beat.

"All right, let's go. I can't guarantee to meet your need for breakfast if Argusten and Radnor have been through the line already."

"They can't be that bad."

Ramsey laughed, loud and sharp, as he drew me into his side and made for the door. "Trust me. They really can be."

7

It turned out Ramsey was correct. Gage Argusten and Cethin Radnor had, in fact, already made it to breakfast. Ramsey pointed them out as we entered the commons. They sat side-by-side in their black uniforms, laughing with a group of guards at one of the far tables. Even from a distance, I could see both of their plates were piled high with food.

Ramsey didn't need to say *I told you so*, it was written all over his face. I rolled my eyes and gave him a gentle shove, and his answering laugh caught the attention of the room. Every eye fixed on us, and I froze, my skin crawling. Ramsey took it all in stride, offering a pointed greeting to the room before taking my hand and leading me forward. While things remained more hushed than when we'd entered, their attention returned to the food and company.

"Take whatever you want." Ramsey nodded to the breakfast spread laid out on a long marble counter near the kitchen.

There was still plenty despite the guards' full plates—enough for far more than two people. An assortment of fresh fruit, baked bread, and eggs was arranged on tiered trays and serving dishes. Steam still curled into the air over the eggs, and I wondered if Ramsey had them make more in anticipation of our arrival.

After I'd gathered my breakfast, I turned to find him eyeing my plate with a frown. He'd been trying to get me to eat more ever since I woke up in recovery, but my appetite since the attack was small. Doctor Jensen said it was a side effect of the medicine and to try to eat more than I wanted to. Easier said than done.

Ramsey grabbed an extra muffin, trying to be subtle as he glanced at me. I had no doubt he'd try to make me eat it when I'd finished my own plate. *If* I finished it.

He led us to an empty wooden table at the front of the room that could easily seat ten people. Ramsey took the spot at the head and gestured for me to sit at his right. I did and busied myself looking around the room, trying to imagine us sitting like this every morning, together and content.

As I reached for my fork and began to eat, the voices of some guards sitting two tables away carried over. They spoke so intently, I couldn't help but listen.

"It's not like we haven't tried that before," one man said with a roll of his eyes. "Hayden's not like his father. Compared to Galen, his powers—"

"Hayden's powers can be overcome. He has weaknesses just like anyone else!"

"Powers or no powers, the rebels are moving closer to the city. We've all noticed it."

"Doesn't matter. We've stopped them before. We'll do it again."

As I stared in their direction, Ramsey's attention shifted their way. He wiped his mouth on a napkin and set down his fork. "Don't worry about that, Khara. Everything's fine."

I shot him a disbelieving look. "It doesn't sound fine."

He chose his next words with care. "Since you were attacked, the rebel forces have been more active than usual. They haven't tried anything directly within Anluan, but we've noticed some of them moving closer to the city. Scouting, we suspect. I'll take care of it. You don't have to worry. You're safe here."

"I'm not worried," I hedged. "I just don't even remember them. Why are they doing this? Why attack me at all?"

Ramsey pursed his lips, a debate raging in his eyes. I held my breath, hoping he would finally give me a real answer. I'd asked before, not long into my recovery, but no one would offer any explanations. Any time I asked, they shifted the conversation to something lighter. I could understand avoiding stressful topics while I recovered, but I was well enough to know now.

"Many years ago, my ancestor, Dharavaya, ruled over the region," Ramsey said at last. "His kingdom was strong. He possessed extraordinary powers, as few did in those days. There are legends of how he received them and what he was capable of, but the important part is he was able to extend gifts to others."

I leaned forward, giving him my full attention. "What kind of gifts?"

"Powers." He smiled tightly. "Dharavaya was able to give others a portion of the power he possessed, though it manifested in different ways based on the person receiving the gift. And yet, it didn't diminish his own power. It seemed to make him stronger. Of course, not everyone would use powers like his for the good of the kingdom. He couldn't impart them to just anyone. So he made sure to only give them to those he most trusted, those who proved themselves worthy. He created a series of trials to test the merits of warriors in the kingdom. If you passed each test, proving yourself brave, selfless, and honorable, you would be gifted with power."

So many questions sprang to my mind, and I longed to ask each of them, but with tension already tightening Ramsey's eyes, I held back. This story was painful for him to share, and I couldn't bear to press him.

"*Shalémo*," he said with distaste, "was deemed worthy in the games. He was granted the power to control light. From that point on, he could call down bolts of lightning that shook the earth. He was immensely powerful. It should have made Dharavaya nervous, but he trusted the system he'd created, and more than that, he trusted Shalémo."

"Because they were friends?" Dread pooled in my gut. I knew somewhere along the way, things fell apart. I was living in some version of the aftermath.

"They were." Ramsey sighed. "Close ones. For generations, the Shalémo line proved trustworthy. Shalémo himself never reached for more power and remained loyal to my family and the region. As Shalémo had children, Dharavaya watched to see what would happen. The magic we're imbued with doesn't pass to each child born to us. It's weighted, in a way."

"Weighted how?"

Ramsey paused, blinking before shaking his head. "Forgive me. I should have realized you wouldn't remember. Only certain children inherit powers through their bloodline. The magic skips at least one generation, often several, before another firstborn is gifted. Some share the same gift as their ancestors before them. Others hold a different power entirely. Descendants like me, those born into power, are viewed as special, chosen. It's an immense privilege and a heavy responsibility."

As Ramsey looked away, his eyes unfocusing, my heart ached for him. How heavy a burden was it for him to not only be gifted with power but rule as Sovereign while fighting to keep our people safe?

"It's only been two years since the war broke out. Hayden—Shalémo's newest descendant—inherited powers at birth, as his father Galen did. That makes at least ten generations in a row where gifts manifested in the firstborn children of their bloodline. Outside of their line, it's unheard of." He sighed, pinching the bridge of his nose. The pained way he looked back at me was enough to bring tears to my eyes. "Hayden and I grew up together. We were friends, though with how close our families were, we lived more like brothers."

"What happened?" I asked, taking his hand in mine.

He squeezed it, his lips tipping into a sad smile. "We wanted different things for Anluan. Neither of us was willing to bend. We always came back from arguments before, but not this time."

"This argument caused the divide?"

"It caused the *war*. There was an attack in the night. Hayden turned his powers against us and twisted others to fight on his family's side. Half of the palace was destroyed, good people died, and Anluan erupted into chaos. It was madness, Khara. The entire city, devastated in a single battle. We're still rebuilding sections of it, not to mention the palace. We had to relocate everything here to the eastern Annex."

"But you beat him—Hayden and his rebels?"

"We've held them back," Ramsey corrected. His jaw clenched and he looked away, slipping his hand from mine. "We're still at war, the battles just don't reach inside Anluan's gates. I've made sure the walls are fortified enough to keep the rebels out and all of us safely inside. But it's taken two years to settle into the control I have now, to rebuild Anluan into what it is today." He pushed a hand through his hair before folding his arms. "It's not enough. Not yet."

My eyes filled with tears again. "Ramsey ..."

"Every day, I wonder if things could've turned out differently. Maybe if I'd—" He shook his head, staring into the distance.

I swallowed past a lump in my throat. His story was full of so much pain, I could feel it in my bones, even without remembering it myself. I stopped trying to hold back my tears. They trailed down my cheeks and rolled over the palm I rested my head in. "I'm sorry."

Ramsey blinked, turning back to me, and softened. "Oh, Khara, don't be sorry. It wasn't your fault."

"I know." I wiped the tears away with the side of my hand. "I meant I'm sorry for your pain."

Ramsey stilled, clearing his throat before giving me a tremulous smile. "Thank you."

"And I'm sorry for asking you to talk about painful memories. But I need to know ..." I hesitated, hating myself for pushing him, but not enough to stay quiet. Any time I'd tried to ask before, I'd been told to focus on my recovery. Now that I was out of medical, I couldn't wait anymore. "What happened when I was attacked?"

Ramsey's face darkened. His shoulders tensed, his brow furrowed, and a shocking, steely glint of anger lit in his eyes.

"Ramsey?"

He shook his head. "Forgive me. I don't like to think about it."

"I can't *stop* thinking about it." The possibilities of what could have happened—how I could have ended up here—consumed my thoughts. Every time my shoulder twinged with pain, every time I stumbled when the migraines raged in my head—it was all I could think about.

He must have seen something in my face, because he nodded and sat straighter in his chair. "You're right. You should know. I'm sorry we kept it from you. That *I* kept it from you. I just thought if you had one less thing to worry about ..."

I understood his point of view. Maybe when I'd first woken up wasn't the best time to learn what had happened to me. I'd been so delirious with pain those first two weeks, I had little recollection of them at all. Mostly, I remembered Ramsey's low assurances in my ear and the debilitating pain that rose and fell in unpredictable torrents. The weeks that followed had been overwhelming as they informed me of who I was, who they were, and how I could begin to recover. Between trying to wrap my mind around all I'd lost and finding ways to breathe through the worst of the pain, I'd been a mess.

Maybe I still was. But I needed to know. It was a visceral thing, writhing deep within my chest. There was so much I didn't understand. So much I was still missing. I'd go crazy if I didn't at least understand *this.*

"We were excited," he said, flashing me a sad smile. "Our engagement celebration was coming up. I'd been so busy. We both had. We just wanted some time together. So we were going to go outside of the city for the morning. You wanted to find some wildflowers to gather for the party—butterfly milkweed. Your mother used to tend them."

Used to. My breath caught at the mention of my family, another topic left untouched during my recovery. But this was a question I didn't dare ask, even now. Part of me knew there would be no good answer. Not when I hadn't been visited by any family throughout my recovery and the conversation was redirected any time I began to ask. So I let it be. I could only handle so much at a time.

"You know it's forbidden to enter the forests beyond the city gates. It's been too dangerous for us to venture out there since the divide. But things had been quiet for a while, so it didn't seem too dire to risk it—not for something that meant so much to you."

Ramsey took a deep breath and stared down at the table. "But the morning we were to go out, I was called away. You said you'd wait for me, but something must have changed your mind. You went out on your own. As soon as I realized you'd gone without me, I stopped what I was doing and went after you. I took some guards with me, just in case. We found you unharmed, but the rebel forces were nearby, Hayden among them. There was a fight—a bad one—and you were caught in the crossfire."

When he looked up, his eyes glimmered in the light, a sheen of tears visible over his fiery gaze. "I swear I'll never forgive myself for it."

"It wasn't your fault," I tried to reassure him, shaking my head. "I'm the one who—"

"Sovereign!"

I startled as the loud call of Ramsey's title rang through the room. My movement jolted the table, splashing tea over the edges of my cup. Pulse racing, I spun to face the speaker.

Three guards strode toward our table from the opposite side of the room. I recognized the tallest—a brunet with tousled hair and pale skin—as Gage Argusten. Cethin Radnor kept pace at his side, his blond hair glinting under the overhead lights. The woman in front of them, I didn't recognize. Her slim twists were gathered into a high ponytail that whipped from side to side as she marched toward us. The fierce look on her face wasn't tempered by her height, though she stood inches shorter than the men behind her.

The gold buttons adorning both sides of her military jacket caught the light with every step, complementing the double strands of a gold chain that dipped from shoulder to chest, where they connected to a large pin of Anluan's crest. An ornate gold tree stood within the navy center. The way the delicate lines of its branches and roots stretched the length of the oval and glinted as she moved was striking. Four golden points connected around it to create a diamond.

Whoever this woman was, she obviously had authority.

"What's happened?" Ramsey asked, his voice steely as he stood from the table to meet them. It was incredible how quickly he switched from my fiancé to Sovereign of Anluan.

"Sovereign, we have"—she paused, her brown eyes darting to me, then back to Ramsey so quickly I might've missed it if I hadn't been paying close attention—"a situation."

"I gathered that, Commander. Would one of you mind telling me what the situation *is*?"

She and Cethin stepped past me so they could lean close to Ramsey and speak to him in urgent whispers. I couldn't hear a word, though I was certainly close enough to if they'd spoken at a normal volume. Ramsey's eyes flashed at whatever he heard, his mouth tightening into a thin line. He gave a sharp nod to the commander, who called for the remaining guards in the room to head out.

A brief touch to my arm turned my attention from Ramsey. Gage stood close enough I could see amber flecks brightening his eyes. He dipped his head to me with a playful smirk.

"Princess, good to see you out and about."

I blinked, my brow creasing. I'd read that old world title in a book during recovery, but hadn't heard it used, let alone to refer to me. "Thank you ...?"

Cethin smacked his shoulder with a scowl. "Stop wasting time. Let's go."

Without another word, the guards charged from the room.

I turned to Ramsey, who attempted an apologetic smile. It didn't quite reach his eyes. "I'll have to leave you for a while, Khara. I have things to attend to."

Nerves fluttered in my stomach. "What's going on?"

"Please don't worry about it. There's no time to explain. I have to go." He glanced at the door, and some of the tension left his shoulders. "Emila's here. She'll stay with you for the day."

She reached us as he finished speaking and they exchanged a loaded glance.

"I've got her," Emila said. "Go."

The way they could have full conversations while barely saying a word bothered me. Part of it was pure jealousy. I wanted to remember them well enough to do the same. The other was equal parts concern and an annoyance I tried to smother. Was I the only one who *didn't* know what was going on?

"I'll reassign some of the guards to watch over you both," Ramsey said, and my brows pulled down as concern overpowered my other feelings. He took my hand and gave it a comforting squeeze. "Just a precaution. You know how overprotective I can be." He pressed a kiss to my cheek. "I'll come find you when I'm finished."

With that, he strode from the room, leaving me alone in the commons with Emila and a slew of worries.

8

EMILA REFUSED TO LEAVE the commons until Ramsey sent two guards to watch over us. At least, that was what she told me. I suspected she wanted to linger so she could take her time waking up.

Just as she polished off the last of her blueberry bread, the commander and Gage returned.

"Finally!" A teasing glint shone in Emila's eyes as she grinned up at the pair. "I'm glad Ramsey stuck us with you and not a recruit."

Gage barked a laugh. "I don't think they could handle the pressure."

"Those recruits," the commander interjected, "are still learning the ropes. They'll do just fine once they're fully trained." She gestured to Gage, meeting my eyes and adding, "I'd be more worried about being saddled with this one."

Gage's hand flew to his chest as he gave an exaggerated look of offense.

Emila rolled her eyes and spoke before either could retort. "Khara, this is Gage Argusten, one of the Tower Guards."

"That means I'm the best," Gage said with a wink.

The commander glared. "It means you're *one* of the best."

"Tower Guards?" I echoed, hating that I had to be reminded of yet another thing I would have known four months ago.

"Tower Guards are the Sovereign's most elite force. We protect Anluan—and more importantly, its leaders—from attacks by the rebel forces. Coryndé Isiraden," the commander said as she brought a fist over her heart and bowed her head, "I'm Commander Charna North, one of the senior training officers for the Tower Guards."

Emila smirked. "Char's a friend. When she's not on duty, anyway."

Charna focused her glare on Emila. "Is this going to be another day where the two of you drive me insane?"

Gage raised a brow. "Is it a day that ends in *y*?"

Their banter was beyond me, and yet I found myself relaxing. Gage's playfulness made me feel less threatened by whatever was taking up Ramsey's attention. Surely if he was cracking jokes like this, the danger couldn't be quite so imminent. Charna's no-nonsense leadership exuded the confidence of someone in total control. With her around, I doubted I'd run into any trouble.

"It's nice to meet you both." I winced at how awkward the words felt. "Again, I mean."

"Don't worry about these two." Emila's voice was soft but sure as she rubbed my arm. "You've met them before, but they're not going to make a fuss about it."

Both Charna and Gage nodded.

"It's not your fault those monsters stole your memories." Bitterness tinged Gage's voice.

"Anyway," Emila said, redirecting the conversation to safer territory, "Ramsey wanted me to show you around and speak to you about your role in Anluan as future Sovereigna. Are you up for it?"

I wasn't sure, if I was being honest. This was already more excitement than I'd had since I'd woken in medical weeks ago. My pills were starting to wear off, and a dull headache threatened to form at the back of my head. But with Ramsey dealing with some sort of crisis, I didn't want to add to anyone's worry. "Where to first?"

Emila grinned. "I know the perfect spot."

When the summer breeze moved across my face, my heart soared with gratitude. I was lucky to have a friend like Emila. Breathing in the fresh air and sitting in a patch of warm sunlight felt incredible after so many weeks stuck indoors.

She'd led us from the commons and down a maze of hallways I'd get lost trying to explore on my own—not that I expected anyone to let me try anytime soon. With Emila leading the way, Charna at my left, and Gage walking behind me, we made our way to a glass hallway that revealed an expansive courtyard garden.

Trees grew in clusters here, surrounded by grassy patches, shrubs, and an assortment of colorful flowers. A cobblestone pathway wound around the outer edge, with additional paths trailing inward toward the center. I caught sight of a few ornate stone benches, placed both under the shade of the trees and in areas of full sun.

It was the best thing I'd seen in weeks.

"This is …" I trailed off, my hand covering my mouth as I took in the garden with wide eyes. There were no words to convey the thrum of life in my veins at the sight.

Emila laughed brightly. "Your favorite place. Ramsey had this built for you. He knew you'd want a space to enjoy the outdoors. You've always loved being in nature, and Anluan's a little lacking in that department, at least within the gates. He wanted you to have a space you could do your art, read a book …" She shrugged and stretched her arms wide, her smile rivaling the brightness of the sun. "Not a bad engagement present, is it?"

I smiled softly. "It's a very good one."

"Come on." Emila waved me farther into the garden. "We can talk over on a bench."

We took a paved path that trailed toward the center of the courtyard. Emila kept a slow pace at my side, which suited me just fine. An unhurried stroll in the fresh air was more than welcome, even with the heat.

When we neared a fork in the path, I glanced to the left. A hedge of rose bushes surrounded a stone bench in an otherwise secluded pocket of the garden. Though trees provided shade nearby, the bench itself sat in full sun. It made such an inviting picture, I crossed in front of Emila and took the path toward it without a second thought.

The closer I came to the bench, the more impressed I was by the display. It was a masterful work of art on its own. The long stone seat curved at the edges, easily making room for four people to rest comfortably. Thick armrests curled on both sides and connected with the high back of the bench where ornate carvings led to a gentle point in the middle. Detailed leaves and flowers filled the backrest so fully that it had to have been a hand-carved commission.

I trailed my palm over the top of the bench, the stone warming my hand. Faint blush roses threatened to cascade over the edges, and I traced a finger over the petals. A sweet and spicy aroma filled the air, tickling my mind with familiarity. Throat tight, I leaned closer to breathe in the scent until tears pricked my eyes. It was silly, crying over the smell of a rose. But there was something about it …

I shook myself, blinking away the tears before Emila or the guards could see. This garden was here for me to enjoy, not to weep over for no reason. As I took a step back, my eyes caught on letters elegantly carved into the front edge of the seat between two curling vines.

Avyanna. Beauty in Strength, Power in Love.

"What does that mean?" I asked, gesturing to the engraving as Emila stepped beside me.

She stared past the bench to the roses swaying in the breeze. "It's in honor of Avyanna, one of our former Sovereignas. She was known as a kind and noble ruler, one Anluan lost too soon. Ramsey wanted to recognize her."

"A memorial." My chest tightened with borrowed grief and the weight of following in the footsteps of a woman so beloved that portions of a garden were designed in her memory.

"Of a sort." Emila hesitated. "We could sit here for a while if you want."

"No," I said, shifting back in the grass and curling a hand over my arm. Resting here when I couldn't remember the history of this woman or her contributions to Anluan felt disrespectful. And I wasn't ready to hear about the reality of becoming Sovereigna in a place dedicated to a woman of this caliber. Maybe once I found my footing again, but not yet.

I turned to take the path back to the fork. Emila hurried to catch up.

"That's fine," she said, her mouth tipping into a small smile. "I need some shade. I'm already baking in this heat."

I huffed, the knot in my chest loosening. "Then we better find a spot where we can both be happy. You'll have to drag me out of this sun. I've gone without it for far too long."

We settled on a bench in partial shade where Emila could avoid the sun while I basked in it. The light seeped into my skin, and I stretched out, smiling as I closed my eyes and breathed deeply. For several minutes, all was quiet beyond the rustle of leaves in the breeze and the chirping of birds.

"Emila?" I broke the silence, turning to face her.

She stared at nothing in particular, but blinked back to herself at her name. "Hmm?"

"Do you know what's going on? Why Ramsey had to go?"

Emila turned toward me, a delicate frown on her face. "Not the specifics. Just that it has something to do with the rebels."

"Oh." Disappointment curled in my chest. I'd hoped to glean something from her.

"You really shouldn't worry about it. Ramsey has it all under control. The rebels have been fighting him over the city for years. He knows what he's doing."

"He told me a bit about why things are the way they are."

Emila sighed. "I suppose he had to. It's not like you can live in Anluan and not hear about it."

In the ensuing quiet, her eyes glazed over. I'd seen enough of that look on both her face and Ramsey's to give her time to think.

"Since the divide," she finally continued, "Anluan's been a rough place to live. The people in the city struggle. Children have lost their parents. Parents have lost children. The people fear what the rebels will do next. The fights have lessened, but each one has been brutal. Any time the ban on leaving the city gates has been lifted, the people who go beyond them disappear. Ramsey's doing his best to make sure we all stay safe, but there's only so much one man can do, even if that man is Sovereign."

Her words landed heavily on my heart. There was so much pain I'd forgotten. So much hurt in my city, my people, my *friends*.

"But," Emila perked up, "Ramsey has you. And once you're married, we'll stand a better chance."

I cocked my head. "A better chance?"

She nodded happily. "When anyone with magic is bonded—whether it's to another gifted individual or not—the power they hold is strengthened. In unity, strength. Your union will help protect Anluan even more. And of course, you help Ramsey just by being here."

It took a moment for any implications to settle in. The one my mind latched onto, the one it let wrap around my thoughts and squeeze tight, was that I had more of a responsibility to Anluan and its people than I'd realized. The weight of it stole my breath. Could I live up to what was required of me without my memories? And if I didn't get them back, what would happen then?

Emila nudged my arm. "Stop that."

I blinked, raising my brows. "Stop what?"

"I can see you over-analyzing from here. You're important. You were just as important five minutes ago before you knew about this, and everything was fine. You need to relax."

I shrugged and looked back out toward the trees. "I'm not sure I know how to do that."

Emila's laugh carried across the courtyard. "Well, that hasn't changed."

The playfulness in her fond smile made my own form. At least here, with the sunlight on my skin and the breeze lifting strands of hair away from my face, I could breathe for a while. At least here, I was among friends. Safe. The rest, I would figure out later.

9

THE SUN SHONE HIGH in the sky when Emila demanded we go inside.

"You need to rest," she said firmly as she led me away from the bench. "This heat can't be good for you."

I wanted to argue. The fresh air called to me as if it were a living thing, a friend I'd been parted from for far too long. I wanted to stay. But my body was feeling the exhaustion of the day, and it would be useless to fight her. It was frustrating that going to breakfast, walking the halls, and spending time in the garden was enough to drain my energy.

Alone, I would have pushed myself to do more. Under the watchful eyes of Emila, Charna, and Gage, I'd be lucky to delay the journey to my room by a single minute.

"What will you do?" I asked as we entered the glass hallway leading back into the building.

Emila shrugged. "I'm sure I'll find something to entertain myself with for a few hours."

"I'll be stationed outside your door," Gage added as he walked behind me.

"As will I," Charna said.

I frowned, glancing back at them. "Is that really necessary?"

Gage smirked, amusement dancing in his amber eyes. "Why don't you ask your fiancé and see what he says?"

"It is," Charna insisted. "We'll be with you until Sovereign Ramsey relieves us from duty."

"Don't worry, Khara." Emila waved a hand at Gage. "If you're lucky, Ramsey will send someone to replace that one soon."

Gage shrugged, his smile not dimming in the slightest. "If my talents are needed elsewhere, I'll go. Until then, sorry, Princess, you're stuck with me."

I furrowed my brow at the outdated title he seemed determined to saddle me with. Maybe this was the way he interacted with people, by teasing and making things light. It wasn't the worst nickname, and it didn't feel like he was actively mocking me. If he were, surely someone would say something.

We reached an elevator and paused while Emila pressed her finger against a wooden panel. The doors opened and she stepped in, motioning for us to join her. As I did, Charna and Gage followed me inside.

Emila hit the button for the twenty-second floor, and the elevator rose fast, making my ears pop. As we leveled out, the doors opened with a soft whoosh.

"We have to switch elevators," Emila said as she stepped into the corridor. "It's a security measure set up after the divide. To get to the residential wing in this tower, you have to have authorization. Only those with access granted directly by Ramsey can go up to the private floors where your suite is. The magic ensures it."

"Only a handful of guards are allowed on your floor," Charna added. "And only when they're actively on protective detail."

I nodded, impressed by Ramsey's thoroughness. He'd taken every precaution to ensure my safety.

As we continued down the hall, a wall of large windows caught my attention. I drifted toward them, knowing the others would follow.

The view was breathtaking. We stood high enough that I could see beyond the palace grounds and out into the city. Buildings filled my view, reaching all the way back to the surrounding wall. A monument stood half-crumbled in a large piazza, several buildings forming a tight circle around it. A second courtyard spanned nearby. Some areas still seemed to be in repair—remnants of the initial battle between the rebels and Ramsey two years ago—but overall, the city seemed inviting. I wanted to immerse myself in its winding streets and get to know it again.

I could just barely see over the top of the wall near one of the gated entrances. Beyond it, trees stretched for miles. I stared, mesmerized by the expanse of forest.

"It's beautiful, isn't it?" Emila asked as she stared out at the city. "Anluan's always been a sight to behold."

"What about—?" I gestured toward the treetops outside the walls.

"Beyond the gates? Forests, mostly. Some farmland. Isiraden is to the east. Somewhere beyond the gates, the rebels have hidden their camp. Couldn't tell you much more than that." She folded her arms. "I haven't been out there in years."

"Because it's dangerous." Emila's brows lifted at my words, and I shrugged, fiddling with my engagement ring. "Ramsey told me I was attacked out there."

Her face fell as she turned away. "It happened somewhere out there. It's forbidden for anyone to leave the city. When the ban's in place, it's a capital offense. Beyond the gate, that's rebel territory. The only reason to go out there is if you have a death wish. No one who's gone out has ever come back, for one reason or another. Except for you."

Dread pooled in my gut. "What happened to the others?"

"The rebels happened. That's why we take breaching the border so seriously. It's not a game. This is war. If you go beyond the gates, you're as good as dead."

"You're dead to me. You hear me? As good as dead! Don't ever come back here!"

The furious voice ripped through my mind in a violent spark of memory. Pain flared in my head, so sharp I cried out as my knees buckled beneath me. I gripped my head in my hands as my heart thundered in my chest.

My hearing faded into a whining buzz. With my eyes squeezed shut, I wasn't sure what was happening around me. I focused on trying to breathe. The pain always seemed to steal my breath.

Hands moved over my arms and against my back, holding me up firmly. I hitched in one breath, then another. A whimper escaped as the prickling of tears built behind my eyes. I let them fall. This pain needed some form of release.

"Khara, can you hear me?" Emila's voice just barely broke through the ringing in my ears. I fought to focus on her instead of the overwhelming nausea. "If you can hear me, squeeze my hand."

Oh. There was a hand, delicate and soft, holding one of mine. I squeezed tight, focusing on the feeling of warmth as I took deep breaths.

"Good. That's good," she said, relief thick in her voice. "Do you need me to call for Doctor Jensen?"

I shook my head. I didn't need the doctor, just my pills.

Emila seemed to agree. "How many pills do you need? Two?"

I squeezed her hand once in reply. This episode was bad, worse than the one I had yesterday. And it came on so suddenly.

"Khara? I need you to take the medicine."

I opened my palm and two pills fell into it. My hand shook as I brought them to my lips and swallowed.

"Here." Emila pressed the rim of a bottle to my mouth. "Small sips."

I followed her instructions, savoring the way the cool water soothed my throat. It wasn't as pleasant when it hit my stomach, but I'd expected that. These episodes always left my gut unsettled.

"Let's give her a minute." Emila's words reminded me of the guards' presence. Of course I'd had an episode with an audience. I'd be embarrassed about it if I had the energy to be.

As the medicine kicked in, the pain dulled, and with it, my senses. It was a strange sensation, one I still wasn't used to. The water didn't wash away the bitterness of the pills, and I longed to take another sip to rid my mouth of the taste.

I blinked my eyes open. I felt off-kilter, disoriented and weak. Emila knelt in front of me, her worried face a shade paler than usual. The guards—Charna and Gage both—had gathered beside her. Gage rested on one knee, leaning forward with a dark look on his face. Charna stood behind him, her face carefully blank as she held a collapsible water bottle.

"I'm fine," I said, wincing at the hoarseness of my voice. I cleared my throat and tried again. "I'm fine."

Someone scoffed. My attempt at reassurance might have been more convincing if I could manage to keep my eyes open.

When I did, I was met with Emila's glare. "You're not *fine*, Khara."

Instead of arguing, I gave into my weariness and blinked blearily at her. "Maybe not, but I will be."

Charna offered the bottle to me, and I accepted with a shaky hand. "Drink. Rest. We'll decide our next steps in a moment."

I sipped, hoping to rid my mouth of the bitterness the pills left behind. When I'd had my fill, I gave the near-empty bottle back. My hand still trembled. "Thank you."

Charna nodded, clipping the bottle back to her belt. The others stayed quiet, their eyes focused on me.

I rubbed my temples and sighed. "We should go."

"Can you even walk?" Gage asked gruffly.

I nodded. "I can do it."

Truthfully, I wasn't sure I could, but I was going to try. Bracing myself, I pushed up from my legs, sliding my back up the wall of windows behind me. The clumsy effort left me dizzy, and I wobbled back toward the floor as black spots burst in my vision.

"Khara!"

Calloused hands held me up and I blinked into Gage's stern face.

"You got her?" Emila asked. The edge in her voice spelled trouble for me.

Gage's head jerked against me. "I've got her."

"I'm fine." It was too breathy a statement to be reassuring. My dizziness was too obvious. Why did my body have to betray me at every turn?

"We're ignoring you now," Emila said, voice tight. "We're going to get you back to your room so you can rest. If you need to stop for any reason, tell Gage."

"It might go faster if he carried her," Charna noted.

I shook my head, regretting it instantly. "I don't need—"

"Remember how I said we're ignoring you?" Emila scoffed. "Gage."

"Sorry, Princess," he said as he carefully lifted me into his arms. "Orders."

Emila led the way, her heels clicking against the marble floor. Charna followed behind, ensuring I stayed protected. With Gage's strong arms holding me up, I knew I was safe, and let myself drift.

I registered the quick lift of the elevator, then the sway of Gage's gait as he carried me down the halls. When the softness of my mattress met my back, I let myself fall completely into rest.

10

WIND BRUSHED AGAINST MY face, the chill on my cheeks invigorating as I ran through the grass. I grinned, looking back, as though someone was there—

Nothing.

Someone was supposed to be there.

My brow furrowed as I slowed to a stop. Spinning around, I spotted a grove, but it was too dark to see through the shadowy opening.

"Khara ..."

The voice came from between the trees, soft and breathy and tinged with sadness.

"Come home ..."

It was a plea, a prayer. One I didn't understand.

"Where are you?" I called into the dark. "Where's home?"

No one answered.

11

I woke with tears trailing down my face and an unsettled feeling in my gut. I knew I'd dreamed, but I couldn't remember the details. Only a feeling of loss I couldn't shake.

Groaning, I brought my hand to my forehead and tried to breathe through the pain. Despite my grogginess, the sharp ache in my head was still present, like a fresh wave had come over me in sleep. It was hardly fair the pain could grow while I wasn't even conscious.

I blinked a few times and looked around my room. It was still dark, and I didn't bother trying to find a clock. Instead, I pushed myself to my feet and clumsily made my way into the bathroom.

The light shone too brightly when I flipped it on. I shut it off and reached for a washcloth, letting cold water soak it through. When I stumbled back into bed, I settled it over my eyes, then up to my forehead.

With any luck, I'd sleep until morning.

Loud knocking roused me from sleep. Muffled calls of my name came through the door as I stretched in bed, my body stiff. The washcloth I'd gotten in the night hung halfway off the bed. I frowned as I took stock of myself. The pain was less, but I didn't feel *well*.

"Khara?" My name carried through the open bedroom door. "If you don't answer me, I'm going to come inside. I need to know you're okay."

Ramsey. I cleared my throat but thought better of raising my voice to call to him. The migraine lingered at the edges of my head, and I couldn't risk it flaring up. Instead, I sat and leaned forward, resting my head in my hands and swallowing back nausea. Sometimes the after-effects of an episode felt worse than the episode itself.

"I'm coming in!"

The front door opened, and Ramsey's quick strides moved toward the bedroom. He exhaled heavily when he stopped in my doorway. "Khara?"

"Hey," I murmured as I lifted my head to look at him.

His eyes creased with pain as he stared down at me, as if he was the one suffering. His mouth pulled down in a frown and his hands clenched and unclenched at his sides. "Hey," he said, voice soft. "I'm sorry for barging in on you, but—"

I waved him off. "It's fine. I was going to come let you in. I just ... didn't get very far."

Ramsey walked to the edge of the bed and sat beside me, trailing his hand up and down my arm. "How are you feeling?"

"I'm okay."

"No, you're not. Try again."

I rested my chin in my hand and sighed. "Did they tell you what happened yesterday?"

"You had an episode. Argusten had to carry you the rest of the way here, and you fell asleep before you'd been in bed five minutes."

"It was a bad one." I ran a hand through my hair, sitting up so I could lean against the headboard. "I woke up in the night, but I just went back to sleep."

He nodded, sadness in his eyes as he tried to smile at me. "Your body needed the rest."

I made a noncommittal sound and closed my eyes. "I'm just so tired."

"I came to take you to breakfast, but I think you may need to rest more."

"No, I should go with you." I pried my eyes open. "I didn't eat much yesterday."

Ramsey's frown became more pronounced. "You're supposed to be eating better."

I knew that. I also knew the nausea plaguing me wouldn't allow it. "I'll try to do better today. I promise."

"Thank you." He gently took my hand and brought it to his lips for a kiss. "You're sure you want to go to the commons? I could have someone bring a meal here instead."

It was tempting, but I didn't want anyone to think I needed to go back to medical. If I stayed in my room, I had a feeling I'd sleep the day away. Exhaustion clung heavily to my mind.

"I could use the walk," I said finally, looking hopefully at him.

His lips curved into a slow smile. "Don't think I can't see how tired you are. I'll follow your lead on this, but if something happens and you need to come back—"

"I'll let you know."

"Preferably *before* you collapse."

I huffed. "I'll try."

"I suppose that's all I can ask. Would you like to shower first?"

I shook my head. While warm water sounded heavenly, I was afraid it would lull me to sleep. Or worse, exhaust me. "Food first. I'll just get dressed."

"I'll wait for you in the other room," Ramsey said as he stood. "Call if you need any help."

He moved to shut the door behind him, leaving it slightly cracked. I slid from my bed, waiting a moment to catch my balance before I made my way to the dresser to find something to wear. The commons was a casual space, so I grabbed a pair of flowing pants and a soft sweater and tossed my hair into a messy bun at the base of my neck. It would do for now.

"I'm ready," I said as I stepped into the living room.

He turned from the window and smiled. "You look lovely."

"I'm sure I look exactly how I feel, and lovely isn't the word I'd use."

"Trust me." Stepping closer until he was right in front of me, he trailed his hands up my arms until they rested on my shoulders. Moving one hand to cradle my cheek, he brushed his thumb back and forth over my skin. "You're the most stunning woman I've ever known. Even at your worst, you're beyond compare."

My cheeks warmed at his words—ones I was sure were an exaggeration—but I did my best to take the compliment. I kept my eyes trained on our feet. "Thank you."

He lifted my chin with his finger. "Don't hide, Khara. Not from me."

My eyes met his, and I was struck still. So much stirred in the depths of his gaze. I wished I could identify each emotion glinting there like the fiery flecks the light revealed. Neither of us spoke. The quiet rhythm of our breathing thickened the air with tension.

Then Ramsey took a step back, letting his hands fall away as he cleared his throat. "Breakfast, then?"

I inhaled a shaky breath and nodded. Breakfast would be a welcome distraction.

Silence filled the elevator as we descended. Ramsey stared ahead at the doors, eyes unfocused and brow furrowed. Whatever he had on his mind was obviously important. I didn't want to disturb him, so I leaned back against the wall, leaving him to his thoughts.

When we exited the elevator, Ramsey laced our hands together. "Forgive me. I didn't mean to get so distracted."

"You seem to have a lot on your mind."

"I do. There's a lot going on right now."

"Anything I can help with?" I asked as he led us into the second elevator.

He smiled as he hit the button for level three. "It's nothing you need to worry about. I want you to focus on healing. This"—he waved his hand dismissively—"is just something I'm going to have to deal with."

I wasn't sure what to say to that, but Ramsey continued before I had a chance to speak.

"Actually," he said as we stepped out onto our floor, "that's one of the things I wanted to talk to you about."

"Okay." I pulled him to a stop and turned to face him.

He blew out a breath, rubbing the back of his neck. "Yesterday we discovered a rebel plot, one that threatens the city." He shifted closer, resting a hand against my cheek. "I don't want you to worry. I promise we're taking care of it. It just means I'm going to be busier than I want to be for a while. You might not see much of me until this is handled."

I sagged. That was all? I could never be upset with him for taking care of our people. He'd spent so much of his time beside me as I recovered. I could handle seeing less of him while he protected Anluan from this new threat.

"Ramsey," I said, placing my hand over his. "I don't expect you to be by my side every minute. Of course you're needed, especially now. Take care of whatever needs to be done."

His eyes softened with fondness as he looked down at me. "You're better than I deserve. Thank you for understanding."

I smiled back and nodded toward the commons. "Breakfast, then?"

"Breakfast," he said with a laugh. "I'll have to step out early, but I already called Emila to come join you. She's going to keep you company while I'm working. And you'll have two guards with you every day until this is resolved."

I sighed. "Is that really necessary? I don't think—"

He tugged my hand, bringing us to a stop outside the room. "We have to limit which of our cameras are in use due to power rationing." He pointed to the corner where a small camera was mounted near the ceiling. Unlike the one I'd noticed while leaving medical, no glow surrounded it. This camera wasn't operational.

"We have magic working to keep the Annex as safe as I can possibly make it," Ramsey continued, shifting my attention back to him. "But I'd never forgive myself if something happened to you because I grew too confident about our security. Please, Khara. Give me this peace of mind."

The earnestness in his face made me relent. "Okay. Two guards."

"You'll hardly notice them."

I doubted that, though I could appreciate the sentiment.

He kept my hand in his, leading us into the commons. People stared again this morning, but the looks were much more fleeting. I had a feeling there'd been a conversation about it since yesterday's breakfast.

Ramsey led me to the same table as before, where two steaming plates sat waiting for us. At my seat, a cup of herbal tea sent peppermint-scented steam into the air. Rich coffee wafted from Ramsey's cup at the head of the table.

"I had one of the guards get us plates before I came to see you," he said as he pulled my chair out for me. "I want to make sure I get to spend as much time with you as possible. I won't have long before someone whisks me away."

"It's great, Ramsey," I said as I took my seat. "Thank you."

He settled into his chair and reached for his coffee. I followed suit, eagerly cupping my tea in both hands. The smell of peppermint strengthened, and I inhaled deeply before taking a sip. Its soothing warmth lowered my shoulders, and I relaxed into the meal.

Not five minutes later, Emila shuffled to the table with a full plate and steaming mug. She slumped into the seat beside me, blinking down at her coffee with glazed eyes. I gently nudged her arm.

She spared me a narrow-eyed glance before pouring a generous serving of cream into her cup. "No talking until I've had at least half of this."

I raised both hands in surrender, fighting a smile.

Ramsey met my eyes and smirked before pretending to whisper. "It's best to ignore her until she's caffeinated."

Emila glared at him and pointedly took a large gulp of coffee before looking away.

"Sovereign."

We looked up and found a small group of guards headed for our table.

Ramsey still had half a plate of food in front of him, but as he shifted to stand, I knew he wouldn't finish it. "Any news?"

The guard shook his head. "Nothing concrete, sir. But we have new reports you should be briefed on."

Ramsey nodded, running a hand through his hair. "Of course."

He turned to me, an apologetic grimace on his face. I wished he wouldn't worry so much about leaving me. I understood the responsibilities he shouldered as Sovereign. I wasn't the only one who needed him, and right now, they needed him more. "Go. I'll be fine. Emila's here."

He glanced at her and raised a brow.

She waved him off without looking up from her coffee. "You heard the woman. We're fine. Go on."

With that reassurance, Ramsey pressed a kiss to my forehead. "I'll assign two guards to you when I finish the initial briefing. Please try to rest when you need to."

"I will." It was the least I could do to ease his mind while he dealt with whatever threat loomed.

He stared at me for another long moment.

"Honestly, Ramsey." I squeezed his hand. "I'll be okay. Go. Anluan needs you."

He nodded. "Until later, then."

"Yes, yes," Emila interrupted, waving her hand toward him dismissively while the other warmed against her mug. "Leave already. We've got important things of our own to catch up on. Like wedding plans."

That got a grin out of him.

"Then I'll leave you to it." He turned to leave but paused after a few steps. "Oh, Khara," he said, his eyes sparkling as he returned to the table. "I have a gift for you."

He reached into his jacket and pulled out a small box wrapped in rich, burgundy paper. As he set it in front of me, he leaned forward to whisper in my ear. "Always remember that I'd much rather be spending my time with you."

The words made me shiver. Or maybe it was the way his breath brushed over my skin. Either way, though I hadn't doubted him, the reassurance was welcome.

With another press of his lips to my forehead, Ramsey turned and led the guards from the room.

As I picked at the remainder of my breakfast, I studied Emila. Her eyes brightened more with every sip of coffee she took. By the time her cup was empty, they were practically sparkling, and like magic, I had my lively friend back.

"You haven't opened it," she said, looking pointedly at the package on the table before staring at me as she started on a second cup.

"I will," I said, fiddling with the rim of my mug. "Later."

"What? Why not now?"

"Does it need to be now?"

"Of course it needs to be now! Your doting fiancé—who just so happens to be the most powerful man in Anluan, in case you forgot—gave you a present. On a whim." She reached across the table and slid the box closer to me. "Don't you want to see what he got you?"

"I do." My curiosity rose as I trailed a finger over the smooth burgundy wrapping. "Of course I do. I just thought I'd open it later. In private."

"*In private?*"

I drew back at her incredulous screech. Grateful the commons had mostly emptied, I sank lower in my seat. "Yes?"

"Khara, come on, don't do this to me!" She set her palms flat on the table. "You're curious. I'm curious. We can both leave this room happy!"

Laughter burst from my lips. "Emila—"

"Khara."

We stared each other down. Emila raised a brow as she leaned closer, a challenge if I ever saw one. My lips twitched at the absurdity. All this over when to open a gift?

The box sat in Emila's shadow and my hand still rested against it. I tapped a finger as I considered. Ramsey hadn't given the gift to me in my suite. He'd waited until we were here. Surely it wasn't anything too personal to open now. And I did want to know what was inside.

Without breaking eye contact, I inched the box to the edge of the table and stopped trying to hold back my smile.

Emila grinned back, her eyes sparkling as she straightened and clapped her hands. "Yes!"

I laughed as I slid a finger under the seam of the wrapping. Magic thrummed as my hand made contact with a small wooden box. Isiraden wood. The box alone would be gift enough, but knowing Ramsey, there would be more to the present.

My eyes widened as I lifted the white marble top. Three delicate gold bracelets sat inside, nestled on a velvet lining. Each band had been engraved with the same flowers carved into my bedroom door.

Emila whistled. "Someone has good taste."

"He does." I picked up one of the bands, admiring the craftsmanship. It was stunning, the kind of jewelry worthy of a Sovereigna.

I froze. Soon enough, I'd be filling that role as Ramsey's wife.

With careful hands, I replaced the bracelet inside the box and fastened the lid. I didn't want to think about that now.

"You don't want to wear them?"

I glanced at my outfit. "They're a little too nice to wear with this, don't you think?"

"Khara, when you have bracelets like those, you can wear them with whatever you want."

I smiled and shook my head. "What's on the agenda for today?"

She didn't comment on the change of subject, though her eyes told me she knew exactly what I was doing. "I thought we'd go to the garden, and go over some of the expectations of you as future Sovereigna. How's that sound?"

Relief washed over me. A better sense of what was ahead would ease the anxiety that kept welling up in me. I hoped. "Like a weight off my shoulders."

Emila quickly downed the last dregs of her coffee and set the mug back on the table. "In that case, we should get started."

12

Two weeks after my interrupted breakfast with Ramsey, I opened my door, ready for another day of Sovereigna lessons, to find Emila bouncing lightly on her feet in the hall. I blinked, taking in the wide-leg pants sitting high on her waist and the sensible flats on her feet. She looked as stylish as ever, but she usually favored flirty dresses and heeled sandals. My brow furrowed and suspicion rose as she beamed at me, a glint of mischief sparkling in her eyes. I'd come to recognize that look as a precursor for either something very good or very bad.

"Are you up for a drive?" she asked, unusually alert for the morning hour.

"A what?"

"A drive! You know, getting out of here, seeing the city from the safety of a moving vehicle?"

My mouth fell open and I tightened my grip on the door as hope rose warm in my chest. I'd been asking when I could go into Anluan during every Sovereigna training session we'd had over the last two weeks. It had been a definitive *no* every time. But if something had changed, if this was being allowed …

Emila nodded, practically buzzing with excitement. "Grab whatever you need and let's go, before someone decides we're better off cooped up!"

I'd never moved faster.

The sun warmed my face as I followed Emila and our assigned guard out of the Annex. Even tinged with humidity, the fresh air was a gift. I spent far too much time indoors. My shirt sticking to my back was a small price to pay for this excursion.

We exited from a side door and stepped onto the path that wound through a neatly manicured lawn. The guard took the lead, striding down the pavement toward the lot where palace vehicles were stored. While I trailed along with Emila at first, I couldn't help lingering behind. I hadn't been outside yet, other than in the garden, and refused to waste the opportunity to take in the palace grounds.

I turned back to the Annex, craning my neck to take in as much of the building as I could. My breath caught at its magnificence.

The Annex towered in the sky, a beautifully crafted mix of limestone and patterned beige bricks. The stone base made up the first few floors before it thinned, stretching up in the center where it hugged four windows on each floor before ending in a shouldered arch. The limestone created a subtle pattern, broken only by the decorative ledges that added dimension beneath the windows on the first and third floors.

Tall, rectangular windows lined the lower levels. They were trimmed in black panes that continued onto the glass and divided it into squares. The glass itself mirrored the surrounding area rather than offering a view inside. I appreciated the extra measure of security as much as the reflection of the lush palace grounds around me.

Without looking away from the Annex, I shuffled back a few steps until I could make out where the limestone changed to light brick. The upper windows, like the ones in my suite, were a blend of straight and arched tops, all trimmed by elegant black lines. The uppermost levels where Ramsey and I lived disrupted the straight look of the building with layers of protruding rooms. Tipping my head further, I could just barely make out the deep navy Anluan flag waving at the topmost point of the tower.

My fingers itched with the need to draw it. How could I have forgotten something so beautiful? If the Annex exuded such luxury, I couldn't imagine how the palace itself looked.

From this angle, I didn't have a great view of it. Standing in the shade of the Annex, I could only make out a bit of crumbled white stone and scaffolding. It was disappointing. I wanted more than a glimpse of the palace, though I wasn't sure I had the energy to grieve over the damage to what had once been a lavish building. And my former home.

I grimaced as I took slow steps backward. Maybe it was for the best we were walking along the side of the Annex instead of the front.

My eyes flicked up and caught a second navy flag billowing in the summer breeze at the far side of the palace. The Annex's twin tower, where I'd learned the majority of the guard trained and slept, reached high enough that the top was visible from here. At least some of the palace grounds had survived the initial destruction of the war.

Emila tugged my arm, keeping me on the path as it curved to the right. "Please don't trip and fall on me. We'll never get to do something like this again if you get hurt."

I huffed, but turned and fixed my eyes on the path ahead. "I have no intention of getting hurt, Emila."

"Doesn't mean you won't."

I hated that she was right. I heaved a sigh. "I'll do my best not to disrupt our adventure."

Emila frowned, reaching for my arm again to bring us both to a stop. "I was just kidding. You know that, right?"

I shrugged, staring at the covered lot ahead of us. My limitations didn't feel like a joke to me. I hated that I was still struggling so much. If outings like this would be restricted if I had an episode, what hope did I have of reintegrating myself into Anluan properly?

"I'm sorry." The regret in Emila's tone was thick enough to bring my eyes straight to hers. "I didn't mean to upset you."

I shook my head, trying for a reassuring smile. "Forget it. Let's just enjoy ourselves while we can."

She gave my arm a gentle squeeze. "Now that, I can do."

As we stepped under the covering, I spotted Gage. He leaned against the boxy, black cab of a vehicle. His grin widened as he watched us approach.

"Good morning, ladies!" He waved to the guard who'd escorted us. "I've got it from here, Wynn. You're dismissed."

Emila glanced at me before crossing her arms and raising a brow at Gage. "You weren't assigned to us today."

"Thought I'd drive you around." He shrugged easily, and the twinkle in his eyes made my lips quirk up.

"*I* am driving us." Emila stepped into his space and held out her palm. When Gage didn't move, she pursed her lips and started tapping her foot. The pat of her flats against the pavement wasn't nearly as impressive as it would've been if she'd worn her normal heels.

"That's very intimidating," Gage commented, flipping a keyring around on his pointer finger. "But as I'm the one with the keys, I think I'll drive."

Emila's chest heaved. As amusing as it would've been to watch her go on a tirade, I preferred to keep the morning's peace intact. If I could ease the tension, even a little, maybe we would actually get to see Anluan before lunch. "Why don't I drive?"

They both froze before slowly turning to face me in an eerie synchronicity that made my heart sink. It was clear neither of them would let me drive. That wasn't surprising. Honestly, I wasn't even sure I knew how. But I hadn't meant to cause the tension that lined Emila's shoulders or made Gage's smile dim.

"I don't think—"

"It was a joke," I assured Emila as I tried not to wince. "A bad one, apparently."

She blew out a breath, tucking her hair behind her ear. "You know I'd let you if you weren't at risk of having an episode. Really, I—"

"It's fine. I understand." I smiled at her, then at Gage, before glancing at the keys in his hand. "What I *don't* understand is why you'd rather stand here arguing when we could be out exploring already."

I bit back a grin as Emila scuffed her shoe against the ground. Gage rubbed the back of his neck with an awkward smile.

I tried to keep the amusement out of my voice. "So, who gets the honor of driving?"

They glanced at each other, eyes narrowed. Before either could speak, Charna strode up behind Gage and plucked the keys from his hand.

"I will be driving you, Coryndé." The look she leveled at Gage and Emila dared them to object. "If you're going off palace grounds, it will be under my protection."

No one argued. The commander would be the safest person to travel with, all things considered. I trusted her to keep me safe.

Gage heaved a put-out sigh, but the way his lips twitched gave me the feeling it was exaggerated. "There goes my excitement for the day. Let me at least put the battery in for you."

Emila rolled her eyes, but Charna nodded.

I watched, fascinated, as Gage unzipped his jacket pocket and pulled out a thin, glowing cylinder. The blue-white color flickered and danced inside the tube. Emila had mentioned the batteries to me—a blend of magic and science that powered much of our technology, like the vehicles. They were fueled by the magic of the Shalémo line, their lightning harnessed into useable energy. With them leading the rebellion, we had no way of replenishing the storehouse. This magic was rare now, whereas it had once been so commonplace the idea of rationing the power would have been laughable.

Something about it called to me. I wanted to reach out and touch it, but a flicker of pain in my head stilled my hand. I gritted my teeth and shoved it down. I refused to end this trip before it began because of another migraine. Not when I was finally about to see some of Anluan for myself.

Though there were reasons maybe this wasn't the best idea.

"Are you sure it's okay for us to use that?" I asked Emila as Gage finished inserting the battery and shut the hood. "You just told me about the rations. I didn't think before, but maybe we shouldn't use a battery just for this. What if the guards need a car and don't have enough power?"

"Ramsey authorized it. We're fine," Emila said, waving away my concerns. "So few people are cleared to use the vehicles, it's not going to be an issue."

"She's right," Gage said. "The guard rarely uses the vehicles anyway. There's not much need inside the city, and we don't leave much anymore. The foresters and farmers have what they need, and most deliveries from the other Diamond Kingdoms come to us. One battery won't break us."

"If it makes you feel better, Coryndé, I'll check up on a few things as we drive," Charna offered. "Then this will be guard business, not just a leisurely trip."

Her idea unraveled the knot of anxiety in my chest. "Please do. Anything you need."

"I'll see to it." She smiled, dipping her head, then moved toward the driver's seat. "Whoever's coming, get in the car. I don't have all day."

Gage rubbed his hands together. "Don't mind if I do."

Emila smacked a hand against his chest, halting his steps. "You weren't invited. I'm sure you have more important things to do."

As Gage hummed a noncommittal sound, I ducked my head to hide a grin and slipped into the backseat.

"One of these days, I swear," Emila huffed, pushing away from Gage and striding to the backseat. She stuck out her tongue as she slammed and locked the door. Shaking her head, she jammed her seatbelt into place.

"And you wonder why the two of you exasperate me on a regular basis," Charna drawled from the front as she ignited the engine. The leather seats rumbled softly beneath us.

I peeked out the window and couldn't help but laugh at the satisfied grin on Gage's face. He waved and sauntered off. Emila narrowed her eyes at me, but she couldn't hide her amusement any more than she could hide the delicate pink flush spreading across her cheeks.

13

THE GENTLE HUM OF the car fed the butterflies in my stomach as we turned onto the main road. I hadn't been outside of the Annex, let alone off palace grounds, since the attack. This drive felt like a lifeline after being so cooped up.

"Where will we go first?" I asked as I pressed myself as close to the window as I could. I didn't want to miss a single thing Anluan had to offer today.

"We'll take the main road, see what interests you," Charna said as she eased onto the pass and picked up speed. "If you want me to pull over at any point, say so."

"Most of the streets in Anluan weren't built for vehicles," Emila added. "They're too narrow, especially in the older districts near Monusbé Circle. But the main road follows the wall around the entire city. It should make a nice enough overview for now."

We lapsed into silence. I didn't mind. I was too enraptured with the sights out my window. The palace grounds gave way to lines of brick and stone buildings—some in states of disrepair, others with obvious construction happening. Remnants of the initial divide two years ago, I assumed. I peered between the buildings, down paved streets and ones lined with cobblestone, desperate to take in any additional glimpses of my home city. They were fleeting—only the barest flashes of life as the car drove past—but they settled something inside me. They made Anluan more real somehow, brought life to the map on my wall and the stories shared with me over the past few weeks.

Charna slowed as we reached one of the gates. The thick, wooden door stood tall, and the surrounding gray stone stretched higher than the wall itself. I couldn't see the top from inside the car.

"Do you mind if I step outside for a moment?" Charna asked, glancing back at me in the mirror. "I'll be quick."

Emila shrugged and turned to me.

"Go ahead, Commander," I said. "Whatever you need to do."

Her lips tipped into a smile as she dipped her head. "I'll return shortly. Do not," she said, turning to face Emila with a stern expression, "leave this vehicle."

"Wasn't planning on it." Emila waved her off, though a smirk belied her innocent tone. "Go on, get to it. The sooner you wrap up, the sooner we can get on with our tour."

Charna shook her head as she shut the door. I watched as she walked to the gate and began to speak to the group of guards gathered out front.

"What are they doing?" It seemed a large number of guards to mind a gate that mostly stayed closed.

"Imports from Branton come in here at the northern gate. Looks like we're expecting one today. Which is good, because we're running low on green olives."

"Oh yes," I said, "going without your olives would be tragic."

Emila narrowed her eyes as she leaned back in her seat. The leather creaked as she gave a theatrical sigh. "You only say that because you don't remember what Branton olives taste like."

"Do I even like olives?" I asked, wrinkling my nose as I tried to remember if I'd had any. My gaze traveled back out the window, watching a few people milling around.

"You know, I'm not sure."

I grinned. "Guess I'll have to try some of yours when this shipment comes in."

"If I feel inclined to share."

"You're claiming an entire import of olives for yourself?"

"Yes. Yes, I am."

I laughed, shaking my head as I turned my attention back to the gate. One of the guards gripped arms with Charna. The rest dipped their heads with an arm crossed over their chests.

I gestured to the scene. "Commander North is well respected, then?"

Emila shifted closer, looking out the front of the car. "She is. And she deserves every ounce of it. I don't think there's a more worthy commander in all of the Diamond Kingdoms. And I'm not just saying that because she's my friend."

The fondness in her words spoke volumes.

"I like her," I said as I watched Charna stride back toward us.

"She likes you too. More than you know."

Charna opened the door and we both went quiet, settling back into our seats. She glanced at us as she sank into the driver's seat, suspicion narrowing her eyes. "What were you two talking about?"

"Olives," I said. "There's a shipment arriving today?"

Charna flicked her eyes to Emila. "You and your olives." She turned her gaze to me in the mirror as she buckled herself in. "Yes, there's a delivery from Branton expected any minute."

"Please tell me they have it under control," Emila said, her hands folded in front of her heart. "Please, Char! I can't stand the disappointment again."

"Disappointment?" I asked.

"I don't think this conversation is appropriate to have in front of Coryndé while she's still recovering."

"She's fine. You're fine, aren't you, Khara?"

I was lost, but not unwell. "Um, yes?"

"A glowing reassurance," Charna muttered. "They have it under control. And if they don't, we'll handle it as we always do."

"But the olives!"

"I'm sorry," I said, my eyes darting between them. "What's under control?"

Emila winced, sharing a look with Charna, who raised a single brow. It was Emila who finally answered, her words slow and careful. "The rebels have been known to *appropriate* our imports."

I blinked. "You're saying they steal our supplies."

"Sometimes, yes," Charna said. "The rebels attack the delivery vehicles. Sometimes they only take certain goods. Other times, the whole shipment."

My heart sped in my chest. Maybe leaving the palace grounds wasn't the best idea. "How soon is the delivery set to arrive?"

Charna turned to face me, calm and assured in the face of my rising fear. "We'll be miles away by the time they open the gate, Coryndé. You have nothing to worry about."

She held my gaze for a long moment. Confidence shone from her brown eyes, slowing my heartbeat back to its normal rhythm. I took a steadying breath and nodded. She returned the gesture.

"If we continue along this road, we'll circle back to the Annex within the hour. If you'd like to shorten the trip, let me know. We can make any necessary adjustments."

"Thank you."

"Want to take your mind off things?" Emila asked as Charna pulled the car back onto the road. "I can quiz you."

Quizzing had become something of a game between us. Rather than force me to study in what Emila referred to as *stuffy old books*, she helped me learn through conversation and stories. After she'd told me enough information about Anluan, the Diamond Kingdoms, or my future duties as Sovereigna, she'd give me the chance to fill in the blanks. So far, it had proven effective.

When I nodded, Emila straightened with a grin, turning in her seat to face me more fully. "Branton's people traditionally have—?"

"—gifts relating to the control of fire," I finished.

"Panra?"

"To the south. Connected to the earth. Rocks, vines, flowers, trees."

Charna nodded, her lips turning up in the mirror. "They make pilgrimages to Isiraden Forest, you know."

"Pilgrimages?" I perked up at the new information.

"The grove is sacred," Charna said simply. "The journey is a rite of passage as Panran children come of age. They come to feel a deeper connection to magic and consider their purpose in the world. To give thanks for the life they have."

"To the trees?"

"To the ones they believe created them, the source of all magic."

"Yes, it's all very fascinating," Emila cut in, waving a hand. "But this is not a religious tour, so—Coroden."

"Air or wind, depending on how you look at it." I furrowed my brows. "Mountain region to the ... east?"

"West," Emila corrected.

I tried not to let the error bother me, but as always, it was a struggle. The weight of my role as future Sovereigna bore down on me. It was too important a position for me to not give my best to it. I tried, but some days, even my best felt woefully inadequate.

These were just basic facts about the Diamond Kingdoms. I wasn't sure how I'd ever manage to keep track of all the other details, like the corresponding titles of the ruling families. Each family had their own titles, unique to their kingdom.

For now, it wasn't a pressing concern. None of them had visited Anluan since the war broke out. Still, the thought of being unable to retain the information and later insulting one of the ruling families made my chest tighten.

Anluani titles were a different story. They were easier to grasp. Ramsey held the title of Sovereign. After a traditional engagement ceremony, I would be recognized as Sovereignaya and officially considered part of the ruling family. My title would be elevated to Sovereigna after our three-fold wedding ceremonies.

That much I could keep track of. It was my future. The rest would have to come with time.

Biting back a sigh, I tapped my fingers against my leg. It was a lot of information to relearn. One mistake didn't mean I was failing. Still, I longed for the benefit my memories would bring.

"Which leaves our eastern allies ..." Emila prompted.

"Fyrth. Kingdom on the cliffs, connected to water, and, according to you, grumpy."

Charna shot a disapproving look into the mirror. "The ruling family is grieving, Emila."

"Grieving?"

"Their Salishonn, Perez, was killed recently."

I swallowed thickly, my stomach sinking. "What happened?"

"We're not sure. Relations with Fyrth are strained at the moment. Salishé Amarine is unreachable, and Salishonno Dax is—"

"*Grumpy.*"

"—unwilling to engage with us at this time."

My heart ached for them. It wasn't surprising they didn't want to deal with anyone else after such a great loss.

"Have we reached out to offer our condolences?" I asked. "That's something I would handle when I'm Sovereigna, right?"

"After the ceremonies, yes," Emila confirmed. "Ramsey's taken care of it already. As much as he was allowed to, anyway."

"It didn't go well?"

"I told you Dax is grumpy." She shrugged, fiddling with the chain of her necklace. "He doesn't want anything to do with us, not until we 'clean up the mess in our kingdom.'"

I winced, watching the blur of buildings through the window without trying to focus on anything. "That seems harsh."

"That's grief," Charna said, slowing the car as we neared a large stone building. "The rebel attack on Anluan was the first uprising in the history of the Kingdoms. It's more than shocking; it's an affront to all we stand for. As we don't know what happened to the Salishonn, it would be unwise to judge Fyrth. Without the full picture, we can't understand their position. Until we do, we trust they have their reasons and show the ruling family the respect they deserve."

Emila sighed, letting her necklace fall against her silk top as she straightened from her slouch. "It must be exhausting being so wise all the time."

Charna rolled her eyes as she parked the vehicle. "I need to check on the storehouse. You'll be all right for a few minutes?"

"Of course." I sat taller and craned my neck to see out the window. "This is where the magic was deposited before the divide? Where power for the battery packs is harnessed?"

"I'll leave the lesson to you," Charna said to Emila, her lips curving as she opened the door. "Stay in the car. Call if you need me."

Emila scoffed as we watched Charna walk across the street and ascend the stairs to the storehouse. "She acts like I'm going to do something reckless."

"Is that so far-fetched?" I nudged Emila's shoulder and unbuckled my seat belt.

"I am the least reckless person in this car, thank you very much."

I laughed, leaning forward to get a better look at the storehouse. Two wide, wooden doors stood at the top of a short staircase, surrounded by white stone that jutted out to form pillars. A line of windows sat on either side of the doors, decorated by domed archways atop thin stone shelves. At the top, some sort of symbol or word had been carved into the stone, but we were too far away to make out what it was.

Part of me longed to get out and take a closer look. But knowing the northern gate could be opened any minute curbed my desire to leave the safety of the car. Maybe it was unnecessary, but I couldn't help being hesitant when it was likely rebels were lying in wait nearby.

"Tell me about the storehouse," I said, eager to fix my mind on something productive.

As always, Emila didn't disappoint.

"It's one of the oldest and most important buildings in Anluan." She shifted back to relax against the door and propped her legs across the seat. "The power we use for most of our technology is stored inside. Before everything happened with the Shalémos, they would deposit their magic into the storehouse. There's power in giving of yourself for the good of others. Their sacrifice added to the potency of their light, and we've been able to harness it to power the city."

"But there hasn't been power added to the storehouse in, what, two years now?"

"Not since the war broke out," Emila confirmed, her face lined with discomfort. "When we lost the Shalémos, we lost access to the power. That's why we have the rationing in place until we can figure out a solution."

"Like what?"

She shrugged. "That's above my pay grade. We have other sources of power, this was just our most common one. Coroden provided us with wind turbines years ago, but with so much forest surrounding Anluan, we didn't have much space for them. It's a small source of power and it'll stay that way unless we clear out some trees from Orveyin."

"Which would reduce our ability to produce our main exports."

"Exactly. So much of the city relies on our wood harvests. It's not a viable option to deforest, not unless we get desperate. We've made use of hydropower through past collaborations with Fyrth, but like the wind energy, it's not enough to power the whole city. Not yet."

I frowned, staring back at the storehouse. There had to be some sort of solution, some way to make our resources last.

Tamping down my worries, I leaned back in my seat and tapped a finger against my engagement ring. Surely Ramsey and his advisors had some ideas. Two years was a long time to consider a solution.

A flash of bright light stole my attention. Brow furrowing, I leaned forward to look out of the windshield. It came again, and this time a thick web of lightning spread across the sky. It was too bright. I blinked against a sudden flare of pain in my head.

"Were we expecting a storm?" I asked, turning to Emila as I pinched the bridge of my nose.

She slid forward until she was almost in the front seat, craning her neck to look at the sky through the windshield. Another web of light crackled, and Emila tensed, spitting out a curse. She pushed forward, draping herself over the driver's seat, and shoved her hand against the steering wheel. The horn blared—a long, harsh sound that grated against my ears and made my head throb.

A rumble of thunder echoed through the air and the hair on the back of my neck rose. Something was happening. My stomach turned with nausea as panic sent my pulse thudding in a fast rhythm against my skin.

"Emila—"

"Buckle up." She lifted her hand off the steering wheel and smashed it back down in another long blow of the horn. "As soon as Charna gets here, we're going back to the Annex."

My breath hitched, my lungs tightening with panic. "It's the rebels, isn't it?"

Emila glanced back, her face tight as she released the horn before blaring it again. "They won't risk coming into the city. We're just going to drive back to the Annex to be extra safe."

I barely managed a nod before Charna sprinted from the building. Emila threw the door open for her before launching back into her seat. Charna glanced at the sky, picking up speed. She was in the car and locking the doors moments later.

"Risk the short way or go around?" Emila asked, voice tight as Charna backed the car onto the side street.

She met my eyes in the mirror. "Coryndé, do you trust me?"

I didn't dare speak, too worried my voice would waver and bring tears with it. My heart was already pounding, a band of pain in my head matching its tempo. Swallowing thickly, I gave a jerky nod.

"Then we're going back the way we came." She pulled the car forward and increased its speed. "We'll pass the northern gate. It may be open, but I will not slow this car for any reason. You have my word that no harm will come to you. Understood?"

"Yes," I managed through my tight throat.

Emila reached over and squeezed my hand. Her leg bounced, but otherwise, she seemed calm. I was the only one panicking. I hated it, even though I had good reason to be upset. These were the rebels who'd hurt me so badly that I was in medical for months. Of course I'd be afraid to face them.

We sped forward and I closed my eyes against the gray blur of the stone wall out my window. The time for taking in scenery was over. All I needed was to get back to the safety of my suite.

Coming out here had been a bad idea. Why hadn't I seen that before?

I dropped my head into my free hand, letting my hair fall in a curtain around my face. It made a poor shield, but was one I relished as I tried to focus on anything other than rebels attacking. My breaths. The rumble of the car. The brush of Emila's thumb over the back of my hand.

"We're nearing the gate. It's open," Charna warned. "I'm going to speed up. We're almost through the worst of it, Coryndé."

Gripping Emila's hand tighter, I sat up and pushed the hair from my face. I didn't want to cower in the backseat as we drove by. I was better than that. Or at least, I wanted to be.

We flew forward and I caught a flash of light flaring through the open gate. My next inhale shuddered, but I forced myself to look. The guards scrambled around in chaotic pairs just inside the wall. A woman lit fire in her palm before sprinting through the open gate. A man darted after her, fishing something from his pocket that went hurtling through the air seconds later.

Charna kept her word, increasing our speed even more as we came parallel to the scene. It wasn't enough to stop me from witnessing the chaotic blur of violence through the open gate.

Vehicles were scattered along the road, people darting in and out of them with crates and boxes. One truck had tipped onto its side. Someone climbed from the window, falling to the ground just before a fireball set the truck ablaze.

Thick tree limbs flew like daggers through the air, slamming into people and knocking them off their feet. From the wall above, arrows soared on unnatural paths of wind to find their targets. More fireballs launched, igniting grass and trees as people dodged. Blinding light flashed in jagged bolts that raised the hair on my arms.

Muffled yells and shouts of pain. Arms and legs driving into each other. A burst of water rushing toward the worst of the flames.

We passed in little more than a blink, but the glimpse painted a grim picture. Pain flooded my head and tears wet my lashes. They fell despite the way I tried to will them away.

"Don't look, Khara," Emila said, tugging my arm until I turned toward her. "You don't need to look."

I bit my lip against the sorrow and fear tightening my chest. Her words came too late. There was nothing more to see. Still, I closed my eyes tight and didn't open them again until we were safely back on palace grounds.

14

THE ATTACK OUTSIDE THE northern gate left me shaken for days. The rebels made off with almost two vehicles' worth of supplies, including Emila's olives. I was assured it was more of an inconvenience than anything. None of the stolen goods were things we couldn't get by without, but that didn't stop tension from building in the Annex. It also didn't stop the increasing demand for Ramsey's time and attention.

The rebel plot the guards had flagged before the delivery attack still wasn't fully known, leaving Ramsey and the protectors of Anluan to try to piece together what might happen next. The guards grew increasingly on edge as the days wore on, but everyone kept quiet about the specifics. Whenever I asked, their answers were vague or directives to focus on my health. Apparently, it was well known that Ramsey didn't want me involved.

Though I could see how much Ramsey cared, it frustrated me. I did my best to appreciate that he didn't want me to worry and suffer any setbacks in my recovery. Still, I couldn't help being curious. I had enough mysteries surrounding me to last a lifetime.

When he was around, Ramsey was a doting fiancé. He brought me a new gift every time he showed up at my door. I tried to tell him I didn't need them, but he insisted it was his right to spoil me. Each gift he presented was beautifully crafted, of the highest quality, and undoubtedly expensive. Satisfaction shone in his eyes as he gave me each one, and I realized he wouldn't stop. He enjoyed giving me presents, and it was nice to see him so happy. I let it go and simply thanked him for each new trinket he brought.

I did my best to hide the headaches that continued to plague me, but it was difficult when the episodes were bad. I'd stumbled, staggered to my knees, and blacked out more times than I cared to admit. But no one forced me back to medical, so I dutifully took my pills and got back up each time an episode overcame me.

Emila remained a huge help. When I was exhausted, she would wait with me in my room. If we were out when a migraine struck, she would make sure I had everything I needed and see to it that I got my pills. Whenever my health was shaky, she would forgo our lessons and talk about lighter things—her fanciful ideas for my wedding, what I should sketch next, silly stories about the guards and officials she'd managed to overhear recently.

We'd taken to a routine of sorts. I'd meet Emila in the commons for breakfast, either walking with Ramsey or one of the guards assigned to me. After eating, we'd visit the courtyard garden to enjoy the sunshine and fresh air as we talked over the things I needed to know. I'd bring my journal and sketch the fountains and flowers, sometimes even Emila and whichever guards were on duty that day. It was a haven of peace amid so much uncertainty.

Each day when we left, I found myself drawn to the same spot—the large windows between the elevators on the twenty-second floor. There was something about the view. I would find myself stepping toward the windows without a second thought, so much so that Emila and the guards started pausing in that area without me having to say a word.

I'd stare out past the city walls, as though the world outside were a mystery all its own. I knew I'd been attacked somewhere beyond the gates, but it felt like there was more to the land surrounding Anluan than what I'd been told. If I could get out there and see it for myself, maybe I could find some answers.

I didn't dare voice any of that out loud. After what happened last time I was outside the gates, not to mention how close I'd been to the most recent rebel attack, I knew Ramsey would lose his mind over the mere suggestion. Emila was likely to have her own sort of fit over the idea.

Not to mention, the pain in my head spiked every time I stared at the spot. It wasn't always debilitating like the first time, but there was inevitably some sort of flare-up in my head.

That had to mean something, didn't it? There had to be a connection.

These thoughts circled my mind at every turn. I lingered in the hallways on floors high enough to give me a view over the top of the city walls—staring and trying my hardest to remember anything at all. It didn't help. It hurt me in some ways. And yet, I couldn't seem to make myself stop.

Eventually, on a day I had to sit against the large windows due to a minor episode on the way back to my room, I confided in Emila. As we waited for my medicine to kick in, I told her about the pull I felt toward the space beyond the city walls.

My brows pinched together as I fought to figure out how to best convey my thoughts. "It's like ... I'm trying to remember something."

Emila tilted her head, pursing her lips as she considered. "You were attacked out there," she said finally. "It makes sense you'd be curious about where it happened."

"But what's out there?" I gestured toward the window. "Where was I when it happened? Why was it somewhere the rebels were monitoring?"

Emila shook her head, her lips tightening into a thin line. "It's not safe out there, Khara. There's nothing more for me to tell you." Tension filled the air as she paused. When she spoke again, her voice was strained, and she wouldn't look at me. "And truthfully, it's upsetting to even think about. What happened to you was horrifying. I wish you wouldn't bring it up."

The waver in her voice struck me. I couldn't forget about what was behind the gates or the questions that swirled in my mind. But I could make sure my desire for answers wouldn't hurt those closest to me.

I wouldn't bring it up again. I could handle being drawn toward the area the same way I was handling my dreams—on my own.

15

THE CITY BUSTLED WITH life, loud even within the car Cethin edged onto the narrow city street. He and Gage sat in front, their watchful eyes monitoring everything we passed. Emila shared the backseat with me, tapping away at a tablet Ramsey had let her borrow for the day. He and Doctor Jensen were the only ones allowed to use the devices due to the power rations, but apparently, something about today was special—and not just because they were finally bringing me back into Anluan.

Taking a vehicle at all had been a debate between Emila and Cethin. He wanted us to walk to wherever they were taking me since a car wouldn't be able to make the full trip anyway. Emila wouldn't hear of it, arguing my condition was too unpredictable to venture that far without one.

Despite it being less than two weeks after the rebels had ambushed the import delivery, I didn't spiral into a panic at the idea of being off palace grounds on foot. I'd been able to reassure myself since then. But I had to admit, I felt more comfortable with riding in the relative safety of a vehicle.

It was Emila's shameless appeal to Ramsey that had won the argument. He'd ordered the use of the car, intent on both my comfort and protection. Any remaining protests had died on Cethin's tongue. No one wanted to contend with Ramsey.

I twisted my engagement ring around my finger as I stared out the window. The farther we traveled from palace grounds, the more people began to fill the streets. Most shied away from us, but some drifted closer, staring wide-eyed at the rare sight of a car winding down the road. Many of them wore dark clothing—blacks and grays, dulled blues and browns—and my eyes seemed to catch on anyone who carried themselves with rounded shoulders and shuffling steps. Emila had warned me that Anluan was still recovering from the outbreak of war and I might see some unsettling things, but my heart still ached at even the smallest signs of struggle.

It wasn't all heavy, though.

Animated crowds also filled the streets. A group of grinning children kicked a ball across an alleyway. At a corner building, a woman waved a stream of water up to rinse the window she'd been washing. Shop owners spoke passionately, their hands flying about as they interacted with their patrons. After so much white and clean and order since waking up in medical, these glimpses of life lifted my spirits.

Cethin pulled the car to a stop on the side of the street, close to a row of faded brick buildings. We wouldn't have been able to turn the next corner in the car. The street was even narrower than the ones we'd already crept down. We'd have to take the rest of the trip on foot, a prospect I couldn't help being excited by. I hated being cooped up when there was so much to explore.

Gage left the car first, moving to stand outside my door before I'd even undone my seatbelt. He opened it for me and led me to the street corner, keeping himself between me and the curious onlookers murmuring across the road.

"Sovereignaya!"

I turned toward the cry of a young voice, barely catching sight of the blurred form racing around Gage before a small body crashed into me. The impact made me sway, but Gage snapped a hand out to steady me. Arms wrapped tight around my legs.

"Sovereignaya, you're back!"

I blinked down, stunned by the blonde girl gripping my legs—not to mention her use of a title that wasn't mine yet. "I—"

I glanced at Gage, who shrugged with a grin. He didn't seem bothered by the display, despite the plan to keep distance between me and the people across the street. Maybe because she was so young.

"Do you remember me?" she asked, tilting her face to stare up at me with shining green eyes. "I saw you at the ceremony. You were beautiful and you waved right at me!"

My confusion grew, but I tried to hide it. Maybe she meant she would be coming to my future wedding ceremonies? Or maybe this little girl knew exactly what she was talking about, and I was the one who couldn't remember some public event of the past. It was far too possible a prospect.

I pushed down the frustration the idea brought and smiled at the girl. "You're coming to my ceremony? I'd love to see you there."

"No, *before*. I already went!"

"I'm sorry," I said, my brows furrowing. "I don't—"

"What are you doing?" Cethin stalked over and ripped the girl from my legs, eliciting a startled cry that pierced my heart. "You think you can touch Coryndé Isiraden like that?"

"Cethin, it's fine." Shock colored my words. "Let go of her."

"It's not fine, and she knows it." He scowled down at the girl, his blue eyes glinting. "Who's in charge of you?"

"She's just a kid, Ceth." Relief filled my chest as Gage lifted Cethin's hand from the girl's shoulder. "Come on, let go. She's what, four years old? Hardly a criminal mastermind. Unless you think the rebels recruit that young."

"This isn't funny," Cethin hissed, turning his attention to Gage. "You may not take anything seriously, but I do. This isn't—"

"Adira, where are you?" A woman's voice carried over the crowd, and the little girl's head whipped in that direction. I followed her gaze to a woman who maneuvered through the crowd while cradling a sleeping baby against her shoulder. "You can't run from Mama like this!"

"Mama!" The girl—Adira—cried out, tears welling in her eyes.

The woman's eyes snapped to her daughter, then widened as she took in the guards standing around her. She raced toward us, crouching in front of the girl. The way she cupped Adira's cheek, sliding a thumb across her skin as she searched her for injury, brought tears to my eyes.

"I'm sorry if she caused any trouble," she said, still staring at her daughter. "She's a good girl, but she'll wander off if I turn my back for a second."

She glanced up, her mouth pressed into a thin line. When she turned toward me, she blinked. Recognition washed over her face, and her mouth fell open.

"*Coryndé*." She said my title so softly, her voice full of respect and what I thought might have been fear. "You—"

"You should mind your children better," Cethin cut in, his voice gruff. "Take the girl and go."

Shock swept through me. All this over a hug from a child? These people were hardly a threat. Had I always been so closely guarded on the streets?

"What do you know about minding children?" Emila huffed, smacking his shoulder as she stepped between him and the family. "You're overreacting. Give them a minute."

Cethin scowled but stepped back, folding his arms over his chest as he returned to watching the crowd. It appeared to have grown in the time we'd stepped from the car. "We're too exposed out here. Hurry up."

Emila sighed, offering the woman an apologetic smile. "Excuse him. He takes his duty to protect Coryndé Isiraden very seriously."

"Of course," the woman muttered, gripping her daughter's shirt as she stood to face us properly. The little girl pressed closer to her mother's side, half-hidden behind her legs.

Shaking myself from my shock, I offered the woman a smile. "Adira just wanted to say hello. No harm done."

Adira peeked out from behind her mother's skirt, blinking carefully at me, and I smiled warmly. With an adorable duck of her head, she smiled back.

"Forgive me, Coryndé," the woman said, stunned eyes glancing from me to her daughter. "I didn't expect to see you here. Not after …"

Not after I'd almost been killed in the rebel attack? I swallowed back my grimace. Did everyone in the city know about what happened to me?

"I'm happy to be back among our people," I offered. "And very glad to have met Adira today."

The girl beamed. Though her mother chuckled warmly, her eyes darted to the guards behind me.

"She's a big fan of yours," she said finally, her hand rubbing idle circles on the baby's back.

"I'm a big fan of hers, too. She gives excellent hugs."

The mother smiled down at Adira, her body losing some of its tension. "That she does." Her eyes flicked behind me again, to where Cethin and Gage stood. "We should be going. It's good to see you out and about, Coryndé."

"Thank you." I bent, holding out my hand for Adira. She grasped it tight. "Next time we meet, I'll be sure to wave. I hope you'll wave back."

She nodded seriously. "I will, Sovereignaya."

I tilted my head, confused once again by her premature use of the title. I glanced at Emila, hoping for some insight on how to handle it, but she simply shrugged with an amused smile.

"That's not—" I cut myself off, shaking my head. She was only a child. I wouldn't be the one to squash her attempt at respect. "I'll look forward to it."

Her mother dipped her head to me before shuffling her children across the street. I stared after them, wondering if my appearance would be as surprising to others as it had been to this family. Maybe it was a good thing I was in the city today. It had been months since the attack, and I'd been sequestered inside the Annex the whole time.

"Let's go," Cethin said, gesturing to the alley with his head.

The set of his shoulders and gruffness of his voice made it clear he'd reached the end of his patience. The last thing I wanted to do was push him further.

Gage sighed as he turned to me and Emila. "He's right. We should keep moving."

I nodded. Letting Emila and the guards take charge of our outing soothed any hints of unease that threatened to arise. They had more experience with the city and its people than me. At least, more than I could remember having.

"Even surly sticks in the mud are right sometimes." Emila raised an eyebrow as she made a shooing motion at Cethin. "Lead the way, then."

16

With Cethin guiding us, we wound down a few streets, walking over uneven cobblestones between brick and aged stone buildings that kept my awestruck gaze sweeping upward. I had to be slowing us down, but no one complained. More than once, my gawking made me fall steps behind Emila, and Gage had to catch my arm so I wouldn't trip over the wooden crates and loose bricks littering the ground. The warm rush of heat to my face didn't quell my enthusiasm, and Gage waved off every apology I made with an amused smile.

After passing through a tight alley, we exited onto a cobblestone square. Lines of weathered brick buildings covered in ivy surrounded an open-air market where hints of lavender, leather, and yeast blended in the air. Tents and carts stood in rows, creating walkways for people to explore the artisans and vendors selling their wares. The faint song of a lively violin carried from somewhere out of sight.

On the corner, a man used wind to toss a laughing boy in the air and hold him up with nothing more than a spin of his hand. The boy's mother dropped a few bills into a wooden box at the man's feet while a gaggle of children clapped and cheered.

A wide smile stretched across my face as I took it all in. Here, finally, was some vibrancy, some promise of life that felt real and tangible.

"Someone's excited."

At Emila's teasing, I turned to find everyone staring at me with various amounts of amusement on their faces. I didn't care. There would be no apology for the joy bubbling within me. I grabbed Emila's hand and pulled her forward. "Let's go!"

Cethin stepped in front of us, blocking our path as he eyed the market with suspicion. When he nodded and moved forward, Gage gestured toward the tents with a flourish. "Princess, I present to you—the market!"

I shot him an exasperated look, though I was sure my smile tempered the effect, then turned to Emila. "Where to first?"

"Wherever you want," she said with a sly look on her face. "But we're waiting on the final member of our party first." She turned to the guards. "He got out early."

This was the first I'd heard about anyone else joining us. I shifted impatiently, eyes catching on rows of soap and hand-dyed cloth. I didn't want to wait. I was far too eager to explore.

"Khara!"

Ramsey's voice rang through the bustle, and I spun toward the sound. He stood at the edge of the market, his navy suit jacket folded over one arm, white shirt sleeves rolled up on his muscled forearms as he waved me over. Even from a distance, the warmth in his expression made my stomach flutter.

"And there he is!" Emila grinned as she took my arm. "Let's go."

She led me toward Ramsey while Cethin and Gage followed dutifully behind. I shook my head as we came close enough to talk without shouting.

"I don't understand," I said, a dazed smile forming on my lips. "I didn't think you were free today."

He shrugged, grinning as he reached for my hand. "I rearranged some things. I wasn't going to miss you experiencing the market again. You love it here."

The low hum of chatter echoed from the rows of vendors around us, and my eyes wandered, taking in the market. A woman displaying potted plants on a stand a few tents down curled her fingers as if beckoning the plants forward, and pink dahlias bloomed.

"I can see why." I turned back to him. "It's incredible."

"One of the longest-standing traditions of Anluan," Ramsey said proudly. "We had to shut it down for a while, but it was one of the things I fought hardest to reopen after the city was destroyed. Our people need somewhere to display their work."

It had to be helpful for the economy and morale too. Ramsey had done so much for Anluan, so much to help the people not just feel protected and safe, but live their lives again.

"Come on." He motioned with his head. "There's a lot I want to share with you. Emila, are you joining us?"

She hung back several steps, that sly smile still gracing her face as she shook her head. "You know, I just remembered that I'm supposed to meet my friend." She shrugged. "What can you do? You two go on. I'll meet up with you later."

"You'll be okay on your own?" I asked. No one let me go anywhere without guards within the Annex and we didn't have the same level of protection out here. It had to be somewhat safe. They'd never risk me being here if the threat were high, let alone Ramsey himself. But I didn't want Emila to be in a vulnerable position just so I could have time alone with Ramsey.

She waved me off. "I'll be fine! I'm a grown woman."

I looked pleadingly at Ramsey, and he gave a short nod. "Argusten, escort Emila wherever she needs to go. If it looks safe, come back and find us."

He nodded and turned to Emila. "After you."

She rolled her eyes. "Fine. I'll see you both later!"

As they walked away, I leaned into Ramsey's side. "Thank you."

He squeezed my hand. "I doubt she would've run into any trouble, but I'm happy to ease your mind. She's a good friend to us both."

"She is," I said. "Now, what did you want to show me first?"

We spent the day exploring as many of the vendors as we could. Leather craftsmen, lace makers, florists, artists, chefs, and bakers all displayed their best work. Every vendor was unique, and I took it all in with wide-eyed wonder. As we passed a candlemaker, he snapped his fingers, and the row of his sample candles lit. I was sure I looked like an enthralled child as I watched the flames flicker to life, but I hardly cared.

At first, the way people reacted to us was awkward. Many times, they stared at me in confusion, as if they were trying to place me. When they recognized Ramsey at my side, something seemed to click into place. Their eyes widened, and suddenly, we were the most important customers of the day.

Ramsey's interactions with the people were incredible to watch. He was charming and open, chatting with everyone as if they were old friends. The people showed him the utmost respect, and many offered complimentary items to us. While we accepted their wares, Ramsey made sure to compensate them anyway.

The glassmakers were my favorite. The older couple was kind and warm, letting me linger in their tent as long as I liked. I inspected each piece of glass, mesmerized by the way the light reflected color onto the pavement and sides of their tent. With their astonishing amount of inventory, there was plenty for me to explore.

"We reclaimed as much glass as we could when Anluan was attacked," the woman told me with a sad smile. "We thought maybe if we could create something beautiful from the ashes of that day ..." She shrugged, gesturing around her as she let the thought trail off.

"From the ashes!"

"We rise!"

Pain flared in my head as suddenly as the voices that echoed through it. I gasped and gripped my temples, my breath catching. The episode was quick enough that I could hide it from Ramsey. The glassmakers, on the other hand ...

I straightened as I focused on breathing. "I'm okay," I said, my cracked tone pleading with them to stay silent. At their nods, I relaxed. "Thank you."

Ramsey strolled over from the entry, completely at ease. Good. He hadn't witnessed my latest episode. "A merchant across the way would like a word with me. Will you be okay here for a moment?"

"Of course." I smiled as brightly as I could despite the lingering pain.

His eyes warmed as he leaned in to kiss my cheek. "I've stationed the guards at the entrance." He pointed to Cethin and Gage, who'd rejoined us sometime during my perusal. "When you're finished, they'll lead you to where I'll be. Take your time. Enjoy the art. If you'd like to bring anything home, note it and it's yours."

"Thank you, Ramsey." I squeezed his hand. "I'll see you soon."

"Until then." He released my hand slowly, nodding to the glassmakers before heading for the front of the tent. He paused to speak to Cethin and Gage, then disappeared into the small crowd.

When I turned back, the glassmakers were trying not to stare at me as they busied themselves with their art. I bit my lip and considered how to handle this. No one had told me I couldn't speak of what had happened to me, and this couple had kept their silence for me once already.

I cleared my throat, stepping closer. "Thank you," I said lowly, glancing to the entry. Gage was watching me, but he didn't seem concerned or overly interested in what I was saying. "I don't know if you know what happened to me ..."

The man frowned. "You were gravely injured in an attack a few months ago."

"Yes. And there have been some repercussions. I'm still recovering. It's been a few days since I've had a bad episode. That's why I was allowed to be here today." I paused, staring at a rainbow of colors cast against the canvas wall behind them as I searched for the right words. "Ramsey is very protective of me. I don't want him to worry any more than he has to."

The couple shared a long look before the man dipped his head. "Your secret is safe with us, Coryndé Isiraden."

The level of respect infused in his words baffled me. Like everyone else, he said my title as if I were someone worthy of deep honor. I wasn't sure how I'd possibly come to deserve it. Was it prompted solely by my connection to Isiraden? They kept telling me I was special because of it. But what use was this connection if I'd still ended up here—memoryless and reeling? I shook the thoughts away.

"It means a lot to me." I dipped my head. "I'm sorry, I didn't catch your names."

He smiled, eyes brightening like shining emeralds. "Jonah Zalmon." He draped an arm over the woman's shoulders. "And my wife, Trinity."

"It's a pleasure to meet you both," I said. "Your work is incredible."

"Here," Trinity said, rummaging through the workstation behind her. She pulled out a glass pendant. "It would be an honor if you would take this. We salvaged this glass from the former school at the edge of Anluan. It was destroyed beyond repair, but we make sure the history of the place stays alive."

I examined the glass, noting the mix of rich yellows and oranges melding with brilliant red. "It's like fire," I said in awe as the light cast its brilliant hues around us.

Trinity nodded, her eyes crinkling as she placed the necklace in my palm. "Many things can rise after a fire, no matter how hot the blaze. Let this piece be a reminder of that."

"From the ashes, we rise," I murmured as I turned the pendant around in my hand.

When I looked up, I started. Trinity's eyes glimmered with tears. Jonah's arms were wrapped over her shoulders again, his attention fixed on the entrance where the guards kept watch. It felt like I'd done something wrong.

"I'm sorry. I—"

"Don't be." She gave me a watery smile. "Don't ever be sorry."

"I'm still feeling a bit fuzzy. The episodes I have ..." I trailed off, shaking my head in hopes of clearing it. "This piece is stunning. I couldn't possibly just take it. Please, let me pay you. I can get Ramsey—"

Trinity folded my fingers over the pendant, shaking her head firmly and holding my gaze. "It's yours."

Something in her soulful, glimmering eyes made me accept.

"Thank you, Trinity, Jonah. I won't forget your kindness."

Jonah smiled warmly at me, his wrinkles making him appear even more welcoming. "For you, it's our pleasure."

Moved by his words, I thanked them again before turning to leave. Gage stared at me, straightening as I moved closer. He nudged Cethin's arm to get his attention and we set out to meet Ramsey.

I ran my thumb over the fiery pendant in my hand. As we stepped back into the sun, the light caught against a line of jagged yellow down the middle of the glass.

17

When I found Ramsey, he stood with his arms crossed while in deep conversation with a vendor. His shoulders were tight, and the corners of his mouth pulled down as he spoke. While the tension was obvious, I couldn't make out what they were saying. Cethin stopped us before we reached them, making sure to keep me between himself and Gage.

The vendor seemed as stressed as Ramsey. He threw his arms, wildly motioning toward the gate. I glanced at it, but there was nothing to see. Whatever issue they were discussing, it wasn't something happening now. Relief washed over me in a gentle wave, and I relaxed again, turning to watch the market instead.

At a booth of scarves a few tents down, a teenage girl stood watching me. While her face was mostly covered by the scarf draped over her head, a few tight curls escaped to frame her face. Her striking hazel eyes drew me in as our gazes met.

It wasn't unusual for me to be stared at. It'd been happening all day. But this girl didn't look away when our eyes met like the others in the market. She stared back, intent and serious in a way that unnerved me. Something about her eyes felt familiar, but by now, I'd learned that didn't mean there was a connection.

Another flare of pain ignited near my temples, and I winced, closing my eyes. It built on top of the earlier pangs, and I wasn't sure how much longer I would be able to hide my discomfort. I blinked rapidly in hopes of clearing it away and chanced a peek to see if the girl was still staring. But she was gone, the scarves on the end display billowing softly in her wake.

Frowning, I turned back toward Ramsey as he finished speaking with the market vendor. He marched toward us with a stormy glint in his eyes that made me take a half-step back.

I immediately chided myself. This was Ramsey. His anger shouldn't frighten me.

"Ramsey, what happened?"

"I'm sorry, Khara." He forced a strained smile, fisting a crumpled paper in one hand. "It appears I'm to be drawn away again. There are urgent matters to attend to." His eyes flicked to Cethin and Gage before returning to me. "Would you like to stay at the market awhile longer? I'm sure we can find Emila and have her accompany you."

"If that's all right." My smile went tight as I swept my eyes over Ramsey, trying to understand what was happening—why he couldn't tell me what was wrong. "There's so much I haven't seen yet. But Emila—"

"Has impeccable timing?" she said as she breezed in out of nowhere.

I blinked. "I thought you were—"

She waved me off. "I did, I'm done, and I'm here now. Just in time, apparently. You off again, Ramsey?"

"Unfortunately. You'll stay with Khara?"

"Of course."

"Thank you." Still stiff with anger, he turned to the guards. "Stay with them. When Khara's ready to leave, drive her back to the Annex and see her inside. Do not let her out of your sight under any circumstances."

"Yes, Sovereign."

"Ramsey ..." I longed to reach him, to ease some of his burden, even if he couldn't tell me what it was. He carried so much on his shoulders. I didn't want him to have to bear that weight alone.

Taking my hand with a gentleness that belied his anger, he brought my hand to his lips for a kiss. "I'm sorry our day was interrupted." He ran a finger over my engagement band. When he met my eyes, he softened. "I'll make it up to you. I promise."

I nodded, lost for words. None of this made sense, and with Ramsey keeping things from me, I had no way to catch up. Though my chest went tight, I tried to release the frustration. He had his reasons. But I wanted to be trustworthy enough for him to share these things with me, wanted to be there for him when ruling became stressful.

If I remembered, he wouldn't feel like he had to be so careful around me. If I remembered, I could *help*. I could be a true partner to him, as his future Sovereigna should be.

For now, all I could do was be the best support I could be—for him and Anluan both.

Ramsey kissed my forehead in a quick goodbye before striding away. With each step he took, his shoulders inched higher and higher.

"Have you had Quincy's bread rolls yet?" Emila asked, shifting my attention from Ramsey.

I blinked, turning to face her. "I don't think so."

Her eyes sparkled. "Then I know where we're going next."

Emila linked our arms and led the way to the bakery, pointing out some of her favorite vendors along the way. The scent of yeast and rosemary hit us several stations before we reached Quincy's. Whatever was baking smelled delicious. We walked up to an assortment of sweet and savory baked goods that made my mouth water. I stepped closer to a case full of fresh loaves of bread while Emila moved to the counter.

It quickly became clear the bread rolls were only a secondary part of Emila's agenda. She flirted shamelessly with Quincy, sparing glances to me and the guards outside the tent for a few moments before giving Quincy her undivided attention. I wondered if he was the one she'd left to see earlier.

I backed away from where Quincy leaned over a raised table with a grin just for Emila. As they spoke, his eyes didn't waver from her face, and her laugh rang freely at his words. I smirked, shaking my head at the blatant flirting as I stepped closer to the sunlight.

I'd been pushing the pain aside as best I could for hours now. I didn't think I'd be able to for much longer. My head was beginning to pound. It was frustrating, always being the one who needed to stop, to rest, to end the fun. I hated feeling helpless, and it was all I'd felt lately.

I wasn't about to interrupt Emila after all she'd done for me. I was the one who wanted to stay out. She was kind enough to oblige, even if she had her own reasons for agreeing. But as the heat of the sun soaked into my skin, nausea churned in my gut. I needed to head back.

A glance behind me showed Emila choosing which rolls she wanted. She'd be finished soon, and until then, I'd rejoin Cethin and Gage and ask to return to the Annex. I wasn't sure where they'd taken up their post once they'd determined the booth was safe, but I knew they weren't far. They took their orders to keep me close seriously.

I found them in the shade. Cethin was alert, his arms crossed as he kept a close eye on the crowd. Gage angled toward him, his posture as loose as ever as they held a hushed conversation. I moved closer, listening intently as their discussion became clear.

"They're getting in somehow," Cethin said, scowling.

Gage rolled his eyes. "I'm not saying they aren't. Obviously, they've found a way to breach the walls if their symbol is popping up again. I'm saying maybe you're giving them too much credit. Maybe their spies are getting in and out through the wall's weaker points. I could point out a few spots they might be exploiting right now!"

He pointed to the market's edge, past where I'd spent time admiring the beauty made by the glassmakers, leather craftsmen, and painters. "I bet someone small enough could get in and out from over there. Might take some maneuvering, but any spies Hayden or his father are sending must be crafty enough to make it work."

Cethin's scowl deepened. "I doubt they're using *that* as an access point into the city." He paused, considering. "But we should check it out."

Gage shrugged. "Yeah, probably. We can take a look tomorrow." He grinned mischievously. "I'll volunteer to test my theory, see if I can wiggle my way through the gap."

"Shut up." Cethin sighed. "We'll do it right. Pretend you know we have protocols, Argusten."

"Just trying to help. You know the protocols won't let us look into any potential access points for at least a week, maybe longer."

"Did you see Sovereign Ramsey earlier? Leaving signed notes is one thing, marking buildings like they have is another. He was fuming over those tags. If we let him know we have an idea of how the rebels are getting in, he's likely to expedite the process."

My adrenaline spiked. The idea of rebels entering the city sent a shiver down my spine. My eyes darted around the area, searching for any sign of them, but the peaceful bustle of the market hadn't changed.

"Maybe," Gage agreed halfheartedly, scuffing his boot on the pavement. "They better get what they need soon. The Sovereign isn't going to mess around, not with—"

"Khara," Cethin interrupted, his sharp eyes meeting mine as I approached. "Is everything all right?"

"Yes, fine." I smiled tightly, forcing my eyes not to wander from my guards. "I just—could we head back soon?"

They studied me carefully, as if searching for any problems I might be trying to hide.

"It's been a long morning," I offered. "I'm tired."

No need to mention the prickling unease of rebel eyes on my back, the simmering urge to barricade myself inside the Annex where they wouldn't be able to reach me.

Cethin motioned to Gage, who nodded before moving inside the tent to gather Emila. "We can walk this way," Cethin said, gesturing toward a path. "They'll catch up."

As we walked, I couldn't prevent the churning worry. Were the rebels really getting inside Anluan? After what happened to me and the raid I'd witnessed, the prospect sent my pulse thrumming wildly. How safe could it be for me to be out in the open like this if they were roaming the city, hiding in plain sight? They could be anyone. I could've stood right next to a rebel today—spoken to one, even.

If that were the case, nothing came of it. The market had been peaceful. No attacks were made. I was leaving unharmed. Had I not eavesdropped on the guards, I wouldn't have known to be wary at all. I blew out a breath, releasing the tension in my shoulders. Spying wasn't the same as attacking. It was a problem, but not an immediate danger. I would have to trust Ramsey and the guards to handle the issue before it escalated.

But if the rebels *were* entering Anluan, was this area the key to how they were doing it? If they could get in, they could get out. I stared at the wall, looking for the gap Gage had mentioned. There was a shadow halfway down the path in the opposite direction. Maybe that was the entry point.

Even as my head throbbed in time with my pulse, my mind pondered over the space. What were the rebels spying on? Did it have something to do with me? Was that why Ramsey was so tense?

I zoned out until Emila's hand rested against my cheek.

"Oh, Khara, you're so warm!" she exclaimed. "Boys, take us home."

"I'm all right, really," I argued feebly. But worry over the rebels still churned in my gut. My nausea was worsening, as was the pain in my head. "I just need to lie down."

She nodded, wrapping her arm around my waist. "We'll get you settled as soon as we get back. I'll even leave a roll in your room for you to eat later. You don't look like you could stomach one now." She turned to the guards as she led me away. "Come on. We've had enough for one day."

Despite my relief to be leaving, I wished her words weren't quite so true.

18

WIND BRUSHED THROUGH THE trees above me. The rustling echoed, a crescendo of fierce white noise that still managed to soothe me.

I stood at the base of an old, familiar tree. I knew I'd dreamed of it before, drawn it more than once since waking from the attack. The peeling bark. The way it seemed to stretch up to kiss the sky.

I felt small beneath its winding branches. Insignificant in the grand scheme of things. And yet, somehow, being here made me feel infinitely significant at the same time. I reached out and pressed my palm to its trunk. The texture was rough against my skin, but not unpleasant. In the quiet, I could have almost sworn a hum of life pulsed from the tree into my hand, like it was greeting me.

"Come home…"

The voice was less startling this time. It had frequented my dreams often enough. I almost expected it now, even though I frequently forgot its messages as soon as I woke. In this place, I didn't have that problem.

I turned, hoping to locate the source. The leaves quieted their rustling as the wind calmed to the gentlest breeze and the tree faded from view.

"Khara…"

I spun, searching the black void. Nothing. How could there not be anything?

"Come home…"

I spun again, looking over my shoulder and searching the dark. A pair of brown eyes appeared, slightly above my eye level. I froze, unable to look away.

Intense longing filled me, and I folded over myself, overwhelmed by the pain it caused. But there was something else, something strong just beneath the surface that I couldn't identify.

"Please," I rasped, desperate for something I didn't even know how to define.

"Come home…"

"I don't know what you mean!" I cried out, burying my hands in my hair.

"Please, come home …"

Tears slid down my face as I breathed, heavy and hitching. I looked up at the piercing brown eyes again as they began to fade.

Find the tree.

These words were whispered more to my heart than my ears, different from the voice urging me to come home, but just as able to make my nose sting with unshed tears. As the words repeated in an insistent echo, a new tree sprang into view.

I took in its height and maturity before watching the rest of the scene fill in around it, one piece at a time. Other trees—towering and strong—surrounding it. A footpath leading into darkness. Tall grass and a smattering of wildflowers.

"Come home …"

19

Tears stained my cheeks when I woke. I rubbed my hand over my face, inhaling deeply.

Come home. The words echoed in my mind, even as the memory of the eyes I'd seen faded. How could I lose the details so quickly when the dream had been so strong?

Flicking on a light, I scrambled for my journal and flipped it to an empty page. I had to get the words down while I still remembered.

Come home. Find the tree.

I tried to scribble notes on the feelings that came over me in the dream, but the specifics were already fading. I remembered feeling pain, the heaviness of the tears that escaped me. But was that in the dream or reality?

I growled in frustration, flipping to the next page and sketching the outline of a pair of eyes. Even if I couldn't remember the details, I knew they existed. Giving them a place in my journal served as an act of defiance against my mind's failings—one I desperately needed.

While the rest of the dream faded, the second tree lingered in my mind. Unlike with the first, I had a fuller scene to work with. I sketched a lush meadow surrounded by a copse of mature oaks, sycamores, and pines. The words *find the tree* echoed in my mind.

By the time I'd finished filling in the details, my stomach was growling. I didn't know what time it was. I'd gone to sleep as soon as we'd returned from the market. Light no longer seeped around the curtains, though, I could tell that much.

Heaving a sigh, I moved off my bed and into the living room, where dim light illuminated the walls in a soft glow. A small paper bag sat on the kitchen counter, "*Eat me! :)*" scrawled over it in Emila's handwriting. I fished out one of the bread rolls she'd left me.

Taking a large bite, I moved toward the mantle above the fireplace where a clock sat. Just shy of midnight. I rubbed my forehead in frustration. So much of the day wasted.

I stared out the window at the walls surrounding the city. They loomed like shadows above the buildings. Spots of light created a beautiful glow around homes and shops. There weren't many lights around the wall itself, but I could just barely see a faint outline of the treetops.

"Find the tree," I whispered, brow furrowing in concentration.

What if the tree from my dream was real? What if somewhere beyond the walls there were answers for me? If I could find that grove ...

I shook my head. Ramsey would never allow it. It was forbidden to go beyond the gates for good reason. The rebels were out there somewhere. I didn't know enough about what they were planning or how they operated to know how to avoid them.

And those were only the outside dangers.

If I were to leave, I could have an episode at any time. It had been days since the last terrible one, but just being out at the market had flared the pain. What if I left and became so debilitated I couldn't move? The rebels could find me, and I wouldn't be able to run. And I didn't even know what kind of animals were out there.

But Gage's words echoed in my head. There was a way to do it. If the rebel spies could get in and out, then surely I could too. As long as I wasn't incapacitated by a migraine.

I bit my lip and stared at the journal in my hand. The drawing of the trees faced up. If I flipped through the book, I would find piece after piece of fragmented dreams and vague memories. Nothing was solid enough to follow. Nothing except this grove.

If I didn't find out if this was a real place, somewhere I'd been, maybe somewhere I'd loved ... how would I be able to live with that? It would eat away at me, drive me mad.

I had to find out.

I had to go there.

My heart quickened. How would I even get out of here? Ramsey had been so upset at the market. The guards had promised someone would be posted nearby at all times until this was resolved. I had no idea how I'd leave my bedroom unaccompanied, let alone make it into the city and beyond the gates.

I pressed my hands over my eyes and took a steadying breath. One step at a time.

Sweeping back into my bedroom, I rummaged through my dresser, fumbling until my fingers landed on a thin sweater. I pulled it on over the top I'd worn to bed, then shimmied into a pair of black pants. I hoped I'd be warm enough without a jacket. I chilled easily, another unfortunate side effect of the attack.

Light would be helpful, but I didn't have anything I could take with me. Outside my window, the full moon glowed. It would have to be enough.

I found a simple leather bag in my closet, perfect to sling over one shoulder and hold supplies. I grabbed the bottle of pills from my side table, though I hoped I wouldn't need them. Better to be prepared in case I did. Moving to the kitchen, I tucked a second bread roll and a water bottle inside.

As I turned and surveyed the room, my eyes fell on my journal. It would have to be my guide once I got to the other side of the wall. I nestled it inside the bag, hoping the water wouldn't leak and ruin it, before adding a few pencils in case I needed to write anything down.

I wouldn't have a way to communicate with anyone. If something went wrong, I'd be on my own. I bit my lip. Was I really going to do this?

Shaking away all thoughts of risk, I shouldered my bag and crept to the door. I held my breath as I pressed down on the handle and pulled. The latch clicked as the door opened, and though the sound was quiet, I winced, tensing in anticipation of being caught. But no sound came from the hall.

Peeking my head out the door, I glanced to the left—nothing—and then right. There sat Gage, next to my door, just out of the way. His knees were bent, his arms folded against his chest, and his head tilted against the wall. His eyes were shut, his breathing deep and even.

He'd fallen asleep.

I couldn't help but think of how much trouble he'd be in if anyone caught him like this. Or worse, noticed I was gone. But not even the guilt of that possibility stopped the compulsion I had to leave.

Stepping farther into the hall, I shut the door as gently as I could. The click of the latch echoed loudly in my ears, and I froze before slowly turning to look down at Gage.

My mind raced, searching for a believable reason I'd be leaving my suite at all, let alone at this hour. There wasn't a good one. My plan to find answers would be over before it began.

But Gage didn't wake. He shifted slightly, chuffing a soft breath as he let one leg stretch straight out in front of him.

With my hand on my chest in a futile attempt to calm my racing heart, I tiptoed down the hall. I reached the elevator, quickly pressing my thumb to the pad to call the car to my floor.

The soft sound of the doors sliding open fueled my haste. Just because Gage hadn't woken before didn't mean he wouldn't at all. If I had any hope of making this work, I had to get away from him. No one could follow me.

I slipped into the elevator, crowding myself near the display of buttons, and jabbed the one for the lowest floor. My eyes darted out the doors, praying Gage wouldn't be roused yet, until they finally closed again. I thunked my head against the back wall, relishing the chill and closing my eyes.

As the elevator descended, I focused on my breath and steeled myself to keep going. All of this would be worth it. I had to know what was out there.

The elevator opened, and I tensed, squeezing myself against the side of the car. When I didn't hear any signs of people in the bay, I chanced a look. Clear, for now. Heart still in my throat, I darted to the opposite wall, pushing the button to call the second elevator. The doors opened immediately, and I rushed inside, pressing the button for the first floor over and over until they closed again.

I leaned against the wall again as the car descended, my hand over my chest. How busy were the common floors at this time of night? I'd never been down there so late, and desperately hoped the car wouldn't stop before reaching my destination.

This time, when the doors slid open, a murmur of voices met my ears. Panic flared in my chest, and I bolted from the elevator. My eyes darted for somewhere to hide, but there wasn't anywhere within the bay. I'd have to chance staying in plain sight and hope they weren't planning to use the elevator, or sneak away before they came too close.

Desperation threatened to send me running, but I held back. Slowly, I peeked around the corner, scanning the hall for the voices. A guard stood at the far end, just outside an open door. She stared at a clipboard, jotting down notes.

Another guard left the room behind her, shutting the door and saying something I couldn't make out.

Maybe they were on some sort of patrol? I couldn't tell. They wore the standard gray uniform rather than the Tower Guards' black, but the uniform itself meant little. Most guards wore them during their downtime as well as while on duty. I wasn't sure it mattered anyway, as long as they didn't see me.

The man moved to a door farther down the hall, entering a code into the keypad. When he held the door open, the woman barely glanced up from her notes before walking inside. The man followed and the door clicked shut behind them.

Moments after they disappeared, I took off down the opposite end of the hall. As quietly as I could, I slipped past closed doors and new corridors. The overhead lights had been dimmed, some turned off entirely, likely to preserve power as part of the rationing. It cast eerie shadows across the floor and walls. I quickened my pace, eager to reach the end of the hall.

As I rounded the corner, new voices rang out behind me, and my heart thundered in my chest. I hurried to get out of their line of sight. They sounded too close. Despite the dim lighting and long shadows, it would still be easy to spot someone standing in the hall. I tried to pull open the nearest door, but it wouldn't budge.

Panicking, I darted to the next. It opened and I slipped inside, trying to stay quiet as I caught my breath.

Waiting there in the dark became the longest minutes of my life. The voices gradually built in volume as they drew near—two guards, talking about how to protect some supplies coming in—and then faded just as gradually. I waited another minute after it went quiet before I gathered my courage and cracked the door. When I didn't see anyone, I made my way into the hall again.

I wasn't entirely sure where I was going. I hadn't exactly gotten a full tour of the building. But I did know there was an entrance down this hallway. We'd taken it to go to the market.

It should've been coming up ... *there*! I breathed a sigh of relief and quickened my pace to the door. It had a small wooden panel and keypad similar to the one outside my room. I pursed my lips. It required access via magic or a code.

Praying I wouldn't alert anyone with my actions, I squeezed my eyes shut and pressed a finger to the scanner. A thrum of magic greeted me, followed by the release of a latch, and my eyes flew open. The wooden panel glowed a soft green. I darted through the open door, marveling as I stepped onto the cobblestone path beyond. The door shut heavily behind me, but I didn't flinch.

I'd made it out of the Annex undetected. Now I just had to find my way from the palace grounds to the wall and into the forest on the other side.

I hadn't expected the outdoor patrols, though it made sense that Ramsey would have guards monitoring the grounds at night, even in small numbers. When I almost walked into the line of sight of a few near the fence, it took me by surprise.

There wasn't much cover on this part of the grounds. Mostly, it was open space, a few paved paths, and a sprawling grass lawn. I pressed my body into the shadows by some shrubs, trying to quiet my breathing while I waited for the guards to pass, hoping they wouldn't notice me. A stick snapped beneath my foot.

"Did you hear that?"

I froze. A beam of light shone in my direction.

Someone sighed. "Probably just an animal."

"Shouldn't we check it out?"

The light made a slow pass across the other side of the shrubs. My heart pounded and I fisted my hand in my sweater.

"If you want to go sifting through the landscaping, be my guest. I'll keep patrolling for rebels while you protect the Annex from squirrels and stray cats. I'll be sure to let Commander North know which enemy scratched you up in our report."

The light moved away as the guard huffed. "You're not funny."

"Debatable. Let's go."

I breathed shakily as they moved farther down the fence line. After I could no longer make out their lights, I made myself wait a few minutes longer, straining to hear any sign of them. Everything had grown quiet when I peeked around the shrubs. Seeing no one, I gripped the strap of my bag and took off toward the fence.

White stone pillars and iron fencing surrounded the palace grounds. In the daylight, it made for an impressive display. Right now, all I cared about was finding a solid foothold. I hoisted myself onto the white stone, then over the iron bars. My foot clanged against them, and I cringed.

"Hey, you! What are you doing up there?"

Panic flared as beams of light bobbed closer. I didn't hesitate. Heart pumping wildly in my chest, I jumped to the pavement below and took off into the streets at a run.

I was far in the shadows by the time I stopped to catch my breath. A painful stitch bloomed in my side, making me cringe as I rested against a cool stone building. Tipping my head back against the wall, I laughed breathlessly. I couldn't believe I'd made it this far.

With adrenaline singing in my veins, I pushed off the wall and started for the market square.

Finding it took much longer than I'd anticipated. I didn't know exactly where I was going. Relying on my memory, faulty as it was, and trying not to be seen as I struggled in the dark made it challenging to find the landmarks I'd noticed that morning.

When I emerged into the familiar square, I shivered. Earlier, the market had bustled with life. Now, it sat unoccupied and full of shadows. The tents remained, though some of the carts were missing and most of the goods appeared to have been moved out. The emptiness held an eerie, unsettling quality. I closed my eyes and pushed down my unease.

When I looked around to check for curious eyes, I saw no one. All was quiet, my breath the only sound reaching my ears. From the moon and occasional lampposts lining the streets, enough light shone to illuminate the path I needed to take.

With determination and a growing need to be on the other side of the wall, I picked up my pace. Jogging down the path, I searched for the potential access point Gage had noted.

As I approached the area, I slowed and inspected the wall for anything out of place. Sure enough, pieces of stone appeared loose, though it wasn't overly noticeable. Had Gage not mentioned it, I doubted I would've given them a second thought. As it was, I noticed the deeper shadow of a crack—a gap in the gray stone at the bottom of the wall.

I nudged my foot against it until the stone started to shift. If I pushed hard enough, it looked like it would slide. I bent, using both hands to lean my weight against it, and lurched forward as it slid aside more easily than I'd anticipated. Heart racing, I reached into the space, stretching my arm as far as it could go into a small, dark tunnel. Right through the city's wall.

Gage's words rang true. Someone small enough could make it in and out of the city if the tunnel went straight through. I adjusted the bag over my shoulder. Wearing it would make movement more awkward, but I needed the pills and the journal. I couldn't leave them behind.

A clattering noise sounded behind me, and I jolted, panic shooting up my chest. No one could find me, especially not here.

I pushed myself through the gap, slipping inside the dark space. There wasn't much room, but it was wide enough that I could turn on my knees to tug the loose chunk of stone back over the entrance until it snuffed out all but a sliver of the soft light from the street.

Breath heavy, I rested my forehead against the makeshift door, letting the chill from the stone seep into my skin. I closed my eyes against the darkness and breathed in the scent of the musty blocks. I'd found the entry point. I could find the grove. This would all be worth it in the end.

When my heart slowed, I slung my bag over my back and crawled forward. I moved slowly, cautious of what my hands and knees might find on the dusty ground. A few rocks dug into my palms, sharp and uncomfortable. I stopped to run a finger over them, but when I found no break in my skin, I gritted my teeth and kept going.

Partway down, my elbow sent something clattering against the side of the wall. I reached out blindly with one hand until my finger ran over a smooth bump on a cylinder. A beam of light appeared, pointing toward the end of the tunnel.

A flashlight. One of the spies must have hidden it here. If it was abandoned, there would be no harm in taking it. But what if someone was counting on it being here when they came back? I didn't want to steal, even if it was from a rebel spy.

What was wrong with me? Being concerned over taking from traitors to my city?

I shook my head and gripped the flashlight in my left hand. I'd need the light once I reached the other side. I could always bring it back and leave it in the center where I'd found it. There'd be no harm in that.

When I reached the opposite end, I propped the light against the wall and moved my hands against the stones in front of me. There had to be another loose piece, the covering to a hole, *something*. I was determined to find it. I'd come too far to turn back now. And if I did, I'd have no guarantee I would be able to try this again. No, it had to be tonight.

As I moved my hands near the corner where the outer wall met the tunnel, I felt a crudely formed hand-hold in the stone. I grabbed it, experimenting with pulling and pushing until it shifted. I pulled to the right, putting as much of my strength into the movement as possible.

Fresh air blew in through a crack as the tunnel wall shimmied open. Moonlight shone down on the tall grass as it swayed in the summer breeze. I continued to maneuver the cut of stone using the handhold until there was a space big enough for me to crawl out.

In minutes, I was inhaling fresh air and resting on my knees in front of the gap. I'd have to replace the covering for this side, but there'd be time for that after I'd caught my breath.

I looked up, wiping the sweat from my brow as I took in the forest before me and the expansive wall at my back. With the sound of crickets chirping around me and leaves rustling overhead, I marveled.

I'd made it out of Anluan.

I HALF EXPECTED SOME sort of alarm to blare, announcing that I'd stepped outside of the city. Of course, if that were the case, the rebel spies would have been caught and dealt with by now. Still, I needed to get away from the wall quickly if I was going to find the tree.

I had no idea which direction to go. Truthfully, I had no idea what I was doing at all. Breaking the law and the trust of my fiancé, all because of a dream ... I had to be mad. When I was caught, maybe I could blame all of this on poor side effects from my medicine.

Shaking my head, I stepped toward the treeline, aiming the flashlight beam in front of me and sweeping its beam slowly from side to side. There wasn't much to go on, even with the moon highlighting things in silhouette. I started walking slowly, heading away from the eastern gate and the nearest light atop the wall, all the while letting my flashlight's low beam pass over the ground at the treeline.

Eventually, I found a footpath. It was grown over, barely a path at all. It would've been easy enough to miss, even in daylight. Steeling myself, I pushed forward into the forest.

There would be no turning back now.

The woods were darker than I'd expected. Tall trees lush with leaves blocked most of the moonlight. As I slowly made my way forward on the footpath, I found myself grateful to whoever left their flashlight in the tunnel. I'd have been stumbling around in the dark without it.

Even with the light, the darkness was disquieting. I was alone, doing something foolish. There were so many reasons I shouldn't wander these woods at night, or at all. And yet, I couldn't bring myself to turn around and go home. Not without finding something to make this risk worthwhile.

As I walked farther down the path, something in the air shifted, almost as if I'd walked through a barrier. Like an invisible force had brushed against my face, making it tingle with warmth. It almost felt like the pressure of a light touch that wasn't quite real. When I took another step forward, the warmth lingered, but the air returned to normal.

I'd never felt anything like it. I paused, turning slowly. I couldn't hear signs of anyone else nearby—just my own breathing, the rustle of the wind in the trees, and the rhythmic chirping of crickets in the grass. Still, I was cautious. If someone was out here, I wanted to know.

Nothing around me changed, though, and I couldn't see a soul. I shook off the nerves as best I could, pretending I didn't feel the hairs standing on the back of my neck or the raised goosebumps peppering my arms.

It was only a few paces down the path that a headache built, making me stop and press my palm to the mossy trunk of a sycamore. *Not now!* I was too far to get any help from anyone in the city, and far too invested in my journey to give up. I shut my eyes tightly, directing my breath to the pain. It helped, marginally, but my time to search would be limited.

Reaching into my bag, I pulled out my journal and flipped through the pages until I found the recent drawing of the tree in the grove—the one I needed to find. With the flashlight aimed at the pages, I took in the details as best I could. This tree's one remarkable feature was a shape where the bark had peeled. It reminded me of the blade of a sword, pointed toward the ground.

I looked around, but couldn't distinguish anything that proved I was headed in the right direction. And yet, I had a feeling I was on the right path. Surely the building throb of pain in my head meant I was close to triggering *something*. Maybe even a memory. The episodes were increasingly linked to snippets that could be nothing else.

At least that's what I kept telling myself. There had to be a purpose to this pain. I couldn't accept anything less.

Besides, something about this pathway seemed eerily familiar.

Journal in hand, I forged ahead. The path twisted, taking me farther to the right, and I followed it without a second thought. My feet moved more surely here, as though they remembered this trail. Like they'd traveled it before. My head throbbed in time with my pulse the farther down the path I went. I did my best to ignore it. If I could just keep going, I knew I'd find the grove. I could feel it in my bones.

After following the bend, I came to a stop. The footpath forked, moving in opposite directions. I frowned, rubbing my forehead. Which would lead me toward the grove?

I tried to look at each trail for any signs—footprints or markings that showed the way—but couldn't make anything out. I'd have to decide for myself, go with my instincts. The thought made me cringe. Without my memory, I couldn't trust myself with much. This seemed too big a thing to chance a wrong decision. But there was no one else here to offer advice or decide for me. It was up to me alone.

I closed my eyes, picturing the trees in my drawing. The way they formed an imperfect circle. The way they varied in type, width, and maturity. The way they gave shade to half the meadow in the midday sun. I imagined myself walking there. When the path forked, I moved to the right without hesitation, reaching my hand out to brush against the flowering bushes as I passed.

My eyes sprang open, and I swiveled the flashlight to the right. Taking a few quick steps in that direction, I let the light fall to the side. It illuminated a cluster of bushes with delicate purple flowers growing on them. Exactly as I'd pictured.

Stabbing pain flared in my head. I gasped, dropping the light to the dirt as I grabbed my head and choked back a moan. This was building into a bad episode, I could feel it.

My legs trembled and I braced against a fall. I couldn't be stuck out here, writhing in the dirt until someone stumbled upon me in the morning. No, I refused to be that helpless. Not tonight.

Steeling myself, I gingerly bent to reach for the light. Spots filled my vision as I came back to standing, and I blinked, holding my arm out for balance until they cleared from my eyes.

With all the determination I could muster, I trudged ahead. This was the right path. It had to be. I would make it to the grove. The rest, I could figure out from there.

A break formed in the trees ahead. The path ended, overrun by tall grass, and beyond it, a shadowy opening barely lit by the moon's glow. My heart raced and slowly, I walked forward, anticipation welling inside me with every step.

It was here. I knew it.

When I reached the path's end, I didn't hesitate. I stepped straight into tall grass that rose past my ankles to brush my calves. Ten steps in, I turned and surveyed my surroundings.

This was it, the grove from my dreams.

Even in the dead of night, it was beautiful. Waves of grass rose and fell in the breeze like a gentle call of welcome, beckoning me to enter in. The barest hint of vanilla wafted in the warm, mossy air. Sycamore, oak, and pine trees stood tall and magnificent, circling the clearing like sentinels of peace. Something about this place made me feel like I could breathe. I hadn't realized how labored the feeling had been until I stood here, dwarfed by the majesty of the trees surrounding me.

Tears blurred my vision as I spun in a slow circle, and the tension in my shoulders loosened. I was comfortable here in a way I wasn't even within the privacy of my suite at the Annex. The courtyard garden couldn't hope to match the peace this place exuded.

I melted into the grass in the center of the meadow, laying on my back and pillowing my head with my hands. Above me, an opening in the trees revealed cloud cover. As it moved, a glimmer of stars peeked through. The sight settled the race of my heart into a steady rhythm.

My headache lingered. The hour was late, and this grove felt safe. Familiarity nestled around my heart like a homecoming. With a sigh, I closed my eyes and decided to let myself rest, just for a while.

I only realized I'd slipped into sleep when a sharp snap jolted me awake.

21

MY EYES FLEW OPEN, and I bolted upright, gripping my bag close to my side. I stayed quiet, intently listening for any other sounds. I hadn't meant to fall asleep, and I chided myself for it. Anything could've happened while I dozed.

At a second snap, I hurried to my feet and spun from my position in the middle of the clearing. I would not be caught off guard by whoever or whatever was out here.

For a moment, there were no sounds but the creaking of branches moving in the wind and the gentle rustle of leaves. Still, I remained alert. Listening. Waiting.

Crack.

My head whipped in the direction of the sound, flashlight raised. A figure stood at the treeline across the clearing. A man. And he was staring at me. I froze, weighed down by my rising panic. No one in these woods would be an ally. This was exactly what I'd needed to avoid!

"You know, if you wanted an audience with me," he said as he stepped into the clearing, "all you had to do was ask."

He moved with a grace that suggested he knew this place well. I flinched back, my mouth going dry, but I didn't dare run. He looked fit enough to catch me. As he came closer, he raised his hand to keep the beam of light from his eyes. It blocked his face from view, but I could make out a few black curls falling onto his forehead. More importantly, I could see the tension lining his jaw, the caution in the way he carried himself.

"What, nothing to say?" he asked as he strode closer, the edges of his jacket flaring open with the movement. "No gloating? That's a refreshing change."

He peeked around his hand, squinting at me. When our eyes met, he froze, his hand falling to his side as his mouth slackened.

"Khara?" My name fell from his lips, soft and precious like a prayer that fit the hushed reverence of the grove. I couldn't miss the relief in his wide, brown eyes.

It was as clear as it had been in his voice. His whole body sagged as if a tension he'd been carrying left him all at once.

I held enough tension for the both of us. I stood straight, muscles tensed to run despite the lingering ache in my head. He knew my name and used it freely, not my title like so many others. The only people who should have been out here were rebels. He had to be one.

I would not go quietly.

He reached out a hand, stepping closer, and I recoiled. I needed to keep distance between us. I was acutely aware I was alone with him. Why had I thought I could leave the city and find this place without any consequences? What had I *thought* would happen?

Mind whirling, I fixed my attention on the man. This time, when our eyes met, his were troubled. Something about him felt familiar, but just barely. Like a remnant from a dream.

A flash of piercing brown eyes. A tree. The grove. Come home.

Pain.

I cried out, stumbling to the side as I doubled over. The pain jabbed, sharp as a blade, building to unfathomable heights. Tears filled my eyes as I clenched my fists and struggled to catch my breath. The pain had never been this bad before.

I barely registered the sound of pounding feet before warm hands grasped my arms and lowered me to the ground. His presence lingered beside me, close enough to feel his body heat against my side.

I couldn't bring myself to pull away. The pain was too great. I sobbed, clutching my head, but the pressure did nothing against the onslaught. The torment and my growing panic stole my breath.

A hand brushed over my forehead before running through my hair. Fingers glanced across the hidden undercut and trailed over my surgical scar. I flinched as the hand stilled, my shoulders rising and curling inward. The fingers drew back. While the touch hadn't hurt, the unexpected reminder of the scar's existence did.

"What have they done to you?"

I didn't bother trying to answer, too overwhelmed with pain to make the effort. Instead, I forced down hitching sobs and choked out a plea.

"Pills." My eyes squinted open, and tears fell freely down my face. "In my bag. Please. *Please.*"

He didn't hesitate, digging in my bag until he found the glass bottle. "This?"

I nodded, holding out a trembling palm in expectation. No matter who he was, he seemed compassionate toward my suffering.

Instead of helping, he remained crouched beside me, inspecting the bottle and the pills inside. "Who gave these to you?" he demanded, anger hardening his voice. When I didn't answer, he tried to meet my eyes. "Who gave you these pills? Have you been taking them?"

"I need them," I said through gritted teeth. "Please, I need them. You don't—" I broke off with a cry as the pain flared higher. Curling in on myself, I groaned and desperately pressed both hands to my head.

"Khara." His voice was firm and calm as he cupped his hand on the back of my head. "This isn't ... these pills won't help you."

I shook my head as a harsh sob escaped. I just needed my pills. The pain was too much.

"I promise you," he urged as he moved to cup my face in his hands, "these aren't what you think they are. They're dangerous. A combination of magic and medicine meant to suppress powers in the gifted. They'll make you worse."

"They take the pain."

"For a time, maybe," he conceded, voice soft. "But they're suppressing your powers. That builds up inside you. Your gift has to have an outlet. You know this. We've known about this threat for a long time. Why would you—?"

He froze, backing up to where I could feel the chill of the air between us again. His face paled, tawny beige lightening with a growing horror he barely held at bay. "Khara, what's my name?"

I stared at him through bleary eyes until a look of understanding and grief surged to life on his face. I shook my head over and over again as I looked away.

"I don't know." Once the words had escaped, I couldn't stop repeating them. "I don't know. I don't know you. *I don't—*"

With a hacking breath, I rubbed the back of my hand on my forehead, then down over my mouth. I blinked to clear my vision, but it only released more tears. Through gritted teeth, I met his eyes and added, "I don't remember anything. Not from before the last attack."

I assumed everyone in the area—in Anluan or the rebel camp alike—would know which attack I meant. Everyone had so far. And why wouldn't they, if it was as bad as I'd been told?

He went quiet, his lips pressing into a tight line as he blinked rapidly. The pain in his expression struck me, and my hand lifted with the absurd urge to comfort him. As soon as I realized, I stopped myself and lowered the shaking limb to the ground. If he noticed my strange behavior, he didn't comment on it.

When I broke the silence again, my voice was thick, exhaustion coloring every word. "You know me? Or of me? I don't understand what you were saying before. Powers?" I squinted at his kneeling form. "Who are you?"

His face fell further, his eyes glimmering in the beam from the flashlight I'd dropped during the height of my episode. "I'd hoped it wasn't true. Or exaggerated, maybe. I thought …" He shook his head. "They told me you weren't yourself, that you'd been seen with Ramsey. Reports mentioned potential memory loss." He looked away, staring at the treeline with vacant eyes. "I guess I thought you'd still know me somehow, even if it were true."

Another rush of pain had me swallowing back a moan. I wanted to keep talking, to learn more about this man. He might've been with the rebels, but he hadn't attacked me yet. He seemed to have information about me he was willing to share. Maybe sifting through it could give me answers, even if it wasn't all true. If I could concentrate past the pain.

I closed my eyes again, shutting them against the meager light. The pain had brought a swell of nausea with it. Soon I'd be too dizzy to stand unaided.

"How bad is it? I can help if you'll let me."

I wrenched my eyes open again. He'd moved closer, his knee pressed into the ground by my thigh. His eyes seemed deeper this close, like there were galaxies inside of them. Before I could think about what I was agreeing to, I gave a jerky nod.

Take the pain.

He softened. "I'm going to help you, I promise."

He sounded so sincere, I couldn't help but believe him.

He reached forward and touched two fingers to my temples. His touch was as gentle as the look in his eyes. "Take a deep breath."

I inhaled as deeply as I could, holding it for a moment before exhaling. As I did, he did *something*.

A warm, tingling heat zipped across my head. The strange feeling of almost-pressure traveled along the path where the pain had taken hold, and as it did, the sharpness lessened. Another trail zipped to my shoulder where a knitting sensation thrummed in my bones. After a long minute, all I felt was warmth, until even that faded.

We stayed in that position, with him kneeling close to me, his fingers gently pressed against my temples while I leaned into his touch, my knees folded under my legs. I focused on breathing until my shuddering inhales turned deep and full, guided by the gentle motion of his breath. The pain faded back until all that remained was the post-episode fuzziness I'd become all too familiar with.

When I opened my eyes, I found him watching me. He hadn't moved—maybe so he wouldn't disturb me, maybe for some other reason entirely. Whatever his motives, I relaxed the slightest bit. What he'd done—taking the pain from me—was incredible. I wanted to know who he was and what he knew about me more than ever.

"Better?" he murmured, studying me carefully.

"Yes," I said, voice hoarse. I cleared my throat. "The pain's gone. I just—I feel fuzzy, after an episode."

He narrowed his eyes, still completely focused on me. Still close enough I could feel the way his chest rose and fell with each breath. Finally, he nodded. "I can only do so much," he said, a hint of frustration in his voice. "Full healing is my father's gift."

He glared at the bottle in the grass before he opened it, removing the few pills I'd brought. Before I could blink, he threw them far into the forest.

My jaw dropped. He'd just tossed my pills away like they were trash. I *needed* them—at least I did when strange healers weren't around. I turned my wide eyes his way.

"You won't need those." He shrugged, and an errant curl strayed onto his forehead. He swept it back into place. "And trust me when I tell you, you don't want them, either."

There was nothing for me to say. He was resolute in his opinion. Besides, I could get more pills. I didn't know how much time I had left with this man, and I needed to know whatever he would tell me.

"You have questions." He kept staring, but waited patiently for me to answer.

"I do."

He flashed me a bright smile, full of the kind of fondness that comes with understanding someone. He knew something about me, something that made him sure of my curiosity.

He settled into the grass, leaning back to give me space. As he motioned for me to do the same, light glanced off the black ink of a small tattoo just under the side of his wrist. Pins and needles ran up and down my legs as I unfolded them from beneath me. When the feeling stopped, I crossed them and sat up tall, chancing a glance at him. He sat watching me, relaxed and patient.

I didn't waste another minute. "You know me."

"I do."

"And I know you," I said with less certainty. "Somehow."

He nodded, gazing intently at me. "You know me better than just about anyone."

I couldn't sense any deceit in his voice. He spoke with a sad sincerity that rang true. More than that, he appeared content to sit with me in the middle of the night and talk. I didn't think he was lying to me. At least, not about this.

My eyes roamed over his face, and I searched my mind for any glimmer of recognition. Surely, I'd remember eyes that deep and sincere, the boyish charm of the long black curls that sat atop his head, or the brilliance of the smile he'd directed my way. I thought maybe if I tried to remember hard enough, something would come to my mind.

Nothing did.

I was afraid to push too hard. I'd just been relieved of the pain and didn't want to risk its return. Even if I did have a pseudo-healer sitting in front of me, resting his face in his palm as he stared openly at me.

But I did see things within his eyes. So much kindness. The same fondness I'd noticed earlier. And patience that rivaled anything I could remember, even during my slow recovery in medical when everyone was catering to me as much as possible. No, this was something different.

I cocked my head. Somehow, I knew this man. Vague impressions of familiarity prickled just beneath the surface, desperate to break free.

Eyes still locked on his, I took a deep breath and leaned forward. I wanted to ask who he was. A better question sprang to my mind, one I wasn't sure I was ready to hear answered: *who are you to me?* Rather than ask either one, I settled for another question altogether.

"What's your name?"

He held my gaze for a long moment, saying nothing. I thought he might not answer at all. He rubbed a rough hand over the tapered hair on the side of his head and blew out a breath. But then he smiled, meeting my eyes again with a gentle confidence I didn't expect.

"My name is Hayden Shalémo."

I jolted upright and froze.

Hayden Shalémo.

This wasn't just one of the rebels.

This was the leader of the rebels himself.

22

My heart skipped a beat before staggering into a gallop as fear stole my breath. *Hayden Shalémo.* Here, in front of me. If I jumped up and ran back the way I came, would he be able to catch me? Would he try to keep me here? Use me to get to Ramsey?

Hot tears brimmed in my eyes. Ramsey would be devastated! What was I *doing* out here?

It had been stupid to leave the city. Going beyond the gates was forbidden for good reason. Why didn't I listen? And what had brought me out here—a dream? I'd put myself in danger, risked everything, to chase down a glimmer of a dream?

Now I sat feet away from the man responsible for my lost memories in the first place. And of course it was him! Through the blur of my tears, I could make out the jagged shape of a lightning bolt shaved into the tapered hair on his right side. My chest tightened as my breaths turned raspy, and I raised a shaky hand to fist in the thin fabric of my sweater. Looking at him made me dizzy, but I couldn't look away. What if he took the opportunity to strike?

"I'm sure you've heard some things about me," Hayden said, each word measured and careful. He looked at me like I was a skittish animal. As much as I hated it, I felt like one. Like prey caught in a trap. "But I need you to know, you're safe here with me. No harm will come to you. You have my word."

What good was the word of a man like him—one who destroyed my city and slaughtered our people? I couldn't believe I was safe here. Not now. We stood on opposing sides of a war I didn't fully understand. But I knew enough to know the senselessness of the destruction and pain Hayden and his rebels had brought on the people of Anluan. On Ramsey. On *me.*

And here I was, alone with him. How could that be safe for me? For anyone?

But there was this look in his eyes that registered despite my fear. My panic slowly shifted into confusion. Hayden seemed open, like he had no desire to hide his feelings. He laid them all out for me to see as they swirled in the depths of his captivating brown eyes. When I tried to discern the emotions, I thought I saw sincerity. Promise. Compassion. But was any of it real? Or was it just a trick so I'd let my guard down?

I slowly settled back into the grass, trying to focus on my breathing. I wouldn't trust Hayden. I couldn't. But I could sit and listen to him for a while longer. If he kept his word, there would be no problem. Maybe I'd learn something that could help with my memories. Maybe I could bring information back to help Ramsey and the guards better protect Anluan.

The potential settled me, and I forced my body to relax, one muscle at a time. Hayden watched, cautious and patient, but with an abundance of hope in his eyes. As I met his gaze, he held a hand up in surrender.

"I won't hurt you," he repeated. "We've known each other since you were thirteen. We used to chase each other barefoot in the grass."

Though I knew he'd been close with Ramsey, the idea of such a long friendship between Hayden and me was jarring. We must have been friends through Ramsey. There was no way I couldn't have been familiar with him when he was practically Ramsey's brother. But if their relationship had fallen apart enough that they could oppose each other in a war, how close could our friendship truly have been?

"I would never hurt you."

My rebuttal formed instantly as Hayden's words brought the attack and its aftermath to the forefront of my mind: *you already have.* But caution stilled my tongue now that I knew who he was. No good would come from accusations.

I looked to the sky, noting the subtle way it lightened as we drew closer to daybreak. Even if I had been at ease in his presence, there wouldn't have been time for a lengthy conversation. If I wanted to sneak back to my suite without getting caught, I had to leave soon.

"I have to go."

Hayden straightened. "You're leaving? I thought you wanted answers."

"I do," I said, a bite of defensiveness in my tone. "But no one knows I'm gone. At least, I hope they don't. If someone's noticed I'm missing, they don't know where I am." I motioned to the sky. "It will be light soon. I have to get back into the Annex before then."

In the ensuing quiet, I worried he wouldn't let me leave. My pulse raced as he frowned, staring into the distance. I still wasn't sure I could outrun him, but

I tensed in preparation. Just as I was about to leap to my feet, Hayden spoke again, conviction lacing his words. "Meet me here tomorrow. I'll wait for you at midnight."

I didn't answer as I stood and scooped the borrowed flashlight from the ground. It had flickered off at some point. I shook it, tapping it against my hand in hopes that would make it work. It didn't.

"Here," Hayden said, holding out his hand. "I bet it's the battery."

I hoped not. There would be no way for me to use the flashlight on the return trip if that were the case.

Reluctantly, I passed it over to him. Hayden deftly opened the bottom and removed the battery. It didn't glow like the ones I'd seen in Anluan. Its magic had been depleted. I sighed. Trekking back through the forest would be a challenge without the extra light.

"Definitely needs charged," Hayden muttered. Before I could blink, a small bolt of lightning pulsed from his fingertips into the chamber. The connection held for only a moment before the battery glowed a faint yellow.

My eyes widened as he replaced it and pushed the switch up. The flashlight beamed, bright as ever. Hayden smiled as he flipped it in the air before catching it and handing it back to me in a fluid motion.

"That should be enough to get you through the forest, at least. Didn't want to risk overloading it, so I only filled it partway."

I nodded, unable to look away from the beam. He'd done all of that with so much ease. Just how powerful was he?

"I mean it," he said, pulling my attention back to him. "Meet me here tomorrow and I'll answer any questions you have. And I'll help you with your migraine problem. We can manage the pain, keep you off those pills."

It was a tempting offer. The way he'd relieved my pain tonight was unlike anything I'd ever felt. But I wasn't sure I *could* sneak out again, even if I wanted to—and I wasn't sure I did. This excursion had been risky enough.

"Khara," he pressed, his fingers rubbing across the tattoo on his wrist, "don't you want to remember?"

Of course I did. But at what cost? I'd thought I would do anything to regain my memories. Look where that had led me tonight! A lot was at stake in Anluan. What if I ruined everything in pursuit of my memories? Could I live with that?

Could I live without remembering my life before the attack?

Head spinning, I bit my lip and backed away. He didn't try to stop me, though his hand twitched toward me like he wanted to before he dropped it at his side. When I was at the edge of the clearing, about to enter the treeline, I turned my back to him. My pulse thundered in my ears, and I braced for an attack. He hadn't moved against me yet, but that didn't mean he wouldn't if he had a good opportunity. I'd taken two steps into the forest when he called out to me.

"I'll wait for you. Tomorrow night, the night after. As long as it takes, I'll be here, waiting for you."

I glanced over my shoulder. Hayden's face was pinched with pain, conveying a brokenness that unnerved me. A rising determination flared behind his eyes as he clenched and released a fist at his side. He meant what he was saying ... or he was a really good actor.

I held his gaze for a moment, saying nothing before I turned again.

"Come back tomorrow night. Please, Khara."

The fragility of his plea shook me, but I couldn't tell him I'd be there. How could I trust him—heir of my enemies, destroyer of my city, the one responsible for countless deaths and my stolen memories? I could barely trust myself, and I was supposed to trust *him*?

Squaring my shoulders, I strode back down the footpath I'd followed into the grove. I could feel his eyes locked on my every step.

I didn't spare a look back.

23

THE JOURNEY BACK TO the Annex was tedious. The adrenaline from sneaking out of Anluan, finding the grove, and coming face-to-face with the enemy had served me well, but the crash left me exhausted.

I didn't feel the same kind of fuzziness that usually came after an episode. I supposed I could thank Hayden for that. Whatever he did, however he took my pain, it didn't seem to have the same side effects as the medicine.

Could he have been telling the truth about the pills? Were they making things worse? Did I even *have* powers? No one had mentioned any to me. I knew of my connection to Isiraden and its magic, but I hadn't thought that was enough to classify me as one of the gifted. If I had powers, I hadn't noticed anything that pointed to them.

Questions consumed me as I wearily trekked back toward the city. Once I reached the wall, I pulled myself into the tunnel and shimmied through. At the halfway point, I hesitated. I didn't want to actively help the rebels, but I also couldn't bring myself to steal, even from spies. I'd feel guilty either way.

Too tired to debate with myself, I turned the flashlight off and propped it against the wall as I'd found it.

There was a hint of light in the sky as I carefully moved the makeshift door in the wall. A shadowy figure stood at the end of the street. They pointedly looked away as the wall shifted, then hurried in the opposite direction. So, some of the locals in this neighborhood did know about the tunnel. I cringed, hoping no one would spot me and report this to the guards.

Exiting quickly, I concealed the entry point as best I could and rushed toward the palace grounds. I kept to the shadows, slipping in and out of alleys so no one would catch me wandering the streets. The thought of explaining what I'd done tonight made me sick to my stomach. It was awful enough knowing I'd betrayed Ramsey. I didn't want to see it written across his face.

As I slipped into another alley to catch my breath, a splash of black graffiti on white stone drew my eyes. Someone had scrawled *we rise* across the side of the building. The *s* caught my eye. A diagonal line connected the ends of the letter and extended past until the *s* looked closer to a stylized *8*. I tilted my head, *from the ashes* on the tip of my tongue before a jab of pain forced my eyes shut.

I shook my head and pushed forward.

No more distractions. I needed to get back.

When I neared the fence surrounding the edge of the palace grounds, I paused in the shadows of the buildings across the street. The palace made an unsettling image in the dark. Though it stretched wide across the lawn, I could just barely make out the collapsed entry in the dim light. I shuddered and looked away. I didn't want to hold this destruction in my memory when I couldn't remember what the palace looked like whole.

I waited with bated breath until a pair of guards appeared to walk the perimeter. They swept a flashlight over the grounds, but their hushed conversation seemed to take up most of their attention. I doubted they saw much trouble at this hour if they were so nonchalant about their duties, especially after I'd been spotted on the fence on my way out.

Several minutes after they'd marched past, I darted across the street. After making sure my bag was securely fastened, I climbed over the iron fence. As soon as my feet hit the ground, I sprinted toward the Annex.

Reentering the building was surprisingly easy. A press of my palm to the door unlocked it with a thrum of magic. Wide access to closed doors was a perk of being Ramsey's fiancée, I supposed.

And this was how I repaid that trust—by breaking it. Disregarding the law and my fiancé's feelings. Having a secret meeting with the enemy.

Guilt weighed down my steps. I didn't deserve trust. I didn't deserve a doting fiancé or the power resting on my shoulders. The people of Anluan deserved so much more than me. So did Ramsey.

I trudged to my suite, exhausted in body and mind. All I wanted was to curl into a ball, wrap myself in one of my plush blankets, and sleep. The thought of rest after such a long night drove me through the quiet corridors.

When I reached my hallway, I froze. If my guard was awake ...

I covered my face and groaned. I hadn't thought this through. I'd just have to face the consequences. Maybe being found out would be a mercy. This secret had already twisted my insides into knots.

I kept my steps intentional and quiet as I rounded the corner and walked toward my suite. Gage's eyes snapped to me as soon as I entered the hall. I fought back a cringe and strode toward him as if I'd done nothing wrong.

He frowned as I came to a stop in front of him. Concern glimmered in his eyes rather than the accusations I expected. "Princess? What are you doing out of your room?"

He didn't ask how I'd left undetected. It seemed we were going to ignore that he'd fallen asleep on duty. But maybe if I went along with it, there could be a mutual benefit. I rubbed my forehead, considering what to say.

He cocked his head. "Should I call someone for you? You look like you're in pain."

I flashed him a weary smile that quickly fell. "That's not necessary. I just need to get some rest."

"Why weren't you doing that already?"

I did my best not to wince, and shrugged instead, feigning nonchalance. "I went for a walk. Couldn't sleep."

There. Not a total fabrication, just not the whole truth.

His raised brows told me he hadn't bought it, but he didn't try to contradict my story. He motioned to the door. "Well, then, you better get some rest."

"I intend to." I eyed him cautiously as I pressed my palm to the center of the door and watched it unlock. The magic of Isiraden wood would never cease to amaze me.

As I shut the door, Gage nodded to me. His eyes glinted with the promise of secrecy. He wouldn't say anything about my midnight wanderings. I wasn't sure if that was a good thing or not.

While I was exhausted, my mind wouldn't let me sleep after I returned to my room. Instead, I lay awake and restless in my bed. I had so many questions after speaking to Hayden. Was anything he'd said the truth? Had we really known each other since I was barely a teenager? He'd insinuated I still knew him well. How was that possible?

Forgetting all that, his implications about me circled my thoughts. Was I one of the gifted? If that were the case, why wouldn't anyone have told me about my powers? There had been plenty of time to bring it up while I was recovering, or even since I'd left medical. Unless they were trying to protect me from something. But how could not knowing about my powers protect me?

Who was using the tunnel in the wall? Should I tell Ramsey about its location? But how would I do that without admitting to what I'd done? Could I face his disappointment if I did? And would I be restricted even more than I already was? My heart couldn't handle that any more than it could handle Ramsey's reaction to the truth.

Surely if Gage had pointed out the area to Cethin, the guards would look into the wall. They would find the tunnel. It wasn't that well hidden if you knew where to look. I could keep quiet, and it would all work out in the end.

I sighed, rubbing my eyes.

I was a terrible person.

24

I was back in the grove, but this time I could see it clearly. More than that, I could feel it. Tall blades of grass tickled against my bare legs. The sun warmed the exposed skin on my shoulders. Wind caressed my face and lifted my hair.

I sighed as the peace of the grove washed over me and I settled on my back in the center of the clearing. I could rest here, and all would be well.

"There you are."

The voice was unexpected, but even with my eyes closed, I didn't startle. The sense of overwhelming peace remained. I was content. Nothing could shake me.

"Here I am," I said, not bothering to open my eyes as my lips twitched upward.

"I've been looking for you," he said fondly. "I should've known I'd find you here."

My smile grew. "You always seem to."

The grass rustled as he moved to sit beside me. "I'd find you anywhere. But yes, finding you here has become a specialty of mine. You really love this place."

I hummed in reply. It was true. This grove had become a haven, a place where I could slow down and just be.

"It's peaceful." I shrugged, dislodging my arms from where they rested against my belly. I didn't mention the way it reminded me of the grove in Isiraden Forest. Sometimes it felt like the sacred grove called to me, sent whispers echoing in my mind. Being here wasn't the same, but it brought a small measure of connection and comfort.

He laughed, and the sound made my stomach flutter. It wasn't his carefree laugh—I hadn't heard that in a while—but it was still purely his, rich and charming in a way I loved.

He brushed the stray hairs from my face. "You know, I hear it's even better when you open your eyes."

I laughed as I did just that, turning toward him. "Better for me, or for you?"

His piercing brown eyes gleamed with amusement.

The eyes I'd been dreaming of.

The eyes I'd looked into last night.

Hayden grinned, affectionate and just a hair mischievous as he leaned closer. "For us both, I think."

I woke with a massive migraine. It was nothing less than what I deserved after gallivanting outside the city like the law didn't apply to me. Still, it was horrible.

Equally horrible, I could remember enough of my dream to feel thoroughly confused by it. What was real, and what was my subconscious running wild after meeting Hayden in the grove? The dream had been so vivid, so lifelike. The migraine was certainly real enough. Some of the details had to be memories trying to surface. But how could I know which ones?

We'd been so familiar with each other in the dream. I'd felt the contentment, the *peace*, as if I were really there. No dream had ever felt so real to me before.

I was in too much pain to grab my journal. I was in too much pain to do anything.

And Hayden had thrown out the last of my pills.

I groaned, covering my head with my pillow and letting my body sink further into my bed. I cursed my stupidity as I pushed back tears of pain and frustration. With my eyes shut tight, I prayed for someone to come along soon—anyone who could let themselves into my room. There was no way I'd make it far from my bed.

When someone knocked at the door, I opened my bleary eyes. The debilitating onslaught of dizziness, nausea, and biting pain wouldn't allow me to get out of bed, but my heart leapt with hope as Emila called my name. When I didn't answer, the knocking grew louder. She shouted for me a few more times before going quiet. I held my breath, praying she hadn't left.

The door creaked open, and I could have sobbed. Emila strode into my bedroom, her tense eyes finding me immediately. She deflated as she took in my state.

"Oh, Khara." She rushed to my side and knelt to meet my eyes. Brushing my hair from my face, she cupped my cheek. "How bad is it?"

I hated that question. Hot tears leaked from the corners of my eyes. "I'm out of pills."

Her face was lined with sadness as she ran gentle fingers through my hair. "We'll fix it, okay? Hang on. I'll be right back."

She stepped into the living room, staying in my line of sight, and called to Gage through the door. "Get Doctor Jensen up here and make sure she brings more of Khara's medicine!"

Gage murmured a response, but I couldn't make out the words. Emila came back, though, so I assumed he was taking care of it.

"Thank you," I said, closing my eyes again.

"You don't have to thank me. This is what friends do."

"Wouldn't know." The joke fell flat, even to my ears.

"You know well enough by now," she chided, taking my hand in hers. "Just let me help you. Doctor Jensen will be here soon. We'll get some medicine in you and you can rest as long as you'd like. Don't worry, Khara. We've got you. You're safe."

"You're safe here with me."

I shook my head as Hayden's words echoed in my mind. I didn't have the energy to think of him anymore today. The steady throb of pain in my skull was evidence enough of that. Besides, this was his fault—my lack of pills and the injuries that made them necessary—and getting worked up about it wouldn't help.

Instead, I focused on Emila's steady presence and the in-and-out of my breath, hoping it would be enough to distract me until I could get more medicine.

25

"You should have called me immediately," Doctor Jensen said, her face pinched. "She never should've gotten this bad."

Emila's eyes narrowed, though her voice remained soft and steady. "I only just found her. I called for you as soon as I realized she needed help."

The doctor made a dismissive noise. Emila crossed her arms over her chest, shifting her weight. I could tell she wanted to argue and appreciated that she held back. My head couldn't take the back and forth today.

Doctor Jensen sat in the chair she'd pulled to my bedside and held out three blue pills. "Take these."

"Three?"

She nodded, face grim. "This is the worst episode you've had, correct?"

Hesitantly, I nodded.

"I thought so. We need to get ahead of this and make sure you don't suffer unnecessarily. The extra dose should help settle the pain, and we'll keep a close eye on you the next few days to make sure this doesn't happen again."

"Why *did* it get so bad?" Emila asked from the foot of my bed.

"If I had to guess ..." Doctor Jensen shifted to look down at me. "You had an episode or two—small ones, maybe—and didn't take a pill?"

I bit my lip. I didn't want to admit she was right. I hadn't taken a pill at the market or after we returned.

"It was just the one," I said sullenly, turning to Emila. "While we were out at the market. I didn't want to ruin anything. It was such a nice surprise."

Emila sighed, giving me a sad smile as she patted my leg. "Khara, we care about you a lot more than a day at the market. I wish you would've said something."

"I had you bring me back here."

"Yes, and when we asked if you were okay, you said you were just tired."

"Well, I was."

Emila and Doctor Jensen shared an unimpressed look.

"Khara," Dr. Jensen began, and I held back a sigh at her tone. A lecture was coming. "You know how important it is to treat each incident as it happens. You could have taken a pill or two when you arrived back in your room. You *should have*. The episode today shouldn't have been this bad." She sighed, scanning her notes. "Other than the incident yesterday, is there anything else you've neglected to tell me? Any episodes, spacing out, anything at all?"

My mind flashed to the dreams I'd been having. The journal filled with what I could remember of them. The pain upon waking. I thought of Hayden's fingertips brushing my temples, replacing my pain with a tingling warmth.

"No. There's nothing else."

She narrowed her eyes. "In the future, you call me. Understood?"

I nodded, contrite. "Yes, Doctor. I understand."

"Good. Any questions before I go?"

"The medicine ..." I bit my lip as I searched for the right words. "I feel fuzzy when I take it. Is that normal?"

Doctor Jensen cocked her head, frowning as she searched my face. "It's one of the side effects, yes. Do you not remember discussing that?"

"No, I do. I remember." I fiddled with the edge of my blanket. "I just don't like the feeling, is all."

Emila patted my leg again. "Can't say I blame you."

Doctor Jensen turned her disapproving frown on Emila before looking back at me. "I understand, Khara," she said, voice clinical and firm. "But it's an unfortunate necessity to curb the effects of these episodes on your body. It's better for you to feel *fuzzy* for a while than to be in such high levels of pain, yes?"

She had me, and she knew it.

"Yes," I sighed. "It's better."

"Then if there's nothing else ...?"

I shook my head. "No, that's all. Thank you, Doctor Jensen."

"Of course. I'll update Sovereign Ramsey on your condition. Get some rest."

With that, she swept from the room. The spark of tension in the air left with her.

Emila shifted to make herself more comfortable, lounging across the foot of my bed. "Always a ray of sunshine, that one."

"Be nice," I chided, though my lips curved into a smile. "She's helped me a lot."

Emila scoffed, picking at the blanket. "Doesn't mean she has to be so uptight all the time."

"She's being ... professional," I said slowly, struggling to find the right word as much as my belief in it.

Emila huffed a laugh. "Well, she was right about one thing. You do need to rest. I'll let you do that."

She gracefully stood from the bed before smoothing her dress from waist to knee. "I'll come back in a bit with some food, then camp out in your living room if you're okay with that."

When I nodded, she smiled.

"The guards changed shifts as Doctor Jensen was coming in, so Charna's out front. Lucky you, upgrading from lowly Gage to the competence of the commander herself." I snorted, and her eyes sparkled. "If you need anything before I come back, let her know."

"I will," I said through a yawn, my eyes already closing. Fatigue swept over me as the medicine took effect, the extra pill making me drowsier than usual.

"Go to sleep, Khara," Emila said softly. "I'll be here when you wake up."

I sighed out a long breath and fell into a dreamless sleep.

26

THE NEXT FEW DAYS passed in a slow but steady routine. I was left to rest each morning—doctor's orders—and had breakfast delivered by Emila or whichever guard came to take over for the night shift. Ramsey brought breakfast himself on occasion, but with things so unsettled with the rebels, his visits were less frequent in the mornings.

He constantly apologized for his absence. While I missed his presence, I hardly expected him to be with me all the time. His dedication to Anluan inspired me, and the situation with the rebels was too important for him to ignore just so I'd have more of his company. I'd taken up enough of his time during my initial recovery when he'd refused to leave my bedside for days on end. I refused to be a distraction.

I began to take my medicine more regularly. The severity of the last episode prompted my caretakers to become more vigilant. They had me swallow a pill at the slightest twinge of discomfort reflected on my face. I often woke in pain, having dreamt of scattered flashes. Fresh tear tracks would trail down my face, though I could never remember why.

The medicine dulled the edges of my pain, but this new batch left me feeling weaker than before. I hated the lethargy dragging down my bones and fogging my mind, but they assured me my body would adjust. I tried to bear it gracefully, though I couldn't help longing for a better way.

Most afternoons, I rallied. I'd leave my bed and go for a walk with Emila, peppering in the physical therapy exercises for my shoulder. She'd answer my questions about Anluan, tease me about my relationship with Ramsey, and give me insight into what would be expected from me once I was his wife. It was a strange blend of enjoyment and overwhelm. Her teasing comments felt normal in a bittersweet way that made my heart lift and ache.

Friendship with Emila was easy in many ways. She understood me, and I could picture our relationship before the attack every time we shared a laugh. She always seemed to know when I was getting anxious about the level of responsibility I'd bear as Sovereigna. She'd make a joke, tell a distracting story, or decide it was time for a break and tell me to sketch something in my journal.

But every now and then, something would remind me of my disadvantage in our friendship. She'd share a story I had no reference for or mention someone I should probably know but didn't. There was too much of our history I couldn't remember. Too many details I only knew through the mouths of others. Too much I didn't ask because I hated that I needed to. Because I didn't want to cast a shadow over the bright spots in my days.

Ramsey hadn't let up the watch of the guards. It seemed like he'd added to the assignment since I'd worked myself into such a debilitating episode. There were always two guards present during the day now, and they stayed closer than they had before. They rotated positions twice during the day and again before nightfall. His most trusted guards were assigned to my suite, though it seemed for the residential floors, one guard was deemed enough. Everyone seemed confident that the magical safeguards put in place throughout the Annex would prevent any issues up there.

Today, we were followed by Gage and Cethin—one of Ramsey's preferred duos—as we strolled through the garden paths. Emila seemed to prefer them as well. She spoke more directly to them than anyone other than Charna and wasn't above teasing either of them at the slightest opportunity.

"Princess," Gage called, holding out an envelope as he drew closer to where Emila and I rested in the grass. "This is for you."

The glossy sheen of navy paper shimmered in the light. I perked up as I accepted it. As expected, an ornate *R* had been pressed into gold wax that sealed it shut. It matched the stack of letters I kept in my bedroom. Ramsey had taken to writing to me throughout the days he was too busy to be by my side. It was a gesture I'd come to anticipate each afternoon.

Khara,

I'm sorry for my absence again this morning. I wish I'd been enjoying your company instead of meeting with the advisors. We're close to figuring out the best way to move against the rebels. I'm hopeful I'll have my mornings back soon, and we'll be able to spend more time together, as it should be.

At any rate, they will have to continue without me this evening, as I have every intention of having dinner with my beautiful fiancée. Just us tonight. I'll meet you at your suite at seven. Know I'll be watching the clock until then.

Yours alone,

Ramsey

"What's that?" Emila asked, peering over my shoulder.

I folded the paper before she could read it, tucking it back into the envelope. Some things were meant to stay private.

"Ramsey's having dinner with me tonight."

Emila smirked, her eyes brightening with delight. "Finally ditching his duties. I knew it was only a matter of time. That man can't stay away from you."

I shook my head as I fiddled with the letter. "He's not ditching anything. I'm sure if they needed him, he'd stay behind. Dinner's not that important."

"Dinner may not be"—she leaned back on the grass beside me—"but you certainly are. Especially to Ramsey."

That evening, I searched my closet for something to wear. Hanging in the back, I found a selection of elegant dresses I was almost too afraid to touch. I'd had no need of finery in medical, and even now, my days didn't require anything so fancy. But when bold red fabric caught my eye, I decided to try dressing up.

While the dress was fairly simple, it was more formal than what I usually wore. But then, Ramsey's invitation had sounded more formal than eating together in the commons. He'd been working so hard lately. I wanted to make our limited time together special.

After slipping into the dress, I did my best to apply some makeup before tackling my hair. Letting the large bathroom mirror guide my movements, I pinned my waves into a low chignon. It took time, but I managed to arrange my hair until it hid the raised scar peeking through the undercut slowly growing in. Avoiding the scar had become second nature. Ramsey's face tightened whenever he noticed it, and I didn't fare much better. It served as too harsh a reminder of what I'd been through. What I'd lost. All the things I couldn't remember.

Shaking those thoughts away, I stepped back and focused on my reflection. The bold red dress suited my olive skin. The fabric hugged my curves without clinging too tightly. I felt more beautiful than I could ever remember feeling. And yet, it was strange to see my eyes lined in black and the daring red color on my lips.

Maybe it was too much.

A knock at the door jolted me from my doubts. It was too late to reconsider. Ramsey had arrived.

I crossed into the living room, clasping the glass pendant from the market around my neck. The fiery necklace rested against my skin, a perfect complement to both the color of my dress and its dipping neckline.

Ramsey stood in the hall wearing a fitted charcoal suit. The unbuttoned jacket and slight rumpling of his shirt spoke of a tiring day. Even as he frowned down at his tablet with exhausted eyes, I couldn't help but think him handsome. He glanced up at the door as it opened before turning his attention back to the screen. But in an instant, his stunned eyes flashed back to me.

"Khara," he breathed. "You look …"

"Is it too much?" I skimmed my palms down the skirt where it hugged my curves.

"Not at all." He shook his head, tablet forgotten as he stepped forward. His hand brushed against my bare shoulder, slowly trailing down my arm, and I fought back a shiver at the touch. He took my hand and lifted it to his mouth for a kiss. "You're absolutely stunning. You just surprised me."

I shrugged shyly as I gestured to the dress. "I wanted to look nice tonight. For you."

He grinned, a smile that reached his eyes and rid his face of all traces of weariness. "Well, you certainly outdid yourself. How would you feel about dinner in my suite? I'd much prefer to keep you to myself, especially dressed like that."

Heat flooded my cheeks, but I nodded. His grin widened as he held out his arm for me. I took it, and we made our way to the elevator.

Ramsey had to press his hand to a wooden panel to select his floor, which sat directly above mine. When his handprint was approved, a thrumming pulse of magic formed a thick presence in the elevator before the wood glowed a soft green.

We rose quickly to the twenty-sixth floor. The elevator opened right into Ramsey's living space, which must have taken up the entire level. It was no wonder it required magical authorization to enter.

My eyes wandered over his suite. The décor was modern yet warm, a perfect fit for Ramsey. Tall windows covered an entire wall, giving an unimpeded view of the city that surpassed even mine. The rich brown of the hardwood floor provided a warm contrast to the crisp, white walls. Soft rugs surrounded the gray couches positioned in front of a large fireplace. Dark wooden bookshelves lined the far wall, covered with books, framed photographs, and plants. It made the space feel less like the rest of the Annex and more inviting, like a home.

"How are you feeling?" Ramsey asked, eyes soft as he led me from the elevator. "It's hard to imagine you as anything other than well looking like that, but I know appearances can be deceiving."

"I'm all right, Ramsey. Haven't your guards reported as much over the last few days?"

"They have," he admitted, dipping his chin. "But I don't want to rely on them. Reports don't tell the whole story. With you, I want to know all I can." He stopped and turned to face me. "So, Khara, how are you feeling?"

"I'm fine, really. Nothing has been nearly as bad as the other day. The medicine seems to be affecting me more strongly," I admitted. "And Doctor Jensen has me taking a dose as soon as I feel symptoms right now."

"And you have Emila enforcing that directive."

I snorted. "I certainly do."

She was quick to open the pill bottle. She'd hand me a blue tablet whenever I showed the slightest sign of pain.

"She means well, but sometimes ..."

Ramsey laughed. "I can imagine you're feeling a lot of *sometimes* with all of us. Me especially. I've been particularly overbearing with you lately, I'm afraid."

His words softened any irritation I'd harbored. "You've been perfectly understandable."

"Understandably overbearing." He flashed me a self-deprecating smile. "I'm trying to be better, Khara. About everything. I know I haven't been around much lately—"

I opened my mouth to absolve him of his guilt, but he shook his head and waved me off.

"Please, don't defend me." He sighed, rubbing the back of his neck before dropping his hand to his side. "I know I have to make sacrifices in order to do what needs to be done. I've accepted that. Some days I just resent that you have to make them, too. Especially right now." He cleared his throat, looking away abruptly. "Anyway, I want you to know I'm sorry. I'm going to be around more. That's a promise."

He looked into my eyes again. Sincerity deepened the subtle amber swirling against the brown of his stare, and I couldn't help comparing the way he looked at me to the way Hayden had that night in the grove. Where Hayden's eyes held piercing depths of tenderness and an overwhelming openness, Ramsey looked at me like I was the most important person in the world, as if I were a treasure he prized.

Ramsey's charm and charisma blended well with his air of authority. He typically held himself as though he was a little guarded, but at times like this, he let me see who he was beneath the mien of Sovereign.

Love from Ramsey was controlled and careful, yet he exuded confidence. Like he knew it was his right to be with me, but he maintained distance to be respectful of my situation. I wondered how it had been before I'd lost my memories. How it might be after I regained them.

If I regained them.

"Khara?" He tilted his head, watching me with concern brewing in his eyes.

I shook my head to clear it. "There's nothing to forgive. You've been working to protect Anluan and everyone in it, including me. How could I be mad at you for that?"

"You're far too good to me."

The fondness in his smile sent my stomach churning with guilt. Ramsey had been my pillar of support since I'd woken in medical. He'd soothed me through the pain and helped alleviate my fears. He'd distracted me whenever I felt overwhelmed and cheered me up on days I struggled to see past my grief. He had never pushed me past my level of comfort as I got used to the idea of our relationship. He gave me space to process my situation without leaving me floundering in it alone.

He'd elevated my needs above his own for months and made sure I knew how much he cared.

You're far too good to me.

Between my missing memories and meeting with the enemy, I kept finding myself thinking the reverse.

27

As Ramsey moved to prepare the table, I wandered to his bookshelves. You could tell a lot about a person by what they kept on their shelves, and I desperately wanted to know more about Ramsey. The less I had to ask him about things I already should have known, the better.

Worn fabric drew my eye to a collection of old books. I couldn't resist trailing a finger across the binding of a set of navy volumes. The titles had dulled from what must have once been bright gold, but that only added to their charm. *A History of the Diamond Kingdoms of Veyhaan* took up much of one shelf. I would have to ask Ramsey if I could borrow them later. A better grasp of our history would be vital as Sovereigna.

Anxiety twisted my insides. My future duties weren't something I wanted to think about. This night was about my relationship with Ramsey. Him, not his title. There would be time for all of that later, preferably when Emila would be around to temper my unease.

I moved on to a nearby shelf and discovered an even older volume, one whose title I couldn't make out against the faded binding. My finger slipped between the pages as I pulled it from the shelf and a thrum of magic ran through me.

I straightened, eyes wide. I'd heard Isiraden paper and ink had been used in old, important books, but I'd yet to see one for myself. If anyone owned such a thing, it would be Ramsey. With careful hands, I opened the cover to find the title: *Mysteries of Magic: A Study of Isiraden Forest.*

The thrum of magic grew as I trailed two fingers over the title and accompanying depiction of an ancient tree. My chest warmed. Something about the gentle hum felt welcoming, like the greeting of a dear friend. It made me want to get lost inside the pages for hours.

With no small effort, I gently slid it back onto the shelf. This wasn't the time, though I hoped I'd be able to find some for it soon.

I brought my attention to the next shelf, where several framed photographs sat atop book stacks and to the sides of potted plants. Picking up the first frame I came to, I grinned at what was clearly a photograph of a young Ramsey. He wore a small pout on his face where he stood, arms crossed, between two regal figures. I could only assume they were his parents. The woman and Ramsey had the same eyes. The man shared his jawline.

I set the frame down and moved to the next. My breath caught. Ramsey was older in this one, though I imagined he'd barely been a teenager at the time. He beamed where he sat on a fallen log, splatters of mud on his face, arms, and clothes. The girl beside him brought stinging tears to my eyes. She sat curled into his side, covered in mud, her hand clutching his arm. The smile on her face was smaller but no less genuine.

She looked exactly as I imagined I would have at that age.

Through blurry eyes, I moved on to the next photo and the next. The girl—*I*—was in so many of them. Hanging off Ramsey's back, my chin tucked over his shoulder and arms wrapped around his neck. Shyly staring at the camera with a flower crown perched on my head. Eyes lit with mirth as I looked at Ramsey, both of our cheeks full, remnants of glazed pastries in hand.

My throat tight, I picked up a photo hidden behind the others. Despite being framed, it bore wrinkles and tears at its edges. A jagged line broke the image so only two-thirds showed.

In this one, we were older. Ramsey resembled himself as he was now, and I clearly recognized myself beside him. It was maybe a few years old at most. He'd thrown his arm over my shoulder, a wide grin on his face. I stood beside him, a soft pink barely visible on my cheeks as I held a wrapped box and smiled at the camera. Someone else stood next to me, their side barely visible before the rip in the paper cut them off.

I frowned. Whoever it was had been lost to the damage.

I moved to put it back when I noticed their arm had also been slung over my shoulder. On their wrist, I could just make out a black tattoo. Squinting my eyes, I barely registered it as a stylized *s* with a line extended through it.

Just like Hayden's tattoo.

"Khara?"

I startled, my heart pounding as the frame clacked back against the shelf. I turned to Ramsey, who stood at the edge of the room, head tilted and concern spreading over his face.

"What's wrong?" he asked, brows dipping as he moved toward me.

"What?"

"You're crying."

I brought a hand to my face, blinking as my fingers came away wet. When had that happened?

Glancing back to the shelf, I sniffed and swiped at my face. "Sorry. I was just looking."

Ramsey frowned, running gentle hands up and down my arms. "At what?"

I grabbed one of the frames, breaking his hold, and held it out to him.

"There are so many," I whispered. "And I don't remember. I don't know why it hit me so hard. I didn't expect it."

Ramsey stared at the photo, his eyes wistful. When I sniffed again, he met my gaze. I tried to reassure him with a smile, but my lips ruined it by trembling. He set the frame back into place and pulled me close, his arms wrapping tight around my back.

The hug ruined my tenuous hold on my emotions. Fisting the lapels of his jacket in my hands, I pressed my head against his chest and cried.

28

"Would it help if I told you about one of the photos?" Ramsey asked as he slid a chair out for me at the dining table.

I slumped into it, worn from my tears. I hated that I'd cried on Ramsey and soured what should have been a pleasant evening. Wearing such a fine dress felt like a wasted effort now. No doubt my makeup looked ridiculous after all that crying.

Ramsey crouched in front of me, brushing a thumb across my cheek. "I'll tell you whatever you want to know. I'll tell you a thousand stories. Just say the word."

Part of me longed to hear them. The desperation to know more of myself—more of Ramsey, more of us *together*—hung heavy in my heart. Another part wasn't sure I could handle it. How would it feel, hearing these memories I couldn't hold on to myself?

I leaned into Ramsey's touch and heaved a sigh. "I'm sorry for ruining tonight."

"Nothing is ruined." He laced our fingers together, working to meet my eyes. "I love being with you. And I'd love nothing more than to share these memories with you again."

My breath hitched. He was so generous, always ready to make things better for me. I had to find a way to make them better for him too. For both of us. I had to find a way to restore my memories.

In the meantime, a story couldn't hurt—at least not more than any other reminder of what I'd lost. I'd faced plenty of them by now. I could face this too.

I shoved down the tears, but my voice still wavered. "You really don't mind?"

He shook his head, his eyes soft as he cupped my cheek. "Not at all." He pressed a kiss to my temple. "Wait here."

As he left, I turned my attention to the table. Despite the rich aroma, I barely glanced at the food steaming on our plates. The candles clustered in the center of the table drew my gaze. My eyes lost focus as I watched the flames dance. I needed to shut off my thoughts for a while. If I managed to get out of my head, maybe the evening could still be salvaged.

By the time Ramsey returned, carrying a stack of frames, I'd managed to settle myself. He offered me a tentative smile as he moved to sit beside me. His eyes roved over my face, his concern shifting to relief as he took in my expression. He placed the stack on the table, moving a single frame to rest facing up where we could both see the photograph inside.

"You eat," he said softly. "I'll talk."

Food barely interested me at the moment, but I dutifully reached for my fork. Eating seemed a fair exchange for a memory. Spearing a glazed carrot, I took a bite and raised a brow at Ramsey.

He huffed a laugh, his eyes darting to the photo of us covered in mud.

"Meeting you was one of the best things that ever happened to me." He traced a finger over the edge of the image, no exaggeration or teasing in his words.

"I didn't have a lot of friends growing up, other than ..." He shook his head before taking a sip of water. "Well, I didn't have a lot of friends. My parents would take us outside the city in the summer. It helped me, being away from so many people. We had a cottage not too far from yours."

"In Isiraden?" I leaned closer, tilting my head at the pines surrounding us in the picture.

"No, that wasn't allowed. Not even for us." He tapped the fallen tree we'd sat on. "This was in the Orveyin Forest, just to the north of Isiraden. That's where we met, and where we spent most of our time."

My lips twitched at the qualifier. "Most?"

"We were children, Khara. What were laws to us?" He smirked, his eyes alight with amusement. "We slipped in and out of Isiraden often enough."

Images of our younger selves darting between cedars and sycamores as we chased each other into the sacred grove filled my head, and I chuckled. "So, you were a mischievous young Sovereigno."

Ramsey's eyes dipped back to the frame, smile turning shy as he rubbed his neck. "Something like that. Though you were far more likely to pull me into trouble than the other way around. The mud all over us? That was your doing."

"Really?"

"Oh yes. We'd had heavy rain and you wanted to race through the forest anyway. You didn't tell me there was a massive puddle at the finish line."

I bit back a smile as I swirled my fork through my mashed potatoes. "How are you so sure I knew about it?"

"You insisted on using that specific finish line and couldn't stop giggling about it. I should have figured it out then." He chuckled, shaking his head. "You didn't run nearly as fast as usual, either."

"So you won?"

"I did, though the race was rigged." Ramsey gave me a pointed look and I couldn't bite back a grin. "But I ran straight into the puddle, slipped on the mud, and fell right onto my back. I was soaked through."

I clapped a hand over my mouth as I laughed, and Ramsey's entire face brightened at the sound.

"That's about how you reacted then too. I was determined to get you back—"

"Of course you were."

"—so I grabbed a handful of mud and threw it right in your face."

My jaw dropped. "Ramsey!"

"I was twelve!"

He laughed, and warmth settled over me. If it got him to laugh like this, I'd listen to hundreds of his stories. He deserved these moments of happiness. We both did.

"Besides," he added, smirk growing, "you gave as good as you got."

"I'm sure I did," I said softly, staring at the photograph. The brightness of our smiles alone told me this had been a good day. Though I was grateful it had been captured, I wished I could remember it myself. Shaking the thought away, I looked back up at Ramsey. "Your clothes look like they were expensive. Did you get in trouble for ruining them?"

"Mother threw a fit, I'm sure." He shrugged, his eyes flicking away. "But that wasn't unusual."

I frowned. He'd never spoken of his mother that I could remember. "What was she like?" I shifted in my seat, itching with curiosity. "Did she ... like me?"

Ramsey grimaced as he reached for his drink.

"Oh," I said, my heart sinking as I stared down at the table.

"If it helps, she rarely approved of me, either."

If anything, that made it worse.

"Ramsey—"

"It's fine," he said, his smile tight enough I knew it was anything but. "She did her best, but my mother wasn't easy to please. She had high hopes for me, but I could barely control my gift. And you ..."

I set my fork down as my stomach stirred with nerves. "What about me?"

"She didn't like how much time I spent with you." He heaved a sigh, and his words picked up speed. "Or that we ran around the forest. Or where you came from, or how you held a position as Isiraden-born that she could never hope to reach. She was jealous and bitter, Khara. None of it had to do with you."

I swallowed thickly. "When did she ...?"

Ramsey huffed, scrubbing a hand over his face. "She's alive, at least last I heard. Ran away one night and didn't bother to take me with her. Never sent word to me after."

Shock ripped through me. She'd run away when she was Sovereigna and a mother? It was unfathomable. What would make someone abandon their son and their duty to their people? And what of his father?

My voice broke. "Ramsey—"

He took my hand and squeezed. "It's in the past. Let's leave it there."

Throat tight, I nodded. "If that's what you want."

His hand tightened around mine. "I have everything I want right here."

In the ensuing quiet, the temptation to bring up my family flared hot in my chest. Questions about my own mother sat on the tip of my tongue. As if he sensed it, Ramsey's shoulders slowly edged toward his ears, his hand clenching around his fork. Dread coiled in my chest. His reaction didn't bode well.

After the heaviness of what Ramsey had shared about his family, I hated the idea of asking about mine. Fear had held my tongue this long. I could wait a while longer. Pushing the questions down again, I settled back into my seat and let the uncomfortable silence grow.

29

Chaos surrounded me. Everything had changed so quickly. How had it come to this?

Rolling booms sounded like thunder, echoing until I couldn't determine where they began. Light flashed, bright and blinding, as a swarm of ashes swirled into the sky on the wind.

My heart raced. I had to stop this. I had to find him. I had to—

"*Khara, please ...*"

My name was the barest whisper, yet it reached me loud and clear, even over the turmoil of the attack. I turned, my hair whipping around as I looked for the source of the voice.

"Hello?"

No one answered.

I turned back to the battle, heart thundering in my chest—but it was gone.

Nothing remained. Nothing but inky blackness.

Before I could panic, pinpricks of light pierced the darkness. They came quickly, one after another, until I stood beneath a starry night sky. All I could see were stars.

The faintest echo of a voice came from behind me. "The stars used to calm you."

I turned, but again, no one was there. Just me and thousands of stars glittering overhead. They felt close enough to touch.

My heart slowed as peace settled over me. A tear of relief rolled down my face. The confusion of the battle was over. I could breathe again.

Sadness lined the voice when it came again, this time more clearly. "You're safe, Khara."

"*You're safe here, with me.*"

Hayden.

I called his name, searching the darkness with more intent. "Where are you?"

"I'm here."

And there he was, standing in front of me, his hands in his pockets and a sad smile on his face.

I should have felt angry or scared. Dream or no, Hayden didn't belong in my head. He was the one responsible for the atrocity I had just dreamed. Instead, I felt inexplicably safer in his presence, and hated myself for it.

"What do you want?" I snapped.

He flinched. Good. He deserved to feel as unnerved around me as I did around him.

"I just—" He paused, a helpless look on his face. "I just want you to be safe. I need to know you're okay."

I frowned. "You're not responsible for me."

"Aren't I?"

He reached out as though he was going to touch my arm.

Before he could make contact, I woke up.

$$30$$

My head ached as I blinked my eyes open. Tears had left a salty trail down my face while I slept. I sucked in a rasping breath, trying to breathe through the pain. It didn't work as well as I'd hoped, but there wasn't much else I could do.

Except take another pill.

They'll make you worse.

The voice in my head sounded a lot like Hayden's. I frowned as I stared at the bottle of medicine on my side table. I'd been taking extra doses for days. The pills were helping the pain. But I still felt off when I took them, disconnected from myself in a way I didn't like.

And I didn't dream when I took the pills. Or if I did, I never quite remembered what I'd dreamed about.

Those little blue pills ... I needed them. I'd told Hayden as much when we met.

And yet, something inside me resisted the idea this morning.

What if I didn't take one? What if I worked through the pain on my own somehow? What if—

I cut off the thought, but it sprang right back.

What if I found Hayden and let him help me?

I huffed angrily, throwing my hands over my eyes. The idea was ridiculous. It was an affront to the role I had in Anluan and as Ramsey's fiancée. I couldn't do it.

But all I could think of as I lay in my warm bed, hands covering my face to block the early morning light, was the echoes of what I'd felt in that dream. Outside of the pain and fear within the first dream—the one already fading from my mind—I'd felt calm, at peace.

Tears stung the corners of my eyes. Frustrated ones, this time. I was so tired of this. Tired of being weak, of needing so much help, of walking around in confusion all the time.

I was tired of doubting and not knowing how to trust myself.

Maybe it was time to take a leap of faith.

For a long moment, I stared at the pill bottle. Then I shoved it inside the drawer, out of sight.

Ramsey cleared his schedule to spend more time with me that day. As we strolled through the garden together, I studied him. He'd lost any signs of discomfort he'd had during our dinner. His smiles came easily, and his eyes were bright as he carried a covered basket in his hand. Stress didn't line his shoulders the way it tended to after his meetings. Something had happened.

He noticed my staring as we ventured onto an inner path and smiled warmly. "What?"

"Nothing," I said, shaking my head and turning back toward the flower bushes lining the trail. "You just seem lighter today."

"I feel it." He took my hand, pulling us to a gentle stop. When we faced each other, his eyes were bright with relief. "We've figured out a plan, Khara. It will take some time, but I think we've finally found a way to beat them. The rebels won't be a threat much longer."

I blinked. I'd expected some sort of good news, but I hadn't expected *this*. He made it sound as if the war would be over soon. His confidence surprised me.

"That's great," I said, though uncertainty bled into my voice.

Ramsey gently brushed the hair from my face. "You don't seem pleased."

I was at a loss for words. Part of me was thrilled. So much would change for Anluan and all its people, in the city and beyond. We could reopen full trade with the other Diamond Kingdoms without fear of raids. Our people would be free to leave the city gates whenever they wished. But another part of me was torn. How much would we lose trying to achieve this victory?

"You're worrying." Ramsey nodded firmly, as if it were obvious. Sometimes it was intimidating that he could read me so well. "Khara, everything is going to be all right. This plan, it's a good one. We'll be able to set things right." He tipped my head up and caressed my cheek. "Finally, after all this time, Anluan will be what it always should have been."

His eyes took on the look of a man with all his dreams in reach.

This was more important to Ramsey than I'd realized. Admiration softened me at the clear display of how much he cared for his people and the kingdom he ruled. As he trailed his hands down my arms to rest against my wrists, tension released from my shoulders.

"And I'll have you to share it with," he added, pressing a kiss to my hand. "You make all of this worth it."

I swallowed thickly. His words were meant to assure me of how much he cared, but I still struggled to accept them. The declaration came with a weight that settled over my shoulders and dripped down until my gut filled with lead.

Who was I to deserve any of it?

My unease faded, slowly replaced by a soft contentment as Ramsey and I lounged next to each other on a blanket in the grass. He'd hidden it in the basket, along with a few books and fresh lemon tarts from the kitchens. It was exactly the kind of surprise I welcomed.

As I lay on my stomach, a book of old Anluani legends open in front of me, I studied Ramsey.

He'd given up on his book already. It rested against the tops of his thighs, propped up by his bent knees. While the weather wasn't as sticky with humidity today, it was still warm, even in the shaded area where we'd settled. Ramsey had removed his suit jacket and rolled the sleeves of his dress shirt up his forearms as soon as we'd sat down.

With both arms bent behind his head, he lay flat on his back, his eyes closed and a small smile playing on his lips. He'd shaved, but kept the light stubble he favored. Even here in the shade, his skin seemed to glow with warmth. A breeze picked up, moving through his hair and shifting the black strands slightly out of place. My lips tipped up.

He looked good like this, casual and content in a way that made me feel more at peace myself. How often was Ramsey able to truly rest as Sovereign? Quiet moments like this made the idea of marrying him a little easier to process. But with all the demands of ruling Anluan, how many of these moments would be part of our future?

"Why are you staring at me?" A knowing grin spread across his face. "Is the book not to your liking?"

My cheeks flushed. He hadn't even opened his eyes, and still, I'd been caught.

"No, it's fascinating." I busied my hands with the book. "They all are. Everything feels new."

"Does that bother you?"

"Yes and no." I traced a finger over an illustration of a winged horse. "On the one hand, I get to experience every story like it's the first time."

"And on the other?"

I sighed. "I wish I remembered these stories. Which was my favorite when I was a child? Did any of them have a strong connection to a specific time in my life? I don't know. They're little things, but ..."

"Just because a thing is small doesn't mean it's unimportant." Ramsey stared at me, his eyes shining with something I couldn't pinpoint. "It matters, Khara. I'm sorry."

"Don't be." I offered him a strained smile. "I didn't mean to spoil our time together."

He frowned, sitting up and turning to face me properly. "You're not spoiling anything. I want to know what's on your mind, no matter what it is. You don't need to try to spare me from your feelings. Let me help shoulder the burden. I want to."

My eyes stung. "You already have."

"Then I'll keep at it. I'd do anything for you."

The weight of his words settled over my heart. Turning back to the book in front of me, I tried to focus on keeping my grief at bay. Despite Ramsey's reassurances, I didn't want to cry right now. This time together was special, and I refused to mourn my losses every time we were alone. There had to be room for more than my sadness if we were going to rebuild our relationship.

My attention on the book didn't bother Ramsey. He seemed to understand, offering a kiss to the crown of my head rather than saying anything else.

I stared at the ornate drop caps at the start of the next tale. The book was beautiful, an illustrated copy of myths and legends with embellishments throughout the pages. The paper held the delightful smell of an old book, even in the open air. It might have been as old as some of the ones Ramsey had on the shelves in his suite.

The reminder of them brightened my mood. I sat up and met Ramsey's eyes. "You have a book about Isiraden and its magic, right?"

He cocked his head. "I do."

"Do you think I could borrow it?" The thrum of magic I'd felt while holding it intrigued me almost as much as the title. Something about it was comforting, and the contents could prove useful. "The books in my suite are mostly fiction, and I'd like to learn more about Isiraden."

Ramsey hesitated, and my smile faltered.

"I don't mind if you borrow it, eventually," he said carefully. "But I can't give it to you right now. I need it as a reference."

"A reference? For what?"

He rubbed the back of his neck. "Just some research I've been doing."

"On Isiraden?"

He nodded, his eyes lighting with passion. "Its magic is something we use, but we've barely begun to tap into its full potential. I've been working with specialists on possibilities to harvest the magic to better Anluan. It looks promising, but there's more to be done."

"It sounds exciting," I offered, trying not to let my disappointment show. It did sound fascinating, but there was so much more I wanted to know about Isiraden and my connection to it. That book seemed like it was the best place to start.

"Very." He reached for my hand and entwined our fingers. "That book is the only comprehensive study of Isiraden we possess. It's connected to all of my notes."

"Could I help with the project?"

Maybe I could read the book that way. And it would give me time to learn more about Isiraden magic. My connection to the forest might even help them make progress.

Ramsey's brows pinched. "I don't think that's a good idea."

"Why not? I could help. Surely my connection to Isiraden would be of value."

"It would," he agreed, smoothing his thumb back and forth across my hand. "But you're still recovering. There will be plenty of ways for you to contribute later. For now, I'd prefer it if you'd rest. Take time to settle in before you dive into any big projects."

A flicker of frustration rose in my chest, but I shoved it down. His reasoning made sense. I just hated feeling so useless. How long would it be before I could actually serve our kingdom the way a future Sovereigna should? What if it took too long? Worse, what if I never fully recovered?

"Hey," Ramsey said, cupping my cheek and distracting me from my fears. "You don't have anything to prove, not to me or anyone else. You're doing well. Healing takes time."

I sighed, leaning into the comfort of his touch. "I know. It's just hard sometimes."

He nodded, his eyes brimming with sadness. "I wish I could make this easier for you. I hate seeing you in pain."

That much had been obvious from the start. Even through the haze of agony that had me squinting blearily at him on that first day in medical, I could see how much my pain tormented him. He carried it like a weight, a thick blend of guilt, love, and fear that I still noticed in him at times.

"It won't always be like this," he promised, tucking a stray hair behind my ear. His nearness made my pulse quicken. I closed my eyes, focusing on my breath. "This will pass, and everything will be better on the other side. You'll see."

They all kept telling me to wait, that my recovery was a process, and healing would come in time. I believed them, more or less. Surely something had to change eventually. Still, I couldn't help the longing that pulled at my heart. How long would it take and what would I miss out on in the waiting?

I sighed, locking eyes with Ramsey. "Is it wrong to hope I see it soon?"

Ramsey's lips twitched as he lowered his hand to mine. "If it is, we're both in trouble."

My huff of laughter broke any lingering tension in the air. Ramsey's grin was blinding before it gentled.

"I can let you know when we're finished with the book." He played with my fingers, and I struggled to focus on his words. "Maybe you can read it then? It may take quite some time, but if you're willing to wait ..."

"I am." What was a bit more waiting while I was at it? "I think it'll help. I'd like to understand more about my connection to the forest."

"Of course."

When Ramsey squeezed my hand, I squeezed back. His answers didn't give me what I wanted, but he'd tried to accommodate the request. That was all I could ask for. In the meantime, I'd have to try to be patient. By the end of all this, I hoped it would come more naturally. I'd certainly have had enough practice.

We went quiet, slowly relaxing back into our places on the blanket as the conversation faded into comfortable silence. With the faintest hint of roses carrying over on the summer breeze, I returned to my reading and let the ancient stories of my people sweep away all other thoughts.

31

Why did emergencies always have to interrupt mealtimes?

Ramsey had intended to spend the entire day with me, ending with another private dinner in his suite. He wanted to cook for me. Instead, we were interrupted in the hall by a cluster of guards. Cethin led the charge. The satisfied smile on his face held an edge I wanted to shy away from.

He nodded to Ramsey, barely sparing me a glance. "Sovereign."

"Radnor." Ramsey nodded in return, standing tall. In an instant, he'd shifted back into his role as Sovereign. Excitement gleamed in his eyes. "What's happened?"

"We found one." Cethin's smile grew sharp. He looked like a predator about to move in for a kill. "We have one of the traitors locked in a cell on the lower level. Commander North is keeping an eye on him."

Ramsey's eyes went steely as the corners of his mouth lifted. "Good. I'll see to him immediately." As soon as the words escaped his mouth, he froze. He turned back to me, wincing. "Khara—"

"Should I go with you?"

Based on my lessons with Emila, my presence as future Sovereigna could be required in these situations. Despite my curiosity, I didn't want to go. Whatever interrogation was about to occur wasn't something I wanted to be involved with.

I grimaced at my cowardice. How could I be what Anluan needed if I was unable to face a bound prisoner?

Ramsey spoke slowly, as though afraid to offend. "No, I don't want to risk you. The traitor may be in custody, but it's best not to underestimate him." His face tightened. "We've been burned before."

I nodded, glancing at the guards behind him. The harsh looks on their faces only fed my discomfort.

"This is important," I said, focusing on Ramsey to quell my unease. "You need to go."

He planted a quick kiss on my forehead. "Thank you for understanding. With any luck, we won't have these interruptions much longer."

"I'll see you tomorrow?"

"Of course." He squeezed my hand before moving back toward the guards. "I should be done with this by then."

The words were casual, but they sparked a sliver of apprehension. I brushed it aside—until I caught Cethin's dark smirk. As he met my stare, a chill ran down my spine. I wanted to turn away, but before I could, Ramsey signaled to the guards. They strode off to deal with the rebel prisoner, leaving only one guard by my side. I had never been more relieved it wasn't Cethin.

With Ramsey occupied, my dinner plans turned into lounging with Emila in my suite. I curled up in the corner of my couch, wrapped in my coziest blanket. As much as I hated to admit it, I still tired if I did too much in a day. Though I seemed to be less fatigued than I'd been in a while, weariness had crept over me. I didn't want to overtax myself. And I hadn't taken a single pill today.

I shook my head, pushing thoughts of the medication away. There would be time to work through those implications later.

"You okay?" Emila asked, dipping a chunk of bread into her soup. Her frown spoke of her worry again.

"Just a little tired, that's all."

She stared at me through narrowed eyes for a moment, then brightened. "I believe you. *This time.*"

I threw a crumpled napkin at her. "I don't lie to you!"

At her unimpressed look, I faltered. I hadn't thought of myself as a liar, but lately, I'd been stretching—if not outright avoiding—the truth. The realization stung.

"Much," I amended. "And I don't mean to. Sometimes I just want to feel like nothing's wrong with me."

Emila softened, setting her bowl aside on the coffee table before turning to face me fully. "You're healing, and you've had a hard recovery. Of course you're going to get frustrated. But you're doing so well, Khara."

I frowned, scrunching my nose. *Doing well?* Most days I was barely functional.

"Really," she persisted as she leaned closer. "You've come so far in such a short time. And you haven't had a bad episode in a few days, right?"

As it often did coming from Emila, the attempt to make me smile worked. My belief wasn't so easily inspired. I wasn't planning on taking the pills as frequently and had no idea what to expect with the change.

The thought surprised me. When I'd shut them inside the drawer that morning, I hadn't realized I'd decided to leave them there. But the more I thought about it, the more resolved I became.

I wouldn't take the pills again. Not unless I absolutely had to.

"So, obviously," Emila continued, "this is an upward swing. And yes, you may have more setbacks along the way, but we're all here for you. You have Doctor Jensen, Ramsey, me. We'll make sure you stay where you need to be."

"I know."

In the face of Emila's unbridled positivity, there was little else to do but agree. But her words gave me pause.

They would make sure I was where I needed to be ... but what if I didn't agree with where they thought that was?

32

THE WIND KNOCKED MY hair loose from my braids, blowing it against my face as I charged through the field. Screams rang out amid deafening shouts and clanging that turned my stomach. I squinted against a light bouncing off silver—a glint of metal.

Amid the chaos came a cry, one I recognized. My heart sped in my chest.

No. No, no, no!

I turned, frantic. I had to stop this. I had to—

Pain stole all thought. It sprang from my shoulder and radiated outward like a strike of lightning along my nerves. I jolted, trying to bite back a scream as my hand instinctively moved to the wound, but I couldn't hold back a cry when it made contact. Biting my lip, I tried to breathe through my nose. Blood trailed down my fingers, staining my dress and dripping onto the grass.

"Khara!"

I couldn't respond. It took everything in me to remain standing.

How did this happen? How had things gone so wrong?

Without warning, the scene warped, jumped. I blinked rapidly, still gripping my shoulder. No wound, just a lingering sensation of pain that was quickly fading.

Thick cedars and an expanse of tall grass surrounded me. I had crested a hill, and my lips formed into a smile. I didn't feel scared, or sad, or confused anymore—only a thrilling sense of delight.

I was running, I realized as the wind whipped my hair around me. It would have made more sense to braid the waves back or toss them into a bun at the base of my neck, but that wouldn't have felt so deliciously free—and I felt so free I could taste it on my tongue, sweet as honey.

I peered over my shoulder, grinning, and spotted Hayden. He was younger, and somehow I knew that I was too. He ran behind me, his eyes alight with joyful determination. I laughed and turned back to watch where I was going, but looking behind me proved to be a mistake.

Hayden caught me around the waist and spun us both. He lost his balance and we tumbled to the mossy earth, laughing breathlessly.

"You're the fastest girl I've ever met," he said proudly.

"And yet, you always manage to catch me," I teased, poking his rib.

His arms tightened around me, strong and gentle in the way I loved so much. "I have a strong incentive to, don't I?"

I smiled and brought my arms over his, pressing myself against his chest. I rested there, catching my breath without a care in the world. Even after breathing came easy, neither of us moved. We lay there until the sun had moved toward the west.

I sighed. "I have to go train."

"I'll wait."

He made it sound like it was the most logical thing in the world. Amusement curled my lips.

"You'll be waiting awhile."

He released me from his hold, shifting so he could meet my eyes. They were fond and warm as he smiled at me, his head propped on his hand. "For you, I'd wait lifetimes."

After so many nights of dreaming of things that split my head into pieces, I thought I'd be used to waking in tears in the middle of the night.

I wasn't.

My head burned with pain, sharp and disruptive as ever. I'd only stopped taking my pills that morning, and found myself instinctively reaching for them. Blowing out a steadying breath, I dropped my hand and fisted it in the sheets. I'd made my decision. I couldn't waver at the first test of my resolve.

I rode out the stabbing sensation, clenching and unclenching my fist as I breathed through the worst of it. My mind wavered between focusing on the pain and swirling with the confusion my dream caused. It was the most vivid one I'd ever had. It felt so real. Had it been a dream or a memory?

I'd wait lifetimes.

Dream-Hayden's voice echoed in my head, reminding me of our conversation in the grove. He said he'd wait for me. Days ago, now. Would he keep waiting, even though I hadn't shown up when he'd asked me to? Would he have the kind of patience to return again and again without any sign of me? Did it even matter to him that much? I couldn't say. But a new urgency stirred to life inside of me after that dream.

I needed to go back to the grove. Tonight.

33

Nerves filled me as I cracked open my door and peeked into the hall. I had no idea who was supposed to be on guard duty. I'd prepared an excuse, hoping it would be accepted by whoever I found. But when I peered out, no one was positioned beside my door. I frowned, but didn't hesitate to take full advantage and slip into the hall.

Sneaking out of the Annex felt less intimidating this time around. Maybe it was because I'd succeeded before with no one the wiser, other than Gage. And he only knew that I'd left my room, not where I'd gone or who I'd spoken to. Maybe it was because I knew where to go this time. Or maybe it was because I couldn't stop thinking about the overwhelming sense of freedom I'd felt in my dream.

Whatever the reason, I nimbly raced across the palace grounds, climbed over the iron fence, and sped into the shadows of the buildings across the street. I didn't slow my pace as I wove through the alleys and side streets of Anluan until I reached the wall near the market.

Once in the tunnel, I found the flashlight, though it wasn't exactly where I'd left it. Someone must have come through since then. I filed that away to think on later, grabbing the light and flicking it on when I made it to the path just inside the treeline.

Tension drained from my shoulders as soon as I started down the footpath. The sense of familiarity in the forest grounded me. The moon's light gave a soft glow to the leaves swaying above. I felt more relaxed than I had all day. At least, until I made it just shy of the grove. There I hesitated, my tension mounting.

What if this was all wrong? What if Hayden was waiting for me because it was a trap? What if he'd stopped waiting for me days ago? I couldn't decide which would be worse.

But the dream. I couldn't push it out of my head. I couldn't forget how it felt to run with abandon, the wind in my hair and Hayden by my side. I couldn't forget the warmth of his smile and his bright eyes. Or his arms wrapped around me.

Taking a steadying breath, I stepped forward only to freeze at the sound of raised voices. One was Hayden's, but there was another that I didn't recognize. I tried not to let it shake me, but I hadn't expected anyone but Hayden to be in the grove. My stomach churned. Was this a trap as I'd feared?

Hayden had the answers I needed. Another man in the grove didn't change that. I would have to be brave to get them. Still, this situation required more care than I'd thought. I would also have to be smart.

Heart thrumming, I edged to the side of the path, tiptoeing over sticks and brush as I inched farther into the trees. Seeing through the foliage was difficult, but that could only work in my favor. The last thing I wanted was to be seen before I knew what was going on.

Peeking through the trees, I focused on their conversation.

"—stayed long past what was agreed to, Sovereigno."

"I know."

"The risk increases the longer you're here—"

"*I know*, Tate."

"Then be reasonable! Come back with us."

"I can't."

"You have a duty—"

"Yes, I do! One you know I take seriously. I've disrupted the imports. I've met with the spies, set the pathways we need! But I have a duty to her, too, and I will not abandon her to—"

"All reports show she's fine! You're hardly needed to—"

"Fine?" Hayden laughed so bitterly that I cringed. "You haven't seen her. I have. What they've *done*—"

"She's with him! What more evidence do you need to know she's—?"

"*Do not.*" The anger in Hayden's voice halted my breath. Thick tension crackled in the air, heavy enough I could feel it from halfway across the clearing. His next words were so low that I couldn't make them out.

It hardly mattered. The rest of the conversation was lost to me as agony ripped through my skull. With a sharp inhale, I staggered to the side, my hands gripping my head. Branches scratched my arms, but I barely registered the sting as my knees slammed onto the mossy path. The pain was fierce, but I had to move. Another rebel was here. It wasn't safe.

I lowered my trembling hands, breath shaky, and looked up. Hayden and the rebel had moved closer, their eyes fixed on me.

"Khara," Hayden said, his eyes wide as he closed the distance between us, "are you all right?"

I blinked back dizziness as I straightened from my hunched position. Now that they'd seen me, it was too late to run. My legs still tingled with weakness. I doubted they would hold me up, even if I could run past the pain lacing my head. There was nothing I could do. I was at their mercy. My pulse raced in my ears, dulling all other sounds.

Hayden crouched, reaching to steady me. I flinched back, but kept my eyes fixed on the older man behind him. He was the one I was most worried about. His crossed arms and the deep set of his frown did nothing to calm me.

"Why did you bring him here?" I asked, unable to keep the trepidation from my voice any more than I could the accusation.

"It's not like that." Hayden held out his hands, palms up. "This isn't a trick. He won't hurt you. I didn't know you'd be here tonight. Tate and I needed to have a conversation, but he's leaving now. It'll just be you and me, okay?"

Heart pounding, I flicked my eyes from the rebel—Tate—to Hayden and back again. The man's arms stayed crossed, but his eyes had softened with pity. I swallowed back my hatred for the look along with the rising bile.

The tension between the two men seemed to have broken. I was the only one stiff with it now.

"I made you a promise," Hayden said, drawing my gaze as he leaned closer. "I won't break it. You're safe."

After one last glance at the other man—who hadn't moved or spoken since I revealed my presence—I nodded.

Hayden dipped his head and blew out a quiet breath before turning to the older man. "Give my father my report. I'm staying. Ask him to send runners—volunteers only."

"Yes, Sovereigno," he said, voice kinder now. Tate stared down at me with unnerving intensity, searching my face like so many others did. "It appears you're needed here after all."

The crease between Hayden's brows faded as his shoulders lowered. "I wouldn't stay if I wasn't."

"Just be careful. For all our sakes." Tate fisted a hand over his heart and bowed his head. Without another word, he strode across the clearing and disappeared into the trees.

I focused on the crackling shuffle of his steps as I tried to breathe through the rising nausea. The surge of pain had compounded what I'd woken up with, and my head throbbed in time with my pulse.

"I'd like to help you," Hayden said gently. He reached toward me as he rose to his feet, but didn't move any closer. His respect for my space loosened the last of the tension from my shoulders. "Will you let me?"

As I stared at his offered hand, I remembered the last time I was here. The way it felt when he pressed his fingers to my temples and took my pain. The relief had been a magic all its own.

I nodded, shifting forward to take his hand, and he pulled me to my feet. When I wavered, he steadied me—one hand grasping my arm, the other wrapping around my back in a silent, steady support I couldn't help but lean into.

Once I thought I could stand on my own, I blew out a shaky breath. "I'm ready."

"Then let's move into the grove. It's a little cramped here."

We moved together, Hayden carefully supporting me with every step. Though the pain still gripped me, I forced my feet to move down the mossy path and into the tall grass. When we'd walked far enough into the grove, Hayden pulled me to a gentle stop.

He shifted to meet my eyes as he slowly slid his arm from my back and released my arm. When I didn't waver, he relaxed and gestured to my face. "I'll need to ..."

I nodded, and with slow, deliberate movements Hayden lifted his hands. He paused, his hands warm where they hovered beside my head. I squeezed my eyes shut in anticipation.

Featherlight, Hayden brushed his fingertips against my temples. Warmth flowed from them and traveled through my head, following the pathways of pain I'd had since waking from my dream. In an instant, the pain subsided. Tingling warmth took its place, and I sighed, sagging.

Hayden moved to brace my shoulders as I focused on my breath. The scent of cedar, cinnamon, and a hint of smoke drifted from his jacket. Something about it niggled in my mind, a whisper hinting at memory, but like everything else, it went no further. With a deep exhale, I straightened. Hayden hesitated before releasing me.

"Your rebel, Tate," I said as the tingling warmth faded. "He called you Sovereigno."

Hayden's brow furrowed as he tilted his head. "Yes."

"Why?"

"As a show of respect for my position." He spoke slowly, his eyes flicking over me like I was a puzzle to be solved. "What else would he call me?"

"I just thought, with Ramsey ..."

"Ramsey can call himself whatever he likes." Hayden's shrug sent an errant curl falling onto his forehead. He tossed it back with a sigh. "Doesn't change the way my people show respect to me or my father."

It was bold, claiming a title he hadn't earned, especially one reserved for born sons of Anluan's ruling family. But what could I do about it? Hayden led a rebellion. He would go by whatever title he wanted, earned or not. And even I had to admit, somehow being the rebel's Sovereigno fit him.

Hayden's eyes roved over my face. "You look exhausted," he said, blunt but not unkind. "You can rest with me for a while."

Without waiting for my answer, he plopped to the ground right where he'd stood, cushioning his head with his hands. He relaxed into the earth, the picture of ease—as if we weren't on opposing sides of a war. As if he trusted me not to move against him. As if we were friends.

I needed to rest before returning to the Annex. That didn't mean I trusted Hayden—or myself—enough to settle in beside him. Instead, I shuffled backward, finding a large tree at the inner edge of the clearing that looked comfortable enough to rest against. I leaned against the trunk, sitting upright so I could keep an eye on Hayden. If he moved, I refused to be surprised by it. But he simply lay in the grass, unbothered and eyes closed.

He was so strange. I was the enemy. Or at least, I was deeply connected to the enemy. How could he lay there like it didn't matter? Hayden was a mystery that needed to be solved—one too dangerous to uncover without care.

He had to feel my eyes on him. He couldn't be that oblivious and stay hidden from Ramsey's guards for so long. And yet, he made no move to get up or start a conversation. He seemed completely content with the silence.

I was not. I pursed my lips, trying to think of what I wanted to say. It always came back to the same thing—my memories.

"You said you'd help me remember."

Hayden didn't move from his spot—didn't even open his eyes—but he nodded. "I did, and I meant it."

Frustration and a glimmer of hope clashed within me. "How are you going to do that?"

He opened his eyes and sat up, turning to sit cross-legged, facing me. The motion was fluid, practiced. I expected him to start a serious conversation, but as he took in my position against the tree, he chuckled.

"What?" I asked, crossing my arms. Nothing about this situation was funny.

"That's your favorite tree," he said, nodding at the trunk against my back. "I can't even tell you how many times I've seen you sitting just like that—sketching, enjoying the sun, resting with me."

I stared at him, dumbfounded, but he just shrugged.

"You want to know how I'm going to help you get your memory back? I think you already have what you need inside you. We just need to pull it out." He leaned forward, meeting my eyes intently. "I'll do whatever it takes to help you remember, Khara. Whatever you need."

"Then tell me something," I challenged, shifting forward. "Something about me, about my life."

"Is this a test?" He cocked his head, his eyes sparkling with amusement. "How will you know if I'm telling the truth?"

The question cut through me like a knife. I'd tried to avoid answering it for my entire recovery. How did I know anyone was telling the truth when I couldn't remember anything about them or myself? My eyes misted with tears at the reminder of my helplessness, at the struggle to trust myself and those around me.

Hayden noticed. Of course he did. He leaned forward until he was kneeling and tried to meet my eyes. I didn't make it easy for him.

"Khara?" His voice was gentle, coaxing. Hard to ignore. But I managed.

I blinked away my tears and frustration, wiping my eyes with my sleeve. Hayden would see, but I didn't care. Let him see a glimmer of the pain I'd been living with—the kind that came not from sudden migraines, but from not knowing yourself.

"I swear, I won't lie to you. Not about anything."

That made me look up. He seemed so earnest, a fiery sincerity clear as day in his eyes. Trusting him would take more than that. I wasn't sure he'd keep his word, but I nodded. I'd hear him out, at least. There would be time later to make up my mind about whatever he said.

He kept his eyes on me. "Was there anything in particular you wanted to know?"

There were many things, really. But one had been bothering me since I'd woken up after the attack. Something I feared I knew the answer to and wasn't sure I wanted to face on top of everything else. Something I'd been too afraid to ask Ramsey or Emila, but thought I might be able to ask someone who wouldn't be able to look at me with pity every day.

Clearing my throat, I let the question slip loose before I could lose my courage. "Do you know about my family? No one's told me anything about them."

Hayden's face tightened. "I do," he said carefully. "Khara, I'm so sorry, but your family ... they're dead."

34

IT WAS EXACTLY WHAT I'd feared. What I'd known deep down. It had been easier to ignore the question and the grief I'd expected to follow the answer. But here, under a cloudy night sky in the hushed grove, I let the sense of loss wash over me. My eyes watered for people I couldn't remember having in the first place.

Hayden watched my reaction intently, his own eyes wet as he stared at me with a downturned face. I wasn't sure why, but the sense of shared sorrow made my heart ache.

I closed my eyes and took a shaky breath. "How?"

"I don't think—"

"You said you wouldn't lie." My voice came out weak as I narrowed my eyes at him. "You promised."

"I did. But I didn't say I would tell you anything you asked. This is a heavy place to start. Are you sure you want to know?"

I swallowed thickly, but nodded. "I want to know who they were. And what happened to them."

Hayden sighed heavily, running a hand down his face. "Okay. You're an only child, at least by blood." He gave me a half-smile that didn't last long. "Your parents lived in a cottage on the outskirts of town, not too far from here. Your father was one of the Isiraden foresters and for a while, your mother taught at a school."

"When did they die?" I asked when he didn't offer more.

He ran a hand through his hair this time, mussing his curls. The other clenched into a fist in his lap. "You were a child when your mother died. She got sick, and your father—he didn't trust my family enough to bring her to be healed."

Had my mother known someone could have healed her? Didn't she want to try to live—for me? My nose stung as I blinked back tears. There were some questions I'd never know the answers to.

"Your father—" Hayden cut off, shaking his head. "You were barely a teenager when he died. Logging accident. Or at least that's the official story."

"And unofficially?"

"No one could ever prove it," Hayden said carefully, "but some believe he was killed."

That wasn't something I was prepared to process. I shoved the shock down before it could give way to pain. My time with Hayden was short. I wouldn't waste it spiraling. My throat tightened with the effort of keeping back tears. I cleared it before asking my next question.

"What happened to me then? I was an orphan, so where did I go?"

"You were on your own for a while. To say your father was a harsh man is putting it mildly. You'd taken care of yourself for quite some time by that point, so you managed to survive well enough. But eventually, you were brought to the palace and came to live with my family. That's when we became close."

I blinked. We'd lived together when I was younger? If that were the case, how did we end up on opposite sides of a divided Anluan?

"I don't understand. You were like family to me, and now we're enemies?"

He flinched as if I'd struck him. "You're not my enemy, Khara. You could never be my enemy."

I laughed bitterly. "No? Then why would you do this to me?"

"I don't know what you mean," he said slowly. "What did I do to you?"

"This!" I jumped to my feet and gestured to my body. "You broke me. I can't remember anything! And you say we're not enemies? Ask me to meet you in the middle of the night? For what, Hayden?" I spread my arms out wide, breathing heavily as my tears began to fall. "What do you get out of this?"

I wanted to shove him. I wanted to run. Most of all, I wanted to understand.

"*Why*?" My voice broke as my shoulders slumped, my energy spent as fast as it'd come. "Why offer to help me? We're not on the same side. You're the one who did this to me! Why would you want to help me now?"

Hayden stared, his eyes brimming with pain and sadness. Something steely began cementing in them, too, but it didn't alarm me. The tears that fell when he blinked did. He held my gaze, letting me see each drop that rolled down his face unhindered.

"Khara," he said my name roughly, his voice tight with pain, "they told you I did this to you?"

Everything left me—my words, my anger, my breath. No one had said it was Hayden directly, but he had been blamed. He led the rebels. They acted on his orders. That made it his fault. And yet, standing here watching tears pave trails of grief down his face, it was hard to believe he would have ordered it.

"Didn't you?" My anger had ebbed and faded into a bone-deep weariness. All I wanted was the truth—without having to uncover what was hidden behind each answer. "Was it you, or one of your rebels? Someone gave the order to attack me that day, and it had to have come from you or your father."

Hayden shook his head, his red-rimmed eyes begging for belief. "I swear, Khara, I did not do this to you. I didn't tell anyone else to either. I never would and neither would my father. *Never.*"

I didn't know what to say, so I said nothing at all. I just sat back against the base of the tree and ran a hand over my face. Covering my mouth with my hand, I stared off to the side for a long moment. With my knees pulled to my chest, I felt safe enough to let the stampede of emotions rampage through my chest.

I wanted to talk to Hayden for answers. How was it I ended up with a thousand more questions?

I took a deep breath and called on my courage. When I turned to face him, Hayden sat rigid in front of me, looking as raw as I felt.

"Okay," I said roughly. "Say I believe you for now. You didn't do this to me, at least not directly." He opened his mouth, but I refused to let him interrupt. "If it wasn't you, why was I attacked? If you care for me as you claim to, how did I end up in the middle of this?"

Hayden frowned. "You're in the middle of this because you're important, Khara. You matter. To both of us."

"To you and to Ramsey."

"Yes."

I considered this, but it brought no real answers. Thinking too much about the intertwining of relationships was bound to give me another headache.

"Something else," I said, shaking my head. "Tell me about something else."

His lips twitched, like he wanted to continue and it pained him not to. But he nodded anyway, deferring to my plea. "What do you want to talk about?"

I wasn't sure where to start. What topic would be safer? It was hard to choose what to ask when I didn't know what unexpected blows could be hidden in the answers.

Finally, I ventured, "You mentioned last time that I had powers."

"What about them?" Hayden straightened abruptly, his voice pitching with concern. "Are you having problems?"

I blinked. "I don't. Have them, I mean. You mentioned me being gifted, but before that, I hadn't considered it a possibility."

The crease between Hayden's brow deepened as he scowled. "They've really done a number on you."

My brow furrowed, but he continued before I could comment.

"You *do* have powers. You were born with them. They must have been gifted to one of your ancestors, but the line remained dormant for a time, until you were born in Isiraden. You're special, Khara." His smile was soft but faded quickly. "Your powers must be blocked somehow if you're unable to access them. I'd have thought going off the medicine they gave you—" He stared at me intently. "You did stop taking those pills, didn't you?"

I shrank beneath his gaze. "I haven't had any today, but the day after I met you, I had the worst episode I'd ever had. I couldn't get out of bed. Doctor Jensen gave me more medicine and upped the dosage. I've had them all week, until today."

Hayden's lips pressed into a thin line. "What changed?"

"Nothing." I looked away. "I had a dream, and ..."

I shook my head, ready to stop talking, but Hayden's eyes lit with curiosity. "Go on."

"I had this dream, and you were in it." Heat flooded my cheeks. "I remembered what you said before, about the pills making me worse, and I just felt like I had to come here and see you. Get answers. It's stupid."

I hugged myself and stared at the swaying grass, determined not to face him. I didn't need to see his reaction to that mess of a confession.

Hayden didn't speak. I wasn't sure if he was just as embarrassed as I was, or simply giving me space. But I couldn't stand the silence.

"What am I supposed to be able to do, anyway?" I asked, rubbing my hands down my pant legs to settle my nerves. I hoped it wasn't anything dangerous ... or any more overwhelming than having powers itself seemed to be.

"You see things," he said, a smile clear in his voice. "Sometimes during the day, but mostly in your dreams."

My eyes flew up to meet his. He nodded, assuring me I'd heard him correctly.

I saw things ... in dreams.

"What sorts of things?" I asked, curiosity and hesitation coating my words.

"I don't know everything about it. Any gifts of the mind are rare. But from what you told me before, you mainly get impressions—as if your dreams are trying to tell you something. They often point you in the right direction. You might dream a glimmer of the future. Other times, you'll see an object, a word, a place, and you'll know it's important."

He smiled fondly, his eyes focusing on something far away. "You took to drawing them out a long time ago. Said it helps you figure out what you need to do with them. You had notebooks full of sketches." His attention returned to me. "It's happened before when you're awake, but only a handful of times over the years. And only when it was pointing out something especially urgent."

"My dreams ..." I thought of how many times I'd woken in pain, unable to remember more than jagged pieces of what I'd dreamt the night before. How quickly those pieces faded entirely. Lead lined my stomach as I spoke the dawning realization: "Whenever I take the pills, I don't remember my dreams."

Hayden's face pinched. He leaned forward as if he was going to comfort me, then thought better of it and sat back. "That makes sense. I'm sorry, Khara. Like I told you, they'll only make things worse. Suppressing powers, especially when you're born with them, has nasty side effects."

"Like migraines." My voice cracked on the words.

Hayden nodded, pain almost covering the anger in his eyes. Almost.

35

I couldn't believe it. The medicine I'd been taking all this time could have been *causing* my pain?

No. Ramsey wouldn't have done this to me. His concern for me shone through everything he did. But did Doctor Jensen know? Was she trying to keep my powers at bay? For what purpose?

I let my head fall into my hands. This was getting far too complicated. I had so much to think about, and I didn't want to do it here in the grove when I felt like I could go into a tailspin at any moment. I felt safe enough with Hayden to sit and talk to him. I wasn't sure how I felt about trusting him beyond that.

"Khara, are you all right?"

I couldn't help but laugh, bitterness saturating my tongue. "No, I'm not." I tilted my head to rest against my hands so I could look at him. "Tell me something else."

"Like what?"

"Tell me what happened between you and Ramsey."

Hayden stiffened. He tousled his hair, blowing out a long breath. "I've known Ramsey since we were young. His family and mine, we've been close for generations."

I nodded, remembering that from Ramsey's account. Hayden raised a brow but didn't comment.

"Generations ago, my ancestor, Shalémo, was born with significant power—the most *gifted* of anyone on record. He used his power to protect the kingdom. Under his care, Anluan grew into a thriving metropolis. Ramsey's ancestor, Dharavaya, was a friend. Eventually, Shalémo gifted him with power. It was a good decision at the time."

My brow furrowed as his words sank in. Shalémo gifted Dharavaya with power? Ramsey had said it was the other way around. I wanted to ask, but Hayden paused, staring into the distance. When he turned back to me, the pain in his eyes stilled my questions.

"Ramsey didn't inherit his powers, exactly. Not the way they are now. He had an inclination for them, but nothing big, nothing offensive. Ramsey could reach out and touch your fears—that's the best way I can describe it. Empathic, but only to fear. It was a burden, one he hated."

My stomach sank. Ramsey hadn't told me that. I couldn't imagine what it must have been like for him. To be a child and feel not only your own fears but everyone else's? Burden wasn't a strong enough word.

"When he came of age, my father gifted Ramsey with power. It's tradition—the firstborn of his family typically receives a gift from mine as recognition of the friendship between our families. But beyond that, I think my father wanted to give him something in hopes it would help him cope. For a while, it seemed to work." Hayden smiled sadly, his eyes bright. "I had my friend back. He could function again. He even used his gifts to soothe fears. We were all so proud of him."

And he had been. I could see the remnants of it in the depths of Hayden's eyes even as they filled with tears. He sniffed, rubbing a hand over his mouth, quick and rough.

"It was a surprise to me when things changed. I didn't see it coming." He cleared his throat, staring down at his hands. His thumb brushed against the symbol on the side of his wrist. "Ramsey wanted more. I thought he was just excited, being ambitious. After so long of watching him struggle, I thought it was a good thing. Looking back"—Hayden shook his head, hugging a knee to his chest—"I should have seen it coming."

A tear trailed down his cheek and he hurriedly wiped it away. "My family has ruled Anluan for generations. We love this place and our people."

I blinked rapidly, my mind stalling over the words. I couldn't make sense of it. His family had ruled for generations? That wasn't right. It had been the Dharavaya line that ruled. *Ramsey's* ancestors. Hayden had promised not to lie, but now he was telling me something wildly off track. Did he think I wouldn't notice?

My mouth opened, then closed as I stuffed my questions down. Any sign of disbelief could halt his story altogether, and that was a risk I couldn't take. I'd listen to his story and process it after, just like I'd been doing since we started talking.

"And Ramsey ... I loved him more than most," Hayden went on. "But he wanted things we couldn't allow. Felling more trees from Isiraden to harvest its magic. Experimenting with the gifted and our powers. Imparting more powers than would be sustainable. My father dismissed his ideas." He broke off, huffing a bitter laugh. "I knew Ramsey was upset. He never tried to hide how he felt. When he was mad, he made sure you knew it. But he calmed down, got quiet. I thought he needed some time, some space to process his disappointment. Now I know he was making his plans."

Hayden's eyes grew distant as he stared at the ground. "We don't talk about it much, but powers are tied to your heart. When you're born with power"—he gestured to me—"it's tied to who you are at your core. When you're given powers, it's tied to you, but it seems to be harnessed by your heart's motives more than anything. If your intentions are pure, they'll serve you well because you're using them well. If you don't ... when you use your powers to cause harm, to elevate yourself over others, they'll change into something else. Morph to match your heart. Ramsey's powers the day he attacked us were new. Dark. Twisted. We weren't prepared."

Tears trailed down both of Hayden's cheeks. His eyes were unfocused, fixed across the clearing like he was seeing something I couldn't. Something that made dread coil in my gut.

"He gathered a group of fighters somehow. Guards, citizens. I still don't know what he told them, but Ramsey's always been convincing. They attacked us in the night, in our private suites. My father and I fought them off as best we could, but my mother ..." He breathed in shakily. "They made sure my father wasn't close enough to heal her. She died before we could get to her."

My heart clenched at the sorrow lining his words. I swallowed past the tightness in my throat. He couldn't be making this up. No one was this good of an actor, were they?

If his story was true, Ramsey was responsible for this pain. But it didn't make sense. Not with what Ramsey had told me. And certainly not with the way he interacted with me or the people around him.

My confusion was growing, but I'd come to listen. This wasn't the time for my questions. I would work out what to believe later, when I wasn't staring grief in the face.

"I tried to reason with him," Hayden said, almost desperately. "I really did. Once I realized Ramsey was the one leading the rebellion, I thought we could stop it. But he wouldn't listen to me. My mother was dead, along with countless others. The city was in ruins—between Ramsey's powers and the ones he'd rallied to join him, even my own ..." Self-deprecation filled his voice as he shook his head. A jagged bolt of light pulsed from his hand before he tightened it into a fist. "There was already too much collateral damage. My father decided we had to run, leave the city to Ramsey so we could get as many people out of the palace as possible."

I winced as I tried to picture the destruction of that night. The palace was still in disrepair, with scaffolding arranged around crumbled sections of what was once a magnificent building. It seemed like little progress had been made in two years. The damage must have been extensive.

"We made it out," Hayden continued. "It was a difficult journey. Many were injured, including my father, but we made it out. Now we're trying to do better, for the people who are loyal to our family and the ones who aren't. Anluan can't be ruled by a man like Ramsey. The darkness he carries now ..."

Hayden blew out a breath and rubbed his hands on the legs of his pants. "Sorry. It's not a pleasant story."

It really wasn't. I wasn't sure it was a believable story either. The accounts from Ramsey and Hayden had similarities, but the differences were striking. It was too much for me to unravel now.

I wiped my tears instead of saying anything, then met Hayden's eyes and offered what I could—condolences. "I'm sorry about your mother."

His watery smile hurt to look at, but I forced myself to stay focused on his face. "She loved you, you know."

"She did?"

He nodded, his smile softening into something more genuine. "You were the daughter she never had. She adored you. Would've done anything you asked without a second thought."

I allowed myself to consider having that kind of love in my life. If he were to be believed, my parents weren't altogether loving—at least my father wasn't. It was nice to believe, if only for a moment, that I'd had someone in my corner. Someone who loved me like a mother when I no longer had one of my own.

Hayden breathed out, shaking himself from his thoughts as he gave me his full attention again. "Was there anything else you wanted to know?"

Of course there was. The more I listened, the more questions I had about everything. Was it possible for their perspectives to be so different that Ramsey and Hayden both believed they were telling the truth? Or was someone intentionally lying to me? My heart constricted at the thought. It was hard enough to trust without my memory. I couldn't start believing I was being lied to or I'd lose what was left of my mind.

Hayden watched me with quiet intensity. He didn't say anything, just waited for me to gather my thoughts. I didn't want to hear any more sad stories, real or not.

Meeting Hayden's eyes, I asked for the one thing I thought I could handle. "Could you ..." I trailed off, hesitant. But at Hayden's encouraging nod, I asked, "Could you tell me something good? Something happy?"

If he was surprised by the request, he didn't show it. "I can manage that."

Settling against the tree behind me, I willed my body to relax as Hayden began telling me some of his fondest memories. They were just what I'd asked for—happy, light, good. As the stars twinkled overhead and his stories continued, my eyes drifted shut. I didn't even notice when his voice lulled me to sleep.

36

Brightness. All I could see was brightness.

Everything was white. Everything was pain.

I blinked, but it did nothing to clear my vision.

I was moving, I knew that. I knew little else.

Light blinded my eyes at regular intervals. My heart raced.

Where am I?

I cried out, a harsh, sobbing sound, as a jolting movement ratcheted the stabbing sensation all at once.

It *hurt.*

My ears were buzzing, but I could still hear voices.

Harsh. Cold. They weren't talking to me. At least, I didn't think they were.

Which is worse?

Loud. Everything was too loud. I whimpered, tried to move my hands to cover my ears.

Pain. White. Hot. Scorching me from the inside out.

I'd thought it was bright before, but that was nothing compared to now. How was it possible for everything to have gone so starkly white? All around me, there was nothing but a keening buzz and pain so fierce I could hardly breathe.

Am I dying?

Finally, I managed a strangled inhale. A wheezing cry of an exhale.

Sounds came back, louder than before and harsh in my ears. And those *voices.* So rough.

Tears pricked my eyes. I could barely see, barely breathe, barely think. But I needed to get away. I had to *go.*

"Hold her down. Now!"

Weight dropped onto me, warm, but not kind. Rough hands, pushing, pulling. I didn't want to go. Wherever they were taking me, I didn't want to—

Something brushed my arm and I screamed. Loud. Harsh. All my pain, forced into sound.

"Watch what you're doing!"

That voice. That voice was familiar.

Help me. Please, help me!

Nothing changed. The pain stayed, thick and harsh and all-encompassing. There were hands holding down my arms, my legs, moving through my hair. The sensations overwhelmed me. Too much. *Too much.*

A prick in my arm. The pinch of straps. The metallic tang of blood.

Was it mine? It had to be mine, didn't it?

I groaned, nausea climbing my throat until I was sure I would vomit.

Someone hushed me. Hands brushed through my hair.

Please. Please, help me. Please!

Spots filled my vision. My heart raced. My eyes stung. My body flashed hot and cold.

I shouldn't be here. I shouldn't—

The pain began to fade, and me with it. I fought against the wave that threatened to pull me under. I couldn't let it take me. I couldn't let them—

Please. It was all I could think as the world faded to gray and darkened until it was black as ash. *Please, please …*

Had I said it out loud?

Either way, it was a worthless plea.

37

"Khara!"

I jolted forward with a cry, scrabbling against the hands pressing on my shoulders. My head connected with something hard, but I didn't stop. I couldn't. I scrambled, crawling forward until I could get to my feet.

I had to get away.

My vision was blurry, and I swayed as pain filled my head, but I couldn't be here. Couldn't let them—

"It's okay! You're okay."

The voice was close. Too close.

No, no, no. I couldn't let them ...

I tried to run but only made it two steps before my knees gave way. My mind swirled with confusion as the chill of the ground seeped through my pants. Grass tickled my hands. A warm breeze slipped past my cheek. I was outside?

Someone slid to their knees beside me. I cried out and tried to move away, but two hands pressed against my shoulders, holding me in place. I let out a keening whine, pain and fear flooding through me. As I folded over, trying anything to relieve the agony, one of the hands moved to cup my head, supporting my neck.

"Khara, please, talk to me."

The voice broke through my panic. It wasn't harsh like the others. Neither were the hands. No, these were gentle and steady. Supportive.

This wasn't one of them. This felt safe. I exhaled and forced my body to relax.

The hands shifted in response, carefully holding me up. "Khara?"

I kept my eyes closed and shifted my head. I was outside, kneeling in the grass. Not there. *Not there.* And I was coherent. Coherent enough, anyway. But the *pain*.

My heart pounded too hard. My breath came in strained pants, my chest shuddering with every inhale. My head dipped, falling onto a tense shoulder that readily accepted my weight. The body heat comforted me, soothing my panic with its warmth. It told me I wasn't there, trapped with harsh voices and harsher hands. It told me I wasn't alone.

"I want to help you," the kind voice whispered. "Please, Khara, let me heal you."

Take the pain. Take it all. I would have begged if my mouth would've cooperated. I could barely focus on my breathing, let alone try to talk. I jerked my head against his shoulder, as close to a nod as I could get.

"Thank you," he whispered, so fervently my eyes pricked with fresh tears.

Fingers pressed against my temples, and warmth traveled in a tingling path around my head, stitching together whatever had been sliced and ripped open until nothing remained but a fading warmth. The pain vanished.

My body collapsed against the one in front of me. The hands fell from my temples, and arms wrapped around me, holding me up. Soft notes of cedar stirred in the air, bringing with them feelings of safety.

My tears fell in steady streams, and I gasped in a ragged breath. As my body shook with sobs, a hand gently trailed through my hair.

A hand in my hair.

I froze, panic flaring again. The hand fell away faster than I tensed, moving to rub my back instead. I relaxed and let myself cry away every trace of fear and hurt. A litany of broken words tumbled into my ear, a steady rhythm of heartbreak.

"I'm sorry. I'm so sorry."

I came back to myself slowly once my tears ran dry. First came the realization I'd been dreaming. All of it had been a dream. I'd woken in the grove with Hayden. He'd been the one talking to me. It was his arms wrapped around me, holding me as I cried.

I sniffed before taking a deep, shuddering breath. Exhaustion overwhelmed any hint of embarrassment. Let Hayden think what he wanted. When I shifted away, he responded immediately, his hands moving to brace me as I sat up.

His grim expression surprised me. His face was wan, as if my fit had sickened him. His eyes were red, and tears still crawled down his face, staining tracks onto his cheeks. When he spoke, his voice was hoarse. "Khara, what *was* that?"

I couldn't ignore the desperation in his voice. My chin trembled, and I bit my lip against fresh tears. I didn't want to cry anymore. I looked away from Hayden and shook my head jerkily.

"It's okay." It didn't sound like he believed it any more than I did. "You're okay," he said with more conviction. "But that dream—what you saw, the way you reacted—"

"I don't know." My voice was hoarse and rough. Shredded. It hurt to speak.

"You were crying out in your sleep. That *scream*—" He cut off, his voice strangled. As he covered his mouth with one hand, his eyes glistened with tears. "Khara, please, what were you dreaming about?"

"I don't know. I really don't." I fought back a shuddering sob. "I don't think I *want* to know," I added, the barest whisper filled with a heartache I wasn't sure how to manage. "I don't think I want to remember. Not that."

Hayden was still close to me, his body warming mine. He leaned forward, sad and silent, and wiped the tears from my face. I closed my eyes and let the others fall. Gentle as could be, he thumbed each one away before pressing a kiss to the top of my head.

I sniffed, moving away from him without a word and scrubbing my hands over my cheeks. I was sure I looked a mess, but Hayden didn't seem to notice. All I saw in his stare was intense compassion and a worry that couldn't possibly be fabricated.

I glanced toward the sky. It was much lighter now.

"I have to go," I murmured, sniffing and wiping my shaking hands down my thin sweater.

Hayden seemed at a loss for words, though his eyes didn't leave me. I was sure he could see how shaken I was, but he didn't move to stop me until I staggered to my feet. He jumped to help, but I found my footing on my own.

"I'm okay. It's fine," I said, unsure if I was trying to convince him or myself. "I have to go."

"Will you come back tomorrow night?"

I met his eyes—those deep brown eyes rimmed in the red that caring for my pain had brought him—and I couldn't say no. "I'll try."

And as I walked away from him and the grove, I found I meant it.

38

I HADN'T GIVEN MUCH thought to what would happen when I arrived back at my suite. But as I poked my head around the corner, my lack of forethought was glaringly obvious. Cethin Radnor stood outside my door, alert as ever in his crisp, black uniform.

I thunked my head against the wall behind me and kneaded my forehead. I was too tired for this. My mind was full of things I needed to think about and things I never wanted to think about again. All I wanted was to curl up in my bed and sleep.

There was nothing I could do to prevent it. I had to reveal that I'd left my room unaccompanied. I would just have to deal with the consequences, whatever they would be.

Taking a deep breath, I prepared to walk into Cethin's line of sight. As I took the first step, a hand fisted in my shirt and tugged. Biting back a scream, I spun and found Gage behind me, smirking as he leaned nonchalantly against the wall.

"Again, Princess?" He clicked his tongue, his brows raised. Exaggerating a put-out sigh, he pushed off the wall. "Stay here. I'm taking over for Ceth. I'll send him off down the other end of the hall. When I start whistling, the coast is clear, and you can sneak back into your room."

I blinked at him, dumbfounded. "You'd do that?"

"Sure." He shrugged. "You're the princess, right? Besides, I'd be going stir-crazy if I were you. A little rebellion can be good for you."

I winced. If only he knew.

"Wait here." He flashed me a quick grin before strolling around the corner as if he didn't have a care in the world. Maybe he didn't. Nothing seemed to bother Gage.

I was too far away to hear what he said to Cethin, but I could make out the murmur of their voices. A moment after they went quiet, whistling echoed down the hall.

I dashed around the corner. Gage had relaxed against the wall, his hands in his pockets. When I reached him, he stopped whistling.

"What song was that?" I asked as I placed my palm in the center of the door. The magic unlocked it with a soft click.

"Just something I heard once. You should get inside. Change your clothes." He paused, tilting his head as he studied me. "You're okay, right? I don't need to call for anyone?"

"No." My words fell fast from my lips as I pushed the door open. "I'm fine. Really. I appreciate it, but I'm fine."

"Okay." He shrugged and looked back down the hall. "I'll pretend I believe you. Go get some sleep. I arranged to be on watch most of the day. If you need anything, I'll be here."

I stepped over the threshold and nodded. "Thank you, Gage."

His lips quirked up. "Don't mention it." He paused, his nose wrinkling as he turned to face me. "Really, though. *Don't* mention it. Okay?"

I huffed a laugh. "I won't if you won't."

His eyes brightened with a flash of admiration. "It's a deal, Princess." He'd likely realized what I had—if one of us was found out, we were both in trouble. "Go get some sleep. You look like you need it."

He had no idea how much.

When I woke later that day, I tried to pretend everything was normal. I was fine. The dream from the night before hadn't bothered me. Hayden hadn't said anything that gave me pause.

For a while, I even managed to do it.

I slept in late, only waking when Emila pushed her way into my bedroom with a worried frown. It took several reassurances before she believed I hadn't had an episode and was just feeling run down.

"I got this for you," she said, tossing a paper bag onto my stomach where I lay in bed.

A mix of peppery bacon, eggs, and maple syrup wafted from it. The blend of sweet and savory made my mouth water.

"Thank you." I smiled as I grabbed the still-warm sandwich by its paper wrap. For once, the thought of bacon didn't send nausea swirling in my gut, and I intended to take full advantage.

"You're just lucky I came today and not Ramsey. That man would have lost his mind if he'd waited for you to answer the door as long as I did."

"You could've come in sooner, you know," I pointed out, taking a small bite. "You have access. So does Ramsey."

Emila rolled her eyes as she made herself comfortable on the edge of the bed. "There's this thing called privacy. Maybe you've heard of it? I'd like to give you some. Though if you keep scaring me like this, I may reconsider."

I softened, picking at the sandwich's wrapping. "I didn't mean to make you worry. I'm really just tired."

"Couldn't sleep?"

"Just a rough night."

Emila made a humming noise. "If you want to keep your secrets, that's fine by me." She fell back and used her arm to prop up her head. "See? Privacy."

It was my turn to roll my eyes. "You're a very good friend."

"That's what I thought you were going to say." She grinned. "What do you want to do today?"

What did I want to do? Nothing. Blissful, glorious nothing. But I had responsibilities, and I didn't want to shirk them. "What do I *need* to do today?"

"Besides relax? You're not required to be anywhere. We could stay here or go to the gardens. Whatever you want."

"Then let's stay here. I'm exhausted."

As I sank back into my pillows, Emila sat up and studied me. "You're sure you're okay?"

If everyone kept asking, I must be more terrible at hiding things than I'd thought. I sighed heavily. "I'm sure."

"Could've fooled me."

"I'm just—" I opened my eyes and sat up, meeting Emila's gaze. "Why did Ramsey choose me?"

She blinked, confusion written all over her face. "What do you mean?"

"Why did Ramsey choose me to be his Sovereigna? What do you think he sees in me that makes him think that this—that *I*—am the right choice?"

Emila shifted to face me fully, her brow furrowing. "Why are you asking me this?"

I shrugged, only a little surprised by the heat of tears gathering behind my eyes. "I don't know."

"No, no." Emila pointed a finger at me. "You *do* know. Why are you asking?"

"I just wonder if I'm right for this. I mean, I'm not exactly ruler material." I huffed a bitter laugh as I tugged at my blanket with greasy fingers. "I don't even know that I'm *marriage* material. I can't remember who I am, let alone my relationship with Ramsey, and I just—"

"Nope!" Emila interrupted, fire in her eyes as she crossed her arms. The ruffles lining the neckline of her dress fluttered with the movement. "I'm not even going to let you finish that sentence. Khara, what brought this on? Of course you're *marriage material.*"

She infused enough annoyance into the phrase that I winced. It did sound ridiculous when she repeated it like that. Still, it was a concern I couldn't fully shake.

It didn't seem fair to enter into a marriage with Ramsey when I was so far removed from who I'd been before the attack. I tried so hard to gather the pieces of myself and make them fit back together, but it proved challenging when I didn't have a full picture to work from. What if I couldn't connect the right pieces and it ruined everything between us?

Emila sighed. Her tone lost some of its bite, but none of its conviction. "And if anyone were to make a good ruler, it would be you. Don't tell Ramsey I said so, but you could rule without him by your side. You already have the people's respect and it's obvious how much you care about Anluan."

I didn't know how the people felt. The few I'd met, however briefly, showed me some form of deference. The titles, the dipping of their heads, even the tone of their voices. But how much of that was genuine? And was any of it actually about *me* rather than my connection to Isiraden or Ramsey? There was no way for me to know, and sometimes that uncertainty bothered me.

My love for Anluan, on the other hand, felt as natural as breathing. There was something about this kingdom—something that went beyond memory and remained rooted in my heart. I cared about what happened to it and to our people, within the city and beyond. I didn't think that would ever change, with or without my memories.

Emila reached forward and took my hand, waiting for me to meet her eyes before she continued. "You were made for this, Khara. I see it. I wish you would too."

I blinked back tears, sniffling as I took in her words. Would I ever be able to believe I was born with that kind of purpose? That I was capable of not just stepping into the roles in front of me but succeeding in them?

Being Sovereigna wouldn't be easy. I'd known that from the start. This life was already challenging, and I wasn't even officially Ramsey's Sovereignaya yet. According to my lessons, my current duties would increase after a ceremony elevated me to Sovereignaya, then again once we were married and I became Sovereigna. There was so much for me to learn and understand before I'd be able to fulfill either of those roles well.

Still, something in Emila's words latched onto my heart like a truth I couldn't ignore. Maybe my lack of sleep was making the situation seem more daunting than it was. Taking a steadying breath, I nodded.

Emila kept staring, her eyes searching mine for something. She must have found it, because she nodded back, then leaned onto one arm to lounge on the bed. "Tell me who made you doubt yourself and I'll give them a swift kick in the shins."

I laughed, but knew she would do exactly that if I told her a name.

"And, Khara," she added, smiling slightly, "Ramsey wouldn't have anyone but you by his side. Never doubt that."

The words rang true. The way he'd sat with me during my recovery, the way he'd held me as I cried over lost memories, the gifts and whispered reassurances of his affection—they all pointed to his commitment to me. He wanted me here, with him. That wasn't something I should doubt.

I gave Emila a watery smile and nodded.

"Speaking of *marriage material*," she added, perking up with a wide grin. "You know we need to start planning what we'll do for your engagement party!"

I cocked my head. "Engagement party?"

"Ramsey hasn't asked you about it yet?" The answer must have been obvious, because Emila covered her mouth with her hand, muffling a curse. "I'm sorry. I thought he would've mentioned it to you by now."

My brow furrowed. "There's supposed to be a party?"

Ramsey had mentioned one when he'd told me about the attack, but I'd heard nothing about it since. Maybe amid the chaos of the rebel plots, he'd forgotten to discuss it.

A slithering sense of unease stirred in my gut. I hated that something as simple as a party could fill me with nerves.

"I don't know if it's my place to say." Emila winced, tucking a strand of hair behind her ear. More confidently, she added, "Ramsey's coming over later, right? Ask him about the party when you go to dinner. I'm sure he was planning on mentioning it soon anyway."

"Yeah, sure."

The thought of a crowded room made my stomach roil. But I could attend a party for Ramsey, couldn't I? It wasn't too much to ask that we celebrate our engagement.

The more I thought about it, the more I realized this shouldn't have been a surprise at all. Of course we'd celebrate our engagement. And once I was Sovereigna, I'd have plenty of responsibilities that included parties of some kind. Maybe this would be a good way to ease into it.

"Hey." Emila broke me from my thoughts, snapping her fingers toward my face. "Don't overthink it. It'll be fine. More than that, it'll be fun!" Her grin turned wicked as she met my eyes. "Plus, we'll make sure you look absolutely irresistible."

My face went hot, and I shook my head as I looked away. Whatever Emila's definition of irresistible was, I wasn't sure I wanted to know.

39

Ramsey arrived at my suite before dinner, wearing a smile brighter than any I'd seen from him in days. The stress he'd been wearing like a second skin had sloughed off. His happiness softened his face, removing the dips and lines that came with ruling a kingdom at war. He had so much weight on his shoulders as Sovereign. It lifted my spirits to see him looking so young and carefree.

He placed a kiss on my cheek, grinning when my face flushed, then offered me his arm. When I took it, he led us to his suite. I hadn't been back since our first dinner—one I couldn't help but feel I'd ruined, even after Ramsey's reassurances. I was determined my grief wouldn't touch this night.

"I lit a fire," Ramsey said as we exited the elevator. He nodded toward the hearth, where flame crackled gently against wood. With his hand on the small of my back, he guided me to the couch. "I know how much you enjoy them."

"I do." I smiled up at him. "Thank you."

"I'll do anything to make you happy, Khara."

His eyes shone, reflecting orange flames that deepened their normal brown. They captivated me, more open here than in the stolen moments we had between ruling and recovery. In their warmth, I saw how comfortable he was with me. In their softness, intimacy whispered of our past. I tilted my head, ready to listen to our shared history, when he glanced toward the kitchen.

"I've had the chefs prepare a special meal for us."

"Oh?" I blinked back to the present, unable to stop my rising curiosity. "What's the occasion?"

"We can talk about it over dinner." He leaned close and pressed a kiss to my head. "Rest here. I'll just be a few minutes."

He left for the kitchen, leaving me to my thoughts. Without his presence to focus on, anxiety crept over me, covering any lingering musings of the past with reminders of the many questions my conversation with Hayden had brought.

Being in the Annex was harder after the previous night's conversation. I wanted to voice my questions, especially to Ramsey. Wanted to dig for answers until I uncovered the truth. But I didn't know how, not without giving away my midnight trips to the grove. While there was still much I didn't know, I knew *that* wouldn't go over well.

I twisted the engagement ring on my finger and frowned. Hayden had to have been lying. His story was too different from Ramsey's. And with the way things were in Anluan, I couldn't imagine Hayden's version being true.

But what did he gain by lying? He'd taken my pain and warned me about the pills. Neither of those things benefited him. Unless he healed me so I'd be more likely to believe him.

There had to be some truth to his words, though. I'd been feeling better since I stopped taking the medicine he'd warned me about, and his explanation of my dreams fit somehow.

And what of my parents? Ramsey never mentioned them, likely to spare me the grief of knowing they were dead. It had happened a long time ago, but this was the kind of wound that left a mark. Maybe he was afraid to force me to uncover those scars while I was still recovering. I could understand that. And, of course, I hadn't asked, too afraid to confirm my suspicions. How could I blame him for not telling me something I wasn't sure I was ready to know?

I shook my head. There was too much to consider. Too many unknowns. If I had my memories, none of this would be an issue. I would know my history, know how I got to be where I was now. I'd know exactly who was telling the truth and who wasn't.

I huffed, running a hand through my hair and fighting a grimace when my fingers glanced over the hidden scar. Pushing my hand down, along with the stinging reminders of my situation, I pressed back into the couch. This night would not be ruined by my pain. I refused to do that to either of us again.

The gentle pad of Ramsey's feet against the hardwood sounded through the room. Smoothing my hair, I tried to ease my face into a pleasant expression. My smile felt forced, but Ramsey didn't seem to notice as he turned the corner and grinned.

"Dinner awaits," he said with an exaggerated bow.

I groaned, hiding a smile behind my hands. "Not you too."

He raised a brow. "What?"

I sighed as I stood from the couch and walked toward him. "Nothing, really. Some of the guards just call me *princess* sometimes. It's usually accompanied by exaggerated displays of deference."

Ramsey barked a laugh. "And by some, I'm going to assume you mean one guard and it's Argusten."

"You're not wrong."

He took my hand in his and led me toward the dining room. "If you're *princess*, he's the court jester. Don't take anything he says too seriously. He's one of my best guards—loyal, from a good family. But one of these days, between Radnor and North, he's going to drive someone to do something drastic." Ramsey smirked, amusement dancing in his eyes. It faded as his lips pulled into a deep frown. "But if he ever bothers you, tell me and I'll deal with him."

The switch from amused ruler to protective fiancé charmed me, even if his concern wasn't necessary. "He doesn't bother me, Ramsey. I can take a joke."

"Good."

As we walked into the dining room, I gasped, my hand rising to my mouth. Gold chargers held white plates in front of our seats at the table. Rich red and soft pink roses blended together in vases of varying heights. Between them stood softly glowing candles. And all around the center of the table, garlands of greenery wove among the candles and vases. The elegant display was far beyond anything I'd expected.

"Ramsey," I whispered, too stunned to say anything more.

"Do you like it?" His lips were close enough to my ear that I shivered.

"It's incredible." I turned toward him, not hiding the shock on my face. "But you didn't need to do all of this. I—"

He placed two fingers over my lips, and I went quiet. His eyes reflected the flickering glow of the candles as he stared into mine. The air thickened as the same sense of intimacy I'd felt before rose between us again.

Something was here, just out of my reach—a shared past spilling into the present.

"You are my fiancée," he said, lowering his hands to my hips. He pulled me closer, and my breath hitched. "My duty is to make sure you get everything you deserve and more."

I still wasn't sure what I deserved. It certainly didn't feel like I deserved *this*—this extravagance, this doting attention. The love of this man who held power and authority with such grace and charisma. This man who never gave up on me and ensured I knew I was loved.

This man who didn't know I'd been spending time with his enemy.

"I don't deserve you," I whispered, staring into the flame of a candle to escape his gaze.

Ramsey brought his hand under my chin, tipping it up until I faced him. "You do," he murmured. "Of course you do."

Slowly, he lowered his lips to mine. The kiss was soft, almost hesitant, and lasted only a moment before he pulled away, just enough to meet my eyes. Whatever he saw there made him shake his head. He cupped my face and kissed me again.

This time, there was no trace of hesitation. Ramsey kissed me as though we were all that mattered. My heart sped in my chest as I moved my hand to rest against his shoulder. It shook slightly and my stomach fluttered. Ramsey's lips lingered as he slowly pulled away, every inhale and exhale a shared breath.

It was the first kiss I could remember.

It was one I'd never forget.

Throughout dinner, Ramsey's spirits remained unshakably high. He avoided all talk of rebels and war, instead telling me more stories of our life together. It didn't hurt as much as I'd feared it would. I hadn't realized how desperately I needed to hear them, to get a glimpse of what life was like for us before the attack.

He was a fantastic storyteller. No one had made me smile and laugh as often as he did when he recounted stories from our childhood. The fondness in his eyes when he spoke of climbing trees, wading through creeks, and sitting together under the stars mirrored the nostalgia in his voice. These memories were precious to him. At one time, they must have been to me too.

"I wish I could remember it," I confessed, picking up another photograph Ramsey had brought over. I ran my finger along the edge of the frame. "Knowing I've lived so many wonderful moments but can't remember them ... it's not fair."

Ramsey's eyes flashed with pain. "If I could give your memories back to you, I would."

"I know." I set the frame down, forcing a smile I wasn't sure he'd believe. I busied myself with moving my fork around what was left of the chocolate cake on my plate. "I don't blame you for anything, Ramsey. I just get frustrated sometimes. Everything feels so new and confusing, and everyone else knows what I'm missing. It's hard to constantly be three steps behind, and that's without my episodes making things worse."

He shifted, entwining his fingers with mine. "You don't have to try to keep up with anything or anyone. You as you are now, that's all I want. That's all I'd ask of you."

His words pricked my heart. What if I wanted more than this version of myself? What would that mean for us?

"I can't imagine how challenging it's been, trying to relearn your life while recovering," Ramsey continued, shaking me from my spiraling thoughts. "I know I haven't been around as often as I'd like. As often as I should be—"

"Ramsey—"

He held up a hand, stopping any argument before it left my lips. "I know you don't blame me, that you understand. It doesn't lessen the guilt. I'm your fiancé. I should be there for you, whenever you need me."

"But you're not *just* my fiancé. You have a responsibility to Anluan. Our people need to know they can count on you, that they're being protected." I leaned forward, holding Ramsey's gaze. "I feel much better knowing I'm not distracting you from doing what needs to be done."

He blinked, swallowing thickly as his gaze fell to the table. "You are a marvel, Khara."

"And you're a better man than you claim to be." I gave his hand a gentle squeeze, drawing his eyes back to mine. "Give yourself more credit, Ramsey. There's only so much a man can do in a day—even if that man is Sovereign of Anluan."

His lips curved into a smile that made him glow, the warmth of it rivaling the candles' flames. "I'll try to remember that." He cleared his throat, taking a sip of wine before turning back to me. "I did have something I wanted to share with you."

"Right," I said, settling back into my chair. "The special occasion."

He nodded, shifting in his seat in a way I'd never seen him do. Ramsey always seemed so in control, so self-assured. It was strange to see him this flustered. Despite a hint of concern, I found myself charmed by it.

"I meant to bring this up a while ago," he said, rubbing the back of his neck. "But with the recovery taking longer than we anticipated and your episodes flaring up the other day—"

"Ramsey," I cut in, amusement overtaking my concern as he rambled. "What do you need to tell me?"

He blew out a breath. Folding his hands on the table, he eyed me closely. "We hadn't set a date for our wedding yet, before the attack."

I blinked. Other than Emila, no one had mentioned the wedding, and all she wanted to discuss were details like dresses and flowers. I hadn't thought to ask when the ceremonies would take place.

"I'm in no rush," he hurried to add. "You don't even remember agreeing to marry me in the first place. I would never ask you to move forward until you were comfortable."

He paused, his lips pursing, and nerves filled my stomach. There was more to this, something he was reluctant to say. Hesitation wouldn't change whatever it was. Best to get it over with.

I leaned forward, my hands twisting a cloth napkin beneath the table. "... but?"

"But we *had* set a date for our engagement ceremony, and I haven't had the heart to cancel. I just kept hoping you'd be better, that we could keep this one thing." He let the thought hang in the air before shaking his head. His next words came slowly, carefully measured as he stared at me. "The gala is scheduled for the end of next week."

A wave of anxiety crashed over me. Only a week away. That was so soon.

But was it really? Ramsey had been planning this for ages. *We* had been planning it, even if I couldn't remember doing so. Would it hurt to go along with it? I'd been told there was a prevailing sadness among the people since the attack. Maybe hosting this event, giving everyone a chance to celebrate and see us together, would be a chance to lift their spirits.

"We can postpone. I should've done that to begin with. I—"

"No," I said, looking up to meet his concerned eyes. "We should have the party."

He ran a hand over his stubble. "You're sure?"

I nodded as I reached for his hand. "I think it will be good. For the people, for us. We planned to celebrate our engagement this way before the attack. I'd hate to let what happened steal this from us too."

"You never cease to amaze me." Ramsey trailed his thumb back and forth across my hand. "I should make sure everyone knows we're still on, then." His eyes went distant, a hundred plans swirling within them before he turned back to me and smirked. "Emila will be thrilled."

The excited look on her face this morning made more sense now. I groaned. "She'll be completely unbearable planning the details, won't she?"

"It's part of her charm."

I laughed. It really was.

We settled back in front of the fireplace after dinner. Ramsey tucked me under his arm, facing the hearth as the flickering flames cast a soft orange glow around the room. It was quiet, the gentle crackle of wood the only interruption to our companionable silence. I was hesitant to break it, but all the talk of the engagement party had raised my curiosity to a level I could no longer ignore.

"Ramsey," I began, shifting from under his arm to face him more fully on the couch. He turned to me with a hum. "Would you tell me how it happened? When you proposed?"

Surprise widened his eyes before he straightened and turned to face me fully. "Of course I will. Forgive me. I should've told you sooner." He huffed a laugh. "Though now I'm wishing I'd had it photographed. At the time, I wanted the moment to be wholly ours. We spend so much time in the public eye as it is."

I appreciated the sentiment. While I hadn't felt overwhelmingly in the public eye since I'd woken from the attack, I imagined that had been achieved through concentrated effort. I was well guarded, and, for the most part, the few people I interacted with maintained a respectful distance. It seemed a horrific injury was one way to secure privacy in Anluan.

"I debated how to ask you for the longest time," Ramsey confessed as he reached for my hand. "You are everything I've ever wanted, Khara. No way I asked you to marry me would ever have been good enough." He didn't notice my frown as he ran a finger over my engagement ring. "Still, I had hope, so I arranged for us to spend some time alone. We went over to the canal—the part where the trees line the waterway. You always loved to sketch there."

Despite not remembering the canal, I could imagine it. It sounded like exactly the kind of place I'd enjoy. Peaceful. Calm. Maybe with some convincing, I'd be able to see it for myself soon.

"We walked together—just you and me, arm in arm. When we reached the space with the trees, we sat on a stone bench against the wall lining the path. You said it was the perfect spot to rest." His eyes went distant, shining in the fire's glow. "It was a cold day, chilly even for autumn, and I'd brought a carafe of your favorite tea for us to share. The cold kept others away. It was like we had the place to ourselves. I might've ensured it by cordoning off the area, but I knew you'd get after me for that." He smiled wistfully. "It was a perfect afternoon. And before the sun set, I knelt before you and asked you to be my bride."

He turned to look at me, his eyes brimming with sadness, and my heart ached. I was always disappointing him. My memory loss didn't just affect me. It hurt everyone around me, especially Ramsey.

"I'm sorry," I whispered. "I wish I could remember."

"None of this is on you." He laced our fingers together and lifted my hand to his lips for a kiss.

A hint of my guilt ebbed with his words. He spoke so sincerely, as if he truly didn't harbor any resentment for the way things were. It softened my heart to him even more.

"You never have to apologize for not remembering. I'll always be right here, ready to remind you."

As he leaned forward to kiss me, the soft glow of the fire highlighting the richness of his brown eyes, I didn't make him wait. This time, I leaned in and met him halfway.

I forgot all about meeting Hayden in the grove. Dinner with Ramsey had gone so well, I lingered in his suite. For once, I felt normal—just a girl swept up in the excitement of a romantic evening with her intended. I didn't want the feeling to end.

When Ramsey walked me back to my suite, it was long after nightfall. The hall was dim and quiet, granting us a few final moments of shared peace. When we neared my door, the guard on duty pointedly moved down the opposite end of the hall, keeping his back to us. My cheeks flushed, though the privacy was appreciated when Ramsey dipped his head to mine for a good-night kiss.

It was tender and unhurried, the perfect end to our evening.

After a final good night, Ramsey nodded to the guard and left me to rest.

It took me a long time to fall asleep, my mind stuck on the press of Ramsey's lips against mine.

40

I STOOD ALONE IN a pitch-black room. There were no walls. Or at least, I couldn't distinguish any. No windows. No doors. Nothing but an infinite black, dark and foreboding.

Did I still exist in this sea of nothingness? I could barely feel the weight of my limbs, barely lift my arms. I was lying on my back, I realized. My arms fell heavy to my sides.

I don't know where I am.

The thought began to spin in my mind, building panic deep within my chest. My heartbeat quickened, pulsing and breaking the heavy silence with the fast, shrill sound of beeping.

My fear grew.

I don't know where I am. I don't know where I—I don't know—

"Khara."

I held my breath. A voice, gentle and calm. Steady. So steady, when I was anything but.

"You're okay. Breathe. Please, just breathe."

I should obey—my lungs begged me to—but the darkness. There was too much of the inky black, and the blaring beeps, and my heart, racing so fast inside of my chest, like it was going to burst before I'd be able to—

"I'm going to fix it. I'll fix it! Just breathe. Please."

Light flared, sudden and blinding. When I lifted a trembling hand to block it, I found no resistance. I gasped, and my body inhaled greedily as if suddenly remembering it needed air. The light grew more vivid, filling the space around me until everything was a shining white. I had to clench my eyes shut against it, but I could still sense the brightness from behind my lids.

"Almost there."

The light began to fade, and I panicked.

I didn't want to go back. I couldn't.

That darkness would take from me. Take something I couldn't afford to lose.

"You're not going back." The voice burned with surety. *"You're safe, Khara. I promise you're safe."*

My eyes flew open. I stood in the grove, surrounded by trees. The moon shone down on tall grass as it shifted with the wind. It was quiet, but Hayden's words echoed in my head.

I promise you're safe with me. He'd said it so many times.

I frowned, turning and taking in the empty clearing. Shouldn't he be here? I called his name, and in the next moment, he appeared in the center of the clearing. It should have been odd, but I went along with the flow of what I now recognized as a dream.

Only a dream.

"I'm sorry," he said, his thumb running back and forth over the symbol tattooed beneath his wrist. "You didn't come, and then I felt how panicked you were. I wanted to make sure you were all right."

I furrowed my brows, not bothering to hide my confusion. If Dream-Hayden was anything like the one in reality, he'd be able to see right through me anyway.

"It's a powers thing. We're ... connected." Hayden winced, his eyes flicking from me to the ground as he rubbed the back of his neck. "It's a long story."

"I have time." Arching a brow, I sat cross-legged right where I'd stood. It was much closer to Hayden than I allowed in our face-to-face meetings. But inside a dream, it couldn't do any harm.

He blinked, tilting his head as he stared down at me with searching eyes—another way Dream-Hayden matched reality. His facial expressions already felt so familiar. After a long moment, he sighed and roughly ran a hand over his head, mussing up his curls before he sat facing me.

He opened his mouth as if to speak, but closed it again just as fast. As he searched for words to explain, he absentmindedly plucked blades of grass from beside him. I waited, content to watch as he used his fingernails to slice through one blade after another.

There was no rush. No need to make every moment count. No fear of an attack or being caught breaking the law. Here, I could just watch, listen, be. The reprieve soothed any threat of impatience in me.

When Hayden finally spoke, his words were slow and disjointed. "I have powers."

I wrinkled my nose. I knew this. *Everyone* knew this. Dream-Hayden wasn't very imaginative.

I grimaced. That meant *I* wasn't very imaginative.

"No, I meant—" He sighed, shredded grass falling from his fingers as he lifted his hands to scrub his face before meeting my eyes. This time, when he spoke, his words rang with confidence. "I have powers. Some you know about—the way I can use light, harness its power, call the lightning. It's my born gift, the known one, and I can heal to a degree. This other ability, it's ... connected to yours."

I straightened, my head spinning. "My dreams."

"Remember what I told you? Your dreams give you impressions, glimpses of things that are important."

Of course I remembered. I'd had a hard time wrapping my mind around it.

"You and I, our powers are linked, to a degree. So we can—*sometimes*—communicate with each other. Through our dreams."

He eyed me warily, his body braced for my reaction. All I could do was blink.

"I don't understand," I said slowly. "You're saying ... *what* are you saying?"

He groaned, burying his face in his hands. "Sometimes, when it's necessary, we can join dreams. You can come into mine, talk to me, influence things." He hesitated, wariness lining his body with tension. "And less often, I—"

My blood ran cold. "You can come into my dreams."

He was actually here. In my dream. As if he were standing right in front of me.

I bolted to my feet, backing away, but there was nowhere to go. Until I woke up, I was stuck here. In a dream. With Hayden.

"You're real?" My voice broke. At his sharp nod, the full weight of the revelation took shape and panic thundered through me. "You can get inside my head. *How long have you been in my head?*"

He lifted his hands in surrender, his eyes wide. "No, it's not like that!"

I turned away, covering my mouth with a shaking hand. Tears filled my eyes, and I clutched my fist in my shirt as I gasped for air. This whole time, he'd had access to my mind. What had he been doing to me? Was that why I couldn't remember? Was it why I'd been so willing to go see him in the first place? Had he put that thought in my head somehow?

"Whatever you're thinking, I promise it's not like that." Hayden's tone was desperate, his words falling fast behind me. "Just listen to me, okay? I don't do this whenever I feel like it. I respect you too much for that, and I'm only able to join your dream if you allow it. It's dependent on your power. Okay? You have to allow it."

I spun to face him, tears paving cold trails down my face. "What do you mean, *allow it*? I didn't—"

"You did," he pressed. "Khara, you called for me."

I had said his name when I ended up in the grove after the light broke through. Still. "That wasn't—"

"We're connected," he said. "It wasn't just that you said my name. Before that, when you were panicking, something in you called for me, and the something in me that's linked to that something in you answered. It's why your nightmare shifted. Understand?"

I laughed bitterly. "No! I don't understand this at all!"

Hayden deflated, his shoulders turning inward before he took a step back. "I can—I'll just go. I'm obviously not explaining this well. I didn't mean to upset you. I would never invade your dreams, even if I could. That's a violation—not just of your trust, but of the connection itself."

He shook his head and ran a hand over his mouth. Mind still spinning, I said nothing, and he looked away. "I haven't even been able to reach you since the attack. I've tried to send you messages, tried to reach out when I thought I felt distress. Once I thought maybe I'd broken through, but besides tonight, I'm not sure it's worked. I'm—" His voice broke. He looked back at me, and the moonlight revealed a glossy sheen of tears in his eyes. "I'm truly sorry, Khara. It won't happen again."

I frowned. Why did he always have to seem so sincere? I had no reason to believe a word he said, and yet, I found myself wanting to.

It was dangerous. Unwise. And apparently, too late.

"Don't just leave." Sniffling, I wiped tears from my face. "I want to understand. Stay. Please."

Hayden's expression didn't lift, but he sat, folding his hands in his lap. He looked so innocent—so *sad*—that I found myself softening.

"Since waking up in the Annex," I said, my feet smashing the grass as I paced, "I haven't been able to remember most of my dreams." I stopped moving to meet his eyes. "I've been writing out the little I can remember when I wake up. There's been this voice …" My eyes lost focus as I tried to remember the phantom words. "*Come home*. It kept telling me to come home."

Hayden sucked in a sharp breath.

"Was that you?" I asked, watching him carefully.

"I didn't think you'd heard me," he said, so quiet I had to strain to hear. "I tried, at first, to make the connection happen. But I couldn't feel it—feel *you*—for the longest time. They told me it was hopeless, that I should prepare for the worst. But I still tried to call out to you, night after night." He inhaled shakily. "Even when I stopped actively trying to reach you, I must have been reaching out subconsciously. How long have you …?"

"I'm not sure." I wrapped my arms around myself, pretending it was from a chill in the air and not my need for comfort. "It's clearer when I don't take the pills."

"Of course it is." Hayden's eyes darkened before he met mine. "Are you still taking them?"

"Not since I last saw you. I feel more like myself when I don't."

"Good. That's good."

We went quiet, both of us lost in thought. I still wasn't sure how I felt about having Hayden here—if he truly *was* here and this wasn't some horrible trick of my imagination. But I didn't feel unsafe. Just overwhelmed.

No wonder no one had spoken to me of my powers. They seemed to be unbearably complicated.

"Your memory," Hayden said, his soft voice breaking the silence. "Do you still want me to help you try to get it back?"

Of course I still wanted my memories back. But did I trust Hayden enough to let him help me do it? Could I trust him not to do something else to my mind without me realizing?

"How would you do that?"

"Honestly? I'm not sure how to go about it. I have some ideas, but it would all be experimental."

I blinked. "Experimental? That's your pitch?"

Hayden laughed, his eyes crinkling as his smile turned fond. "It's all I have right now."

He paused for a moment, his brow furrowing, and I could see his mind whirling. How could I be so good at reading him already? Maybe he was telling the truth about me knowing him better than anyone.

"I'd use my healing ability," he said, a bit more confidently this time. "That's where we'd start. I think if I can push the power to your mind, it could heal whatever's damaged. I told you this isn't my forte?"

"You said it's your father's gift."

Hayden nodded. "My father, Galen, was born with healing magic. My grandfather gifted him a portion of the family's lightning power later. My father imparted some of his healing ability to me after the war broke out, to help with"—he waved his hand in the air—"all of this. Too many people have been hurt. He didn't want them to have to wait for him if I was nearby. But I'm limited in what I can do until I inherit more power from him when I officially become Sovereign."

I couldn't help but think the title would fit Hayden, just as it fit Ramsey. But this conflict would come to an end eventually. One of them would have to lose their title to the other. Likely more than the title.

My stomach clenched, and I stiffened as visions of death and fates far worse sprang to mind.

Hayden's eyes fell on my rising shoulders, and he moved on. "Short version: I can heal you partway, enough that maybe you'll start to remember. If you stay away from those pills," he added, voice tinged with bitterness, "then I think your dreams will become more clear."

"How will I know my dreams are actual memories, not my subconscious playing tricks on me?"

He tilted his head, regarding me with a piercing stare that could see right through me. "You'll know."

"But *how*?"

"You have to trust yourself, Khara." His eyes bored into mine, full of meaning I couldn't quite grasp. After a beat, he sat back, breaking eye contact. "You'll know."

I wasn't going to hold my breath. Without my memories, trusting myself wasn't something I could do. At least not fully. "So how do we do this?"

He raised a brow. We both knew I was changing the subject, but I didn't care. I raised a brow back. Hayden sighed, but his lips quirked up.

"I don't think we can do it like this. Meet me tomorrow night at the grove. We'll start then."

This time when I told him I'd try, I knew I'd keep my word.

When I woke the next morning, groggy and blinking the sunlight from my eyes, I remembered my dream.

I sat up, ignoring the head rush, and reached for my journal and pen. I wrote every detail onto the page. The initial dream, full of darkness and fear. The light breaking in and the shift to the grove—to being with Hayden. I hastily scrawled out every word I could remember him saying, especially about powers. At the end of the page, I wrote out his invitation: the grove, tonight.

When I finished, I realized my head barely ached. For the first morning I could remember, I felt okay. Almost normal. Or what I imagined normal would be.

I didn't need to consider taking a pill.

I didn't even try to smother the smile that spread across my face.

41

THE ENGAGEMENT PARTY BECAME a point of focus for me. By the way Ramsey had talked about it, I assumed the details were taken care of and all I'd need to do was show up. Apparently, I was wrong.

A knock sounded at my door earlier than normal. I opened it and an exuberant Emila burst through, already talking a mile a minute.

"I'm so glad you said yes!" she gushed, striding into the living room with coffee in hand and throwing herself back against my couch. "I mean, of course you would. Why wouldn't you want a party? But I did wonder. You've been doing all right lately, but I know you still get tired, and you haven't been around too many people yet. Easing in, I get it. But, oh, this gala is going to be the talk of the century! You're going to look so gorgeous, Ramsey won't be able to take his eyes off you! I can help you choose your gown, right? Please say yes!"

I blinked as my brain took a long minute to catch up. When I realized what she was talking about, I rolled my eyes. "Good morning, Emila. How are you today?"

She scoffed. "Oh, please. Don't give me that! We're best friends and if I can't barge in here ready to plan every detail of this party—that's only *one week away*, mind you—what's the title even good for?"

I laughed as I settled beside her on the couch and nodded toward the cups in her hands. "Is one of those for me?"

"Of course." She handed one over. "Like anyone needs to see me hopped up on two coffees. Well, a coffee and a tea. I snuck you one with caffeine."

I took the cup, inhaling notes of bergamot and rose. She'd brought one of my favorite blends. "Thank you, Emila." She waved me off, but her smile was pleased as I tasted the drink and sighed. "Now, what about the party? You *are* talking about the engagement gala, right?"

"What other party would there be? Now, I know the basics are taken care of. Ramsey filled me in on where we're at with the planning process. There are still decisions to be made, and while I am more than happy to dive in myself, it *is* your party. You only get engaged once!" She scrunched her nose. "Well, in theory, at least."

I shook my head, taking a long sip of my tea. "Assuming I don't end up engaged twice, what do I need to do to make this the best party of the year?"

"That's the spirit! Here." She dug a thick stack of papers out of her bag.

My eyes widened. "How long have you been working on this?"

She had the grace to blush, though her grin didn't fade. "Okay, you caught me. I've been involved since the beginning. But Khara! Someone had to keep the plans moving forward while you were stuck in medical, and who better than me?"

I reached for a few of the pages, smiling as I took in the handwritten notes and sketches. "I'm just teasing. Honestly, you're doing a better job than I ever could."

"True."

We both laughed, scooting closer so we could look over the plans together. As Emila added more and more papers onto the stack, I winced. "This will take us all day, at least."

She shot me a wide, wicked grin. "Don't worry. I've cleared our schedules."

Emila hadn't been kidding. The two of us spent the entire morning together, our planning only broken when Commander North insisted we have lunch. After we ate, we worked through the evening. Ramsey stopped by to see me, but Emila quickly shooed him off. She barely let him come in for a hello and a chaste kiss, but Ramsey was a good sport about it. He laughed warmly and told us to have fun before leaving again.

Gage brought dinner. "Emila, Princess," he said jovially as he set bags of food on the table, "I come bearing gifts!"

Truer words had never been spoken. The food smelled incredible, and I was starving. I broke away from Emila and rifled through the bags. A selection of soups, salads, and sandwiches filled them. I sighed in relief.

"Thank you," I said fervently, taking one of each. "I'm so hungry, I was about to eat Emila's party plans."

"I would've killed you," Emila called from the couch without looking up from her notes. "Then who'd enjoy this lovely party I'm planning?"

I shot Gage a wry look. "You'd think she's the one getting married."

His smile faltered, but faster than I could blink, it was back and bright as ever. The change had been so abrupt, I wondered if I'd imagined it in the first place.

"Not one word, Argusten," Emila ordered, glancing up with narrowed eyes.

"Not a one, ma'am."

He flashed her a mischievous grin. Emila's cheeks dusted pink as they stared at each other.

I bit back a grin of my own.

That night, I didn't even bother trying to sleep. Cradling a cup of tea, I settled in with my journal, waiting for enough time to pass so I could slip away from the Annex undetected.

I began to sketch, wrapped up in a blanket on the couch. I let my hand move without thinking about what I wanted to draw. The rhythmic motions soothed me—the slide of the pencil across the paper, the gradual filling in of lines until they became three-dimensional.

Eventually, I finished the piece, feeling lighter than I had all day. Drawing always managed to settle my heart. I looked down, taking in what I'd made, and dropped my pencil. It rolled across the rug at my feet, but that hardly mattered.

I had drawn a perfect likeness of Hayden.

I hadn't meant to, but there he was, fleshed out in detail. He stared up at me, his eyes piercing through the page with fire and hope. His head was tilted so I could see the jagged bolt of lightning shaved into the side of his head. I'd even included that errant curl that always fell onto his forehead. He looked so real, I found myself almost as mesmerized by the drawing as I was by Hayden himself.

I slammed the journal shut and stood.

It was probably late enough to leave.

When I opened the door, Gage was mysteriously absent from his post. He had realized I'd been leaving at night. Maybe he thought he was giving me time to explore the Annex on my own. I hoped he realized how much he was risking by doing so.

Did I even realize how much *I* was risking?

Maybe we were both fools. Any time a reason this was a bad idea came up, I ignored it. I kept pursuing this, kept making these meetings with Hayden happen.

It was for my memories. Mostly. I needed to remember who I was and how I came to be here—in Anluan, with Ramsey. I needed to know if the story Hayden had told me about us being close was true.

Somewhere inside my memories, there was a key, one that would help me make sense of all of this. I just needed to find it.

42

Now that I'd done it a few times, sneaking out of the Annex was almost anticlimactic. My heart still beat heavily in my chest as I sped down dim hallways and waited for guards to pass before climbing the iron fence marking palace grounds. There would be real consequences if I was caught, and the idea of that particular confrontation was enough to make me nauseous. But I didn't doubt that I could make it onto the streets and beyond the city walls anymore.

The flashlight still sat in its place about halfway down the tunnel. Crawling through the dust was barely cause for a second thought. I was surprisingly comfortable with it all. Maybe I was some sort of criminal mastermind at heart.

When I made it to the grove, Hayden wasn't in his usual spot in the center of the clearing. He stood closer to the treeline. Our eyes met right away.

"Hayden." I nodded, trying not to fidget under his gaze. It was different now that we'd interacted in my dream.

"Khara." He smiled. "You're earlier than I expected."

"Yes, well ..." I struggled to figure out what to tell him, not wanting to seem overeager. I definitely wouldn't admit to drawing his face to pass the time. Heat spread across my chest and crept up to my cheeks. He *could not* find out about that. I cleared my throat. "I wanted to make sure I could get here."

Hayden's smile grew, his eyes sparkling in the moonlight. He'd caught the blush. The heat in my face built. "Well, your timing works for me. I'd have waited all night if I needed to."

I blinked, startled by his sincerity. "*Why?*"

It wasn't the first time he'd said something like that, and I could read the truth of it in his eyes. He meant it, every time, but I couldn't figure out the reason.

Raising a brow, he walked backward into the grove. "Am I that much of a mystery?" Though he tried to sound lighthearted, I caught a tinge of sadness in his voice. "I thought you would've figured that out by now."

Frowning, I crossed my arms and followed him into the grove. "Everything's a bit of a mystery to me these days." I shrugged, trying to make light of it, but he saw through that too.

"It's okay. I know I'm not ..." He shook his head with a sigh before giving me a tight smile. "Never mind, Khara. Don't worry about it."

I wasn't sure I was capable of forgetting any of the things he said to me. Something about him screamed *important*, beyond being the rebel army's leader. There was something personal here, something I was missing. He was like a word on the tip of my tongue—familiar, but just out of reach.

I desperately wanted to recall everything about him. Good or bad.

For now, I had to let it go. I gestured to my head. "How are we going to do this, then?"

Hayden turned to face me fully. My memory problem seemed a welcome distraction. "Let's settle in first," he said, voice following the far-off look in his eyes. A little dip formed between his brows as he took in the grove. The thoughtful expression made him seem younger, reminding me that he could only be a few years older than me at most.

Hayden moved toward the trees on one side of the clearing. He spun in a circle, using his foot to smooth down the tall grass until a flattened patch formed. As he sat, he gestured for me to do the same.

The patch was small and forced us closer than normal. I sat cross-legged in front of him, my knees touching his. My heart picked up speed, but I did my best to ignore it. It wasn't anything to get worked up over. Hayden had healed me before, and it was fine.

But before, he hadn't been sitting so close that I could see a constellation of faint gold specks in his eyes whenever the moonlight hit them.

I blinked and shook my head, quickly looking away. Too quickly for someone like Hayden not to notice. To his credit, he didn't say anything.

"I'll need to touch you." His eyes were soft and so full of kindness, my breath faltered. He waited, his gaze locked with mine. He wouldn't move until I said it was okay, and that made me feel even safer.

"That's fine," I whispered.

Maintaining eye contact, Hayden leaned in slowly, reaching toward my head. I could feel the warmth of his hands before he touched my face. When he placed his index fingers against my temples, trailing his thumbs to rest against my jawline, a zapping pulse of electricity surged between us. While it wasn't painful, it startled me enough that I jolted forward with a gasp.

"Sorry!" Hayden froze, but didn't remove his hands.

"What was that?" I asked, breathless.

"Side effect of my powers." He grimaced. "I'm sorry. I didn't know that would happen."

"It's fine. It didn't hurt."

"Good." He exhaled deeply and relaxed. "Okay, I'm going to start the healing process again. If you feel any pain, tell me so I can stop. No memory is worth you being hurt."

I wasn't sure I agreed. What was a little pain if it meant recovering all I'd lost?

Hayden's expression tightened. He narrowed his eyes as if he knew what I was thinking.

Slowly, I nodded. When his stare didn't waver, I sighed. "I'll tell you."

He took a deep, steadying breath. "Then let's give it a shot."

Hayden closed his eyes, his brow furrowing in concentration as he gently increased the pressure of his fingertips against my temples. I took a deep breath and closed my eyes too. Then, much like the times he'd healed me before, the warmth came.

At first, it was the same. Gentle warmth. A tingling line of energy that moved from my temples to wrap around my head as though it were a living thing searching for pain to cover and cool into submission.

And then it shifted.

It felt like the power flowing into me hit a wall. I furrowed my brow at the strange sensation, squeezing my eyes shut tighter. It wasn't painful, just uncomfortable. Hayden must have felt it, too, because his fingers pressed more insistently against my head.

With the movement came an increase of power, a surge I'd never felt before. It hit the same barrier in my mind, forcing a sharp gasp from my lips. This time the flow of power *was* a little painful. I pulled back on instinct, and Hayden's hands immediately fell away.

Breath ragged, I brought a hand to my head. An odd dizziness swept over me, and I closed my eyes against it.

Hayden touched my arm as he leaned toward me. "Are you all right?"

"Give me a minute."

He sat back, staying quiet while I waited for the feeling to pass. When it did, I opened my eyes. As expected, Hayden was staring intently at me. His eyes roamed over me, trying to see something that wasn't visible from the outside.

"I've never felt anything like that before," he said, his eyes narrowed in thought.

I shook my head, as clueless as he was. "It didn't feel like when you healed me before."

"What was different this time?"

I could tell from his tone he was already working to solve this mystery. He was so intent on helping me regain my memories, it amazed me. Was helping me going to benefit him somehow, or did I matter that much to him?

I focused on his question, sorting through what had happened. "At first everything was the same. It felt warm, and there's a trail of tingling energy that moves through." His nod encouraged me to continue. "Then it felt like that energy was hitting a wall inside my head. Like something was blocking it from where it wanted to go. I don't know."

Hayden shifted, sitting up straighter. "It felt like a wall to you? Like a barrier?"

"Exactly like a barrier. And then when you started pushing, it felt like the power hit the barrier, hard. It was uncomfortable before, but this time, it started to hurt."

His face crumpled. "I'm sorry, Khara. I—"

I waved my hand in dismissal. "It's not your fault. I was more surprised than anything. Do you know what's going on?"

"Someone did this to you," he said, his lips turning down. "I've thought so before, but this makes me sure of it."

A wave of chills swept up my body. "Did something to me? Like what?"

He ran a rough hand through his curls, looking away for a long moment. The way his body tensed prompted my muscles to stiffen as well. When he turned back to me, jaw clenched, his words made my stomach turn. "I think someone intentionally messed with your mind to take your memories."

43

MY WHOLE BODY WENT cold. It wasn't an accident. This had been intentional? The idea that someone could alter my mind was worse than any nightmare I'd had. The notion made my stomach roil.

"Who would do that to me?" I demanded, my voice tight with horror. "Who *could* do that to me?"

He winced, regret on full display in his eyes. "I don't think you want me to answer that right now."

Indignation flared in my chest as I caught his insinuation. Anger felt better than the overwhelming horror. I embraced it, pushing it into my words. "You think it was someone at the Annex? Like who, Ramsey? Don't be ridiculous."

Hayden frowned, but didn't back down. "If you can't imagine he'd do this sort of thing, I won't try to convince you. But think about the people around him. Do you really trust them all? Who's had access to you, Khara? After the attack, when you were at your most vulnerable, who cared for you? Were they actually helping you, or doing something else entirely?"

The words were like a slap in the face. I turned away, blinking rapidly against the tears building in my eyes. I didn't want to think about this. The idea that anyone would do this to me was painful. I refused to even consider Ramsey being involved. He would never do something so horrifying and invasive. Doctor Jensen would have had enough access to do it. Or one of her assistants. But did they have the means? The thought of any of them hurting me while I was supposed to be safe, was assured of it over and over again ...

I hitched a ragged breath and glanced at Hayden. He softened as he took in the turmoil written all over my face.

"Khara ..." His voice sounded almost as wrecked as I felt.

I shook my head, bringing a hand over my mouth. I couldn't spiral over this. If Hayden's suspicion was true, there was nothing I could do about it right now.

Taking a deep breath, I pushed the overwhelm away so I could focus on why I was here. "Forget who did this to me. How do we fix it?"

Hayden rubbed a hand over his face as he thought it over. "Without knowing exactly what they did to you, I don't know that I can. We can keep trying to shift things in your mind, bring healing to the areas that are accessible to me. Maybe there are enough places near this barrier—or even cracks in it—that will allow me to send power through. My father might be able to do more, but I would never ask you to make that decision right now."

I had a feeling that would be a one-way trip. If I made my way into the rebel camp—wherever it was—I doubted I'd be allowed to leave and go back to Anluan. They might not hurt me, not if Hayden's treatment of me was any indication, but surely they wouldn't be able to let me leave afterward. Not with the information I'd be able to share with their enemies.

How did I get here, straddling the line between sides? If Hayden's story was to be believed, I'd been standing near it most of my life. Friends with Hayden, practically family. Tied to Ramsey.

"So without going to your father," I said slowly, "we just try again?"

Hayden nodded. "It's the best I can do on my own."

"Then we try again." I wiped my eyes. "Go ahead."

Hayden hesitated, but I let him see all my determination. It didn't erase the weight of my sadness or the sickening feeling of violation at his theory. But it did strengthen my resolve to undo whatever had been done to me.

He leaned forward and brought his hands to my temples. "Tell me when it starts to hurt."

I nodded tightly. "Just do it, Hayden. Please."

Power flared to life in his hands, traveling in gentle trails into my head. I received the warmth gladly, letting the familiar path of tingling energy work its way through my mind. It pressed against the barrier, and I focused on breathing deeply, in and out. It was uncomfortable, but not painful.

"I felt it." Hayden's breath warmed the side of my face. "I'm going to try to go around it, repair anything I sense. Hold on."

I kept breathing as he did just that, doing my best to pay attention to the strange feeling of the energy's movement in my head. The barrier seemed smaller than I anticipated. As the power flowed around it, I sensed an oval shape behind the barricade, inaccessible in my mind. Somehow I could tell it was flat, like a rock you'd skim across a lake.

The energy traveled in a path around the barrier a few times. The tingling sensation returned as something knitted together in my head. My breath hitched as it did, and Hayden started to pull away.

"Keep going," I said. "It's not hurting me."

He pressed his fingertips back against my skin. Everything was warm as the energy moved along the barrier, but there were no other signs of change.

"Take a deep breath. I'm going to try to push against the barrier again."

I nodded, bracing myself for the pain.

It wasn't as harsh as last time. Hayden gradually increased the amount of force he used. The pressure built, wrapping over the wall and trying to reach beyond it.

I inhaled deeply and exhaled for a few beats longer. In and out. Tried to focus on my breath rather than the way the discomfort built alongside the pressure. Eventually, I couldn't distract myself any longer and whimpered.

Hayden's hands flew away from my head. He frowned, his eyes full of concern. "Khara?" He tilted my head up so I was looking at him. "Are you okay? Was it too much?"

"It just got to be a lot." I inhaled shakily as the pain settled.

"You were supposed to tell me when it started to hurt."

"And in a way, I did."

He huffed a frustrated laugh as he ran a hand through his hair. A curl fell out of place, and I fought a pained smile as he tossed it back. His hair would be a tangled mess by the time we parted ways. "It's almost a relief that you still do this."

"Do what?"

"Try to get away with doing things on your own." His lips quirked into a small smile. "You moved past a good bit of it, but I imagine it's hard not to fall back on the habit when you don't remember the trust that led you away from it."

Did I trust Hayden? I blinked as realization settled over me. I did trust him—enough to be here. Enough to let him try to help me recover my memories. It was more than I could say for Doctor Jensen. But did I trust him enough to reveal when I was vulnerable, in pain?

"It's okay," he said, his eyes glinting with sadness. "Really. None of this is your fault. I'm just grateful you're here. That you trust me enough for this."

I played with a blade of grass between my fingers. After a moment, I cleared my throat, glancing back up and meeting his eyes. "I do trust you with this." Sighing, I let my lips tip into a wry smile. "I don't know why. I probably shouldn't. But I do."

Hayden's grin brightened the entire grove. "I'll take what I can get."

44

THE HEALING PROCESS TOOK longer than I'd thought. What felt like a few moments had taken closer to an hour by the time all was said and done. I wanted to try one more pass through the barrier, but Hayden wouldn't budge. He didn't want to overload me with too much in one day. It was a smart decision, but I still had to tamp down my disappointment.

I had to admit, though I'd barely done anything, I was worn out. So much so, I thought I'd fall asleep where I sat. When my blinks came slower, my eyes heavy with the need for sleep, Hayden shifted, drawing my attention.

"Here." Moving to sit against a tree beside me, he slid closer until his shoulder brushed against mine. "You're exhausted. Rest for a while. I'll keep watch."

The idea of falling asleep with my head pillowed on his shoulder was tempting. It was also too much. Despite being exhausted, I wasn't sure I would be able to fall asleep this close to him.

Limbs heavy with hesitation, I pulled away. I didn't want to hurt Hayden's feelings, but I wasn't ready for this. "I'll just go."

I stood to leave and grimaced. My legs tingled with pins and needles after having sat for so long in one position. I tried to take a step away and stumbled.

"Khara!" Hayden reached to steady me, quick as lightning.

"I'm fine." I kicked my legs out to return full feeling. "My legs just started to fall asleep."

"*You* are starting to fall asleep. I don't like the idea of you traveling back to Anluan on your own, not when you're so tired."

I glanced at him over my shoulder. "I'll be fine, Hayden. I really should go."

He met my eyes with that intense concentration again. I could always tell when he shifted from looking at me to studying me. It was still a little disconcerting.

Whatever he saw this time was enough for him to relent. He sighed heavily. "I know I won't be able to convince you to stay." Fondness shaped his voice despite his obvious concern. "At least let me walk you to the wall. Please. I just want to make sure you stay safe."

I frowned. It sounded like a big risk for him to venture so close to the city. If someone were to spot him, it would mean trouble. For him and for me. I had no doubt it would cause a fight, right then and there.

"I don't think that's a good idea. If someone were to see you ..."

"Don't worry about me." He smiled wryly as he stood in a fluid motion. "I'm near Anluan more than you'd think. This won't be nearly as dangerous as my usual activities. But if it makes you feel better, I'll make sure I remain a shadow in the trees. I won't follow you to your entry point."

I blinked. "Wait—you know where I'm getting in and out of the city?"

"Who do you think put it there in the first place?"

My brows flew up. Maybe it shouldn't have been such a surprise, but I hadn't considered he had been the one to create the tunnel. To risk being so close to Anluan to build it himself ...

"Wasn't that dangerous?"

"Of course it was." He gestured to the path as he began to walk toward it. "But life is nothing without risk. You have to take chances if you want what lies on the other side of your fear. Come on." He turned toward me, mischief dancing in his eyes as he walked backward in the grass, his arms out wide. "Let's take a risk."

My mind swirled with potential horrible endings on our hike to the city. Hayden moved with ease, leading the way and pushing back the occasional tree branch for me as we passed by. Considering he was in more danger than me if we were caught, his relaxed demeanor felt entirely unfair.

He kept trying to steer my mind away from my worries as we walked, his voice warm as he told me stories about himself, his father, and growing up in Anluan. Once, he even mentioned me. He shared nothing too serious or revealing, just light-hearted anecdotes that kept me focused on his voice rather than my fears.

When we made it just shy of the treeline, Hayden stopped. "Here we are. You're feeling all right?"

"*Yes,*" I said, exasperation shaping the word. "And I promise I'm telling the truth."

"Good." He leaned against the tree at his side. The softness that overtook his smile as he stared at me was more tender than before. "Then I'll stay true to my word and wait here. Please be careful on your way through the city. You're—" He sighed, thumb brushing back and forth against the tattoo on his wrist, though his eyes never left me. "Just be careful, okay?"

I stared back, caught by the depth of his earnestness. The air grew charged as we stood, eyes locked on each other. I couldn't make sense of it—of *him*—but there was no denying the thickening of the air or the pull in my chest daring me to try. A summer breeze carried soothing hints of cedar and cinnamon over us ... before shifting my hair right into my face.

The moment shattered.

Blinking rapidly, I shuffled back a step, ducking my head as I tucked the loose strands of hair behind my ear. I cleared my throat, folding my arms and looking anywhere but at Hayden. "Thank you for your help tonight."

"I'll always help you." His words were a vow, one I found I didn't doubt. "Tomorrow night, meet me back in the grove. We'll keep going."

For the first time, I made him a promise of my own.

"I'll be there."

45

Gage stood with his back propped against my door when I peered around the corner of the hallway. Despite his relaxed demeanor, his sharp eyes spotted me right away. He grinned and lifted his fingers in a playful wave as I hurried toward him. His amusement felt like we were keeping a secret—which, when I thought about it, was exactly what we were doing. Other than Hayden, he was the only one who knew about my evening excursions, though he didn't know where I went or why.

"Nice night?" he asked, grin still in place as his eyes roved over me for signs of illness or injury.

"Wonderful," I said. "How was yours?"

He shrugged, stepping aside to give me access to the door. "Can't complain. My ward's been awfully quiet. She must be really tired."

My lips quirked as I pressed my palm to the center of my door. "I'm sure that's very true."

"Oh, it is," he said, tone full of mock-seriousness. "But I know nothing. Saw nothing. You're not here right now. You're snug in your bed, sleeping the night away."

I scoffed, but couldn't hide my amusement as I opened the door and slipped inside. "Well, I best not make a liar out of you."

Gage turned back to follow the door as it closed. "I wouldn't worry about that, Princess. I'd make a pretty good one on my own."

I chuckled. Gage Argusten wasn't someone I looked at and thought *liar*. He was too cheerful and good-natured. I just hoped he could keep my secret.

Closing the door, I made my way to my bedroom and unearthed my journal. I tossed it onto the bed before rummaging for fresh clothes. I needed to make notes before I forgot anything that had happened. I changed into a soft set of lounge clothes and curled up in my robe. Sitting cross-legged in the middle of my bed, I began to write.

Barrier: Magic? Science? Possible source of memory loss. Who's responsible?

I frowned at the page. Hayden seemed convinced someone here was behind this. Maybe it was prejudice toward his enemies. Maybe it was a hunch. Maybe he was correct. It was hard to say. All I knew was I wanted to know who did this to me—no matter who it was.

Because Hayden was right about one thing. Sometimes you had to take a risk in order to get what you wanted. I wanted my memories back. Maybe finding the person responsible for me losing them was the place to start.

Morning dawned far too early. With it came Emila, surprising me with how awake she was at the early hour. She'd clearly had coffee already. That, or event planning alone was enough to energize her. She'd brought the engagement party details for us to work on, but my exhaustion wouldn't allow me to focus. I couldn't match her energy level and it showed.

The third time I yawned, blinking heavily as Emila prattled on about floral arrangements, she stopped talking and studied me. There was no hiding my puffy eyes or the dull tone of my skin. Even if I'd had a way, I was too tired to try.

Emila frowned, her brows drawing together. "You look terrible."

"Thanks, Emila." Huffing, I straightened on the couch. "That's very kind of you."

"Oh, stop. You know what I mean." She tilted her head, leaning toward me. "Did you get any sleep last night?"

I tried to wave her off, reaching for one of the sketches she'd laid out on the coffee table. "I slept, just not enough."

Emila glanced at her notes and sighed, plucking the page from my hand. "Well, there go our plans for the day."

"What?"

"Khara, you can't possibly be up for this. You can barely keep your eyes open!"

"It's fine. We need to get this done."

"Wrong," Emila said cheerfully, shuffling her papers back into a thick stack. "*I* need to get this done. You need to go relax in a nice warm bath. After that, we'll get some breakfast."

"There's no time—"

"We're making time. Trust me. Everything will work out."

She stood and disappeared into my bedroom before I could respond. I sighed, slumping back into the cushions and letting my eyes fall shut. Running water broke the quiet, the soft sound of the filling tub loosening some of the tension in my shoulders. Soon, notes of eucalyptus and mint wafted in from my bedroom. With each inhale, my body relaxed further, until I drifted into a doze.

"Come on." Emila's voice was soft as she dropped a hand on my shoulder. "I have everything ready."

With her arm looped through mine, I shuffled into the bathroom and froze. She had transformed the space into exactly the kind of sanctuary I needed. The mint and eucalyptus filled the air more potently here, but it was gentle, a harmonious swirling together of scents that relaxed rather than overwhelmed. Foamy bubbles floated on the water filling the clawfoot tub. Dim light came from a slew of candles she'd arranged in clusters over the sink and ledges. More flickered on the floor, far enough from the tub there'd be no risk of me knocking them over.

My throat tightened. "Thank you."

"You deserve it." Emila gently squeezed my arm. "Now, do you have it from here or do you need my help?"

"I can manage."

"Then I'll leave you to it. There are towels and a robe over there." She gestured to the side where two plush towels sat atop a chair near the tub. My slate blue robe hung from the hook behind it, the satin sheen visible even in the soft candlelight. "Take your time. Rest. I'll check on you in a bit."

She stood on her tiptoes and pressed a quick kiss to my cheek before slipping out, pulling the door closed behind her.

The promise of rest gave me enough energy to toss my hair into a knot on top of my head and undress. The moment I sank into the tub, fragrant water enveloped me in a warmth that loosened my muscles and deepened my breaths. I tipped my head against the edge of the tub and closed my eyes.

I hated the exhaustion weighing down my bones. So many things required my energy during the day. Between the engagement party, wrapping my mind around my present and future duties to Anluan, and continuing my recovery, I was spent.

Using my nights to meet Hayden in the grove took more of my limited reserves. Maybe returning every night was a bad idea. There was only so much I could handle at a time. But enduring days like this would be worth it if the sessions restored my memories. What were a few sleepless nights and weary mornings in light of that hope?

No good would come from turning my mind in circles. I would stick to my plan to meet Hayden and continue to pursue my memories.

But first, I would take the opportunity to rest.

Sinking deeper into the tub, I let the crackle of burning wooden wicks and the gentle rhythm of my breath lull me into a doze.

46

Cardamom, clove, and ginger greeted me when Emila placed a steaming cup on our usual table in the commons. I inhaled greedily as I wrapped my hands around the mug, picking up additional notes of cinnamon and black pepper. From the tea's shade of brown alone, I could tell Emila had added just the right amount of milk.

"Emila, you are my favorite person."

She grinned as she settled into her seat and slid a plate of steaming eggs in front of me. "Don't let Ramsey hear you say that."

I took a long sip of my tea, relishing the blend of spice and honey. "One sip of this and he would understand. It's incredible."

She laughed, the bright sound filling my heart as much as it did the air. Taking a swig of her coffee, she glanced around the room before smirking behind her mug. "Contraband tends to taste all the sweeter."

"It's caffeinated?" I whispered, brows raised in surprise. The next sip warmed me even more. "That's twice now you've broken Doctor Jensen's rules. I'm starting to think you're a bad influence."

"You look like you need it." She shrugged. "Besides, who ever claimed I was a good influence?"

"You're the one making sure I stick to Doctor Jensen's rules."

She scoffed. "Of course I am. Your recovery actually matters."

I tilted my head as I raised my cup. "And this doesn't count?"

"No."

"Why not?"

"Because I said so, that's why." She set down her coffee, crossing her arms. "Just enjoy it, Khara. One cup of mildly caffeinated tea isn't going to kill you. Doctor Jensen knows it too. If she wasn't such a stuffy old bat—"

I snorted. "How *did* I think you were a good influence?"

Her eyes narrowed, but the mock glare couldn't hide the sparkle of amusement in her eyes. "You think this is bad? I used to get into all kinds of trouble. The streets of the Eastern District are full of whispers of Mischievous Mila to this day."

"Are they now?" My smile grew at the thought of a young Emila earning that reputation.

She hummed. "Mostly from my mother."

I covered my mouth but couldn't hold back my laughter.

Emila heaved a dramatic sigh. "There wasn't much to do, and I was easily bored. The neighborhood paid for it."

"And what whispers would I hear if I wandered your old neighborhood today?"

Emila leaned forward, taking the bait as I'd hoped she would. "One summer day, not much different from this one—that's how most of these stories start—Mischievous Mila freely roamed the neighborhood. Her mother was working, and school wasn't in session. There was nothing to do, no one to entertain the poor girl."

"How tragic."

"Very. So she gathered up her mother's cosmetics and trudged into the streets, wandering until she found him—the perfect, unsuspecting victim. You see, old Mr. Meldyn took to sleeping beside his food cart. He'd claim it only happened on rare occasions, but those like young Mila knew better. It happened every afternoon like clockwork."

I smiled into my tea. Sipping it soothed my weariness, while Emila's dramatics helped in a way all their own.

"Some would have stolen a snack from Mr. Meldyn, but not Mischievous Mila. Theft was beneath her. No, she loved to *create*."

"Oh no." I clamped my lips together as laughter warmed my chest.

"Oh yes." Emila nodded, lips twitching. "Old Mr. Meldyn was in serious need of a makeover, and young Mila was more than happy to provide it."

"What did you do?"

"What didn't I do? I painted his lips cherry red, dotted blush along his craggy old cheeks, applied glitter polish to his nails ... I would've lined his eyes, too, if he hadn't scared me half to death when he woke up during the eyeshadow!"

My shoulders quaked as I smothered my laughter in my hand. Emila grinned, shrugging before she took another bite of her eggs.

"He was furious! I think that's the fastest I've ever run." She paused, her eyes going distant before she shook herself. "Second fastest, at least."

Something about the tightness in her smile told me to leave the correction alone. "What did your mother say?"

Emila laughed, and brightness returned to her eyes. "That I should've done a better job choosing the lipstick. The shade of red didn't work with his skin tone!"

Our laughter blended together, loud and unrestrained in the quiet of the commons.

"She didn't mind your mischief, then?"

"Oh, she minded." Emila's smile softened as she fiddled with the handle of her mug. "She made me apologize to old Mr. Meldyn and buy a pack of roasted pecans from him at double the cost. But my mother always said I reminded her of her sister when she was my age. Her eyes would twinkle, she'd go all soft, and I would get away with far more than I should have."

"That sounds nice."

"It was."

We eased into silence, and I imagined the warmth of having a mother whose love wasn't dimmed by mischief or mistakes. Had mine loved me with that kind of fondness?

I shook the question away. There was no way for me to know and no use dwelling on it.

"That was just you, though," I said, eager to turn my mind back to something light. "And one incident is hardly enough to label you a bad influence."

Emila tilted her head and nodded. "True. There are plenty more stories, though."

"I'm listening."

"Well, then." She leaned forward on her elbows. "Let me tell you about the time I convinced an entire group of children to help me build a stray cat colony in an Eastern District alleyway."

"That sounds like charity, not troublemaking."

Her smirk had me grinning before she'd spoken another word.

"It would appear that way," she allowed, sipping her coffee. "Until we get to the hair dye and the founding of the Furmidable Feline Training Program." Though she tried to remain serious, her lips twitched again. "And Khara, we recruited strays from all over Anluan to our cause."

A bark of laughter escaped me as amusement shoved my weariness aside. I leaned forward, my heart lightening as I let myself get lost in Emila's stories.

While I enjoyed the slow morning, it didn't prevent my weariness from flaring when Emila and I stepped into the hall. My fatigue went beyond what food and laughter could alleviate. I rubbed my forehead with a sigh, drawing Emila's attention.

She frowned as she studied my face. "You really are exhausted, aren't you?"

"I really, really am."

Her face fell. "Are you feeling bad again? We can call Doctor Jensen and—"

"No." After what Hayden had speculated, the thought of Doctor Jensen examining me made my stomach turn. I didn't know if I could trust her. Until I did, I wanted nothing to do with her.

Emila caught my arm, pulling us both to a stop. "What's going on, Khara? You're starting to scare me."

I ran a hand over my face. "Nothing. I'm fine." At her incredulous look, I doubled down on my statement. "Really, I'm just tired. There's been a lot going on—between my recovery, learning about all the responsibilities that I have, or will have, the engagement party, and then there'll be the *ceremonies* and I just—"

"Whoa, okay!" Emila cut me off, bringing a hand to rest on each of my shoulders. "Breathe. You're feeling a little overwhelmed, yes?"

Tears stung my eyes. I hadn't thought to use that word, but it was exactly what I was feeling—more than Emila could know. Besides what I'd mentioned, I had all the things I couldn't tell her filling my head.

How would I get my memories back? How much could I trust Hayden? Would the experimental healing sessions actually work? And if they did, what if I didn't like what I remembered? How could I figure out who did this to me—and why they did it in the first place?

So many unknowns. So much confusion. It was exhausting, and not just physically. My mind and heart were tired too.

"Oh, Khara. You'll be okay." Emila smiled sadly as she wiped away a tear that slid down my face. "Everything's fine."

It wasn't, but I could try to believe it would be. For now, I was willing to pretend. My nod was forced, and it didn't stop the tears, but I was trying. That had to count for something.

"Let's take a break today. You can go back to your room. Maybe take a nap?"

"Sounds good," I said, voice wavering. All I wanted to do was sleep.

Emila gave my arm a gentle squeeze. "See? Nothing is happening that can't wait. You'll feel better about everything after you get some rest."

I could only hope she was right.

47

I stood staring up at the thick branches of an old oak tree. The wind rushed by, sending leaves dancing down to rest on the forest floor.

My eyes trailed along the path taken by a red leaf as it zipped from a branch and swirled away on the wind. I turned my head to watch, then followed after its movement.

Leaves already littered the wooded path, and the autumn air nipped at my face—crisp, but not unwelcome. The pine-scented breeze swirled like it was alive. I closed my eyes and smiled. It felt like greeting an old friend.

"There you are!"

Though it meant losing track of the leaf, I turned toward the voice.

"I thought we were meeting by the market," a young Ramsey said, his brow furrowed in confusion.

"I thought I had more time." Playing with the sleeves of my sweater, I offered him a sheepish smile. "I'm sorry, Ramsey."

He shook his head, but his smile was fond. "Don't worry about it. I had a feeling I'd find you out here."

I looked around, taking in the brilliant hues that signaled the shift from summer to autumn. "It's beautiful."

Ramsey shrugged, obviously not seeing the forest the same way I did. "I guess so. Are you ready to go?"

I wasn't, but I nodded anyway. I'd already kept him waiting too long. It would be rude to make him wander the forest with me when we'd made other plans.

Ramsey started back the way he came, leading us out of the forest and toward the city. I let my hand brush against the oaks and sycamores I passed along the way, smiling at the feel of their rough bark against my skin.

Texture. Life. There was so much to admire in the forests.

As we left the trees and made our way to the city gate, a familiar voice rang out.

"Khara! Ramsey!"

Hayden jogged toward us, grinning as he waved. Ramsey's shoulders tensed as I waved back.

I frowned. Hayden was his best friend. Were they fighting?

"Hayden," Ramsey greeted with less enthusiasm than normal. His jaw was tight.

"Hi, Hayden." I smiled warmly. I wasn't sure what had gotten into Ramsey, but I hoped my welcome made up for it.

"Are you headed to the market?" Hayden asked, fisting his hands in his jacket pockets to ward off the chill.

I nodded. "Ramsey and I made plans to go."

There was an awkward beat where Ramsey looked at Hayden with an expression I couldn't place. For as long as I'd known them, they'd been able to have conversations with just their eyes. I teased them about it often.

"You could come with us," I offered, unable to stand the silence any longer.

"I don't want to intrude," Hayden said, tousling his curls with a careless hand. "My parents let me out of lessons early since it's a nice day. But I should probably train with my powers more. I can catch up with you later."

Ramsey softened and rubbed the back of his neck. "No, it's okay. It'll be fun to go together."

Hayden hesitated. "You're sure?"

"Of course." Ramsey nodded, his lips lifting into a slight smile. It didn't fully ease the strange tension in the air, but it helped. "Come on, let's go before all the good pastries are picked over."

The rest of the way to the market, I walked between Ramsey and Hayden. I wasn't sure why, but it felt like the conversation didn't flow quite as freely as usual.

48

Strange pressure filled my head when I woke from my nap. The dream had been vivid, the feelings so real. Was it a dream, or could it have been a memory? Maybe Hayden's healing *had* done something last night.

My journal sat cracked open on my bedside table, and I winced at my recklessness. I needed to be more careful about where I left it. Not that I thought anyone would go rifling through my things, but I didn't want anyone to read it. What was written on those pages was private.

I turned to a fresh page and wrote out the dream, noting every word spoken, every emotion I felt. The idea of the three of us being friends, going to the market together—it being normal for us to do that in a peaceful Anluan—formed a lump in my throat.

If this was a memory, we were so far removed from it now.

I shut the book, consumed with a restlessness that demanded I move and do something. After tucking my journal back in its hiding place between the mattress and bed frame, I smoothed my hair and walked to the door.

Commander North stood at attention when I opened it. She met my eyes, nodding in greeting. "Did you need something, Coryndé?"

I stepped out, shutting the door behind me with a wry smile. "I was going to find Emila or Ramsey. There's only so much lying around I can do in a day."

The corners of Charna's lips twitched. "I can understand that. I'll accompany you wherever you'd like to go."

"Thank you."

Again, she dipped her head. One thing I appreciated about Charna was her brevity. She could speak volumes without saying a single word, and she did it with such confidence—a talent I wished I could learn.

As the elevator bay came into view, nerves twisted my stomach. There was no reason for them. Commander North was trustworthy, and I enjoyed her company. But as the doors opened, unease settled in my chest, and I had to blink back a spark of pain.

Distraction. I needed a distraction.

"Commander, could I ask you a question?" I ventured as we entered the elevator.

"Of course."

"You seem to know a lot about Panra." I leaned against the side of the car. "Have you ever been there?"

"I have." A smile pulled at her lips as she selected our floor. "I was born and raised in Panra."

I hadn't expected that. For whatever reason, Charna seemed like she'd always been a steady presence in Anluan.

"I'd love to hear about it," I said. "Panra sounds incredible."

"It is. The city was built using the gifts of Panran people long ago. It's a masterpiece of wood and stone, layered throughout the forest and stretching to the sea. The palace itself rests in the treetops. Remarkable craftsmanship with impeccable views. You won't find anything like it outside of their kingdom."

"I'd love to see it one day."

"I hope you will. They would welcome you heartily, Coryndé."

"Maybe when the war is over," I murmured, spinning my engagement ring on my finger. Until then, any sort of travel felt out of reach, no matter how appealing it seemed.

As the elevator opened, the unsettled feeling rose again. I blinked against the light and something hazy that tried to settle over my vision. It dispersed, and I tentatively stepped into the bay. Charna exited behind me, watching me carefully.

"Why'd you leave Panra?" I asked before she could say anything. I wasn't sure what was going on with me, and I didn't want any questions.

Charna moved toward the entry to the office wing. "I visited Anluan when I came of age."

Ramsey's office and those of his most trusted advisors were located on the same floor. The access level required to enter was almost as high as the one to get to my suite. A press of Charna's hand against a wooden panel near the door granted us entry.

She held the door open and gestured me forward. "While here, I discovered things I decided to honor with my life."

"Isiraden?" I asked as I ducked inside and glanced around. A few people roamed the halls, dipping in and out of offices, but it was mostly quiet.

Charna tilted her head as she moved to take the lead. "Isiraden, the ancient tree, the ones who formed it. Even you, Coryndé."

"Me?" I paused, my heart constricting. Being held to the same level of respect as ancient magic and the gods who supposedly created it sent fresh overwhelm rattling through my chest.

"You don't seem to grasp the measure of grace given to you," she said, a sad smile pulling at her lips as she turned, careful to ensure that those in the hall gave us a wide berth. "There is a reason you will make a perfect Sovereigna. Your connection to Isiraden ... some things go beyond understanding, even with science and magic at hand."

That wasn't hard to believe. Many things felt beyond my understanding. Including how I could be a perfect Sovereigna.

"Due to the reverence of your position, you hold sway over the people. They will heed your words more than they would for most."

"I find it hard to believe they'd all listen to me," I admitted, watching her carefully.

She inclined her head. "Not all would. But you don't need all. You simply need enough. And that, you already possess. You also hold the heart of our leader. This kingdom will bow to you, Coryndé. Isiraden is the heart of Anluan, and you are the heart of Isiraden."

Nerves beat against my stomach, weakening my voice. "Please call me Khara."

This time, her smile wasn't tempered. "I'm afraid I can't do that. Your title isn't mere formality to me, Coryndé. You earned my respect long ago. It would take a great deal for me to lessen my opinion of you. Come."

Charna led us forward again. I hugged my arms around my waist, watching my feet shuffle against the tiles. Would meeting with Hayden like I had be enough of a betrayal to change her mind?

"You're shouldering a weight beyond what any of us can comprehend," she added. "It's understandable that you'd feel as I believe you do."

"And how's that, Commander?"

"Overwhelmed. Uncertain. Perhaps even afraid."

I cringed, fiddling with the thin sleeve of my sweater. "Am I so obvious?"

Her eyes locked on me. Despite the discomfort of their weight, I didn't look up.

"No," she said kindly. "But after the traumas you've endured, I believe anyone would doubt themselves. And you face more responsibility than most."

When I ducked inside an empty room to the side of the hall, Charna followed.

"Do you think I can do this?" I asked, feeling far more vulnerable than I liked as I met her eyes. My hands gripped the sides of my sweater. "Be a leader, someone worthy of both of my titles. Coryndé Isiraden *and* Sovereigna."

"You're already worthy," Charna said. "And by the time this season fades to the next, I have no doubt you'll be exactly where you're meant to be."

My eyes pricked with heat at her certainty. "I hope you're right."

"You have a well of strength inside you, Coryndé. It's my honor to watch you wield it."

49

RAMSEY WAS ENGROSSED IN a meeting when we arrived at his office. A handful of advisors sat around the table while Ramsey stood, bent over a large map. A gray-haired man nodded, pointing to a corner of the map as he spoke.

The atmosphere seemed tense. Their words were indistinguishable, but they spoke quickly, in low tones. Whatever they were talking about had to be important. Suddenly, I wasn't sure visiting Ramsey was such a good idea. He was busy. I shouldn't interrupt.

Before I could voice my doubts, Charna knocked on the door. Through the glass walls, six heads swiveled toward us. Ramsey met my eyes and stood straighter, flashing me a charming grin. He held up a finger, and I nodded. I could wait as long as he needed.

Ramsey addressed the room again, receiving sharp nods all around. Then hands gathered the materials they'd been pouring over, clearing the table of all traces before he had even made it to the door.

He stepped into the hall, the murmur of his advisors following him before the door closed again. He kissed my cheek in greeting. "How are you feeling? Emila let me know you were having a rough morning."

My eyes followed the bustling movement in the room behind him. "Should you get back to them? I can—" I motioned with my thumb down the hall.

"No, no," Ramsey cut me off, taking my hands in his. "You're my priority. They'll manage for a while on their own, trust me."

Whatever was going on looked important, but I knew he hated it when I questioned the time he spent with me. "If you're sure ..."

"I am." Ramsey gestured for us to start down the hall, away from his office. "And you didn't answer my question. How are you?"

"Better. I just needed more sleep."

He chuckled. "I imagine Emila's been a little intense with the party planning."

"It's been a lot." My smile tightened as I thought of all the reasons I'd felt overwhelmed that morning. I quickly added, "But I'm so grateful for her help! I'd have no idea where to start without her."

Ramsey frowned down at me. "Maybe I should have taken care of the planning myself. I thought you'd like to be involved. I didn't mean for it to overwhelm you."

"It's not that bad," I assured him. "Everything just seems so much bigger and more confusing when I've had less sleep. I'm sure I'll be fine moving forward. Besides, there's less than a week until the gala. I can manage that long."

He tilted his head, considering. "Well, despite all the details and planning, I hope you're looking forward to it. It's about us, after all." He paused, turning so he could look into my eyes. "Because if not, say the word and I'll cancel the whole thing. You matter more to me than any party."

Tension drained from my shoulders. Having the option alone eased some of my stress. I wouldn't do that to Ramsey—or to anyone else looking forward to the gala. Still, the permission to cancel brought a wave of relief with it.

"I'll manage, Ramsey," I said, smiling softly. "But I appreciate the offer."

"Of course." He smiled back, his eyes alight with happiness. "As I said, you're my priority, Khara. Always."

Every time he said it, my stomach fluttered. My heart swelled with gratitude for his support, but in the same instant, it cracked with guilt. I was hardly living up to my side of our relationship.

"Thank you," I whispered.

"You never need to thank me for that."

Ramsey squeezed my hand before leading us forward again. Charna followed at a distance. I appreciated the attempt at privacy. Of all the guards, she did that best—likely one reason she was so trusted within Ramsey's inner circle.

We made our way from the office wing to the elevator bay. I wasn't sure where he was taking me, but it wouldn't be anywhere stressful. Ramsey always made sure to attend to my needs—especially on days like today, when he felt he should be more present with me. I wasn't the only one harboring guilt in this relationship.

I leaned into Ramsey's side as we waited in front of the elevator. He held me close, and I inhaled the citrus and ginger notes of his sandalwood cologne. His thumb brushed soothing circles over my arm, and I relaxed further. My gaze drifted to the large, arched windows on the side wall, taking in wispy clouds and a bright blue sky. Maybe Ramsey planned to take me outside since it was such a beautiful day.

My attention floated back to the elevator as the cab arrived.

The doors slid open, revealing a wild-eyed man glaring daggers at us.

"*You*," he snarled, his eyes narrowed in unbridled anger.

His face was pale, his clothing stained with patches of crusted red-brown. He lunged toward us, a blazing, ill intent on his face that sparked fear in my heart. Faster than I could blink, he threw his shaking arms forward.

One minute, I was pressed to Ramsey's side.

The next, I went flying, blown back by a burst of wind.

50

I crashed into the wall behind us, knocking down a painting as I collapsed to the floor. Dazed by the impact, I barely registered a grunt of pain from nearby.

Ramsey pushed to his feet, his body lined with tension. While he maintained the cool air of control that suited him so well as Sovereign, his flinty eyes and clenched jaw gave away his anger. I'd never seen him so furious as he took a slow, deliberate step forward.

My eyes darted around the room, searching for Commander North. The eruption of wind had pushed back toward the office wing. As she climbed to her feet, she pressed a button on her watch and the overhead lights shifted into a dull, flashing red. Carefully, she moved closer to the confrontation. It was clear this man was unstable. With his powers, that made him even more dangerous.

Ramsey didn't seem afraid. He glared at the man, his arms raised in preparation to attack.

My heart pounded furiously. Who *was* this man? What did he want?

"I see you managed to make your way out of your cell, Lachlan." The hatred in Ramsey's voice startled me as much as the other man's ire.

Lachlan laughed bitterly, highlighting the tight lines around his steely green eyes. "Your power only goes so far, *Sovereign*. It was never going to hold me forever. It didn't even hold me very long."

"Yes, well," Ramsey said tightly, his attention fixed on the man's face. "Allow me to rectify that mistake by dealing with you directly."

"I'm not afraid of you."

A dangerous glint entered Ramsey's eye. Between one blink and the next, they almost seemed to swirl with gray. When he spoke, his voice was low. Deadly. "You should be."

The man glanced at where I trembled on the floor. His eyes darted back to Ramsey almost at once, but then he whipped his head fully toward me. "You shouldn't be here."

I shivered at the intensity of his gaze, the madness in his eyes. He kept his hands extended toward Charna and Ramsey, but his focus was on me.

"What are you doing here?" he demanded. "*You shouldn't be here!*"

My mouth went dry. The way he screamed the words sent chills running over my head and trailing to my chest. Realization settled over me. He was going to do something terrible.

The intuition did nothing to help me.

He whipped his hands toward me in a low arch. An explosion of wind slammed into my side, knocking my shaking arms out from under me. Before I could tumble across the marble floor, the burst of air lifted me and flung me toward the wall of windows.

I flew straight through the center. The gust of wind was too powerful, the glass too fragile to hold. The window shattered, the sound echoing in my ears as a startled scream ripped from my chest. I fumbled to grab something—*anything*—to stop my fall.

I barely managed to grab onto the black mullion, wrenching my arm as momentum jerked me to a stop. I dropped to where the window met the floor, my legs fumbling for purchase against the tower's brick. Jagged glass bit into my palms and the angle of my hold was awkward, but I clung with all my might. Blood trailed down my hands, slicking my grip as I scrabbled one hand over smooth marble, desperate to pull myself up. Shouts rang out inside, but I couldn't process any of them. I was too focused on hanging on.

My feet slid against the brick below me, but I kept trying to find a foothold. Adrenaline flooded my body, and my arms began to shake. I cried out as I slipped backward, terrified I'd plummet to my death.

"Khara!"

I looked up, blinking against a thin trail of blood creeping onto my eyelid as Ramsey crashed to his knees before me, paying no attention to the glass shards crunching beneath him. In the moment our eyes met, his whirled with fear. I slid back another inch, a panicked cry shattering from my throat. I couldn't hold on much longer.

"One of you, get over here!" Ramsey roared, sparing no more than a glance behind him.

He darted closer, glass tinkling with the movement, and reached under me to wrap his arms around my chest. I had to release my hold on the walls as he heaved me up. Eyes shut tight, I clamped my mouth shut against a whimper.

"I've got you. I've got you!" Ramsey repeated as he lifted me toward him. It wasn't clear if he was trying to reassure me or himself.

Another pair of hands joined his, and together, they hauled my shaking body back over the edge. One set of hands released me as soon as I slid back through the opening. Ramsey's pulled me closer. Pressed against his chest, I could feel his heart galloping. He clutched me tight, wrapping a hand around the back of my head to keep me in place as we both breathed raggedly.

When he'd caught his breath, Ramsey jerked away, cradling my face in his hands. He tilted it this way and that, inspecting my face before scanning what he could see of my body without moving. "Are you all right?"

He noticed my hands then, smeared red where my palms had torn. His eyes narrowed and he turned, barking orders at the guards I hadn't noticed filling the space behind us. "Someone get me a med kit!"

"I'm okay," I said. But between my wavering voice and trembling hands, there was no hiding how shaken I was.

"You're not."

"You shouldn't *be here*!"

I flinched at the prisoner's scream. I hadn't noticed he was still in the room.

In that moment, Ramsey looked capable of murder. If he hadn't been holding me, I knew he would've attacked the man. Instead, he turned his head halfway and ground out an order. "Get him out of here. *Now!*"

The guards sprang into action, no less than three handling the prisoner—including Cethin. The man's hands were bound behind him with thick black cuffs that seemed to stop his power, at least temporarily. I slumped into Ramsey, relieved.

"Radnor." Ramsey's voice was a dangerous kind of quiet. "Leave him to me. I will be seeing to him personally."

The dark promise made me shudder. Ramsey frowned, wiping traces of blood from above my eyes. I sighed in relief. With the blood on my hands, I would've only made it worse.

"You're going to be okay." His panic seemed to be fading, but his next breath was unsteady. He was more shaken than he was letting on. Pulling me closer, he kissed my forehead. "You're going to be okay."

"Sovereign," Gage said as he drew near, "I have the kit you asked for. I called for Doctor Jensen as well."

Ramsey nodded. "Thank you."

Gage's face was stony as he nodded back. I'd never seen him look more serious. "If you need anything else, I'll be here. The others have the situation in hand. Commander North said she'll oversee returning the prisoner."

Again, Ramsey nodded, distracted by the kit in front of him. He ripped open a package of gauze and pressed it against my left hand. I hissed and jerked away.

"Sorry. I'm sorry." Ramsey winced in sympathy.

"Move aside, Sovereign."

I stiffened at Doctor Jensen's sudden arrival. I hadn't seen her since Hayden told me his theory about my memory. The thought of letting her touch me when I wasn't sure if she'd played a part in whatever had happened to me was sickening. My heart thundered in my ears, and I swallowed thickly.

I didn't see a way out of this.

51

"Doctor, her hands." Ramsey shifted away to give her space to work.

"Let's get her out of this mess." Doctor Jensen frowned as she shuffled glass shards away with her foot. "Your office or mine, Sovereign?"

"Mine's closer." Ramsey gripped my forearms, gently pulling me to my feet and holding me steady when I wobbled in place. I grasped his arms and gasped at the stinging in my palms. His eyes hardened at the sound. "Come on," he said lowly, moving me forward a few steps to tuck me into his side. "Lean on me, Khara. I've got you."

I nodded, already feeling spent, and shifted my weight so Ramsey propped me up. He moved slowly, mindful of every step. The lights had gone back to normal—no more red glow, no shrill alarm. If it weren't for a million tiny shards of glass and the blood trailing from my hands to the floor, it would have been like nothing had happened.

I grimaced at the dripping blood, not interested in getting a look at myself. I was sure it was horrific—sticky blood on my face and trickling down my neck, staining my hands.

"Almost there." Ramsey's encouragement soothed me as we made our way back into the office wing. Once again, I was grateful for his attentiveness. Furious as he was about the attack, he still pushed his feelings aside so he could help me.

That was a relief. I hadn't liked the look in his eyes earlier.

I shuddered as my thoughts shifted to our attacker—Lachlan. They'd said he was a prisoner. One of Hayden's rebels. It was alarming, being attacked by someone connected to him, especially when I'd been safe in Hayden's presence for so long.

I would ask him about it the next time I saw him. I needed to understand.

Ramsey opened the door to his office and ushered me inside. The room had been cleared, the table free of documents and the advisors nowhere to be seen.

A leather couch sat against the wall near bookcases that lined the far side of the room. Ramsey led me to it and knelt in front of me, lifting my chin so he could look into my eyes. I tried to smile, but my lips trembled with the urge to cry.

Ramsey softened further, pained sadness extinguishing the last embers of his anger. He placed his hand on my upper arm, running his thumb back and forth over my sleeve. "You're going to be okay. And I promise you," he added, soft voice tinged with determination, "Lachlan will pay for what he's done today."

I blinked rapidly, hating that I was on the verge of tears. I didn't want to start crying, especially with Doctor Jensen in the room. But I couldn't stop the way my next breath came as a hitching gasp.

"Oh, Khara." Ramsey sighed, pulling me close. As he held me, I began to cry in earnest.

"I don't understand." My voice shuddered with the sobs I struggled to suppress. "Who was he? Why did he do this?"

Ramsey's arms tightened, the pressure of his hold turning painful. He released me just as quickly, his arms sliding back into a comforting hold. He smoothed a hand over my hair, mindful of my injuries even as he ignored the blood.

"He was a rebel spy. We apprehended him the morning I had to leave you at breakfast. He's been in our custody ever since. Somehow," Ramsey gritted the words through his teeth, "he was able to escape his cell this afternoon. Believe me, that will not happen again."

I nodded, letting the information sink in and quiet my sobs. The man was a spy for Hayden. Had he been ordered to attack me? If that was the case, why wouldn't Hayden have hurt me himself by now? If this spy *didn't* have orders to attack me, then why would he? Something didn't add up, but I was too exhausted to figure it out.

"Sovereign," Doctor Jensen cut in as she approached, "I need to take a look. Her injuries shouldn't wait."

Ramsey carefully shifted aside. "Of course. Thank you, Doctor."

She waved away his thanks, focusing her attention on me. "What hurts the most? Your hands?"

I nodded, my jaw clenching as I leaned forward, resting my arms on my knees so she could inspect my torn-up palms. "I think there's still glass in there."

Doctor Jensen's knees creaked as she knelt in front of me. She took my left hand, evaluating the injury, then set it back down to examine the right, tilting it to the side before letting go. Frowning, her eyes scanned my face.

"You're right." She sighed, glancing from me to Ramsey. "There's glass embedded in both palms. The good news is the bleeding has slowed. I'll need to clean the wounds, remove the shards, and apply a few sutures. Are you okay to do that here?"

It would be uncomfortable wherever we did it, but I didn't want to be back in medical, not even for this. "Here's fine, as long as Ramsey doesn't mind."

"Of course I don't." He turned to the doctor. "Do it here."

"I don't have everything I need. You had a med kit in the hall?"

Ramsey nodded as he stood. "I'll get it for you."

My heart lurched. I didn't want to be left alone with Doctor Jensen. Unfounded or not, Hayden's theory about my memory loss had left me suspicious. How could I trust this woman to help me if she might be responsible for such a horrific violation?

But Ramsey strode out the door, leaving the two of us alone in the office.

52

DOCTOR JENSEN ROSE FROM the floor with a huff, grabbing one of the chairs from Ramsey's table and rolling herself back to me.

"That's better. These knees aren't what they used to be." I said nothing, but made an attempt at a smile while she considered me. "You haven't called lately. You've been well since we upped the dosage of your pills?"

The pills I'd started flushing down the toilet after a few days of staying far, far away from them? I nodded, keeping my smile carefully in place. "I'm doing much better."

Doctor Jensen's smile sharpened. "I'm happy to hear it. Sovereign Ramsey must be thrilled. He was rather worried for a while there. We all were."

Something in her tone gave me the impression she didn't mean it.

"I seem to be feeling much better now." I paused, briefly holding up my hands. "Well, not currently, but that couldn't be helped."

"Nasty business, all around. I don't condone the undue harsh treatment of prisoners, but that man deserves what's coming to him. Anyone stupid enough to go after the Sovereign and his fiancée ..." She shook her head, eyes glinting as her tone darkened. "On his own head be it."

What did *that* mean?

I didn't want that man running around unchecked. He deserved to be locked up, maybe even in one of the more secure prisons outside the city. He'd have no hope of another escape if we sent him to one of the penitentiaries shared between the Diamond Kingdoms. According to Emila's lessons, Kilhelm stood closest to us, but it was isolated near the southeastern coast. It would easily hold a rebel prisoner and keep enough distance between us that I'd feel safe.

But the implication of Dr. Jensen's words chilled me.

"We shouldn't dwell on him any longer." She reached into her small satchel, removing tweezers, a pair of gloves, and a medical wipe. "You need to focus on your recovery. You're doing quite well, Khara. I'm very pleased."

I smiled tightly. "Thank you."

"This will sting," she warned as she pressed the wipe to my hand. I clenched my teeth to keep back a pained hiss. "You may feel some pinching as I remove the glass. Would you like some medication?"

"No," I blurted, instinct driving me to lean away from her. Doctor Jensen's eyes narrowed. I hid my wince and tried to backtrack. "I can handle it. I'm on so much medicine already. I don't want to take any more than I have to."

Doctor Jensen searched my face. I wasn't sure what she was looking for, but I didn't like it. Finally, she nodded. "I can't say I blame you. You've had to deal with a lot of medication lately."

My shoulders slumped in relief. Surely she wouldn't have forced me to take it, but I wasn't sure what would happen if we were ever completely at odds.

"Ready?"

When I nodded, Doctor Jensen got to work. With deft precision, her skilled hands removed each shard. No matter what I thought about her potential involvement in my missing memories, I had to admit she was good at her job.

Ramsey returned as she was working on my left hand. It seemed to have more glass embedded in it than the right. The removal stung, and I couldn't help but grimace.

Ramsey placed the med kit on the floor beside Doctor Jensen. "How are we doing?"

"As well as can be expected." I tried to smooth out my grimace, but the pained sympathy in Ramsey's eyes spoke of my failure.

"Your brave fiancée didn't want any medication to dull the experience," Doctor Jensen commented lightly.

I bristled at her tone. Ramsey turned to me, head tilted and brow furrowed. I shrugged, wincing when the movement knocked Doctor Jensen's tweezers against the gash in my hand. "I don't want to take any more medication. I can handle this. It's not that bad."

Ramsey frowned. "What about the sutures?"

I bit my lip. I hadn't thought that far ahead. Panic had fueled my refusal, and despite my determination to stay away from any drugs Doctor Jensen suggested, I faltered. Stitches would be painful.

Doctor Jensen paused her work, turning to face Ramsey. "I can send someone to fetch a local anesthetic if she wants, but if she prefers to go without, we should respect that."

Ramsey's frown deepened, but he nodded. He settled beside me on the couch, close enough that our legs touched. He was stiff with distress over all of this—the attack, my injuries, and my refusal to accept pain relief. I wasn't sure I would make it through suturing without it, but I appreciated Doctor Jensen taking my side.

When she finished removing the glass from my hands, Doctor Jensen cleared away the remaining blood. She paid careful attention to the area nearest the cuts, determining the largest two gashes needed suturing. The rest would be okay with bandages, but I would have to spend at least a few days with my hands wrapped. It wasn't ideal, but it was better than flying out a window to my death.

With my hands tended to, Doctor Jensen stood, turning her attention to my head. "No glass. But this cut needs a stitch or two as well." She wiped the blood from my forehead before sitting so she could look me in the eye. "This will be unpleasant. Are you sure you don't want medication? You'd be much more comfortable with an injection."

I stared at my hands. Was it worth it to endure more pain just because I had doubts about Doctor Jensen? Doubts that came from Hayden, who had definite biases against the people around me.

I turned to Ramsey. "What do you think?"

"I think I'd rather not see you in pain ever again." He gently squeezed my forearm. "Please, Khara, consider it. If not for yourself, then for me."

I wavered under the weight of his words. Ramsey trusted Doctor Jensen to do this, and I trusted him. He would be with me the whole time, just like he always was. I took a deep breath. "I'll take the anesthetic."

Doctor Jensen nodded, satisfaction curling her lips. "I'll call for an assistant to deliver it. Excuse me."

Ramsey deflated as she left the office, burying his face in his hands. He took a long, shaky breath, and fresh tears welled in my eyes. I hated putting him through so much pain. When he looked up, his eyes were wet. "Thank you."

Mindful of my injuries, I leaned my head against his shoulder. "I don't mean to make you worry."

"Hazard of the job, I'm afraid," he said wryly. "I'll always worry about you. There will always be some level of danger to you as my fiancée. While I'll never like it, I'll have to learn to live with it."

I'd never like the danger either, not to myself or to Ramsey. But like him, I'd have to learn to live with it. Maybe once the war was over, things would be better. Safer. Peaceful. The way it should be.

Doctor Jensen returned, followed by one of the assistants I vaguely recognized from my time in recovery. The young man never seemed to smile. It wasn't that we didn't get along. He was simply so impersonal there'd never been a chance to try.

Ramsey relaxed once the suturing began and I didn't react in pain. He leaned back, head resting against the top of the couch, hands fisted over his eyes. It had been a long day, and it wasn't over yet.

Doctor Jensen made quick work of treating my wounds. When she finished, she cleaned and covered the smaller cuts before wrapping a bandage around both of my hands and placing one on my forehead.

"The bruising will have to fade on its own." She moved my face to the side, assessing me. "It's not too bad."

"Any idea how long it will take?" Ramsey asked. He sounded so tired.

"It's hard to say. A few days, a week—maybe longer."

"The engagement gala is less than a week away." I sighed, turning to Ramsey. "Maybe Emila can help me cover them?"

"I'm sure she could, but please don't worry about it." He cupped my face. "You're stunning, bruises or no. We're not going to let a traitor like Lachlan"—he spat out the name with distaste—"ruin our celebration."

I hadn't seen my face yet, so I didn't know how badly bruised I was, but if Ramsey was okay with it, I could be too. Besides, I had faith that Emila would be able to help. If the bruising faded some, maybe with a little care, no one would even notice.

Ramsey smiled, but exhaustion crept over its edges. I hoped he'd take a break to rest soon. He deserved it. We both did. Though I'd been able to rest this morning, I felt like I was right back to where I'd started when Emila had barged into my room.

"If that's all, Sovereign," Doctor Jensen said, packing the last of her things, "I'll be heading back to my lab."

"Yes, of course. We don't want to keep you any longer than necessary." He stood and moved to shake her hand. "Thank you, Doctor."

"Yes, thank you," I echoed. Even if I couldn't bring myself to fully trust the woman, I couldn't ignore the way she'd helped me.

She nodded to us both, shouldering her bags. "Call me if you need anything else."

With that, she swept from the room. As the door shut behind her, I slouched into the couch and closed my eyes. Without her presence, I felt like I could breathe again.

53

Ramsey and I parted ways not long after Doctor Jensen left. Both of us were exhausted. My face ached and my palms began to sting as the numbness faded. I wanted nothing more than to wash the blood from my hair and fall into bed.

Fortunately, Ramsey felt the same. He suggested we take time to rest, but the dark look he shared with a guard we passed in the hall made me wonder if he had other plans. Ones involving the man who'd attacked us.

I shuddered. That was a question better left unasked.

Ramsey walked me to my suite, ensuring I had Gage and another guard stationed outside, just in case. I was still so shaken by what had happened, having extra protection wasn't something I would've argued against even if I'd had the energy for it.

Gage was far from his usual self. He nodded to me as I entered my room, but he didn't smile or crack a joke. It seemed the attack within the Annex had sobered everyone.

Alone in my suite, I let my shoulders slump and leaned my head against the wall. I inhaled shakily, letting myself feel everything—the confusion, the fear, the surety I was about to fall to my death. The pain, the anxiety, the exhaustion.

What a day this had turned out to be.

I took a deep breath and shuffled into the kitchen, where I rummaged until I found two bags that could cover my bandages. It would be a challenge to shower, but I didn't want to wait for anyone to help me. I needed to wash the blood—and this day—off of me.

In my bedroom, I kicked off my shoes and went in search of fresh clothes. Mine were stained with blood. Probably not salvageable. A shame, really. I'd loved the simple outfit.

I grabbed a pair of lounge pants and the softest shirt I could find. I would follow through on my plan—shower, then curl up in bed. With any luck, I could rest all night.

But I was supposed to meet Hayden in the grove.

I shut my drawer with more force than necessary. Leaning my weight against the dresser, I shoved down my anger. This wasn't Hayden's fault. At least, I didn't think it was. Still, something dark coiled in my stomach at the thought of what had happened. Hayden was connected to Lachlan. It might not have been fair to suspect Hayden—he'd always been kind to me—but I wasn't willing to ignore the connection either. I wasn't sure I'd make it to the grove, anyway—not with how stiff and sore I felt.

It didn't matter now. All that mattered was washing the blood from my skin.

Warm water worked wonders. I'd hit the glass hard and my back was paying for it. But the water soothed my muscles as it cascaded down my skin. I slumped under the spray, resting my forehead against the shower wall as I let the water run.

Once clean, what little energy I'd had was gone. My bed called to me. I wasn't sure if I'd sleep. I wasn't even sure if I wanted to. What would my dreams be like now that I'd been attacked again? But I had to try.

Stepping from the shower, I wrapped myself in a plush towel and moved in front of the mirror. I couldn't put off seeing the damage anymore.

I wiped the condensation from the glass in a rough line. Exhaustion rimmed my eyes, but I barely spared them a glance. The darkening bruise on my forehead demanded my attention. It wasn't nearly as large as I'd feared, but it was tender and looked like it would be darker by morning. The edge of a cut peeked through my hairline.

I looked away. How many scars would I have because of this war between Ramsey and Hayden? In the end, when someone came out the victor, would it even be worth the struggle? As I turned out the lights and crawled into bed, I was confident those were questions I didn't want answered.

54

It was pitch black. Nothing, all around me.

Biting cold seeped into my legs from where I sat on the hard ground, inciting shivers that racked my frame. The scene began to shift, a wall forming behind me, its rough bricks digging into my too-thin shirt. The darkness stayed, fading into night rather than nothingness. The change did nothing to make me less desperate.

My fingers were numb. Fear curled around my chest, tightening my lungs. If the cold didn't kill me, the aching loneliness would.

I hated this dream. And somehow, I was aware it *was* a dream. I gasped for breath around a sob, searching my surroundings for some light. There wasn't nearly enough.

How do you shift a dream?

I closed my eyes and thought of light. Imagined it pulsing and dancing around me.

Ramsey's voice, young and on the verge of tears, whispered on the wind. "I've been looking everywhere for you."

Relief coursed through me, echoing like a remnant of something real, something I wanted to see. But it didn't erase the tremors of cold and fear assaulting my frame. I kept my eyes shut and called for the light. Behind my lids, I saw the change begin.

"You're coming home with me," Ramsey whispered. The phantom warmth of his arms wrapped around me, tight and protective. "Okay? You're coming with me. I'll keep you safe."

The words were said with such conviction, a tear slid down my cheek.

When I opened my eyes, the scene had changed. Light swirled in the empty air in brilliant bursts. They moved above my head as though they were sentient, their alluring beauty calming my lingering fear.

If imagining the light worked, I didn't see why I wouldn't be able to direct my dream to something better. I closed my eyes again, picturing a soft mix of grass and mossy earth beneath my feet. I imagined the smell of a summer night, the rustle of leaves in the wind, and the twinkle of a thousand glimmering stars in the sky. I thought of the grove and all of its beauty.

When I thought of Hayden, too, I opened my eyes.

The grove was calm, peaceful—everything I'd hoped it would be. Hayden wasn't in sight. While it was odd for him not to be lounging in the clearing's center, it was a relief too. I didn't want to talk to him right now.

I wondered if I should, though. Before I went off to meet him again, maybe I should ask him about Lachlan attacking me. If Hayden had planned it, had any part in it whatsoever ...

With a sigh, I sat in the middle of the tall grass, stretching out until I was lying completely on my back, staring up at the sky.

I didn't want to believe Hayden was involved. Right or wrong, I liked him. He was helping me restore my memories as best he could, a kindness that had begun to endear him to me. But whenever I stopped to let myself consider it, there was something else. Something more. Because we grew up together, maybe.

Not for the first time, I wished for my memories so I could better know myself and the circumstances surrounding me. I was tired of being two steps behind everyone else.

Gathering my courage, I decided to try to pull Hayden into the dream. The connection had taken place before because I'd called for him while distressed, but I wasn't about to manufacture a nightmare. This time, I hoped simply calling for him would be enough. I wasn't sure how else to go about it.

So I pictured Hayden. His piercing eyes staring into mine. The way his hair ruffled in the wind. How his smile started in his eyes more times than not.

"Hayden?" I called out. "I don't know how this works ... but if you can hear me, I'd like to talk to you. It's Khara," I added, wincing. Surely he'd have known that. But I hadn't known it was him when he was the one calling out to me. Not for a long time.

Of course, I wasn't sure if Hayden would even be asleep. I'd fallen asleep maybe an hour before dinner. Most people would still be awake. Would the message go through if he wasn't asleep? Would it go through at all?

If it didn't work, maybe it was a sign that I wasn't meant to—

"Khara?"

I shot up at the sound of Hayden's voice. One minute, I was alone in the clearing. The next, there he was, standing in front of me.

"Hayden. You're here!" Surprise laced my tone, but I couldn't help it. I really hadn't expected it to work. I'm sure my shock was just as obvious on my face.

His eyes danced with amusement. "You called for me, yes?"

"Well, yes. I just wasn't sure ..."

"How this works," he finished, nodding and sitting cross-legged in front of me. "You said as much. If you haven't figured it out yet, you just call for me."

"That's it?"

"That's it. Well, that, and you have to want it. Deep down."

I decided to file that away to think about later. I had other answers I wanted more.

"Do you know what happened today?"

"No." Hayden's brow furrowed. "Should I?"

I searched his face. Either he was an unbelievable liar and I, a severely poor judge of character, or he really didn't know the attack had occurred. Relief lowered my shoulders. My inclination was to believe he didn't know about it. But could I give him that trust, given what I'd experienced?

I eyed him carefully. "There was an attack."

Hayden stiffened. "An attack?"

I nodded, playing with the hem of my sleeve. "There was this man. A prisoner. One of your rebels, they said. He looked ... crazed."

Hayden's eyes clouded, his expression pained. "What happened?"

"I was visiting Ramsey in his office. He was going to take me somewhere. I never found out where. The elevator opened and there was this man. He was so angry with Ramsey. They were going to fight. Ramsey called him Lachlan—"

"*Lachlan* attacked you?"

"If that was really his name, then yes. At first, he was just interested in Ramsey, but then he saw me. Something changed. I don't know ..."

I stared into the distance as the moment replayed in my head. Suddenly, it was like I was reliving a nightmare. His arm, spinning toward me. The burst of wind whipping me off my feet. The thud of impact as my back hit the glass an instant before it shattered, and I was sure I was going to die. My hands scrambling for purchase. Glass biting my palms. Barely grabbing the edges in time. Blood-slick fingers slipping.

"Khara, it's not real. Come back."

I blinked, Hayden's voice shattering my concentration and bringing me back to myself. When I turned my head, he was kneeling beside me on the glass-covered floor in the Annex. I looked at my hands, but they weren't bloody anymore. Just stitched and wrapped. I lifted my fingertips to my forehead and traced over the raised bruise there.

"Khara ..." Hayden's voice broke. I turned to him, catching the glint of tears in his eyes. He reached out as if to touch me, but stopped, bringing his hand to cover his mouth instead.

"I'm okay," I murmured, pushing to my knees. I didn't want to sit in the glass any longer than I had to.

"Did Lachlan say anything before he did this to you?"

I tried to remember. He'd said something—shouted, more like. But what was it?

"He did, but I'm not sure I can ..."

"Can you go back in your memory? If you revisit it like you did, the parts before he—" Hayden's voice broke as he rubbed his tattoo. "Before he threw you out the window. It should play out for us."

I didn't particularly want to relive it again. But the information seemed important to Hayden, and I saw no reason not to give it. I wanted to understand too.

Closing my eyes, I thought back to Ramsey and me walking to the elevator. The doors opened. Lachlan surprised us. We were blown backward by a gale of wind. Charna raised the alarm. Red lights, a dim but glaring warning. Ramsey and Lachlan facing off. His attention shifting ...

"What are you doing here? You're not supposed to be here!"

The wind whipped underneath me, lifting my feet from the ground, and I went flying. The glass broke. I was going to die, fall to my death—

"Okay. Okay, Khara, come back. It's all right. You're safe."

When I blinked out of the memory, all I could see was the way Hayden's eyes brimmed with tears. As soon as my vision cleared into focus, he wrapped his arms around me and buried his head against my shoulder. The hug was a surprise, but not unwelcome. Revisiting the attack again left me shaken. My heart pounded in my chest, my pulse thrumming fast.

"I'm sorry," he breathed into my shoulder. "I'm so sorry."

"Did you do it?" I asked, my voice broken. "Did you order him to attack us?"

"What? No!"

"Don't lie to me," I begged, swallowing back tears as I gripped his shirt. "Please, I can't—"

"I'm not lying." His hands tightened around me. "I didn't do this, Khara. I wouldn't."

I pulled away and he let me go. As I blinked back tears, he met my gaze. His eyes begged for belief.

"Setting aside that I'd never put you in danger that way, think about our movements. We haven't attacked the Annex or anywhere else in Anluan. Not in two years."

"You've attacked the supply trucks."

"*Outside* the gates. And we don't hurt anyone more than we have to. We distribute the supplies where they're needed throughout the kingdom."

"Why not leave that to Ramsey? Shouldn't he be the one handling that?"

Hayden scoffed. "One would think."

I ignored the slight. "And what about where those supplies are needed inside the city? You make your raids sound so noble, but how much of what you take goes to your rebel camp?"

"Some of it does." He ran a hand over the lightning-like design shaved into his hair. "But not all. Everything we do is thought out. This?" He motioned to the scene around us, shaking his head. "Why would we do this? Why something of this scale, in Ramsey's own building, with a single man half out of his mind? It doesn't make sense. You have to see that."

Nothing made sense to me anymore. That was the problem.

I heard one thing and saw another. Experienced something and had no context for it. How could I trust what I saw when I couldn't trust my own mind?

"You want the city, don't you?" I pressed, staring at the littering of glass and blood—my blood—on the floor. "Isn't that what all this is about? Controlling Anluan?"

"No. It's about doing what's right."

"And who gets to decide that? It's easy to believe your enemy's the one in the wrong. How do you know *you're* doing the right thing?"

Hayden offered me a strained smile as he shrugged. "Facts. Logic. Heart. And because I don't rely solely on myself. I have good people around me, Khara. My father guides me, even when he gives me the authority to move on my own. Our advisors have input on every major decision. I listen to the stories of the people who've run from Anluan since the divide. I look around me and I see the consequences of what Ramsey's done. I know what he's doing, where it will lead, and it's wrong."

I swallowed thickly, shaking my head. "It's so easy for you to judge him."

"It's not easy for me at all. But it's necessary. I won't pretend he and I are on the same side. He's wrong, Khara." His eyes locked with mine, heavy with grief and pain and a certainty that made my throat tighten with tears. "One day, you'll see it too."

I didn't want to think about it anymore. Didn't want to argue with him or explore the uneasy feeling this conversation left in my chest.

Answers. That's what I wanted. We'd gotten too far off track. This was supposed to be about what had happened today. Nothing more.

I cleared my throat. "If you didn't tell that man to attack me, why did he do it?"

Hayden shook his head, rubbing a hand over his mouth. "I can't say for sure."

"But you have a theory."

He nodded.

"Tell me."

"I don't think you understand the severity of what's going on." He dropped his arms and his thumb brushed over his tattoo again. "When Ramsey captures one of mine, he's not kind to them."

I blinked, letting the words sink in. I remembered the fierce anger in Ramsey's eyes as he'd spoken to Lachlan. The hatred.

"What does that mean?" My voice wavered in fear of the answer. The Ramsey I knew, he wouldn't—I didn't even know what I was denying.

Hayden sighed, his eyes going distant. "Ramsey has special officers. They're trained in getting my people to talk. They do whatever it takes to break them. Whatever means are necessary to get the information Ramsey wants is acceptable—to them and to him."

"You're saying Ramsey allows this to happen?"

"I'm saying he's the one who authorizes it. And I wouldn't be surprised if he participates."

I blanched. That couldn't be true. He wouldn't torture someone, especially not for information. I'd never seen anything from Ramsey that violent or cruel. And yet, that look in his eyes today, the way he'd vowed to make Lachlan pay. I couldn't ignore that either. I bit my lip, fighting back tears.

"War is ugly, Khara," Hayden said, the ache of it layered in his eyes. "He may try to keep it from you, but don't think that means it isn't happening."

Silence fell, weighing down my chest.

"My best guess is that Lachlan was able to escape. But by then, whatever they'd done to him ..." Hayden shook his head. "You were right to say he looked crazed. That wasn't the same man I know. When he saw you, I think he wanted to get you away from Ramsey. Make sure you were safe."

"I *was* safe," I argued, but my voice was weak.

Hayden gave me a sad half-smile. "He wouldn't have thought so. To him, it would've looked like you were in trouble. He would've wanted to save you from sharing his fate."

"By throwing me through a window?"

He grimaced. "Like I said, he wasn't himself. Had he been in his right mind, he could've controlled the power, used it to lower you to the ground. He remembers you from before. I really don't believe he wanted to hurt you."

I puzzled over his choice of words. If Lachlan knew me when I was growing up, did he not know the history of what had happened since? Then again, even I didn't know my full history. Maybe it wasn't so unlikely this man could have missed something that felt so obvious to me.

I didn't want to think about it anymore. Was it possible to be tired within a dream? If so, I was swiftly reaching that point. I closed my eyes and thought of the grove again. Being there would help me settle. When I opened my eyes, we were back in the clearing, standing in the center of the grove.

Hayden glanced around, brows raised, before turning to me. "You're getting good at that."

I shrugged, moving to lie down in the grass. "It doesn't feel very challenging now that I've got the hang of it."

He settled on his side at a respectful distance from me. I appreciated the space, though in the real world, I would've made sure there was more. I still didn't want to get too close to him when I was so vulnerable.

I sighed, closing my eyes and breathing deep. I wanted to rest—truly rest. But I still had questions I wanted answers to.

"What's your tattoo mean?" I asked, blinking over at Hayden.

He raised his brows, moving his arm into the grass between us. The stylized *S* with a line through its center faced up. "This? It's my family's symbol."

"Not the rebel symbol? I saw it tagged on a building once."

"It's my family's mark first and foremost." He rubbed a finger across the tattoo. "I guess you could say it's become part of the rebellion, though. The people use it sometimes."

"We rise," I murmured, my vision going distant. When I blinked back, I cast my eyes from Hayden's open stare to his tattoo. After a brief hesitation, I reached for his wrist. "May I?"

He nodded and placed his arm in my hand. I brushed a thumb over the dark ink, and a thrum of magic greeted me as it faintly glowed. Hayden sucked in a breath.

"Sorry." I let my thumb drift away from the tattoo without releasing my hold on his wrist. "I'm not sure why that—"

"It's Isiraden ink," Hayden said softly. "I had it done for my birthday when I came of age. The magical properties amplify my powers. I don't usually feel it when I'm not actively using them, but your connection must have triggered it. You'd be able to feel it anyway."

"I always do," I confessed. "That thrum of magic? It's everywhere."

"It's not like that for the rest of us. Not so evident. That connection is special, a bond only you possess."

"Isiraden magic," I murmured, drifting my fingers over the ink again. This time, we were more prepared for the hum of magic that passed between us. I tilted my head, inspecting the tattoo more closely. It appeared completely ordinary, a simple, well-crafted design. Fascinating. "That's why it glows."

He nodded. "Like calls to like. We believe the gifts originated in the sacred grove, that the magic flowing in our veins was granted to our ancestors from the same source. When I use my powers, it calls to the Isiraden magic in the ink, and in turn, it calls back to me. That's the working theory, at least. There's a lot about the magic we don't know."

"The mysteries of magic," I murmured, my eyes growing heavy. When I blinked them open again, Hayden was staring at our hands. The awareness that I'd been holding his wrist for too long crashed over me in a wave. I released my hold, biting back an apology. I had to be more tired than I'd thought.

Pillowing my arm under my head, I settled on my side. Hayden followed my lead, pulling his arm back to his side without a word. The relief only made me more tired. With a sigh, I closed my eyes.

"Were you asleep?" I asked, my voice thick with weariness.

"When you called for me?"

"Yeah."

He chuckled, the sound soft and warm. "I was."

"Why? It was early."

I'd only been asleep because of the attack. That, and my lack of sleep during the nights lately.

"Well," he said, amused, "because I was tired. I've been sneaking away to this clearing to see one of the most amazing women I've ever met."

I snorted, peeking over at him. "You must be meeting someone else after I leave."

He smirked, but something serious gleamed in his eyes. "I could meet every woman in the world, in this place or any other. Not one of them would be nearly as incredible as you. You, Khara"—he paused, his smile growing as he shook his head—"you're one of a kind. Always have been."

I wasn't sure what to do with that. What was it that made Hayden—and Ramsey, too, for that matter—say such overwhelming things about me? I could never live up to the pedestal they'd put me on. I wasn't anything special. I was damaged, even. What was I missing? What could they possibly see in me that I couldn't see in myself?

"You're thinking too hard."

Hayden's voice was soft, gentle and kind in a way I was growing so fond of. We locked eyes and his gaze held me in place. I didn't know what made my breath halt when he stared at me like that, but it was a constant I wasn't sure I'd ever get used to. The depth in those brown eyes was enough for me to get lost in. Like trying to count the stars, I doubted I'd ever find an end.

I licked my lips. "I always think too hard."

"You don't need to." He cupped the side of my face. If we'd really been in the grove and not conversing in my dream, the wind might've drowned out his words. As it was, they echoed in my heart until they settled, like they were sinking into my bones and melting into my soul.

I closed my eyes, breathing in the cinnamon and cedar that drifted from his shirt even inside my dream. My shoulders lowered. Hayden didn't move his hand from my face, and I found I didn't mind. The warmth was soothing, the comforting touch welcome after such a stressful day.

"I'm so tired," I said on a sigh.

He was frowning when I opened my eyes. "Then you should rest."

He spoke as if it were the simplest thing in the world. *If you're tired, rest. If you're thinking too much, stop.* Could it be that simple? I wished it was. Exhaustion clung to me.

My eyes drifted shut. I felt like I could fall asleep right where I was. Though I was dreaming, I still felt like I wasn't quite resting yet. Maybe conversing with Hayden didn't allow me to reach the level of rest I needed.

"I'm supposed to meet you in the grove tonight," I murmured, not bothering to open my eyes.

"I won't mind if you sleep instead." He smoothed loose strands of my hair back from my face, tucking them behind my ear. His voice was tinged with sadness when he added, "You had a trying day. Let yourself rest. If not for yourself, then for me."

I wasn't sure I should do anything for Hayden. I was engaged to Ramsey. They were on opposite sides of a war whose darkness I was only beginning to see. And yet, this felt like something I could readily do. Not because of Hayden, but for me. It was time to take care of myself and not worry about everyone else.

"Okay," I said, blinking my eyes open and letting them fall shut just as quickly. "Do you need to go for me to fall asleep? Really fall asleep, I mean."

The fondness in his chuckle was warmer than the summer sun. "I'll break the connection. It's easier to rest that way. If one of us is talking, it's harder to stay asleep, and even if I stayed quiet, there's a certain amount of energy you have to expend to maintain the connection. It's subconscious, but it still requires something of you. It's better if I go. I want you to rest well tonight."

I nodded, stifling a yawn. "Should I meet you in the grove for real tomorrow?"

"If you can get away," Hayden said. "I want to try to heal more of the area around the barrier. Maybe even try to better understand what it is." Frustration leaked into his voice as he spoke of it. I was too tired to feel it myself. "The more I learn, the more I can relay to my father and some of the others—see if we can find a way to safely get rid of it for you."

It sounded like a dream come true. In theory, without this barrier, nothing would stop my memories from surfacing. Getting rid of it would fix my problems, and I was prepared to do whatever it took to make that happen.

"I'll get away. Tomorrow night, I'll meet you in the grove."

Hayden's smile grew into a bright grin. "Okay, then. Tomorrow night. I'll be waiting for you."

I nodded, then pulled back and lay down in the grass. I didn't say any more goodbyes or make more promises. I let myself relax into the cool earth, my head lying heavy on the ground. As I exhaled deeply, my heartbeat slowed and my mind settled. The wind danced through the leaves, the gentle rustle blending with the distant chirp of crickets until the sound lulled me to sleep.

As I drifted off, I heard the softest words, carried as if on the wind.

"I'll always wait for you."

55

When Emila arrived at my suite the following morning, she took one look at my face and gasped, flinging her arms around me. I flinched as her hands tightened around the array of bruises stretching across my back. She dropped her arms as if she'd been burned and pulled away. Her face went ashen, her eyes rounding with horror as she got a good look at me. I'd never seen her so shaken.

I knew how terrible I looked. The time I'd spent staring blankly at myself in the mirror had been enough to make me cringe. Weariness left shadows beneath my eyes. A purpling bruise crept into my hairline, keeping company with the single stitch at my brow. And then there were the hidden things—the yellow, blue, and purple bruises stiffening my back and the dark rows of stitches in my palms, covered by bandages. Yesterday had left its mark.

"As soon as I heard what happened, I rushed over here!" Emila cried. "But Gage wouldn't let me in. Said Ramsey dropped you off to rest, that you looked dead on your feet. I wasn't going to listen to him, obviously." She rolled her eyes, though they shone with unshed tears. "But then he was so serious—I don't think I've ever seen Gage be that serious—and I had to leave. I ran into Ramsey later and he said it'd be best to let you be until you called for someone. I figured if anyone had your best interest at heart, it'd be Ramsey. So I stayed away."

She shrugged as though it didn't matter, but pain laced her expression. It had hurt her to listen.

I pulled her back into a hug, softer than the first, but full of the same sense of reassurance. "I'm fine," I said. "I slept almost that entire time. It's okay you weren't here. Really."

Emila sniffed and nodded as she pulled away. Her cheeks glistened in the light, and she quickly wiped away the stream of tears. "Ugh, look at me! All blubbery. I'm a mess." She shook herself and bounced in place a few times. "Whew, okay."

She looked up at me, wiping her face again and wrinkling her nose in distaste. "No more of that. Let's do something fun. Are you up for something fun?"

My lips twitched. "Depends on your definition of fun."

"Would I ever have you do something you didn't want to do?"

"Yes," I said. "Gleefully."

She gasped, her hand flying over her heart before she shrugged with an impish grin. "You're probably right. But not today."

Her words were cheerful, but an undercurrent of seriousness lay behind them. Emila was willing to temper her enthusiasm and take it slow, just for me. The gesture warmed my heart. With a soft smile, I agreed.

Something fun turned out to be a simple trip to the garden. At Emila's encouragement, I gathered some of my art supplies—simple pencils and charcoal to play with while we sat outside. Party planning had been put on hold, at least my part of it. The latest attack bought me another day of rest. I tucked my supplies into a bag, eager to sketch the trees and flowers in the courtyard. I needed to escape my troubles for a while.

Commander North met us in the hall. I glanced around, but saw no other guards. After everything that had happened, I assumed Ramsey would've assigned more guards to watch over me. Especially since Charna had been thrown around yesterday herself. Shouldn't she have been given time to rest?

"Coryndé," Charna greeted us, dipping her head.

She showed no outward signs of pain as she stood at attention. There were no bandages or bruises to be seen. Her uniform was as pristine as ever. Still, my chest tightened.

"Are you all right, Commander?" I asked, studying her carefully. "Yesterday was …"

I went quiet, wrapping my arms around myself. There were no words for what had happened yesterday.

"You don't need to worry." Her eyes swept over me, lingering on the areas marked by the attack. She frowned, her brows dipping as she lingered on the bruise at my hairline. "I'm fit for duty."

"I wasn't asking because I think you're incapable." I gripped the thin sleeve of my sweater, hoping I hadn't offended her. "I asked because you were slammed into the wall. I just want to make sure you're okay."

Emila stepped closer, glancing between the two of us as she adjusted my bag over her shoulder. "You were hurt, Char?"

"I can speak to Ramsey," I offered. "He can assign someone else. You deserve to rest as much as I do."

She sighed, amusement crinkling the corners of her eyes. "Your concern is appreciated, but I'm fine. I assigned myself to be with you today."

I blinked. "Oh."

Emila huffed as she shook her head. "Of course you did."

Charna didn't respond, other than to gesture down the hall. "To the garden?"

"Yes, we're letting this one bask in the sun to her heart's content today," Emila said. "But don't think we can't tell when you're changing the subject."

"I'm not sure what you mean," Charna said, the hint of a smile playing on her lips.

"Right." Emila laughed, knocking Charna's arm before moving down the hall. "Absolutely no idea."

I shook my head, smiling as I moved to follow. Commander North stayed a step behind me. As Emila rounded the corner and moved from sight, something in the air shifted. The question I was holding back circled in my head. Charna's eyes were on me, but she didn't speak.

"Can I ask why?" I blurted, wincing as I glanced at her. When she didn't react, I continued. "Why assign yourself to guard me? You could be resting. And you must have more important things to do."

She chuckled, the sound warm and rich in a way that put me at ease. "Do you remember our conversation yesterday?"

"About why you moved here?"

She hummed. "When you give your life to something, it is rarely convenient. Duty requires sacrifice. It can get messy. Complicated. That doesn't make it any less worthy."

"So you consider this your duty—to stand beside me after what happened yesterday?"

"To a degree." She paused, and I stilled beside her. "It is my honor to protect you, Coryndé. But I'm here today because I want to make something clear to you."

The air thickened with seriousness. "What's that?"

"I want you to know that you have no need to fear the rebels."

No need to fear the rebels? They'd hurt me—broken my body and stolen my memories. Struck fear into my heart when they raided the supply trucks. Kept me and everyone else barricaded inside the city walls for two years. And yesterday—

My mind flashed to the terror of it all. The crazed hatred in that man's eyes. The brutal impact of fierce wind. My back slamming through glass. The way my breath left me and struggled to return. Dangling from the window, terrified that my hands would slip before help arrived.

But then Hayden broke through. His eyes, filled with hurt anytime he was faced with my accusations. The way he'd reacted to seeing the attack play out in my dream. The sense of comfort I felt in his presence. The warmth that came with his healing. The promises he'd made about my safety.

But where was that protection yesterday? It hadn't mattered when it counted. Despite our conversation in my dream last night, I wasn't sure what to do with that.

I blinked back to the present and found Commander North's eyes fixed on me.

"That man is taken care of," she said, holding my gaze with a sincerity that made it impossible to look away. The weight of a vow hung in her gaze as much as in her words. "This place is secure. And I will personally ensure that you are protected. Today and the days beyond. You have my word."

Heat pricked behind my eyes. Throat tight, I nodded. "Thank you, Commander."

The dip of her head felt like it sealed an agreement.

"Hey, what's the holdup?" Emila called, poking her head around the corner.

"Nothing," I said, offering a watery smile to Charna before I turned the corner. She followed, her presence a comforting weight at my back. "We're coming."

We spent hours in a partially shaded section of the garden. Charna kept a watchful eye from a few paces away, despite my invitation for her to join us. Emila sat atop a picnic table, picking apart a bagel and dipping the pieces into a small container of strawberry preserves. She seemed content to cycle through watching me draw, staring up at the sky, and leaning back with her eyes closed. Maybe I wasn't the only one who needed a day to rest.

I didn't pay much attention to what I drew. The sketches came, some faster than others, and I lost myself in the process. It wasn't until Emila leaned over my shoulder that I came back to awareness.

"Who's that?" she asked, pointing at the drawing.

I looked at the page and jolted, my heart speeding in my chest. I'd drawn Hayden lounging in the center of the grove. What could I say to Emila? Did she know what Hayden looked like? Surely she did. He was notorious! The people had to have been warned to watch out for him somehow, and his family had been well known before the divide.

But was he recognizable in my drawing?

I bit my lip as Emila stared, her head tilted toward my journal. I had to tell her something. She was too focused on the sketch for me not to.

My lips trembled as I forced a smile. "I'm not sure, actually. Must just be a picture I had in my head."

Emila didn't move for a long moment, her eyes still locked on the page. Finally, she turned to me and shrugged. "When inspiration strikes, I guess you have no choice but to follow its lead."

I forced myself to laugh, but it sounded strained to my ears. I held my breath as I waited to see if Emila noticed. When she changed the subject, I closed my eyes and let out a breath.

With a trembling hand, I flipped to the next page and forced myself not to rush through the next few sketches. I needed to move past the drawing of Hayden, but I couldn't garner any more attention. As quickly as I dared, I sketched Emila leaning back on the picnic table, a delicate flower tucked behind her ear.

It turned out that Emila was confident in her ability to help me cover up the bruise on my face. That afternoon, she did what she could to erase the evidence of what had happened, however temporarily. It took time, but when she was finished, I leaned close to the mirror, my lips parting in awe.

"Emila, you are incredible," I breathed, tilting my head in a vain attempt to glimpse evidence of the bruising. "Where did you learn to do that?"

She ducked her head as she shrugged and focused on putting the makeup away. I blinked at her in the mirror, unused to seeing her bashful. When she stayed quiet, I turned to face her and raised my brows.

She heaved a sigh, but her smile told me she wasn't actually upset. "My mother is one of the best cosmetologists in the city. I learned from her. She has a shop, not too far from the market."

"The makeup you took as a child ..."

"Was of excellent quality, I can assure you, though the old man didn't appreciate it."

I laughed. "I'd love to visit your mother's shop one day. Have I met her before?"

Emila's eyes flashed with something I couldn't identify. It faded quickly, but a new tension lingered in the air. "No," she said slowly. "I don't think you've had a chance to meet."

"We should change that. One of these days, we'll go visit."

The corners of her mouth lifted, and she nodded, her eyes going soft. "I'd like that."

I smiled back, already looking forward to it. From the few stories I'd heard of Emila's mother, I was bound to love her. I hadn't been to the Eastern District yet, not past the market. There would be plenty for me to re-experience around her mother's shop. Who better to show me than Emila?

"In the meantime," she said, stepping forward and turning me back to face the mirror, "why don't we do something with this hair?"

56

As soon as I opened the door to my suite, Ramsey engulfed me in a hug. His arms held me loosely, mindful of my injuries, but the press of his hands against my sides was firm enough to bring a sense of safety. I sighed into his chest as I hugged him back. He wasn't going to let anything happen to me. Not again.

"I'm sorry it's taken me so long to come see you."

"Ramsey—"

"No, I should have been here first thing this morning." He pulled away, running a hand through his hair. "I had a lot to deal with yesterday. I was up half the night."

It showed. Tension lined his eyes like it did when he nursed a headache. His hair hadn't been as styled as usual even before he'd mussed it with his hands. I frowned, taking in the dark circles beneath his eyes and the wrinkles on his shirt. He looked as frazzled and exhausted today as he had when we parted ways yesterday.

"I had to make sure everything was covered. That you were safe," he added, pacing in front of me. "But then I slept later than I intended and by the time I woke up, demands were being made of me that I couldn't ignore." He stopped pacing, staring down at me intently. "I'm sorry, Khara."

"Please forgive the man already so he can go get some sleep. He's a wreck," Emila chimed in from the couch.

Ramsey blinked. He obviously hadn't registered her presence. "Emila," he greeted, nodding slightly as he straightened.

She waved him off and stood from the couch. "Don't worry about it. I'm not one of your average subjects. You can be a human being around me." As she reached my side, Emila gave my wrist a gentle squeeze. "I'm going to go, give you guys some time. Send for me if you need anything, okay?"

I nodded. "I will. Thank you."

"Sovereign." She dipped her head to Ramsey with a smirk. "Do us all a favor and get some sleep, yeah?"

Ramsey huffed a weary laugh, rubbing a hand down his face. "I think that's a good idea."

"Mine always are."

With that, Emila breezed from the room.

As the door shut behind her, Ramsey shook his head. "How'd we get lucky enough to have her around?"

"You're asking the wrong girl," I teased. "I wish I knew."

Ramsey's smile dimmed. "You could ask her, you know. I'm sure she'd love to regale you with the tale of how you met and became fast friends."

She would, and I knew it. It wasn't that I didn't want to know. I hadn't asked because every time I had to, it chipped away at me. I had all these people in my life, people who loved and cared for me, and I'd forgotten them. It wasn't fair—to me or to them.

So I'd done what I had to: completely ignored the problem for as long as possible. Asking how we became friends would make the lack of those memories too real. Besides, with any luck, I'd remember soon. Hayden's plan could bring all my memories back, and then I wouldn't need to ask anyone where I'd met them or how we'd formed our relationship. I'd just know.

I looked up, taking in Ramsey's bloodshot eyes and the red rim that spoke of a sleepless night, and frowned. Had he slept at all?

"You really do need to get some rest," I murmured, tracing the dark circle under his eye with my thumb.

"I know." He captured my hand with his, his thumb brushing back and forth against my skin. "But I needed to see you. Needed to know you were all right."

"I am." My stomach fluttered at his concern, but it didn't ease the pang in my heart at his appearance. "There's some bruising on my back, and of course, on my forehead."

His brow furrowed as he searched my face. "I don't see—"

"Emila worked her magic on me."

Ramsey's head tilted as he blinked. "What?"

"Her talent with makeup? Her mother is a cosmetologist and Emila picked up the craft. We're going to visit her mother's shop soon, I think." I gestured to my face. "Emila hid the bruise for me. I needed to make sure we could cover it for the party."

"Of course." Ramsey pressed a kiss at my hairline. "Forgive me, Khara. My mind is addled. I'll feel better once I've slept."

"You could go now, you know," I offered lightly. I didn't want to push him, but he needed to know I'd be okay before he'd leave. I could give him that. "I can fend for myself for dinner or call Emila back. You should rest."

"What if I call for dinner to be brought here? We can eat together and then I promise, I'll go straight to bed."

Spending time with me was important to him. I understood the feeling. After this last attack, I felt raw and vulnerable. Unsettled. It had helped to sleep. And to be near Hayden.

I froze, my brows pinching. Shouldn't I have felt unsettled until now, when I was with Ramsey?

"You can stay," I said, forcing the thought away. I took Ramsey's hand and led him to the couch. After pressing him onto the cushions, I tossed my softest throw blanket over his lap. "I'll ask the guard to have someone deliver our food. We can sit together while we wait."

Within the hour, I'd eaten a warm meal on the couch while pressed against Ramsey's side. He slumped into the cushions, slowly chewing as he stared into space. He didn't speak for a long time, content with the silence and my head resting on his shoulder. On another day, I might've let him drift off and spend the night. But if I was going to leave to see Hayden, Ramsey couldn't stay.

My heart clenched as I squeezed my eyes shut. It did nothing to block out the truth. I was a terrible fiancée.

"Ramsey?"

"Hmm?"

"You should go upstairs, sleep in your own bed. You won't rest well like this."

He shifted but didn't get up. "That's debatable." The sleep coating his words did nothing to temper the smile in his voice. "I'd like to think I'd sleep rather well with you."

Heat filled my cheeks, and I bit my lip, unsure of what to say. Luckily, I didn't have to decide.

Ramsey sighed heavily, stretching his legs and moving his head from where it rested on top of my own. "But you're right. I should sleep in my own bed."

As I shifted away from Ramsey, he straightened and rubbed a hand down his face. "I'll be going then. Breakfast tomorrow? I'll come walk with you, like we used to before everything around here went to madness."

"Not too early?" The last thing I needed was to spend all night with Hayden and be caught coming home by Ramsey. Or miss out on sleep entirely due to an early breakfast. "You need rest, and truthfully, so do I."

"Of course," he said. "We'll make it more of a brunch. I'll come by midmorning."

I smiled, my shoulders loosening. "I'll be ready."

He leaned forward, caressing my cheek as his eyes bored into mine. They traveled to my lips, then back to my eyes. "You're the most important thing to me, Khara," he said, voice low and serious. "The most important thing."

He inched closer, bringing his lips to mine. I wasn't used to kissing Ramsey yet. My hands fluttered uselessly in my lap while my heart sped in my chest.

I didn't remember much about kissing. The only experiences I could recall were my very recent ones with Ramsey. But I knew what kissing him felt like—fierce passion, the kind of love that clung to your side and claimed you as its own. He was both soft and insistent, urgent and unhurried.

I didn't remember much about kissing, but I knew this: Ramsey was very good at it.

When he pulled away, he lingered before my lips, each exhale warm against my face. I wasn't sure I'd ever catch my breath, but I made a noble attempt.

"I don't want to go," he whispered.

The admission sent goosebumps flitting across my skin. I found myself grasping a hand in his shirt and stealing another kiss, moving the other to curl around his neck.

He deepened the kiss, and for long, languid moments, all I knew was Ramsey. His lips on mine. The brush of his tongue. His hands skimming up and down my back. I'd never felt so close to a person before.

In an instant, it became overwhelming. I tensed and pulled away. At first, Ramsey followed, chasing my lips until he noticed I wasn't responding. He leaned back, running his hand from my hair to my cheek.

"Are you all right?" His eyes were dark, but his desire was quickly being overshadowed by concern.

"I'm fine. That was ..." I trailed off, lost for words as I tried to catch my breath. "I just got a little overwhelmed."

Ramsey grinned. "I'll take that as a compliment."

I huffed a laugh, relieved he wasn't disappointed in me. "You should. You should also go get some sleep."

He groaned, but his smile didn't dim as he threw his head against the back of the couch. Mischief lit his eyes as he peered over at me. "If that was my good-night kiss, I think I'll sleep rather well."

"Go rest, Ramsey," I said, biting back a grin. "You're cracking up, and that's no way to rule a kingdom."

He laughed warmly. "You're right, as always."

Heaving a sigh, he stood and reached for my hand. With our fingers laced together, we made our way to the door.

"I'll come get you in the morning," he said, lifting my hand to his lips. "Rest well, Khara."

I bid him good night as he slipped out, then watched until he disappeared around the corner. When I shut the door, I leaned against it and tilted my head toward the ceiling. My fingers brushed across my lips.

I didn't remember much about kissing, but I was certain this was one I wouldn't soon forget.

57

Leaving to meet Hayden after kissing Ramsey felt like more of a betrayal than usual. Guilt churned in my gut as I made my way out of Anluan, but I stuffed it down. I needed to get my memory back. This was how I had to do it. In the end, everything would be better for it, including my relationship with Ramsey.

At least, that's what I told myself as I shimmied through the tunnel and made my way into the forest.

When I arrived at the grove, Hayden was waiting for me, just like he'd promised. As soon as he saw me, he leapt to his feet. His eyes roamed over my body, lingering on my forehead as if trying to catalog every mark from the previous day's attack.

"You made it," he said. "How are you feeling?"

My fingers drifted over the bruise at my hairline. "It doesn't hurt much."

"I hate that you're in pain at all." He stepped closer, raising his hand. "I could heal it for you."

"You can't. Ramsey would notice."

A dip formed between his brows. "Right."

Silence settled over us like the humidity in the air, heavy and uncomfortable. I cleared my throat, fiddling with the bottom edge of my thin sweater, then quickly changed the subject.

"I slept for a long time after you left my dream, and woke up feeling better than I have in days. I needed the rest."

"Good." A fond spark lit in his eyes as he studied me again. "It looks like it helped. Your eyes are bright. You look alive."

Was that from sleep, or from kissing Ramsey so fully? Heat rose to my cheeks. I didn't want to think about Hayden being able to tell what Ramsey and I had been up to. "What did you want to try first tonight?"

Hayden's expression fell, but he smiled again so quickly I wondered if I'd imagined it. "I'd like to try to feel out the wall in your mind again. I know it has the potential to cause you pain, but I really think that's what will be most helpful. We need to figure out what was done to you in order to fix it."

I frowned, but nodded. Pain was no stranger to me. I could handle it. "I'll do whatever you need me to."

He tilted his head. "You'd do whatever I ask?"

"Within reason," I said slowly, fully aware of who I was speaking to. "Why? What else do you want me to do?"

"Nothing." The look in his eyes was indecipherable. "You just keep surprising me, is all."

I could tell he wanted to move on, so I let it go. If he wanted something from me, he could ask later. If not, well, I supposed Hayden was entitled to keeping some things to himself too.

We spent the first hour in silence. Hayden sat in front of me, close enough to touch, as I focused on breathing deeply. When he placed his fingers to my temples, the familiar rush of warmth and the gentle tingling path wove themselves through my mind. At times, the odd knitting sensation made itself known again—a sign Hayden's power had found something to heal.

After a while, he shifted. "I'm going to press in here. I think I might've found a crack in whatever this barrier is. Hang on, okay? If it gets to be too much, tell me."

I nodded slightly, bracing myself. The moment I exhaled again, the power Hayden emitted changed despite the pressure of his fingertips remaining steady. The tingling grew to a pulse that bounced against the barrier.

Something was different this time. Past the discomfort and pain of the attempt, a pathway of healing energy brought warmth into my head. Like a tiny hole existed in whatever barrier was in my mind and a wisp of power had broken through.

It was progress. And that, more than any amount of pain, made me want to cry.

"Are you okay?" Hayden asked, voice strained.

"Fine," I said hoarsely.

"You're crying."

I didn't care. I barely felt the wetness on my cheeks. These tears weren't born of pain, and for that alone, I'd embrace them. These were tears of hope, of relief, of healing. What we were doing was working; I could feel it. And it was the greatest thing I'd experienced in weeks.

While Hayden pushed the healing power for a moment more, I allowed my tears to fall unhindered. They rolled down my chin and dripped onto my shirt. When he let go, I exhaled before opening my eyes.

He stared, searching me intently. I didn't feel much pain. It had started to fade as soon as Hayden had finished whatever he'd been doing. There was weariness, that same tired feeling I'd experienced the last time he'd gone searching for things to heal inside my head, but that was it. Otherwise, I felt fine.

Hayden must have seen it reflected in my face. He deflated, rubbing a hand over his eyes before straightening. "You're okay? Really?"

I nodded, sniffing and moving to wipe my eyes. "It felt different this time, but it wasn't too painful."

"Different how?"

"It was like something made it through the barrier." My smile grew with my excitement. "It was like even when the pain hit, I knew power was getting through the wall of whatever's in my head."

"Then it's working. What we're doing here is actually working."

He sounded as relieved as I felt. And when Hayden let himself fall back into the grass, not even bothering to uncross his legs, I let myself embrace the notion that maybe the two of us really were in this together. Maybe he wanted me to have my memories back as badly as I wanted them for myself. Maybe he wanted me to have them back *because* of how badly I wanted them.

"Thank you." I couldn't keep the words back any more than I could stop the next round of tears. "I don't know why you'd—" I cut myself off, shaking my head. "Just—thank you, Hayden. I need this. I need it so much."

A sob broke loose, and I buried my face in my hands. Having this hope when everything felt uncertain on the good days and lost on the bad—it was more than I could have asked for. Like a dream overtaking a nightmare.

"Hey, it's okay." Hayden's voice was soft as a blanket and just as comforting as he wound his arms around me. They were warm—gentle and kind in a way that fit how he'd approached me from the start.

My tears fell harder.

I didn't understand how someone so compassionate could be the enemy. I didn't understand what had happened between him and Ramsey. How could two people who each looked after me with such care be the cause of a kingdom-wide war?

Hayden rubbed soothing circles on my back as I cried into his chest, surrendering myself to the moment. There were no enemies. No war to think of or sides to choose. I let myself simply exist—breathing, crying, and, in a way I never would've anticipated, healing.

When I'd shed all my tears, I didn't move. I let Hayden hold me. Maybe it was wrong. He wasn't my fiancé. I wasn't even entirely sure he was my friend, though I was beginning to believe he had been at one point. But tonight, he'd been as much of a friend to me as anyone. For once, this felt right. I wanted to stay.

"You're going to be okay," he said, his hand moving gently through my hair. "I will do everything"—his voice caught, choked by tears as his arm tightened around me—"*everything*, Khara, to fix this for you. I won't give up. Not if you do, not if everyone else does. I won't ever give up. Not on you."

I thought I'd spent all my tears, but my next gasping breath shook my chest. Before I knew it, I was crying again. Hayden held me through it all. I couldn't fathom why he'd make so bold a promise to me. Didn't see how I deserved the level of dedication he gave me. But if he was so willing to give it, I let myself consider that maybe I deserved more than I thought.

58

WE SPENT HOURS IN the clearing, trying to nudge Hayden's healing power through the barrier. A few attempts felt like something shifted and broke through. Most ended with me in pain, cradling my head as tears streamed from my eyes.

Hayden wanted to stop every time it happened, but I refused to allow more than a short break. We were making progress, and I wasn't about to slow us down because I couldn't handle a little pain. Any time I expressed those thoughts, Hayden glared at me. His frown was the most put-out expression I'd ever seen, but I didn't let it change my mind.

Finally, after another mishap left me gasping for breath and sick with dizziness, we called it a night. I wasn't sure I could take anymore, and I could see that Hayden wouldn't have tried again, even if I pushed. We had both reached our limit.

"What do you need?" he asked, laying a hand on my arm.

I shook my head, too focused on quelling the growing nausea to answer. I hadn't felt this bad in a long time.

"I'm going to try to heal the symptoms," Hayden said, determination lining every word. "Hang on."

Part of me wanted to beg him to do it. Another wanted to beg him not to. What if he just made it worse? But I couldn't voice either, and Hayden moved a careful hand to my forehead.

For a few moments, we stayed there—him with a palm pressed to my forehead, me curled in a ball on the grass. Then I felt the first blessed tendrils of relief. The warmth swept through me, moving to fill my entire body before it faded into the residual soft tingling I was getting so used to.

I chanced a deeper breath. No headache; no dizziness. My lips curved into a tired smile as I shifted my eyes to Hayden. "It worked."

He slumped backward, rubbing his forehead. Settling into the grass again, he pulled his knees to his chest and rested his head on them. "Good."

I frowned at the exhaustion thickening his voice. "Hayden?"

"Just a side effect."

I jolted upright in alarm. He hadn't mentioned anything about side effects before. "What side effect?"

He reached out to stop me. "Khara, don't move too fast—"

I batted his hand away, narrowing my eyes at him. "*What side effect?*"

He sighed, pinching the bridge of his nose. "The healing powers aren't my natural ability. They're inherited, and only partially at that. Until I have them fully, I'm limited in ways my father isn't. That includes the amount of energy I can expend at a time."

"Which you went over tonight because I pushed you to keep going." A lead weight dropped in my stomach. This was my fault. "I'm sorry. I didn't—"

"It's not on you. I knew what I was doing."

"Then why didn't you say something? Or just stop?"

"You needed this." He shrugged, weariness unable to hide his sincerity. "I want you to have everything you need."

My chest constricted. "I never know what to say when you talk like that."

"That's okay." Hayden huffed a soft laugh. "You never really have."

I snorted. At least I was consistent.

Hayden insisted on escorting me back to the city. I didn't bother arguing. Despite his condition, I knew I wouldn't sway him. My eyes lingered on him as we walked, mindful of his slower stride and heavier breaths. Neither of us spoke, but the silence was just as comfortable as if we had. I even found myself enjoying the hike as I trailed my hands against the leaves hanging over the footpath.

"How long does it take you to feel well again when you're like this?" I asked at the edge of the forest.

"It depends," he hedged. "Sometimes only a few minutes."

I wasn't about to let him avoid the question, not when the answer directly affected me. Brows raised, I crossed my arms. "And times like tonight?"

Hayden frowned and stayed silent. I raised my chin, holding his gaze. I wasn't going to move until he told me. He sighed. "Probably a full day. Maybe two."

My jaw dropped. *Two days?*

"We're not doing that again. I don't care if I'm on the verge of getting everything back. You're not going to drain yourself to fix me." His mouth formed a thin line and I scowled. "I mean it, Hayden! We're not doing this to you again."

He sighed and ran a rough hand over his face. "I won't let it get this bad again. But I don't regret it, Khara. I'd give everything I have if it means you're—" He broke off, shaking his head as he looked away. "I'd let this get far worse for you. That won't change."

I didn't like it, but he'd made up his mind. He wouldn't deplete himself on my account during our sessions. For now, that was all I could hope for.

"Thank you," I said, eyeing the raised roots on the ground, my arms still folded tightly against my chest.

"You're welcome." He heaved another sigh. "I appreciate you trying to look out for me."

I smirked, chancing a glance at him through my lashes. His eyes lightened with amusement, his lips twitching until we both fell into gentle laughter.

"I'm not coming back tomorrow night," I said when our laughter subsided.

He furrowed his brow. "But I thought—"

"You just told me it would take you at least a day to recover. We're not doing this tomorrow night. I'll come back the night after."

He pursed his lips, his thumb running over his tattoo again. "I don't suppose you'd come back anyway …?"

I bit my lip. It was hard enough to sneak out for this healing experiment. To take the risk just to spend time with him felt like tempting fate. "I don't think that's a good idea."

He shook his head, smiling sadly as he shoved his hands into the pockets of his jacket. "I shouldn't have asked. I understand."

I wasn't sure he did, but decided to take him at his word. "So, two nights from now?"

"I'll be waiting for you."

"You always are," I said, the words fonder than I expected.

I thought of Hayden's answering grin the whole way to my suite.

59

I HAD KNOWN IT would be tough to see Hayden and then meet Ramsey for breakfast, but even a midmorning meal seemed like a lot of effort for my weary body as I forced myself from my bed.

I'd dreamed of strange snippets throughout the night. None of it made much sense, but I scribbled what I could remember into my journal. The ghost of a hand in mine. The flutter of nerves in my belly. Whispers of conversation carried on the wind, so quiet I could only pick up a word or two before the voices fell away. A pounding in my chest and the urge to run. Slamming into someone whose arms wrapped around me. The rise of a relief so fierce it moved me to tears.

None of it felt complete, like a full memory. They were strands of thread, knotted together in a messy heap that I needed to untangle in order to make sense of them. If any sense *could* be made of them.

I'd barely finished dressing when Ramsey knocked on the door. When I opened it, Gage had gone and Cethin stood in his place. I frowned, my stomach churning.

Maybe it wasn't fair of me to react that way. Cethin's actions, while harsh at times, were driven by his dedication to his duties. His loyalty didn't deserve the dislike that curled in my stomach. Yet the nagging feeling remained. I tried to shove it aside as I greeted him while Ramsey slipped inside my suite. But I couldn't help being relieved when the door closed and put distance between us again.

I turned to Ramsey and took him in. His eyes were brighter, no longer accented in red. The dark circles had faded. His tailored suit was crisp, the black fabric a thoughtful complement to the warm brown of his skin. His hair was once again parted just so. I smiled. He looked every bit the Sovereign of Anluan.

"You look better."

"I feel it too." He flashed me a devilish grin. "Though I will say, I'm tempted to work through the night more often if it means a send-off like the one you gave me last night."

The kiss. My chest blazed and the heat spread to my face. I pressed a hand to my cheek as I stared down at the hardwood. My hair fell in a curtain, covering my face.

Ramsey chuckled. My stomach fluttered as he moved closer and gently tilted my face up. "There's no reason to hide. We did nothing wrong."

I knew that. And yet, it felt strange to be open with him like this. I'd enjoyed our kiss—oh, had I enjoyed it—but hearing Ramsey tell me how much he desired me, while flattering, still made me a little uncomfortable.

"I know." I closed my eyes, searching for the right words. "I just—"

"You're not used to it yet."

It was exactly that. My body loosened as I nodded. Ramsey took my hands in his, brushing a thumb across my skin.

His brows dipped as his face fell. "Was I overeager? I didn't mean to—"

"Oh, Ramsey, no. That's not—" I sighed, ducking my head and forcing myself to speak. "I very much enjoyed last night."

All doubt vanished from Ramsey's face. His smile grew into a blinding grin as he squeezed my hands. "That's all I needed to hear."

Brunch with Ramsey was worth waking up for. He'd spoken to the staff, and they'd prepared a spread fit for royalty. Waffles were piled high on a serving tray with fresh cream and an assortment of juicy berries on the side. Crispy bacon and miniature quiches in a variety of flavors rounded out the meal. It was heavenly.

With a fresh mug of tea warming my hands, I listened to Ramsey tell lighthearted stories of guard training days gone awry and childhood adventures. I didn't have much to contribute by way of stories, but I shared one of my small adventures with Emila. It wasn't overly exciting and likely something he was already aware of. Still, Ramsey leaned forward in his seat, head tilted and bright eyes fixed on me as he took in my every word.

"I'm glad you have each other," he said as he laced our fingers together on the table. "She's the kind of friend I wish we'd both had when we were young."

"At least we had each other," I said, trailing my thumb against the side of his finger. "Besides, from what she's told me, the three of us would've ended up in far too much trouble."

He laughed. The bright sound filled my chest with warmth. This was the side of Ramsey I loved to see—open and happy, without the weight of ruling Anluan and fighting rebels pressing down on him.

"I'd imagine that's true." He grinned, wide and charming in a way that made my heart skip a beat. "Anluan might not have survived us."

"I don't know," I said, glancing from our laced hands to his eyes. "I think maybe Anluan could survive anything. We're still here, aren't we? Despite everything."

Ramsey's face softened. He turned his attention to our hands, brushing a finger back and forth over the top of my engagement ring.

"We're still here," he said finally, raising his eyes to mine. My breath caught at the smoldering intensity of his stare. "Nothing could keep me from you, Khara. Not in Anluan. Not outside of it. I'll always be here."

I swallowed thickly as he raised my hand and pressed a kiss to my knuckles. I wasn't sure what to do or say. That declaration wasn't one I could match yet.

Affection for Ramsey had made its home deep in my heart, but I wasn't ready to categorize it as love. I didn't remember what love felt like, wasn't sure how to claim it again. Ramsey hadn't said he loved me yet either. Not out loud anyway. I wasn't sure whether to be relieved or concerned by that.

We danced around each other, inching close one moment and sliding away the next. Ramsey seemed to know every step while I struggled to keep the rhythm, afraid to be drawn too close but terrified of pushing him away. We tried to blend the past I couldn't remember with who we were in the present and a plan for the future that drew closer with each passing day.

I had no doubt Ramsey would bind himself to me tomorrow if he could. Despite my fondness for him, I wasn't ready to do the same.

And he understood—sometimes more than I did. He waited for me, let us rebuild what we'd once had while assuring me of how much he cared. Ramsey's devoted attention made my stomach churn with guilt. I didn't deserve his love. The night before, I'd kissed him—passionately and without hesitation—and then gone off to meet his sworn enemy. I cared about him, and yet, I kept sabotaging our relationship.

Whenever I tried to reconcile my choices, I always came away feeling worse.

Ramsey smiled as he released my hand. I tried to return it, hoping the tightness pinching my face wasn't as obvious as it felt while I reached for my cup. He would be devastated if he knew what I'd done. What I was *doing*.

As Ramsey launched into another story, I swallowed a mouthful of tea and vowed to never let him find out.

The rest of the day was full of decision-making. Emila found us as we finished our meal and made quick work of pulling us along as she gushed over party details.

Which color did we want for the table linens? Did we want to have cake or miniature dessert trifles? Would we like red floral designs or a combination of colors?

While it wasn't my favorite way to spend a day, I had to admit it was a decent one. Time flew as we looked over Emila's ideas, signing off on them or making changes. With Ramsey beside me, I found myself relaxing into the process. It didn't feel as overwhelming when he helped make decisions and bantered with Emila. It was even kind of fun.

We'd almost finished when Ramsey was called away to attend to urgent business. He apologized profusely, but I waved him off. I'd grown used to the interruptions and could hardly fault him for handling his duties as Sovereign over planning our engagement gala. Emila and I were more than capable of handling the rest of the arrangements on our own.

Ramsey kissed me goodbye, more deeply than usual, before leaving with a parting grin.

Emila smirked, her eyes sparkling with amusement.

Heat rose in my cheeks. "Don't say it."

She grinned down at her plans. "I wasn't going to say a word."

60

THE FLASHLIGHT WAS MISSING from the tunnel when I snuck out to see Hayden the following night. Frowning in the dust, I searched blindly with my hands. Nothing.

I sighed, resigning myself to using the little natural light available. Hayden would be able to call some light using his powers when I reached the grove. At least, I thought he would be able to. Shaking myself, I blinked past the start of a headache and crawled through the dark.

A warm breeze brought instant relief from the musty tunnel air. Taking a deep breath, I glanced around and pulled the wall covering back into place.

Behind me, a branch snapped.

I froze. Every sound—from my shaky breaths to the whisper of wind in the leaves—felt too loud as I strained to listen for further signs of movement behind me. When I couldn't make anything out, I slowly turned and scanned the shadowy forest. It was too dark to see much, but chills rose at the back of my neck. Someone was out there. I could feel their eyes on me.

Turning back wasn't an option. I needed to see Hayden, needed to keep working on regaining my memories. I had to hope I could make it past whoever or whatever was lingering in the forest. If I could get to Hayden, he would help me.

Steeling myself, I broke into a run.

The darkness did me no favors. I missed the pathway and ended up crashing through the brush, alerting anyone nearby to my presence. My heart hammered, but I didn't stop. Not when branches scratched my cheeks and whipped against my arms. Not when a set of pounding feet thudded behind me. Not when a hissed whisper called out and the steps multiplied.

Heat pricked my eyes. Were they rebels or guards? Did it matter? If they caught me, I'd never know if the healing experiment would work. I wouldn't be able to meet Hayden anymore.

Hayden. I was leading them straight to him.

The realization stole my breath. My concentration fell and I did with it, tripping over a fallen limb and crashing onto my knees. My hands landed in the brush, where something gouged my palm. I cried out, the sound muffled against the dirt.

That was all it took for them to catch up with me.

Someone skidded to a stop, nearly slipping on the mossy earth. "Get up. Slowly."

My hands stung, and I bit my lip against the pain and growing fear as I pushed myself to my knees. The tip of a blade pressed into my back.

"Don't try anything."

I nodded, the movement jerky, but it was enough. The blade moved from my back as I carefully stood.

"Face me."

I turned, my heart pounding so fast it hurt. The man didn't have a flashlight, but what little I could make out of his clothing didn't look like a guard uniform. A rebel, then. Would he know who I was? I couldn't count on him to be like Hayden. What happened in the Annex with Lachlan still plagued my mind.

The man squinted at me, tilting his head before whistling. "Over here! Bring the light."

A whistle sounded twice in return from opposite directions. At least two others were coming. A knot formed in my chest. No. I wouldn't let them hurt me.

My breath came in a shaky inhale and the man raised his hands. The blade glinted in the moonlight. "Relax, all right? We won't hurt you unless you make us."

A bitter laugh caught in my throat. Had I made them attack me the first time? Was it my fault that Lachlan threw me out a window?

Two beams of light bounced across the forest floor, accompanied by rustling leaves. They were too close. I had to escape.

I needed Hayden.

The man shuffled closer as the flashlights behind him neared and began to point up from the ground. His eyes widened a fraction, just before I whipped

my hand out and jabbed the base of his throat. He grasped for his neck, dropping
the blade as he doubled over.

A beam of light threatened to blind me as it swept over my face. I didn't
hesitate. A hissed curse sounded from too close behind me. Blinking back spots,
I turned and ran.

"Wait!"

I didn't stop at the woman's voice.

A man groaned just after. "He's going to roast us for this." Louder, he called
out, "Please, we didn't mean to—!"

I tuned out their cries as I crashed through the undergrowth. I wouldn't stop
until I made it to Hayden in the grove.

There was nothing stealthy or cautious about my arrival. All I cared about was
reaching Hayden. He'd promised to protect me, and I would hold him to it. After
what happened last time, he owed me that much.

Hayden was pacing when I crashed into the clearing. I barely paused when he
whipped toward me, his arm raised and a blue-white glow coming from his tattoo.
Feet from him, I slid to a stop and managed a breathy call of his name. He closed
the distance between us, his arm falling to my back as I bent to catch my breath.

"What is it?" He crouched to look at my face, his frown deepening as he took
in the sweat on my brow and the way I sucked in gasping breaths. His voice
hardened. "What happened?"

"Led them here," I said as I lowered myself to my knees in the grass. "Didn't
know what else to do."

He barely had time to tense before cracks and rustling sounded behind us.
Hayden whirled, lightning sparking around his arm as he raised his hand toward
the opening.

"Whoa! Sovereigno, it's us. It's us!"

"*Callum?*"

"Yes!"

Hayden lowered his arm slightly, glancing at me before turning back to the
rebels as they entered the clearing. The man I'd attacked lagged behind the other

two, still holding his throat with one hand, but the blade was gone. The others—a middle-aged man with a full beard and a woman wearing a long braid over her shoulder—stood with their hands raised in surrender, their flashlights pointing up.

I turned to face them fully, still panting as I clenched a fist in the grass. My hands stung with the movement, but the pain distracted me from the jittery anxiety coursing through my veins.

Hayden would handle this. I'd be fine.

"You chased her here?" The incredulity in Hayden's voice was apparent, as was the hint of anger. His eyes narrowed as they fell on the man with his hand to his throat. "What did you do?"

He opened his mouth to speak, despite the pain it would no doubt cause. The woman put a hand on his chest to stop him.

"She came out of the tunnel as we were heading back," she said calmly. "We'd already turned the lights off. We couldn't see her clearly."

The bearded man—Callum—nodded. "When she ran, we followed. Niko caught up to her first."

My hands trembled. I did my best to hide them in the grass. "And held a blade to my back."

"What?" Hayden barked, taking a step in front of me.

"Didn't know it was you," Niko rasped, doing his best to meet my gaze around Hayden's body. "I'd never—"

"We had to find out who you were," the woman said, her eyes steady on me before she looked to Hayden.

He sighed, running a hand over the lightning design shaved into the side of his head. "I take it you didn't explain yourselves?"

"Didn't have time," Callum said, smirking as he stroked his beard. "Coryndé got to Niko first and bolted before we got there."

His amusement rankled. I forced myself to stand, crossing my arms. "My last unexpected encounter with a rebel didn't end well. Excuse me for being more proactive about my safety after being thrown through a tower window."

A heavy silence fell over the clearing. The pain on their sobered faces almost made me feel bad for snapping. But I was still too keyed up, the lingering traces of fear having not yet faded. I didn't try to fill the quiet.

"We're sorry," the woman said after a moment. "Truly. We would never hurt you, Coryndé. We had to be sure."

I frowned. "Be sure of *what*?"

"Whenever we run into someone leaving the city, we have to find out who they are and what they want," Hayden said. His eyes remained fixed on his people.

"Not everyone who comes out here is on our side," the woman explained. "We ask questions to find out how to handle the situation."

"And if you don't like their answers?" I asked sharply, remembering what Emila had told me. Those who went beyond the gates didn't come back.

The woman shared a shocked look with the others. They eyed me warily, as if they weren't sure how to answer.

Hayden softened, letting his arms fall to his sides as he turned to me. "We take them in, if they're looking for us."

How often did that happen? What would make citizens of Anluan want to leave and find the rebels to begin with?

"And if they aren't?" I pressed.

"Then we find out what they *are* looking for. People don't leave the city without reason. It's a heavily punished crime if you're caught."

"So why would they risk it?"

Hayden smiled sadly. "Why do you? There's something out here that's worth the risk."

I swallowed thickly. That was something I could understand. Some things wouldn't leave you alone until you heeded their call.

"Some struggle to feed their families in Anluan. Some are afraid to stay. Some intend to join family living in one of the other Diamond Kingdoms. We do our best to help them if they want us to." Hayden shot a pointed look toward the trio across from us. "Usually, we're pretty good at it."

"Apologies, Sovereigno," rasped Niko. He dipped his head, first to Hayden, then to me. "Forgive me, Coryndé. It wasn't my intention to hurt or scare you."

I glanced at Hayden, who sighed, but nodded at the man. His tattoo still held a faint glow, but he didn't seem worried. Frustrated, maybe. But he showed no signs of concern about me being in danger.

My eyes trailed over both men before landing back on the woman. They all seemed sincere, albeit a bit sheepish. Despite myself, I softened.

"Apology accepted." I flicked my eyes to the man's neck and hesitated. "Sorry about your throat."

Hayden ducked his head, fighting to hide a smile behind his raised fist.

To my surprise, Niko grinned. The expression only looked a little pained. "Don't be. It was a good hit."

The woman smirked. "We'd expect nothing less."

I tilted my head, confused, but when I glanced at Hayden, he just shook his head.

"Let me heal it," he said, gesturing Niko forward. "Then you should head back."

Niko tried to wave him off, but when the woman elbowed him in the side, he relented. He approached Hayden without fear, smiling at me as Hayden reached a hand to the side of his neck. There was no visible sign of the healing, but Niko's shoulders relaxed after a moment. When Hayden released him, Niko cleared his throat, then beamed.

"Good as new. Thank you, Sovereigno."

"Of course." Hayden clapped him on the arm. His voice went firm, ringing with more command than I'd ever heard as he leaned closer. "But the next time you draw a knife on her, you'll be left to deal with the consequences on your own. Are we clear?"

I blinked. While his tone lacked any threat, the intensity of his words surprised me. Niko's bark of laughter surprised me even more.

"Clear as day. It'd be nothing less than what I'd deserve. You've nothing to worry about from me."

The others inclined their heads in agreement. They didn't seem to think anything of the exchange.

"Good." Hayden offered them a wry smile as he stepped back and ran his hand against one side of his undercut. He gestured toward the path that would lead back to the city. "You should get back. Move forward as we discussed."

The woman's gaze lingered on my face, and I tried not to fidget beneath her searching eyes. She turned to Hayden. "You're sure you don't want to—"

"Nothing's changed," he cut in. "You know what to do."

The group glanced at me, their faces sober. "Yes, Sovereigno."

They moved to leave, and I realized I hadn't even caught the woman's name. It seemed rude not to ask, but the less identifying information I had about them, the less it felt like a lie to keep things to myself. So I bit my tongue against the question as she dipped her head and left.

"Coryndé, a pleasure as always," Callum said as he swept his fist over his heart and dipped his head. His eyes sparkled in a way that made my lips twitch despite myself.

"Get out of here, Callum," Hayden sighed, but amusement laced his tone. "And be careful. No unnecessary risks."

Callum raised a brow. "Same to you, Sovereigno."

61

WHEN THEY'D GONE, HAYDEN deflated, his shoulders rounding forward. He frowned at the grass for a long moment as if he'd forgotten I was there, clenching and unclenching his hands at his sides. I wanted to ask about what *moving forward* entailed, wanted to make sure the rebel plans weren't something that would hurt anyone in Anluan. But Hayden spoke as though hurting our people was something he actively sought to prevent. At the moment, his demeanor concerned me more.

I touched his shoulder. The contact stung, and I hissed, drawing back just as fast.

His head snapped up. "You're hurt?"

"Just scraped my palms when I fell," I assured him as I cradled my hand. "They're tender, but I'll be fine."

Gingerly, he reached for my wrist, his brows pinching as he frowned at the new wound amid the line of stitches. It wasn't bad. Some torn skin where I'd hit a branch at the wrong angle, a scrape from glancing across a rock, fading indents from where the debris pressed but didn't break through. Superficial wounds. More annoying than anything.

Hayden traced a finger over the lines of my palm, careful to avoid the damaged skin. My fingers curled at the featherlight touch, and as I shivered, our eyes met. The intensity of his gaze stilled my breath.

"I'll heal it first," he said softly, tracing the edges of my hand. The sensation was almost too much. "You never should've been hurt because of me."

"This wasn't because of you." I broke his gaze to stare at my palm. "And it was mostly an accident anyway."

"Accident or not, you were hurt by my people. That's on me."

I didn't know what to say. Maybe he was right. I'd thought as much myself after the attacks I'd suffered through. But it didn't seem fair to blame him now.

I shook my head, staring at the soft sway of sycamore branches as a breeze rolled through. "Then heal me. Heal me and make it right."

"I will," he whispered roughly. When I looked back at him, his eyes held a glassy sheen. "I'll make it right."

I wasn't sure we were talking about the same thing anymore.

Before I could ask, Hayden grasped my hands. Pressing his thumbs across my wrists, he let his other fingers cradle the back of my hand. Tingling warmth washed over me, encompassing my hands before trailing up my arms and running down to my legs, searching for more to heal.

The scrapes on my palms knitted together again as though nothing had happened. The dull ache in my knees faded. The shakiness I'd felt evaporated. Just as my stitches began to itch, the energy tapered off. His healing power still amazed me.

I swallowed thickly, my eyes flicking to Hayden again. He stared at my palms, his thumbs brushing back and forth against my wrists.

"It worked," I whispered, just for something to say. There was a strange tension building in the air, and I wasn't sure I liked it.

"It did." He sniffed, raising the back of my hand to his lips. The kiss was as much an apology as his words. "I'm sorry I needed to heal you in the first place."

He released my hands and stepped away, the abrupt separation leaving me cold. Hayden went quiet, folding his arms at his waist as he stared blankly at the treeline, his jaw tight.

I crossed the distance between us, unwilling to let whatever this was lie. When I rounded in front of him, close enough to get a good look at his face, I tilted my head. Tension lined his eyes. I hadn't noticed earlier, but he wore the same outfit he had the other night, though his shirt now sported more wrinkles. His hair was mussed as if he'd been sleeping, his curls smashed together in places. Stubble lined his jaw. While it suited him, it further pointed to a lack of care that made me frown.

"What's going on?" I asked, trailing my hand down the arm of his olive jacket until I reached the rolled cuff just past his elbow. "Something's off with you."

He smiled sadly as he ran a careless hand over the back of his head. "You always did see right through me." He sighed, staring at the ground. "I'm just thinking. I've had a lot of time to think lately."

The answer was a clear avoidance. But as I took in the weariness on his face, I relented, pushing down my questions about what was bothering him and what the rebels were doing. If he wanted a distraction, I'd give him one for now.

I glanced around the grove, searching for evidence as a theory formed in my mind. "Did you sleep here?"

"Not here, but nearby."

I gaped at him. "Why?"

He chuckled, meeting my eyes with a seriousness that held me in place. "I never go too far from here. Not since I started meeting you."

This entire time, he'd been living in the forest? He had a home to go back to, people to lead! Why would he stay here?

He caught the dawning horror on my face as realization set in. "It's fine, Khara. You don't remember, but I actually like camping in the forests. This is just a more extreme version of that."

"But *why*?"

He looked at me with so much longing it stole my breath. His eyes bored into mine as if he were trying to tell me his greatest secret, but I couldn't translate it into words. I could only feel the magnitude of it as it brought stinging tears to my eyes.

"I'm not typically nearby." He paused as if struggling to find the right words. "If I were to go home, I wouldn't be close enough if you need me. I made you a promise. I don't intend to break it."

Tears fell when I blinked. He brushed them away.

"Please don't feel guilty about this," he whispered, cupping my face. "I would do far more for you than sleep under the stars for a few weeks."

A few *weeks*. He said it as if it were nothing, but I knew better. I knew the power he held, the position he was in. I knew how attentive Ramsey and his advisors were to the current situation. Hayden should be spending his days doing something other than waiting for me to return to the grove.

And yet, here he stood. Unashamed of his choice to wait for me and do what he could to help. Completely sincere in his request for me to let his decision stand without adding the strain of guilt onto my shoulders. As far as I could tell, truth lined his every word.

"Okay," I said. There was nothing I could do to change his choices. Feeling guilty over them would only weigh me down. His actions were his own. I could only be responsible for mine.

The corners of his lips lifted as he stared into my eyes. In a slow, careful movement, he leaned in and pressed a kiss to my forehead. "Thank you."

Deep in my bones, I felt like I should be saying those words to him instead.

Hayden didn't work on healing me for as long as he had the other night. I was glad. I never wanted to see him as spent as he'd been after pushing himself like that. He wasn't his father. We both needed to appreciate his limitations while we experimented with recovering my memories.

We ended on a high note. The power flowed into a space slightly larger than the one from two nights ago. I wasn't sure what that would mean, but I couldn't keep my excitement at bay. I wrapped Hayden in a tight hug and laughed when he finished healing me for the night. He smiled, and while it was genuine, it was more worn than usual. Maybe he hadn't fully recovered from the other night.

"Pay attention to your dreams," he said as we parted ways—again, at the edge of the forest near the city. "They'll likely start to tell you things you've forgotten."

I didn't mention they already had, and I had no idea what any of it meant. "I will."

"Tomorrow night?" Hayden asked, his body braced as if he anticipated disappointment.

"I can't tomorrow. There's a party," I finished lamely. "I have to be there."

He nodded, staring at the brush at his feet. His thumb ran back and forth across the tattoo on his wrist. I stared, trying to figure out what he was thinking, but it was no use.

"The night after?" I asked, infusing as much hope as I could into my voice.

He gave me a tight smile. "Of course. I'll be here."

A strange tension filled the air as I walked away. It settled over my body like a second skin, weighing down my shoulders and prickling against my scalp. The entire way back to the Annex, unease sank like a heavy stone in the pit of my stomach.

62

When the time came to get dressed for my engagement gala, anticipation tightened my chest. I hadn't seen Ramsey all day. Emila said it was tradition for the couple to be separated prior to the party to ensure good fortune for their marriage ceremonies. Plus, she assured me it would make my entrance that much more dramatic.

The thought didn't excite me the way it did Emila, but I didn't argue or complain. She'd done so much for us. This night was hers as much as it was mine and Ramsey's. I didn't want to dull her excitement.

When a team arrived at my suite to help me prepare, I pasted a smile on my face and tried to enjoy myself. My anxiety proved difficult to hide. I played with my hands and bounced my leg up and down until Emila finally had enough.

"What's wrong?" she asked, kneeling in front of me as a stylist arranged my hair.

"It's just nerves."

"It's okay to be nervous. This party *is* a big deal. At least to everyone who matters."

I snorted. "Thank you. That made me feel much better."

"Well, I'm not going to lie to you." She softened and patted my knee. "You have nothing to worry about. They triple-checked security after the incident with that rebel. Every precaution has been taken. We're safe."

"Right."

I twisted my fingers in the soft fabric of my pants. No one had mentioned Lachlan since the day after he'd attacked me. I hadn't asked what had happened to him, either. I was too afraid of the answer. Too afraid to find out he was still in the building. Too afraid of what it would mean if he wasn't.

"The details all came together beautifully," she continued. "I checked in on the grand hall and it looks almost as good as the palace ballroom."

"I'm sure it looks amazing. I was never worried about that."

"Good. Your faith in me is inspiring."

I huffed a laugh, doing my best not to move as the stylist continued braiding my hair.

Emila smiled, leaning forward and taking my hand in hers. She gave it a light squeeze. "Khara, the people love you. Ramsey *really* loves you. You look incredible—just wait until you get a look in the mirror! No one will be able to take their eyes off you. And even if that weren't the case, you're an incredibly kind and wonderful person. No matter what happens tonight, you'll always have that."

Her words didn't ease my concerns completely, but they did help me settle. I didn't know about the people loving me. I hadn't been around enough of them to find out one way or another. If Emila said they approved of me, I'd have to take her word for it.

But I did know Ramsey. I knew the way he looked at me while I was lying in bed, choked with pain during those first terrible weeks of my recovery. I knew the way he looked at me before he captured my lips with his. They weren't so different, always anchored in the same deep love.

I glanced at my bed where a long, white box sat tied shut with black satin ribbon. I hadn't seen the dress in person yet, only the sketch Emila had presented to me for approval. Still, I knew Ramsey would be mesmerized by me in that gown. I'd already seen him struck by me when I wore far less stunning ensembles.

I turned back to Emila, took a deep breath, and nodded.

With a delighted grin, she stood and clapped her hands. "That's the spirit! Now, let's get you in your gown. We don't have much time before you'll be presented to Ramsey."

After slipping into the dress, the team led me to stand in front of a large mirror they'd placed in my living area. My reflection shocked me. The golden gown hugged my curves, accentuated by patterns in the delicate beadwork that covered me from bodice to skirt and caught the light with every move I made. The neckline dipped, exposing more skin than I thought I'd feel comfortable with when I first saw the design. But staring at myself now, I was struck by how stunning it was. How stunning *I* was. I looked like a woman worthy to stand beside Ramsey—tonight, as his Sovereignaya, and after our marriage ceremonies, as Sovereigna of Anluan.

My eyes trailed to my shoulder, where I could just barely glimpse the scar left by the initial rebel attack. Lines of beading on a sheer overlay hid most of it. I turned to the side, mindful of the gown's train, and gathered my hair over my shoulder. Between the makeup they'd applied and the lines of beading down the back, my bruises from earlier in the week weren't visible. The stitches had been removed from my hands that morning, the bandages no longer required. With any luck, no one would look closely enough to find evidence of what had happened to me.

The jewelers presented me with a box—a gift from Ramsey. Inside sat a long, gold necklace and matching anklets unlike anything I'd ever seen. The thin, layered strands glimmered in the light, and I traced a finger over them in awe. The lead jeweler smiled proudly before moving to clasp the necklace on me. It rested delicately against my skin, creating a perfect complement to the gown's neckline and beadwork. In the light, it would command attention.

I would command attention.

As I stared at the shimmering necklace, the jewelers slid rings onto my fingers. Another knelt to clasp the anklets into place. When they'd finished, they stepped behind Emila to join the rest of the stylists. Their reflections stared at me with shining eyes and satisfied smiles. Emila caught my gaze and beamed.

Now that I was fully ready to be presented at the party, I understood their reactions. My eyes welled with tears as I took it all in. Thick black eyeliner created an alluring contrast certain to draw anyone in to meet my gaze. A soft peach color lined my lips and provided a bit of shine. My hair had been twisted into a partial up-do with intricate braids woven in. More blended into the gentle waves that fell to my mid back.

I resembled the princess Gage always teased me about being. In this gown, knowing I was about to be on Ramsey's arm, I looked like I deserved to be here. Staring at myself in the gilded mirror, I could even begin to believe that I did.

63

A CACOPHONY OF SOUND hit me as the guards opened the thick double doors to the Annex's grand hall. I did my best not to flinch, steeling myself to step into the room for my entrance with a long exhale.

Emila had lamented the loss of the palace ballroom all day. Apparently, it had been magnificent before the war and would've been a much better venue for an engagement ceremony of intent. But as I caught my first glimpse of the grand hall, my breath caught. I couldn't imagine a more ornate space.

A line of chandeliers hung from golden embellishments that curled along the ceiling. Each one glimmered in the light streaming in from a wall of windows that overlooked the palace grounds. Candles flickered on banquet tables and the intricate wooden shelves that divided the far wall. Gold trim decorated the white walls, a stark contrast to the deep brown of the hardwood floor. And the flowers—Emila's designs had come to life in a stunning display of elegance. They stood tall on navy table linens and cascaded in garlands until they kissed the floor.

Everything was stunning. Grand in a way that made the enormity of the moment press against my chest until my hands tingled. I smoothed them down the skirt of my dress, too aware of the crowd at the bottom of the stairs to shake out my hands the way I wanted to. Heart thrumming, I stepped forward.

A hush fell over the room as I arrived at the top of the stairs. There were so many people. I tried not to fidget, hyperaware of every eye fixed on me.

I deserve to be here.

I hoped repeating it to myself would stop the butterflies in my stomach from fluttering so wildly. I took a deep breath, picturing the way I'd looked in the mirror and the confidence I'd felt in that moment. The movement made the necklaces shimmer against my skin.

I deserve to be here.

My eyes roamed over the silent crowd, taking in the wide eyes and appreciative glances. The silence lasted only a moment before it turned into a startling eruption of applause. My hand gripped the wooden banister and a welcome thrum of magic rose to greet me. The tightness in my chest loosened. With careful steps, I began to descend the staircase, searching the room for any sign of Ramsey.

Guests moved aside, creating a pathway down the middle of the room, and finally, I spotted him. Ramsey stood in a tailored black suit, staring up at me as if I were the only one in the room. Light glinted off the Anluan crest pinned to his lapel. Several golden strands cascaded from it and wrapped around his back. His awed expression shifted into a wide grin that made my breath catch. Somehow I managed to keep myself together enough to make it to the bottom of the stairs without tripping.

Several guests dipped their heads in a bow as I walked by. I nodded in kind, offering a nervous smile to each person as I passed. It hardly mattered to me that the other ruling families of the Diamond Kingdoms weren't present. Emila stressed how insulting it was for them not to attend, but I understood why they wouldn't want to risk the journey. Besides, our people were the ones who truly mattered, and they were gathered all around me.

As I scanned the crowd, I noticed the glassmakers from the market. My smile widened as I waved to them. They bowed their heads in respect but stood a bit stiffly. It seemed I wasn't the only one feeling out of my element. I hoped there would be time to speak with them later. They'd been so kind to me.

Ramsey stepped forward to meet me, stealing my thoughts as he slid an arm around my waist and pulled me into his side. "You," he whispered in my ear, "are a vision come to life from my greatest dream."

Heat spread across my face, and I ducked my head, but my smile didn't dim. Ramsey chuckled, tipping my face up as he leaned in for a kiss. Cheers sounded around us, and Ramsey beamed when he pulled away. His eyes gleaming with pride, he linked our hands before facing the crowd.

"People of Anluan, I present to you Coryndé Isiraden, Khara Laveya—my future bride and your future Sovereigna."

More cheers broke out as glasses were raised high across the room. Everywhere I looked, I found faces full of joy. In the corner, the musicians began to play, and the air filled with celebration. I pressed myself further into Ramsey's side as my eyes heated. Our people really did seem to approve of me. Relief lightened the remaining weight in my chest until it lifted altogether.

I stayed by Ramsey's side for the next hour. Per tradition, we were the first to christen the dance floor. Emila had the honor of tying our wrists together with silk cloth before Ramsey swept me around the room with all the grace of a practiced dancer. It surprised me how well I kept up. My muscle memory seemed to be better than the rest.

After our dance, Ramsey led me to the side of the room, pulling us away from the crowd. He grinned as he looked me up and down, making no effort to hide his pleasure before he pulled me close for a deep kiss. "Khara, you exceed every expectation. You're absolutely stunning."

The heat in my face felt like it might never fade. I glanced away, catching sight of Emila wearing a smirk on her face as she blatantly stared at us from across the room.

I inclined my head toward her. "I had some help."

He followed my gaze. "I should thank her at some point, shouldn't I?"

We both waved, and Emila raised her glass to us. The navy satin of her jumpsuit glinted in the light as she blew a kiss before flitting off to enjoy the party. She'd more than earned it with all the work she did to make this night happen.

"We should rejoin our guests," Ramsey said.

His eyes told me he'd much rather stay in the shadows with me, but we had responsibilities to attend to, even at a party. I nodded, and he led us back into the crowd.

As soon as we made our way to the front of the room, we were presented with glasses of champagne. Two chairs sat like small thrones overlooking the ballroom. Ramsey took the one on the left and motioned for me to sit at his right. The ornate wood hummed with magic when my hand brushed it.

From the back of the room, a man cried, "To Sovereign Ramsey and Sovereignaya Khara!" A slew of others echoed the toast. Ramsey winked at me before clinking his glass against my own. The new title, officially mine tonight, made my heart race. One step closer to being Sovereigna. One step closer to being

Ramsey's wife. I sipped my drink, letting the fizzy strawberry notes distract me from the nerves threatening to rise again.

When the room returned to the standard thrum of music and revelry, I leaned toward Ramsey. "What do we have to do now?"

"There are two more ceremonial traditions throughout the night in honor of our threefold wedding ceremonies. We'll declare our intent before the people and share wine from the same cup. A few women will place a gold headpiece in your hair to signal the people's acceptance of you as their Sovereignaya and future Sovereigna. Mostly, though"—he finished the last of his champagne and sprang to his feet, presenting his hand to me with a flourish—"we dance."

Ramsey's smile was infectious. A broad grin spread across my face as I took his hand and let him lead me back to the dance floor. As we spun and stepped together, any hint of anxiety faded. I shut down my tendency to overthink and let myself fully revel in the celebration around me.

When I exited the ballroom hours later, it was with Ramsey by my side. Our laughter spilled into the hall, blending with the music still playing inside while we snuck away, hand in hand. My cheeks were flushed from strawberry champagne and the ongoing celebration in the air. As we slipped into the elevator, I pressed close to Ramsey's side. He pulled his arm over my shoulder, hugging me closer. His heartbeat thrummed through his suit jacket.

"You enjoyed yourself, then?" His fingers played with the delicate strands of the headpiece pinned in my hair.

"I did." I shifted to look up at him. "It was beyond what I expected."

He chuckled. "Sometimes we dread a thing we later come to love. I'm glad this was as much of a celebration for you as it was for me. That's all I wanted—for you to enjoy tonight as much as I knew I would."

He brushed his hand up and down my arm, lingering at my shoulder. His fingers skimmed to my neck as he moved to play with the golden strands of my necklace. The grand hall had been warm with so many people filling it, but here in the elevator, with Ramsey's fingertips brushing against my skin, I had chills.

I looked up at him. His eyes shone with intent, and his gaze flitted to my lips before he lowered his face to mine. The kiss started warm and pleasant, but soon began to consume with heat—like the slow burn of sitting in the garden under the midday sun.

The elevator doors opened, and Ramsey broke the kiss. My breath was ragged, my body flushed. I blinked at him, dazed, and Ramsey's lips lifted into a sly smile. He pressed a quick kiss to my hand before leading me into the hall, tucking me into his side as we walked toward my suite.

With his arm wrapped around me, his hand rested against my waist. He traced small, slow circles with his thumb that made me shiver.

In the quiet, I realized we were completely alone. No guards. Just us.

Ramsey turned and pulled me into another kiss. His lips moved against mine, warm and insistent. His hands wove into my hair, his fingers wrapping in braids and waves and gold chains. My back connected with my door, and for once, I barely felt the thrum of magic. How could I, when Ramsey's lips were on mine, his hand tangling in my hair? I could hardly breathe, hardly think as his hand drifted up my side.

He broke away, pulling in ragged breaths as he leaned his forehead against mine. "I love you," he said in a breathy, desperate exhale. "Khara, I love you."

My breath caught. Ramsey expressed his love in grand gestures—in extravagant gifts, protective details, and time stolen around his duties. He'd been dancing around the words as he led us in the complicated steps of our relationship over the past few months. I knew he loved me, but he had never spoken the words directly.

I pulled his mouth back to mine, feeling him smile against my lips before he deepened the kiss. By the time we parted, we were both gasping for breath.

Ramsey leaned into my neck. "I love you," he repeated, placing a kiss to my skin. "I want to give you everything." He paused, kissing a trail up my neck until his mouth lingered at my ear. "And I will. Everything this city has to offer, it's yours. I'll see to it. I'll give you everything, Khara."

He moved his hands to cradle my face before he captured my lips again. His hands skimmed down my hips and back up to my sides. "Let me show you."

His words hung heavy in the air. He played with the strands of my necklace as his other hand skimmed my side. The whole time, his eyes bored into mine.

Being this close to him was dizzying. I could feel each of his breaths as if they were my own.

Something inside whispered for me to stop. To slow down until I was sure I was ready for where this night would take us. I hadn't said it back, wasn't sure I could utter those three words to him. But with my mind spinning at his touch, I didn't know why my head and heart were at war in the first place. Ramsey loved me. We'd promised ourselves to each other before our people tonight. I was his Sovereignaya now. My place in Anluan, with Ramsey, felt more real than ever.

"Let me show you," he repeated, his eyes dark with intent.

And I gave in—to him and wherever this night would lead.

Holding his gaze, I trailed my hand down his arm and laced our fingers together. With my other hand, I reached back, opened the door, and pulled him inside.

64

WAKING WAS A SLOW affair. I blinked into the dim light of my bedroom before letting my eyes fall shut with a deep sigh. It was still early. That, or the curtains were drawn too tightly to let in much light. It didn't matter. I was more than content to rest in bed.

As I sank deeper into the mattress, my mind filled with hazy images of the night before. Dancing with Ramsey. Declaring my intention to marry him before our people. Kneeling as representatives pinned a golden headpiece in my hair. Officially receiving my title of Sovereignaya and our people's acceptance.

Chest warm at the thought, my lips lifted into a smile. The gala had gone better than I'd imagined. And after—

After. My heart sped, and I slowly slid my hand across the bed, searching. But even before my fingertips found nothing but the smooth chill of my sheets, a churning unease settled in my stomach.

Something was wrong. Ramsey wasn't here.

I blinked my eyes open, shivering against a chill as I tugged the sheets further over myself. Sitting up, I glanced around the room.

"Ramsey?"

I waited for a response that didn't come. Beyond the bedroom, my suite was quiet. There were no hints of Ramsey's presence. Just an empty space in my bed where he should have been and a dullness slowly creeping over my heart.

Gathering the bedsheet around myself, I slid from the bed. Though I couldn't remember setting it out, my robe sat waiting on the chaise. I slipped the smooth satin over my skin, trying to ignore the tightness growing in my chest. I tied the robe closed and stared blankly across the room.

I wasn't sure what to do. If Ramsey had left, surely he'd written a note offering some form of explanation.

After a quick search, I found it on the kitchen counter. The words had been hastily scribbled and didn't offer much. He'd been called away on an urgent matter and would see me later. More of the same. And yet, this morning it felt vastly different.

I refolded the letter, tapping it against the marble as my frown deepened. I understood the demands of Ramsey's position by now. He could be called away at any time. But after last night, this wasn't what I'd expected. I'd thought he would be here with me. Thought we'd matter enough to share our morning after the way we'd shared the night.

My throat tightened. Was I not enough to keep him? Had I done something wrong? What was so urgent he couldn't have woken me to let me know he had to leave? My chest ached with the longing to speak with him, to have him give me an attentive look that would ease my fears and make all of this feel like a bad dream. But he wasn't here, and that brewing insecurity made me wonder if being near him would bring relief at all.

Regret simmered in my gut. Last night, I'd felt the rush of Ramsey's love, let myself get wrapped up in it. Now, left alone in my suite, nothing felt the same.

I crumpled his note and threw it in the trash. This wasn't a letter I wanted to keep. It would only remind me of the sting of this moment. Of how twisted up my insides felt. Of being abandoned.

As I stared at the floor, the light caught on my gold anklets. Yesterday, these gifts felt like a symbol of love and beauty. Now, they simply felt like chains.

With tears filling my eyes, I strode back to my bedroom. Maybe a shower would settle me. Something told me it wouldn't—just as surely as something had tried to tell me that giving myself to Ramsey last night was a bad idea.

I ignored it exactly the same.

The warm water of the shower shifted to a cold spray, and still, I lingered until my body was reduced to shivers. I tugged on my clothes with jerky movements, hating the tightness of my muscles and the inexplicable urge to *move, leave, run* skittering under my skin. I paced the living room, squeezing my hands into fists that I released just as fast.

I doubted I'd feel any better until I saw Ramsey. I could go find him, talk to him and relieve the knot in my stomach, but I hesitated to do so more than usual. I didn't want to interrupt whatever was so important that he'd left me in the way he did. And part of me was afraid to go only to discover it wasn't something important after all.

If it were night, I'd escape to the forest. Working with Hayden on my memory appealed to me more than anything.

I finally settled on taking a nap on the couch in hopes the time would pass more quickly. With any luck, I'd dream of something good.

When I woke, I didn't feel any better. Grogginess pushed against my mind until it faded back into the unease that had gripped me so tightly before I'd fallen asleep. I flung off my blanket and sat up. My eyes flicked to the bedroom where I'd tossed my linens on the floor to be washed. Just as quickly, I looked away, my breath shaking as I pressed my fingertips against my eyes.

A glance at the clock revealed it was almost time for dinner. I'd slept longer than I intended. There was no way I was going to go sit in the commons to eat. I couldn't handle being around so many people. Eating alone didn't appeal to me either, but the thought of having Emila in my suite, gushing over me and Ramsey and the party, made my heart constrict.

No. I'd tell the guards I wasn't feeling well and request everyone give me privacy.

And tonight, I'd go to Hayden.

65

ONCE I ENTERED THE forest, it felt like I could breathe again. My shoulders relaxed the closer I came to the grove. While a knot of unease lingered in my stomach, it was bearable out here in ways it hadn't been in my suite.

Hayden looked up from where he lounged in the grass as soon as he heard the underbrush rustle beneath my feet. I did my best to smile as I entered the clearing, but couldn't quite manage it. Hayden sat up slowly, his smile dimming as concern lit his eyes. In one fluid motion, he stood and jogged to my side.

"Are you okay?" he asked, gingerly touching my arm.

When I didn't look at him, he lowered his head to meet my gaze. That was my downfall. Those eyes could see through any façade, and they were always so full of tenderness. I couldn't hold back my tears.

"Khara ..." He cupped my face with all the gentleness in the world, brushing the tear away with his thumb. "Please, what's—"

He cut off abruptly, gently angling my head to the side. From the corner of my vision, I caught the flash of his eyes as he stared at my neck. His hands fell, and he clenched them into fists.

"What happened last night?" His voice was firm, as though he suspected my answer and knew he wouldn't like it. "Did Ramsey do this to you?"

My hand drifted to my neck, brushing over the skin Ramsey's lips had bruised. I closed my eyes. I'd nearly forgotten about that.

"I'll kill him." Hayden's voice could've set fire to the earth.

My eyes flew open, and I let my arm drop. I'd never heard him speak so harshly—or so calmly about doing someone harm. Maybe for the first time, I was seeing the Hayden everyone spoke of—the fierce ruler of the rebel army, the enemy of Anluan.

I spoke, though my voice was hoarse. "Don't say that. He didn't—"

"He touched you! How far did he—?" Hayden's voice cracked, and he shook his head as he cut himself off. His fists trembled at his sides, sparks jumping from them as he paced before me.

"If you think he forced me to sleep with him, you're wrong," I said shakily. His power stormed the air, crackling with his anger. It smelled like it was about to rain. "It wasn't like that. After the gala, we just—I—"

Hayden shuddered, from his clenched fists to his shoulders. "If he didn't force you into his bed, then why? Why would you ever—?"

I flinched at the harshness of his tone, and Hayden stopped abruptly. He took a deep breath, unclenching his hands. He met my eyes, and while his still blazed with fire, they filled with softness as well—and something so broken it made me want to weep.

His voice was quiet when he spoke. "Why would you choose him?"

I faltered under the weight of his gaze. Any answer I could give felt like it would be the wrong one. There was something more going on here. Something beyond my reach, niggling at the back of my mind. The knot in my gut had only solidified since he started talking.

"He—he's kind to me." I bristled as Hayden scoffed, shaking his head. "He is! Ramsey loves me. He was by my side the entire time I was recovering from the attack. The attack *you* were responsible for!"

Hayden's head tipped toward the sky as he laughed. The sound was so bitter, I took a step back.

"You think he's kind to you? It was his fault you needed to be in medical at all! Ramsey was with you because he knew if I found out where he had you, nothing would've stopped me from coming for you. He would've had to fight to keep you."

The words didn't make sense. Still, my heart leapt to my throat and squeezed.

"He was with you because he had to make sure that whatever he did to you took. Because otherwise, you would've left him by your own power. He was with you out of *necessity*."

Thin, crackling bolts of lightning sparked from Hayden's hands. They jumped and pulsed with his words as his tattoo began to glow. But I could hardly pay attention to his power. Apprehension and denial warred in my gut, violent as my pounding heart, until a sickening fear crept up my throat.

It didn't make sense. I didn't want it to make sense.

"He doesn't love you, Khara. He's obsessed with you! He may call it love, and he may do his best to mimic it, but if you look closely enough, you'll see through the cracks." Hayden turned from me, his body shaking, his voice wrecked. "You don't belong with him."

"He's my fiancé," I whispered, the only defense I could muster.

"No, he isn't!" Hayden spun to face me again, his eyes swirling with anguish. "*I am.*"

66

THE WORLD CAREENED TO a stop. Everything around me turned slow and muddled. I couldn't hear anything beyond the wild beating of my heart and the ragged build of my breath as I tried to comprehend the words he'd just spoken.

Ramsey wasn't my fiancé. Except he was. Because I'd just declared my intent to bind myself to him in an ancient ceremony in front of half of Anluan.

But somehow, *Hayden* was my fiancé?

It didn't make sense. Nothing made sense.

A muttered curse sent my dazed eyes floating back in Hayden's direction. Lightning crackled from his hands. With detached interest, I watched it grow and pulse faster. The light moved in time with my racing heart, and I wondered if Hayden's was beating just as fast.

He bit back a pained moan, clenching his fists tight. The ink of his tattoo had shifted from its usual black to a shining blue-white. Exertion lined his face, his brow beaded with sweat, and my breath caught at the intensity of his concentration.

Before I could blink, Hayden let out a loud cry and flung his hands to the sides, palms wide open.

Bolts of lightning shot from him, lighting up the night and shocking my world back into motion. I buckled, breath catching in my throat. All I could do was blink as my eyes adjusted to the brightness.

Loud cracking echoed in the clearing as bolts of lightning rammed into the trees. Branches crashed to the ground under the force of his power. I shielded my face with my arm, staring in shocked awe. I'd never seen anything like it.

Hayden's eyes were wide, flashing with flecks of near-white light as he hovered over the grass. He seemed to have forgotten me ... and the fact that we were trying to have a covert meeting. Someone was bound to notice the flashes of light and the booming thuds of trees falling to his power.

"Hayden!" I tried to shout, but my hoarse voice was lost in the ruckus. I took a deep breath and tried again. "Hayden, you have to stop!"

His head tilted toward me. The lightning slowed until Hayden forcefully brought his right hand to clap against his left. One final, brilliant bolt of lightning flared to life and smashed into a tree deeper in the forest with a boom that rattled the ground beneath me.

I panted in the grass, eyes wide as Hayden settled, shaking out his hands at his sides. The glow of moonlight glistened on his cheek before he wiped a trembling hand over his face.

He moved toward me, his eyes searching mine for a moment before he knelt and extended his hand. I hesitated, glancing from it to his face.

"I won't hurt you."

The words were somber, but rang with the weight of a vow. It was enough for me. I clasped his hand and let him pull me to my feet.

As I looked around the grove, my hand flew to my mouth. Trees were felled on both sides of the clearing. Smoke rose where small fires had just begun to fade.

I turned to Hayden with wide eyes. He frowned at the once-peaceful refuge, digging his fingers against his still-glowing tattoo. At his side, his hand trembled.

"I need to go," he said hoarsely.

My heart lurched. He couldn't leave, not after what he'd just said. Not after what he'd *done*. There was too much I didn't know. Too much I needed to understand.

"What you said—"

He shook his head, his pained eyes glancing between me and his shaking hands. "Khara, I really have to go. I can't do this right now."

"But—"

"I have to go."

He turned and hurried away from me. I blinked rapidly, but couldn't stop the spill of tears. I called after him, hoping he'd at least respond to one last thing.

"Hayden, I'm not ... Ramsey's not my fiancé?"

I hated how small my voice came out, the way it wavered with tears.

Hayden stilled at the edge of the clearing, turning his head back toward me. "No. He's not."

I inhaled, capable of no more than a ragged breath as something fragile splintered inside my heart. "And you are?"

He nodded, his expression pinched. His hands trembled, sparks jumping from his skin as his tattoo glowed brighter. "I have to go. I'm sorry."

Without another word, he disappeared into the trees.

I was alone again, and more unsure than ever about what to do. My hands shook. Each labored breath filled my nose with smoke and ozone. My knees buckled, and a sob burst from deep within my chest as I collapsed to the ground. My eyes stared at nothing, and slowly, one shaky breath at a time, that's what I let myself feel.

Nothing at all.

67

Time passed in a haze. I don't know how long I stayed on the ground, curled in a ball, desperate not to think or feel. This was too much. I didn't understand any of it. How could I? Everyone around me had been lying. Keeping secrets. Withholding things I had every right to know. Without my memories, how was I to make any sense of it?

A rustle near the clearing's edge froze me in place. The last thing I needed was to be found here, alone and vulnerable in a grove that could only have been destroyed by one thing. One *person*.

But it was only Hayden who shuffled back into the clearing, his shoulders curled inward as if they were too weary to continue carrying his burdens. His hair was mussed, his eyes rimmed red. He looked every bit as devastated as I felt.

"I'm sorry." He scrubbed a hand down his face as he closed the distance between us. "I shouldn't have—I didn't want to tell you that way."

Had he planned to tell me at all? The question stuck in my throat as I tried to blink back my tears. They crept down my face, running over the remnants of earlier salty tracks, and Hayden's face fell further.

"Khara ..." My name came out as more of a sob than anything. He reached for my hand, but I shrank back.

If his story were true, I didn't see why he would want to touch me now. If it wasn't, I didn't want him to touch me. Even if it *were* true, I didn't want him to. I wouldn't deserve it.

"Please let me explain."

It wasn't his plea that convinced me. It was the way he stepped back, respecting my need for space though he clearly wanted to come close. I gave a sharp nod and wiped my tears. I would listen to what he had to say. And maybe I'd finally get some real answers.

"What I told you before was true," Hayden said.

We sat in the grass as we usually did, but with more space between us and none of Hayden's usual ease. He sat up straight, except for where his shoulders still curved forward, his muscles taut as he rubbed his left wrist.

Maybe he was as afraid of this conversation as I was.

"After your father died, you came to live in Anluan with my father and me. Ramsey brought you to us. You and I were friends, and eventually, we became more. It was the greatest day of my life the first time you kissed me." A hint of a smile pulled at the corners of his mouth. "Well, until the one you agreed to marry me."

His eyes searched mine for a reaction, but I had nothing left to give. My energy was spent from crying, and I was so tired of trying to figure out how to respond. He fiddled with the grass at his side, nodding as if he understood. Maybe he did, if he knew me as well as he claimed.

"Ramsey—" Hayden broke off, shaking his head. "He was like a brother to me. But he wanted you for himself, and when you agreed to marry me, something in him splintered. That wasn't long after my father and I had rejected his proposal to experiment with the gifts. He started to resent me and my father both. I think that's why he did what he did."

He looked at me pleadingly, and the words spilled from his lips in a rush. "I swear, I didn't realize how deep his pain went until he attacked us. I was trying to give him space, and then I was consumed by everything going on between us and my duties as heir. I would've tried to fix it if I'd known he wasn't handling it well. I never thought he'd attack the way he did."

I wasn't sure which attack Hayden was apologizing for—the one that destroyed Anluan or the one that destroyed me. It didn't matter. Tears dripped from my chin onto my hands as I cried for Hayden and Ramsey both. Two brothers torn apart, all because I came between them.

Bile burned the back of my throat. I was the cause of so much pain. There was blood on my hands. "This is my fault."

"No." Dismay lined Hayden's face. "Khara, none of this is on you."

"But I'm the reason!" I covered my face with trembling hands. "I am the reason Ramsey hates you. I am the reason he attacked the city. I am the reason so many of our people are *dead*!"

My body shook as I tried to force back the emotion building in my chest, but I couldn't anymore. I believed Hayden. His story felt right—vaguely familiar in a way that terrified me.

The pain was too large to contain. It burst out in a jagged sob, born of all my grief and guilt.

In a breath, Hayden closed the distance between us. He knelt before me, gently prying one hand from my face to hold in his. I broke, and Hayden let me, pulling me to rest against him. He didn't try to stop my sobs. He didn't offer empty words. He just remained a steady, silent presence beside me as he let my grief stain his shirt.

"I'm so sorry," he whispered when my sobs eased into quiet tears. He placed a kiss to the top of my head. "I'm so sorry I keep hurting you."

The tender words pierced my heart like a sword. "I should be saying that to you."

I felt him shake his head, but he didn't say anything else. It was quiet beyond the rhythm of our breaths and the gentle sounds of the grove I'd grown to love. My energy depleted, I sagged into Hayden's side. His strong arms shifted around me, adjusting his hold to take my weight as he moved to sit on the grass. He didn't seem to be in any hurry to let go of me. I could tell he had missed this—missed me—by the way his hands gripped me tighter before relaxing again, as if he was making sure this was real.

I wasn't sure what moment I'd decided he was telling the truth. But I *had* decided, and now I could feel the rightness of it in my bones.

For the first time since waking in medical, I was close to the answers I'd been looking for. They were just far more devastating than I'd imagined.

68

"Wʜᴀᴛ ʜᴀᴘᴘᴇɴᴇᴅ?"

I didn't want to disturb the fragile peace that had settled between us. I didn't want to have to think about anything else. My head already pounded in time with my pulse. But I needed to know the truth. All of it.

Hayden shifted so he could see me without releasing his hold. "What happened to you in the attack?"

I nodded, bracing myself. Whatever it was, however bad, I needed to know.

"It was our wedding day." Hayden's voice broke, and I went completely still. His grip tightened around me. "I don't know how he knew. It'd been well over a year and a half since he'd stolen Anluan. We were so disconnected by then. Someone had to have told him about the ceremony, where we'd be that day. We've been trying to figure it out." He shook his head, looking away. "We'd finished our ceremony of intent and were starting the private binding ceremony when we heard the shouts."

I pushed myself to remember. My efforts only resulted in flares of pain that made spots dance in front of my eyes. The memories of that day—*our wedding day*—were gone, just like everything else.

"Ramsey brought a group of guards with powers. They attacked the people. My father stopped the binding ceremony and went to see what was happening. He called for me, and I knew. I knew it was bad."

He turned to face me as fully as he could without removing his arms from my waist, like he was afraid if he let go, I'd disappear.

"As soon as I stepped outside the tent, I was pulled into the battle. It had barely begun, and it was already—" He broke off, shaking his head as if it would relieve him of the memory. "There was never any keeping you out of a fight." The fondness in his tone was at odds with the deep sadness in his eyes. "I never would've asked you to stay behind. Maybe I should have, but"—he sighed—"I never want you to be anything less than who you are."

I swallowed thickly, pressing my face into his shoulder.

Hayden leaned his head against mine. "Do you want me to stop?"

I shook my head. "Keep going."

"I lost sight of you. It was chaotic, but between me, my father, and the able fighters present for the ceremonies, Ramsey's guard wasn't large enough to overwhelm us. We were able to fend them off. I didn't figure out it was a distraction until it was too late."

Dread coiled in my gut, and I took in a shaky breath.

"They fled, and some of our people gave chase, but I went to find you. When I couldn't, I called for you. You would've answered," he said. "Even if you were injured, you would've made sure I knew where you were. But there was nothing. I started running, telling people to search for you. We didn't find you, but we found where you'd fought. There was so much blood."

Hayden's voice cracked and he sucked in a tremulous breath. He squeezed me tight, like he was making sure I was still there, still real and solid in his arms. I didn't mind. My heart needed the reassurance too. Hearing this story unsettled me in a way I couldn't shake. I took a deep, steadying breath, and he slowly loosened his grip.

"You were gone. There were signs of a fight all around, so much blood. Sohaila was hysterical when we found her. She wasn't badly hurt, but she was scared. She didn't know where you ended up, just that you'd told her to run when you came to help her. That's what she was doing when she heard you scream."

Sohaila. I didn't recognize the name, but I latched onto it. There was something about it ... My head throbbed as I tried to remember. But there was no memory to grasp, just familiar pain.

Hayden shifted, moving one arm from my side to reach toward his neck. "This is all I found. It was tossed aside in the grass, covered in blood."

With careful hands, he lifted a long chain from under his shirt and extended it toward me. It held three brass beads and a long, pointed shard that reminded me of a dagger.

"It's yours," he said. "You never would've taken this off. I gave it to you." His thumb brushed over the beads. "It was an engagement present."

My mind flashed to delicate golden strands shimmering around my neck. Golden anklets clasped above my feet. I shut my eyes and pushed Hayden's hand—and the necklace—away.

To his credit, Hayden didn't say anything. He simply pulled the chain back over his head and let the necklace rest against his chest.

"They tried to tell me you were dead." His voice went hollow. "We searched for you for days, made plans to break into Anluan and get you back. I reached out to you in your dreams every night, but it was like you weren't there. I couldn't break through."

The brokenness in his voice crashed against my heart like a wave threatening to overtake me. This was what he felt knowing I was alive, when he held me safely in his arms. I couldn't imagine what it must have been like for him when he didn't know.

"They told me you must be dead. That Ramsey ... that he'd killed you." His eyes flashed with grief. "I couldn't accept that. I *wouldn't*. Because if he'd killed you, it would've been to get back at me, and I never could have lived with that."

"It wouldn't have been your fault," I whispered. My heart longed to comfort him, to tell him that I was right here, but it felt too much like a lie. I wasn't really here, was I? At best, I was a ghost of the woman he loved, an echo of who he truly longed for.

He chuckled, but the sound was tinged with pain. "You're still you, you know?" He met my eyes and let me see everything he was feeling—all the pain and loss. All the hope he still held. "You're confused and you're in pain, but you're still you, Khara. I can see you through everything they've done to you."

My voice wavered. "I'm not so sure."

"I am."

His words were soft but certain, sincere in a way that couldn't be ignored. I tried to accept them, to let them wrap around my heart, sink inside, and make it their home.

It didn't work. But staring at Hayden, I thought maybe one day, if he were there to remind me, I could find a way to believe them for myself.

69

THE POUNDING IN MY head grew worse the longer I stayed pressed to Hayden's side in the grass. We'd both settled into silence. In the lull, I let myself get lost in my thoughts.

I tried to picture the day of the attack. The day of my wedding. Tried to feel the soft fabric of a gown against my skin. Tried to picture Hayden, dressed in his best, looking at me with love and promise in his eyes.

Screams rent the air, startling me into releasing Hayden's hands. We snapped our heads to the flap of the tent, and I braced myself. It had been safe here, but peace was fragile. It seemed ours was broken.

I couldn't quite make out the shouts, but they soon mixed with terrified screams that told me everything I needed to know. Booms echoed in the air as the ground shook beneath my feet.

Galen's face, so full of joy moments before, turned grim. His eyes blazed with rare fire, but even that was softened by his sadness. "I'll go."

Hayden had barely nodded before Galen ran from the tent. A moment later, he yelled Hayden's name. We shared a knowing look, and Hayden's face filled with regret. "Khara ..."

"I won't stay here, Hayden."

It wasn't anything he didn't already know, but I felt better for saying it. Today wasn't supposed to be this way. But if war was to leave its mark on this moment, I refused to let him face it alone.

He kissed me, quick but fierce. "Be careful."

"You too."

As he ran after his father, I glanced at my gown. With a pang of regret, I lifted the hem and pulled sharply, ripping the skirt to midthigh. The screaming hadn't stopped since the first one sounded moments ago. I had to be able to move. A gown was an easy sacrifice to make.

The images flashed through my mind in quick bursts. With them came an agony so fierce it forced me to curl in on myself. I cried out, clutching my head so hard my fingers ached.

"Khara, look at me!"

The pain gripped me too fiercely to focus on Hayden's words. It was too much. It had to stop. I groaned, my eyes squeezed shut as warm tears rushed down my face in a steady stream.

"You need to breathe!"

Hayden's plea registered, and I tried to inhale. Air filled my lungs in ragged jerks before quickly leaving again. It hurt. It hurt so badly.

"I'm here. I'm right here." His calloused hands pressed against the sides of my face. "Khara, you have to listen to me. Can you hear me?"

I barely managed a sharp nod.

"Good. That's good." His relief was almost tangible. "I'm going to help. Can you look at me?"

The thought of opening my eyes made me whimper. Hayden carefully brushed my tears with his thumbs. He didn't rush me, just waited until I gathered myself. I took a deep breath, peeled my eyes open, and immediately slammed them shut with a moan. Even the moonlight was too bright.

This was the worst my migraines had ever been.

"I'm sorry," Hayden said, over and over again, his forehead pressed against mine. The words were barely a breath, but with him so close, I heard every one. "I'm so sorry."

I barely managed to crack my eyes open, biting back a moan as Hayden sat back to meet my gaze. His hands never left my face.

"It's your head again? A migraine?"

"Memories," I gasped.

His brows lowered in thought as he tilted his head, then shook it. "We'll come back to that. I want to try healing you."

Exhausted, I nodded and closed my eyes. His hands shifted to my temples and the familiar warmth followed, trailing across my mind and soothing the pain.

Or most of it.

I frowned. It had taken the entirety of my pain before. What was different now?

"Are you still hurting?" Hayden asked, voice strained.

"Yes. Not as bad, but it's still there."

A pulse of power surged, and I gasped at its force. It rushed against the barrier in my mind, seeping into the cracks Hayden had been exploiting in our sessions. My muscles tensed, and I bit back a cry. This time there was no discomfort, only a sharp, stabbing sensation that traveled from head to chest.

"Is it working?" Hayden panted.

I was afraid to open my mouth, too sure I would scream. A low moan escaped, and Hayden's hands left my head faster than they'd come.

"I'm sorry." His fingers hovered close but didn't touch. "How much does it hurt?"

I breathed shakily and rubbed my hand against my chest as if it would lessen the fire coursing through me. Hayden had to have seen, but we were past the point where I'd be able to keep it a secret anyway. I opened my eyes to search his face. It had gone ashen, as if all the blood had drained from it. His eyes were locked on the hand that still rubbed circles over my heart. He didn't say a word, but the look in his eyes spoke volumes.

"I'm fine," I croaked.

His face pinched with anger. "No, you're not. Khara—"

"It's fading, Hayden," I interrupted with a tired glare. "The pain is fading."

He deflated, bowing his head into his hands and tugging at his curls. When he looked at me again, his eyes were rimmed red. My heart sank. Had I always hurt him this much?

"I think it was too much at once," I said, my voice heavy with exhaustion. "That last pulse felt like …" I frowned, words escaping me. "It hit the barrier in my mind and that's when the pain started. It's not your fault."

Hayden shot me an incredulous look. "I shouldn't have—"

I shook my head. This was too much—the pain, the memories, the revelations from Hayden's story. I couldn't handle any more. Not today.

"I need to go," I said, shakily moving to my feet. My head throbbed at the change in position. I rubbed my forehead, standing tensely until the black spots faded from my vision.

"You can barely stand!"

"I need to go. I can't—" I fought back tears. "Please, just let me go."

"Khara—"

"I need to go."

"Where? Back to Ramsey? After what he's done—"

Anger flared hot in my chest. "I know what he's done. I was there!"

Hayden flinched as if I'd struck him. When I wasn't swaying with exhaustion, I'd care enough to hate myself for it. For now, I was too numb to let it be anything more than my chance to escape.

I didn't want to go back to Ramsey, but I didn't want to stay in the clearing with Hayden either. The restlessness inside me was too strong to smother, my heart too fragile to stay. One wrong word and I would lose my tremulous hold over the wave of emotions I was trying to keep at bay.

What I wanted was time. Time to sort through what Hayden had told me. Time to process the memory that had broken through. Time to figure out what Ramsey was doing. I needed time to unravel all the secrets and lies so I could take my life back.

I barely heard Hayden's soft call to be careful as I walked away. Barely registered his promise to wait for me as I entered the trees. My entire focus settled on putting one foot in front of the other. Falling into my bed had never been so appealing. For someone who wanted to remember so badly, tonight I couldn't help but wish to forget.

70

Days passed in a haze of guilt, shame, and increasing suspicion.

When I woke the morning after learning the truth, I regretted leaving my bed. So much so that I crawled back into it and curled into a ball under my blankets.

Hours later, I ignored the resounding knocks at my door. When the soft shuffle of footsteps pricked my ears, I peeked my head from the covers and found Ramsey in my bedroom doorway.

His face fell as he spotted my red-rimmed eyes. "What's wrong?"

"Just sick."

My voice sounded dull and lifeless, a fitting match to my mood. Ramsey frowned as he moved close and sat on the edge of my bed. He pressed his hand to my forehead, and I did my best not to tense while my insides roiled at his touch.

"Would you like me to stay with you?" His eyes shone with a concern I wasn't sure was real.

Before, I might have found the offer gracious. As Sovereign, his time was valuable. His willingness to spend it with me instead of tending to his duties meant a great deal. Now, I wondered about his motives. Did he want to stay for me or himself? Was I anything more than a tool he could use in his war plans?

Either way, I could barely stand to be in the same room as him.

"No," I said. "I just want to sleep."

He nodded, running his hand up and down my arm. My skin crawled with every pass. "I'll come by to check up on you later, then."

When the door shut behind him, I turned over in my bed and cried.

Emila came next, waking me from a restless sleep. I wasn't even sure I was tired anymore, I just wanted to pass the time. If that meant sleeping the day away, at least it was a reprieve from my tangled thoughts.

Emila's brows pinched as she took me in. "Are you okay?"

"I'm not feeling well."

"Should I call for Doctor Jensen?"

Her concern seemed genuine. It always had. But now that I knew who I was, I couldn't help but question who *she* was. Were we truly friends? Maybe her concern wasn't for me at all. Maybe it had to do with whatever was done *to* me.

"Don't call her," I said. "I'm just going to sleep."

I pulled the duvet to my chin and closed my eyes. When Emila left without another word, I didn't feel guilty. I had no capacity for it.

When I woke again, the bedroom was dark. I blinked into the shadows, my eyes prickling with the sting of tears. I wanted to shut my eyes again, fade back into sleep. If I wasn't awake, I wouldn't be aware of the shame festering in my gut.

I'd believed Ramsey. I'd let him lure me into a place of trust and into my bed. In doing so, I'd betrayed Hayden. Betrayed myself. Despite being unable to remember whatever vows I'd made to Hayden before we were ripped apart, an overwhelming sense of guilt still gnawed at my insides.

I shuffled from bed to stop my spiraling thoughts. A note in Emila's handwriting sat on the table, telling me to open the door when I was ready for dinner.

My heart twisted. So much for not feeling any more guilt.

I clenched my fist, crumpling the page as I fought back tears, and opened the door. Commander North turned to face me. She inclined her head before bending to pick up a covered tray from the floor.

"Thank you," I said, attempting a smile to soften the terse way the words came out.

She frowned, tilting her head as she studied me. "Should I call someone for you, Coryndé? You don't look well."

I huffed a bitter laugh. "That won't be necessary, Commander. Thanks for the food."

"Of course." Her nod was sharp, her eyes sharper still. What did she see when she looked at me? What did she know? "I'll be here till after sunrise, should you need anything."

I thanked her again, but had no intention of calling on her. I refused to seek help from anyone here.

In my dreams, I saw Hayden.

He ran, laughing as he chased after me. He cried, face devastated as he realized I'd slept with Ramsey. He spun me in a dance in the middle of the clearing, his eyes alight with joy. He shook with power, lightning shooting from his fingers. He watched me throw a dagger with a smirk on his face. He reached for me, his face lined with fear.

I couldn't distinguish memory from imagination. I didn't care, as long as Hayden himself didn't enter my dreams. I was too much of a coward to face him. By now, he had to have realized that this was my fault. I'd betrayed him too horribly to be forgiven.

Better to stay away.

I managed another day of feigning ill. Lying in bed all day wasn't ideal, but it was better than trying to face liars and secret keepers. Better than facing reality. Better than trying to pretend.

I didn't want to have to *pretend* anymore. Not when I was shattering under the weight of the truth.

Ramsey and Emila wanted to call the doctor. Despite their persistence, I insisted we wait it out.

"If I'm not better in two days," I said, "you can call her then."

Though neither liked it, they relented.

"Please come back."

Hayden's voice was the barest whisper carried on the wind in my dream. I refused to let him in. This distant, quiet plea was all he could manage.

"Please, Khara. Let me see you."

I hated hearing him beg. But I hated myself for everything that had happened more.

I didn't let him enter my dreams.

I didn't deserve his presence.

On the third day, I woke and blinked dully at the ceiling. My body ached from lying in bed. My eyes were dry, my side sore, and I desperately needed to shower. I groaned, stretching my legs as I flung an arm over my eyes.

I hated how I felt. My thoughts and feelings had twisted into a thorny mess that tore into me any time I tried to untangle it. My mind hissed at me again and again—*what is wrong with you?* Shame left a heavy coating over every thought, weighing down my heart.

Nothing felt right. I dreamed of Hayden more and more, but the fleeting visions weren't helpful. They only made my heart ache. So many moments lost. And now that I was getting glimpses of them, I felt like I'd lost *him*.

How could Hayden ever want to see me, let alone be with me? It didn't make sense. Surely he was angry with me. I was furious with myself.

Flinging off the covers, I sat up, running a rough hand through my knotted hair. Anger felt better than shame or sadness. With anger, I might be able to function.

I pushed my way out of bed to take a shower, channeling as much resentment as I could toward Ramsey and whoever was helping him.

I would figure out exactly who that was. I would uncover what they wanted from me. And I would find a way to take back everything they had stolen.

The fire igniting in my gut turned the sick feeling of shame to ash.

71

WHEN RAMSEY CAME BY late that morning, he entered my suite without bothering to knock. He hadn't since the first day of my feigned illness, not wanting to risk waking me with his arrival. As if I weren't hyperaware of every time he stepped foot into my space.

I glanced at him from my seat on the couch where I sat sketching in my journal as he stuttered to a stop in the entryway. The curtains were open. Light poured into the room for the first time in days. I had showered, braided my hair, and put on fresh clothes. After the last few days, the change had to be shocking.

He blinked, shaking himself before moving closer. "You're up."

I forced a smile. "I feel a lot better today."

Ramsey's shoulders drooped. "I'm happy to hear it. I was worried something had gone wrong, that I'd have to call Doctor Jensen."

What did he mean *something had gone wrong*? I filed his words away and forced my grip on my pencil to loosen. The last thing I needed was for Ramsey to notice the tension coursing through me. I flicked my eyes from my sketch back to his gaze.

"No need. I feel fine now. Really."

The corner of Ramsey's mouth tipped up. His eyes lightened as he moved to sit on the arm of the couch. He nodded toward my open journal. "It's beautiful."

"Thank you." I stared at the cottage I'd drawn. Wildflowers lined the yard amid tall grass that led back to the surrounding forest. The windows were open, but I hadn't sketched anything inside the house. I didn't know where I'd seen this place before. It felt familiar, like I'd been there. But of course, I couldn't know if I had.

Ramsey glanced at his watch before shifting to face me. "Would you like to have a late breakfast? I didn't expect you to be up, so I made plans for the afternoon. But I have time for a meal before I'm needed."

My stomach growled, and I frowned, anger brewing as Ramsey laughed like everything was normal. I sighed and shut my journal, tossing it onto the coffee table. There would be no break from pretending, not if I wanted to end this.

"It appears I'm hungry."

Ramsey grinned as he stood and offered his hand to help me from the couch. "Let's fix that."

Though my entire being screamed against it, I took his hand and let him pull me up.

As determined as I was to uncover the truth, I was woefully ill-equipped to do so. I tried to figure out where to start, what questions would be the right ones to ask. By the time we arrived at the commons, I gave up. This was too important to rush into. I needed a plan.

Ramsey ushered me to our table and urged me to rest. When he left to get our food, I didn't argue. I needed the moment alone.

It was late for breakfast. Most of the guards were already on duty and most of the advisors were likely working in their offices. My eyes swept over the room, pausing on the far side where I noticed Gage standing by the door. He studied me, his eyes darker than I'd ever seen them. I cocked my head, unsettled by his seriousness, and lifted my hand in an awkward wave. He nodded back, then turned and left the room.

Before I could think more about it, Ramsey returned with heaping plates of food. "You haven't eaten much the last few days," he said. "Take whatever you want. I'll eat the rest."

While I was hungry, my appetite was small, and my stomach churned. I scraped some eggs onto the empty plate he set in front of me. A piece of toast and a handful of fresh berries filled the rest. Ramsey looked like he wanted to shove more onto my plate, but he refrained. Smart man. Maybe he could sense my anger, or at least that something was off with me.

The silence grew heavy. I needed to be more careful.

"Thank you, Ramsey." I was surprised the words didn't stick in my throat, but they came out clear and sincere. "It's nice to eat together again."

He placed his hand over mine and rubbed his thumb over my engagement ring. "You know I love to spend time with you. It's all I want to do."

"What else do you have to do today?" I asked as I speared a blackberry with my fork.

Ramsey shrugged, pulling his hand away and leaning back in his seat. "Nothing too exciting."

"Did you finalize your plans for the rebels, then? The threat is over?"

He winced, but kept his smile in place. "Not exactly. We haven't enacted our plan yet, but we'll be ready soon."

"So you'll be with your advisors today? Finalizing it?"

"In part."

I took another bite of fruit and swirled some blueberries around the plate as I chewed. Something about Ramsey's casual demeanor struck me as off. He'd been ecstatic about the plan just days ago. Why wouldn't he want to tell me about it?

"Khara ..." I looked up from my plate and met Ramsey's probing eyes. "Are you sure you're all right?"

"I am. I promise." I set my fork down to grasp his hand. "Being sick just took a lot out of me. I'm sure tomorrow I'll be feeling like myself again."

The way he stared made me want to hold my breath, wait to see if he would notice the differences my knowing made. Instead, I sipped my tea as though everything was fine.

Ramsey gave a decisive nod. His smile morphed into a megawatt grin as he leaned forward conspiratorially. "I'm sure Emila could be persuaded to leave you alone another day for the sake of your recovery."

A scoff from behind made me jump. "She most certainly could *not* be persuaded."

Emila slid into the seat beside me in a fluid movement that barely ruffled the skirt of her dress. She glared at Ramsey, who laughed brightly, before she turned to face me. "You wouldn't do that to your best friend after completely ignoring her for three days, would you, Khara? No. No, you would not."

Ramsey choked on a laugh, and even I had to fight a grin. Emila had always been spirited, full of life in a way I couldn't help but admire. The thought that she might be a skilled actress only pretending to care gutted me. It was almost as horrifying as what Ramsey had done.

She bumped her shoulder against mine. "Come on, I was just kidding. If you need to rest, I'll let you. Maybe just don't shut me out this time?"

I grimaced. "I'm sorry." Despite everything, a large part of me even meant it. "I didn't mean to be so ..."

Emila perked up and opened her mouth to interject, but Ramsey cut her off with a glare and firm shake of his head. He must have guessed the unflattering direction her words would go as well as I could.

I snorted, unable to stop a smirk from forming this time.

She waved her hand, grinning back. "All is forgotten."

If only I could forget my suspicions so easily.

72

Ramsey left us after brunch. Before, that would have disappointed me, but today I was relieved. It was easier to pretend with Emila, easier to believe she cared and was just as clueless about my past as I had been. It was wishful thinking, but I couldn't help hoping all the same.

She'd been one of the first people I'd formed a connection with after waking in medical. She'd distracted me from my pain, made me laugh, and helped me feel less alone. She'd been a good friend—or at least a good likeness of one.

We walked the gardens, basking in the sunlight that filtered in through a partly cloudy sky. Humidity clung to my lungs with every step. The breeze that usually lessened its intensity was absent. My shirt stuck to my skin less than ten minutes into our stroll, but I didn't complain. Even struck by humidity, I could breathe better out here than anywhere inside the Annex.

"Hey, Emila?" I asked as we made our way toward a table in the shade. "Do you ever wish you were gifted like Ramsey and some of the others?"

She stilled for so brief a moment I wouldn't have noticed had I not already been watching her so intently. Before, I would've missed her reaction. Today, I saw everything.

Smiling tightly, she shrugged and continued walking. She lifted her hair from the back of her neck and twisted it into a small knot, pulling a tie from her pocket to hold it in place. "Sure, I guess. Don't most people in Anluan?"

I hummed. "Probably."

We reached the table and settled next to each other on the wooden bench, facing out. Emila knew how much I loved to watch the trees sway across the lawn. She knew so much about me. Maybe too much.

"Why do you ask?"

I shrugged, picking up a blade of grass and slicing through it with my fingernail. "I just wonder what it would be like." Throwing caution aside, I added, "I dream about it sometimes—that I have a power." I forced a laugh, proud of how natural it sounded. "Ridiculous, right?"

Emila stared at the trees in front of us, face drawn. Her voice wavered as she chuckled. "Yeah. Dreams can be like that sometimes."

Her reaction solidified the knot forming in my stomach. She knew me—the real me. She had to. And if she knew now, she had to have been in on it the whole time. I clenched my hand into a fist, focusing on the prick of my nails against my palm to temper my anger.

"Tell me a story," I said when I found my voice again.

"A story?" Emila's eyes filled with bemusement. "Like what?"

I shrugged and leaned back to rest my arms against the tabletop. "Tell me the story about how I got here."

"What?" Emila's brow furrowed. More than confusion, concern shone in her eyes—along with a glint of fear.

"Well, I'm about to be tied to the Sovereign of Anluan. I don't remember most of how that happened. Tell me about how I fell in love with Ramsey and overcame the odds to be his Sovereignaya and future bride. Who better to tell the story than my best friend?"

Relief rang in Emila's laugh. The fondness in her eyes pierced my heart. "You're so strange sometimes, Khara."

"Is that how the story begins?"

She snorted, moving to lean back against the tabletop. "No, but maybe it should."

We both laughed, though mine felt stilted. It was hard not to laugh around Emila. Hard to remember she was probably more enemy than friend. Hard to smother the affection between us that had been a lifeline over the last few months.

"You really want me to tell you that story?" she asked incredulously.

I sighed, sensing how desperate she was to change the subject. "I guess I could make Ramsey tell me later."

"That's a fantastic idea." She grinned wickedly. "It would make for excellent pillow talk."

My blush was equal parts shame and anger, but Emila laughed, mistaking it for modesty.

"Oh, come on, you're engaged! And as your friend, I'm entitled to some teasing. I know you two left the party together. Sick or not, I can't believe you haven't spilled any details yet!"

The air thinned. My heart started beating so hard I thought it might burst. My words came out clear and steady but not strong. "I'm not talking about that."

"Not even a little something?"

"I'm not talking about it."

Emila raised her hands in surrender. "Okay! Not talking about it. Sorry."

I turned from her, closed my eyes, and breathed. I was okay. Everything was fine. I repeated the words to myself over and over until I could believe them.

In the late afternoon, a new guard jogged over to meet the one on rotation. Emila said something about our regular guards taking a break while I was sick. I didn't know either guard present, but sat straight as the one on duty strode toward us.

"Coryndé Isiraden." He dipped his head. "It's time I bring you inside now."

I tilted my head and glanced at Emila, who shrugged. "We were going to stay out awhile longer."

"Orders, Sovereignaya. I'm to report inside, and Sovereign Ramsey was adamant that I shouldn't leave you unattended."

I bristled, both at the use of the title that tied me to Ramsey and at my lack of freedom. "If he asks, tell him I dismissed you. You won't get into any trouble. You can send someone else to us when you report to wherever you're needed."

His face tightened. "I'm afraid I must insist. Sovereign Ramsey is calling for all of us."

I blinked. In all the time I'd been in Anluan, Ramsey had never called for the whole guard. I turned to Emila, whose brows rose as she met my eyes and shrugged again. At least this time, I wasn't the only clueless one.

"If you would hurry, ma'am. I'm not to leave you alone and I'll be late if we don't move."

I closed my eyes and sighed. "Lead the way."

He bowed his head, a small smile turning up the corners of his mouth. "Thank you, Sovereignaya."

I nodded back, doing my best to be gracious. This wasn't his fault. He had to follow orders. But now that I knew the truth, these restrictions were unbearably stifling. As we walked back into the chilled air of the Annex, I couldn't help but grit my teeth.

I spent the rest of the afternoon tucked away in my suite. Emila bore the confinement with more grace than I did. While I was content to wallow, she tried to put things into perspective. She spoke of how much Ramsey loved me and how he wouldn't do something like this without a reason.

I was sure he had a reason. I was just as sure it wouldn't be good enough.

We passed the time as best we could. I grabbed my journal and sketched while Emila read a random book from my shelves. I considered taking a nap, but didn't want Emila to think I was pushing her aside. Or worse, that I was sick again and needed to see Doctor Jensen.

After a heavy sigh, Emila tossed the book aside. She stood, stretching her arms and making her way over to me. She tilted her head as she stared down at my open journal. "That's pretty."

The echo of Ramsey's earlier words made me snort. "Thanks."

She frowned, crossing her arms over her chest. "I mean it! You're so good at this."

I sighed and dropped my pencil. "I know you meant it, Emila. Thank you." Grudgingly, I added, "Sorry."

Her lips twitched. "It's okay. I know you're frustrated. I'm sure Ramsey will get an earful later." She looked back at the sketch. "What is that anyway?"

I hadn't been paying much attention. It was far too common for me to lose myself while sketching. My eyes widened when I registered the three circles leading to an elongated triangle. My necklace, the one Hayden had shown me in the clearing. The one he'd been wearing since the day I was taken from him.

"Just a design," I hedged. "Thought it might make nice jewelry. Earrings, maybe. Or a pendant."

Emila hummed. "Both, I think. Does it mean anything?"

Once, I was sure it meant everything. It haunted me that I couldn't remember. It didn't feel like a lie when I shrugged and said, "I'm not sure yet."

73

Hours later, Ramsey arrived at my suite with his arms full of food. He'd lost his suit jacket at some point. His shirt bore new wrinkles and he'd pushed the sleeves up his arms. Despite the slight dishevel of his hair pointing to a tiring day, the satisfaction in his smile reached his eyes.

"I wasn't sure if you'd had enough food," he said as he set two bowls on the kitchen counter.

I couldn't hide my agitation. "Ramsey, you've had us locked up in here for hours."

He had the decency to look sheepish, running his hand through his hair and giving me an embarrassed smile. "I know. I'm sorry it needed to be this way. I had to call in the guard to go over—"

"It didn't *need* to be this way!"

Emila placed a hand on my back, quietly gripping my shirt from her position beside me on the couch. It felt like a warning—one I wasn't about to listen to.

"If you trusted me at all, you'd let me have some freedom here!"

His mouth fell open, though he shut it just as fast. A steely glint flashed in his eyes before he gave me a patronizing smile that sent my blood boiling. "I know it must be frustrating, but—"

"Do you?" I tipped my chin up, folding my arms tight against my chest. "I have barely had a moment to myself the entire time I've been recovering, and when I have, it's because I'm locked in here with a guard posted out front. Someone is always two steps behind me at most, always watching me. How would you feel if I did that to you?"

A heavy silence descended over the room. Ramsey swallowed thickly, his eyes drawn to the floor. It should have been a picture of repentance, but I suspected it was for show. Or maybe a way for him to release the anger that had him clenching his fist so hard that his fingers were paling.

Emila's grip tightened where she clutched my shirt. She'd made no move to leave her place at my back or insert herself into the conversation. She stayed, but for once, didn't participate. I hated that I took comfort in her presence.

Ramsey knelt in front of me. When he looked up, his eyes were dark. I took the opportunity to search him. He was difficult to read, but I still saw that steely glint in his eyes.

"I didn't realize you were so unhappy." He reached his hand out, palm up. When I didn't move, he untangled my arms to take my hand. He gave it a quick kiss, a pleased gleam in his eye that made me shiver. "Tell me, Khara, what would you have me do?"

I narrowed my eyes. Was this a trick? Some kind of joke? "Let me move around on my own. I can take care of myself!"

He chuckled darkly. "I know you can. Usually. But you've not been yourself, and I can't have you getting hurt. What if someone were to attack again?"

I huffed, trying to pretend I wasn't still shaken by that day. "Everyone says it's safe now. You've told me so yourself! Now you're telling me you didn't fix whatever problem allowed that man to escape his cell in the first place? The likelihood of it happening again is—"

"*Any* likelihood is too much for me. I won't risk you."

His declaration twisted my gut into knots. He didn't want to risk me getting hurt, or uncovering the truth?

"There has to be a compromise." I hesitated before bringing my hands to cup his cheeks, holding his gaze. "I'm suffocating, Ramsey."

He tensed beneath my fingers. A flash of pain lit the amber depths of his eyes before he steeled himself. "I'm sorry," he said, more firmly this time. "I can't risk you. I won't. For the time being, this is how it has to be. I promise I'll deal with this threat soon. We can loosen your security then."

I deflated, dropping my hands from his face and slumping back into the couch. Emila stayed silent beside me, but shifted closer. Ramsey blinked, seeming to notice her for the first time.

"Would you like something to eat?" He stood without waiting for a response. It was more a statement than a question anyway. He'd brought food, so he was going to have me eat.

"I'm not hungry." It was petulant, but I didn't want him to win anything else. I refused to let him keep taking my choices from me.

"Just a little something, then." Ramsey set a bowl in my lap and gave another to Emila. "I had them make your favorite. Imports from Branton arrived this afternoon, so we had fresh olive oil."

I took the fork he offered with a sigh. It would probably be best if I *did* eat something and go to bed. Being in my room with Ramsey this late in the evening put me on edge.

Emila cleared her throat and speared a green bean. "Thanks, Ramsey."

He nodded. "Thank you for staying with her today."

The exchange made me feel like a child. I simmered in my anger, not even tasting the roasted tomatoes and seasoned rice as I shoved a bite in my mouth.

Emila winced as her eyes flicked to me, but she forced a smile for Ramsey. "Of course."

After several moments of tense silence, Emila stood and smoothed down her skirt, flashing an apology to me with her eyes. "I should go. Thank you for dinner, Ramsey. I'll see you tomorrow, Khara?"

I nodded, my tension mounting. "Sure."

When she left, I would be alone with Ramsey. My stomach plummeted.

He saw her to the door, then sank beside me on the couch and wrapped his arm around me. The proximity was stifling.

"Don't be upset with me, Khara." he said, voice velvety and rich against my ear. "You know how much I love you, what I'd do for you."

He moved closer still, pressing his lips to the corner of my mouth. I turned my head, meeting his eyes. They held a possessive gleam, one matched by his chilling, wolfish smile. Had he always looked at me this way? How had I never noticed?

Goosebumps covered my arms and a warning flush swept over my chest. This would not end well if I allowed it to continue.

"Forgive me," he murmured. "I just want to protect you."

When his lips pressed to mine, they moved with hunger. This kiss wasn't a profession of love. It wasn't born of desperation to protect. This kiss was a claim, and it revolted me.

I pushed against his chest, turning my head away. He trailed his lips down my neck instead, and I shuddered. "Ramsey."

He hummed, but didn't stop. My eyes stung with tears.

"Ramsey!" I put all the authority I could muster in my voice as I shoved against his shoulders. As soon as his lips left my neck, I stood. "Stop."

He tilted his head. "What's wrong?"

I breathed heavily, wanting to cry and shout and most of all, run. What *wasn't* wrong? But I stood my ground. "We're not doing this."

His eyes, dark with lust, narrowed. "Why not?"

I wasn't sure what to say. It couldn't be the truth. But how to lie convincingly? I bit my lip and said the first thing that came to mind. "I'm exhausted and feeling sick again. I think the time in the sun set me back." I paused, then added, "And honestly, I'm still angry with you."

Ramsey's face pinched before he brightened, a devilish spark in his eye. "Let me make you feel better, then."

"You can't kiss away my anger."

"I could try."

He smirked as if he'd already won, as if he expected me to give in. It only served to fuel my rage.

"No, you can't." I looked away, jaw clenching, and crossed my arms. It was pitiful protection, but the only form I could give myself. "I'm going to bed."

He eyed me shrewdly for a moment that seemed to stretch into eternity. "If you're sure," he said finally, settling back against the couch cushions.

"I am. I need to rest."

"Then I suppose I'll wish you good night."

"Good night, Ramsey," I said dutifully, attempting a smile I knew would fall flat.

"I'll see you in the morning."

The words rang with promise. Veiled beneath was something more, something that set my senses on edge. I shut my bedroom door and crawled beneath the covers, hyperaware of Ramsey lingering in the next room. I stared at the ceiling and focused on my breath, certain sleep wouldn't soon find me.

74

"You're really not going to tell me?"

Hayden's eyes shone with mischief. "I'm really not."

I laughed outright and shook my head. If my eyes were dancing with half as much joy as his, I'd understand the awestruck look he was giving me. He was beautiful like this, so alive. I'd let him plan a thousand surprises if it meant more days where he looked like this.

I'd thought this sort of playfulness had been lost to us. Since Ramsey overtook Anluan, Hayden had been more cautious. He grieved not only his mother, but Ramsey, too. As devastated as I was over the losses, I could only imagine Hayden's pain.

How could someone so close to us become unrecognizable, seemingly overnight? How could I have been so blind to Ramsey's misery?

"Don't do that," Hayden chided.

"Do what?" I asked, though I knew. We both did.

"It's not your fault."

"It's not yours, either."

I pressed a hand to his cheek, and my engagement ring sparkled as it caught the light.

Our lives had turned upside down since word of the proposal got out. Hayden carried so much guilt over what had happened with Ramsey. I could read it in every line on his face, in the whirls of sadness that clouded his eyes. He blamed himself, even more than I did.

He brought my hand down and kissed it. "It doesn't feel that way."

"Feelings lie," I said. "It's not wrong for you to love me, Hayden. And it's not wrong for me to choose you back."

His whole body softened. "If I didn't know any better, I'd say you're perfect."

I huffed, wrapping my arms around his neck. "Good thing we both know better, then."

Hayden grinned and pressed a kiss to my lips. I could almost taste his happiness.

"Close enough for me."

I lay alone in the grass, the chill of the ground seeping through my clothes. Darkness had overtaken the clearing in the moon's absence, but the stars gleamed where they filled the sky. I sank deeper into the soil as I stared at them.

"Khara, please…"

I clenched my eyes shut against Hayden's voice. This sounded like the real him, not a fragment of a dream.

"Come home."

Tears pricked my eyes, and I couldn't stop myself from murmuring, "You don't want me."

I tensed as a wave of longing washed over me. Its ache was almost physical, and I wanted to beg for relief. As suddenly as it came, it was gone.

"I love you. Please, come home."

Had Hayden done that? Could he do whatever that was?

"Why would you want to see me, let alone love me, after what I've done? I don't deserve it."

"You do. To me, you always will. Please…"

The words shifted into an echo of fragmented memory. His words rang with the same feeling they had then. *Close enough for me.*

I considered the happiness of the moment he'd pressed his lips to mine. How tenderly he'd held me in the clearing when I was in pain. Hayden had been so gentle with me since I'd found him again with no memory of who he was. So much longing and desperation laced his voice now.

Despite everything that had come between us, could he still want me? The thought was absurd, and yet, I couldn't help but hope it was true. "You really want me?"

I woke with a gasp, my fist clenched in the blankets. Tears fell as I sat up in bed. I scrubbed them away with a careless hand. My room was still dark, but I couldn't tell how much time had passed. Wasn't sure if Ramsey still lurked in my suite. No matter what time it was, I didn't want to face him.

Here at the Annex, I couldn't help being tense and angry, when I let myself feel at all. Numbing had become my first defense against the overwhelming sense of wrongness in and around me.

I was grieving. For so many things.

My tears fell faster as the recognition of what I was truly feeling settled. Grief hung heavy and uncomfortable in my chest. It made me want to run almost as much as Ramsey's advances did. But after Hayden's whispered reassurances in my dream, this pain made me want to run straight to the grove where he waited for me.

I glanced at the clock through bleary eyes. Three in the morning. I had enough time to go see Hayden if I could sneak away.

I slipped from my bed and crept to the door. Finding it closed filled me with relief. I'd half-expected to wake to Ramsey sleeping beside me, one arm slung over my waist to keep me close. I shuddered, grateful to have been wrong.

The door creaked as I opened it, and I froze, holding my breath. There was no way he would've missed the noise. I poked my head out, scanning the room.

It was empty. Ramsey was gone.

I slid to the floor in relief, letting out a hysterical sound that couldn't decide whether it was a laugh or a sob. I bit my fist to stop it. I had to gather myself if I wanted to leave. The only person to contend with now would be the guard posted outside my door.

I almost sobbed when I found Gage standing attentive on the other side.

His face fell as he took in my appearance. "Princess, you okay?"

His voice held a warmth that made me believe his concern was genuine. Still, I couldn't afford to trust him beyond what I already had. As far as I could tell, he hadn't spoken a word about me roaming around in the night. I could trust him with that secret, at least. If he told anyone, he'd be in more trouble than I would.

"I'm fine." We both winced at the hoarseness of my voice. I cleared my throat. "I'm fine. I just—" I motioned vaguely toward the end of the hall.

Gage nodded and shut the door for me. "You're sleeping soundly. All is well."

"Thank you, Gage."

"No need to thank me. But you better get moving." He glanced at his watch. "My relief will be here just before eight."

That would give me a few hours at best to go to the grove and return. Would I even come back this time? I frowned and shoved the thought aside. That was a question for later. After a nod to Gage, I jogged down the hall and out of sight.

75

As soon as I entered the forest, I abandoned stealth in favor of speed. My feet crashed over sticks and brush, a series of cracks and rustles echoing in my wake as I raced down the path. All I wanted was to feel safe again, and I knew where to go to feel it.

I spotted Hayden lying in the grass as I rushed toward the grove. As soon as he heard me coming, he snapped into a crouch, small bolts of lightning dancing in his palms. I skidded to a stop inside the treeline, meeting his eyes before I bent forward to catch my breath.

For a moment, neither of us moved. All I could hear was my panting breaths as I braced my hands against my thighs and watched the glow of the Shalémo symbol on Hayden's wrist dim.

He stared at me as if I might disappear at any moment. "You're here."

I nodded, unable to stop the way my lips tipped up at his surprise though they fell just as fast. Maybe he hadn't been in my dream after all.

"I thought you said—?"

"I did." He stood and took a tentative step forward. "Of course I want you here, Khara. Of course I want you."

Hearing it in a dream was one thing. Hearing it face-to-face was another. Relief rushed over me, and with it, a fresh torrent of tears that I tried to choke back.

"I don't understand why. Why do you want me here? Why do you want me at all? I forgot you. I've been with Ramsey all this time. After everything I've done—"

Hayden strode toward me, skirting the charred remains of a felled tree as he shook his head. "You have done nothing to make me question my love for you. *Nothing*. I told you, Ramsey's at fault, not you. You didn't know."

"I still let him—"

He pressed a gentle finger to my lips. When I went quiet, his hand slid to my cheek. "You didn't know. You can't make an informed decision when all you know are lies. I don't blame you for what happened. You shouldn't blame yourself, either."

It was too late for that. Blame had been my constant companion since I learned the truth. I wasn't sure I'd be able to forgive myself. I blamed Ramsey too. Of course I did. But I couldn't forget the way I'd opened up to him. How I'd become so comfortable with him that I was willing to bring him into my bed. I'd chosen him that night. Even if it was a manipulation, I'd agreed to it at the time. What did that say about me?

"Please stop." The pain in Hayden's voice stabbed my heart. "I know what you're doing. It's not your fault."

"I feel like a terrible person." My voice broke under the weight of my confession.

Hayden pressed his forehead to mine, and I closed my eyes, my throat tightening further. "You're not one."

He spoke with such confidence I couldn't help but meet his gaze again. The affection held there echoed the warmth of his touch. I let his words settle over me, his absolution a balm to the tatters of my heart.

A small smile played over his lips as he added, "Feelings lie."

The words from my dream. "I said that to you once."

Hayden jerked back. "You remember that?"

"I'd been dreaming of us before you spoke to me. It was too vivid to only be a dream."

"You remembered that day?" A wistful smile spread over his face. "It was a good one."

"I didn't see much." I hated to temper his happiness, but I wouldn't pretend. Not with him. "I don't know where you were taking me or what the surprise was. Just that there was one."

"I was taking you to a grove a lot like this one. I'd found it a few days before, during a scouting mission. I couldn't wait to show you. I knew you'd love it."

I managed to tear my eyes from the soft smile on his face to look around the grove. Despite the cracked trees and felled limbs—damage from Hayden's powers on my last visit—it still held a peaceful presence. I took it in with a fresh sense of wonder.

"You found another place like this?"

He nodded, his eyes soft and bright with memories I didn't share anymore. "Wherever we end up, groves are our place. Always have been."

The words swept over me, soaking into my soul. And yet, I found myself staring at the ground. Shame rose from my belly and wrapped around my throat.

"What's wrong?" His hand touched mine, soft as the breeze. "Khara, please look at me."

I shook my head, mashing my lips together so I wouldn't cry. All I'd been doing lately was crying. I was tired of it.

Silence stretched between us. It was quiet long enough that I started telling myself all the reasons why Hayden really *was* upset with me. What I'd done was awful. I didn't deserve for him to be so gentle with me. I didn't deserve his kindness, let alone his love. How could he love me after everything?

The next thing I knew, he had me wrapped in his arms. One hand rested against the back of my neck, holding me close to his heart. The other rested against my lower back.

Every muscle in my body tensed. Hayden's heart beat a steady rhythm against my ear, calm and unhurried. My face pressed to his chest, I breathed in the hints of cedar, cinnamon, and smoke from his shirt. As the heat of his body seeped into mine, I started to relax.

I fought it, tensing again in his arms. I didn't deserve it. I couldn't *trust it*.

"I love you," Hayden said, his voice breathy against my hair. "It might not make sense to you right now, but I do. I love you more than anyone I've ever met, more than anyone I ever will. Past, present, future—*I love you*. Please let me."

I couldn't argue with that. I didn't want to.

With a sigh that shook my body loose, I leaned into Hayden's hold. His arms shifted, tightening around me until I was surrounded by safety.

He meant this. He meant every word. I could feel it in the warm, gentle puff of air he breathed against my hair, the confidence of his stance, the lack of hesitation in his nearness. I could feel the way he loved me and it was the most incredible, baffling thing I'd ever known.

It would take time to fully trust his love. But I could at least try to accept it.

I brought my arms up to rest against Hayden's back.

"It doesn't, you know," I said finally. "Make sense to me."

He huffed a laugh, resting his forehead on my shoulder. "I figured."

"But I believe you." I gripped him tighter, hoping he could sense the truth in my words the way I could in his. "I'm trying to keep this. Keep you."

His lips quirked into a smile against my shoulder. "I know what happens when you try. If I have your attempt, I know it'll work out for us in the end."

My lips curved upward. His belief in me left me feeling more confident of it too.

I wasn't sure how long we stood beneath the stars with our arms wrapped around each other. I didn't want to let go. This sense of warmth and safety wasn't something I was eager to give up. With Hayden's heart beating steadily in my ear, mine seemed to start mending again. Being near him was healing in its own way, even without his powers.

I sighed as I finally pulled away. Hayden hesitated before releasing me. As soon as his arms fell away, I missed the contact, but apprehension kept me from returning to it. Fear whispered not to take too much. Not to get too comfortable too soon. I'd made that mistake before. Best to be careful now.

Clearing my throat, I gestured to the grass. "Could we sit?"

"Of course."

We moved farther into the clearing and settled in the grass. Hayden sat close to me like he would during our healing sessions. Our knees would brush if either of us moved, but the proximity wasn't as unnerving to me as it'd been before I learned the truth. This felt like something I could get used to. Something I wanted to be familiar with again.

I fiddled with the grass in front of me, letting the cool blades slip between my fingers as I snuck glances at Hayden. He tapped a finger against his tattoo as he stared into the treeline. There were probably a million things we needed to discuss, but I had no idea where to start. Part of me wanted to forget it all and just rest here with him for a while.

The breeze shifted one of Hayden's curls onto his forehead. I fought a smile and the urge to tuck it back into place. There was something charming about the way it always fell into his eyes.

Hayden shook himself, pushed the curl back, and turned to me. "I have a question."

I plucked a blade of grass and rolled it between my fingers. "Then ask."

"Why did you stay away for so long?"

I winced and kept my eyes on my hands. He deserved an answer—I'd left him waiting for days—but I doubted he'd like the honest one.

"I didn't want to," I admitted. "When I went back to the Annex, I locked myself in my room for three days. I was overwhelmed and ashamed and being numb was easier than facing everything. And I was so sure you'd want nothing to do with me. *I* wanted nothing to do with me."

I risked glancing at Hayden and caught the stricken look in his eyes. "I'll say it as many times as I have to until you believe it. It wasn't your fault."

"I just feel like I should've known." I sliced the blade of grass in two with my thumbnail. "Like I should've stopped him."

In the edge of my vision, he shook his head before staring off into the trees. My confession settled between us, heavy, but not unbearable when shared. The silence had just begun to feel awkward when Hayden softly tipped my chin up so he could look into my eyes.

"He manipulated you. Maybe you should've known, but you didn't because he's done something terrible to you. He took *everything* from you." His jaw clenched and a spark jumped from his hand. He shook it out, pausing to breathe deep. "Ramsey is a liar and a murderer. All of it's on him. Don't think for a second that I blame you for any of this."

Before I could figure out how to respond, he shifted, kneeling in front of me and taking my hands in his. "Khara, with all that I am, I promise I'm still yours. As long as you want to be with me, you will be. I still choose you. I'd say my vows in my next breath if you asked me to."

The sincerity in his eyes shone brighter than the stars above us. He meant this. He really would tie himself to me, right in this clearing.

My eyes stung with tears and my heart sped as the truth settled over me. "You really love me."

The astonishment in my voice was so obvious, I winced. But I couldn't help it. The depth of his commitment was stunning.

Hayden laughed, the sound wet, but deep and joyful all the same. His eyes sparkled with peace, and the fondness he directed at me couldn't be denied. It made his words all the more believable. "I really do."

He brought my hand to his lips for a kiss. A slow, shy smile formed on my face as acceptance warmed me from the inside out.

I lost track of time. It should've consumed my thoughts, but I was too content in the quiet of the grove. Too content in Hayden's presence. We didn't speak much as we lay on our backs, side by side in the grass. Next to each other, but not quite touching.

I could have inched closer. Hayden would've welcomed me into his arms. Part of me longed to do it. I imagined resting my head against his chest and letting the gentle rise and fall of his breaths lull me to sleep. It was tempting, but the larger part of me didn't want to risk it.

It was too soon. It would take time for me to fully accept this. His love. *Us.*

The stars dimmed as the night sky faded to a lighter blue. Dawn grew too close to ignore the passing time. I sighed, rolling to face Hayden. We needed to talk. He mirrored my position, facing me with an open expression.

"What do we do now?" I asked, my fingers lazily tracing patterns in the grass.

"What do you want to do?"

A million possibilities flew through my mind. I wanted so many things, I couldn't pinpoint which I wanted most. I did know one thing. "I don't feel safe in Anluan anymore."

Hayden frowned, but nodded.

"I don't want to go back there tonight."

"Then don't," Hayden said, as if it were that simple. Maybe it was.

"Will you stay with me?"

"Of course I will," he said, barely letting me finish the question. "But if we're going to sleep, we should have better cover."

76

Hayden led me into the trees on the far side of the clearing where a makeshift shelter stretched between a cluster of trees. While it provided some cover, it wouldn't do much if it rained. A backpack was propped up against a tree, while a pile of blankets formed a thin bed on the forest floor. Nearby, remnants of a fire smoldered, the light haze of smoke scenting the air.

"I settled here after the first night I found you in the grove." He rubbed the back of his neck as he watched me take in his camp. "I've had to move around a bit. It wouldn't be safe for me to stay in one place for so long. But this spot's my favorite."

I blinked before locking my eyes on him. "You haven't gone home at all?"

"I wasn't about to leave you that long." He bent to pull a blanket from the shelter. "I've met with representatives from our camp and made moves with some of our teams, but I wanted to stay in case you needed me. Besides, it's pretty comfortable here." He sat at the base of a thick cedar just beyond the shelter and patted the ground. "Come sit with me for a while."

It didn't look very comfortable, but I joined him anyway. It would have been difficult for the two of us to fit under the shelter. We would've been practically on top of each other. Heat rose in my cheeks. Staying out here was better.

The patch of dirt was dry and clean, no harder than the grassy clearing. I mimicked Hayden and leaned against the trunk. The bark was smooth and not nearly as uncomfortable as I'd expected.

Hayden grinned as I settled in with a sigh. "See? I told you."

"Do you often sleep sitting up?" I asked, blinking heavily.

"Sometimes." He chuckled. "You can use me as a pillow if you'd like. I won't mind."

I'd resisted earlier. I probably should have again. But I was too tired to object. I would've ended up resting against him if I'd fallen asleep in our position anyway.

So I leaned against his side, tentatively resting my head on his shoulder. I barely felt Hayden's arm wrap around me before I drifted to sleep.

A sharp snap startled me awake. Beside me, Hayden sat alert, one tense arm held out in front of me. I wasn't sure if he meant to protect me or keep me back. He motioned for me to be quiet, and I nodded, barely breathing as thin streaks of lightning flashed in the browns of his eyes. The flare of his power highlighted flecks of amber, making them all the more mesmerizing.

Hayden shifted to stand with practiced ease. I barely heard him, and we were close enough to touch. As he rose, he pulled a throwing knife from a leather holster around his ankle. Though he was ready to draw on his powers if necessary, they could attract too much attention if used at the wrong time. We'd been lucky we weren't found before. I doubted we had much luck left.

I followed Hayden's lead, standing as quietly as I could. I'd heard nothing alarming since the initial snap of the branch, but I knew better than to let my guard down. Someone else was here. I could feel it.

"There you are!"

A head popped into the copse of trees, and I let out an embarrassing squeak before covering my mouth with my hands. Hayden threw his blade so fast I didn't even notice until it landed with a thunk in a sycamore tree just behind where the head had been.

Gage walked out into the open, hands in his pockets and a wide grin across his face. He glanced at the blade stuck in the tree and raised a brow at Hayden. "Yeah, I figured that's about how this would go."

My heart raced. Had Gage followed me here? Was he going to hand us over to Ramsey?

He turned to me, and his grin grew mischievous as he took in how close I stood behind Hayden. "Now, that's more like it!"

Hayden's body drained of tension. He sighed heavily as he stalked past Gage to wiggle his blade from the tree. "What are you doing here, Gage?"

His words were laced with a fond exasperation I couldn't understand. They knew each other? Every time I thought I understood what was going on, something like this happened and reminded me how much I still didn't know.

"Khara wasn't back yet." He shrugged, an impish grin on his face. "I came to find her." His smile fell as he glanced between me and Hayden. "Ramsey's going to call for her early this morning."

That didn't necessarily mean anything bad. Ramsey visited me early in the morning often enough. Still, my stomach churned. So much had changed in such a short time. And I still didn't understand what was happening *here*.

Hayden rubbed his forehead, then let his hand fall heavy to his side. He looked as worn down as I felt. "We need a plan, then."

"That's why I'm here."

I pointed at Gage, my head spinning. "I'm sorry, *why* are you here?" I turned to Hayden, trusting he wouldn't lie. "Why is he here?"

"It's okay," Hayden said as he clapped Gage on the shoulder. "He's with us. Gage has been spying for me since he joined Ramsey's guard after the divide." He smirked, his voice teasing when he added, "He's insufferable, but he has his uses."

Gage shoved Hayden's hand off his shoulder. "Insufferable? I'm a delight!"

He turned to me, offering a tight smile. In the moonlight, I caught a glint of sadness shining in his eyes. "My family, they don't understand what's really going on in Anluan. They believe in Ramsey, always have. Not me. Hayden and his father have always been good to me, despite my family's issues with their rule. I wasn't on palace grounds the night it all went down. My parents—"

His jaw tightened as he stared at the ground. He shook his head and didn't finish his thought.

"When I finally caught up with you and the Shalémos a couple of weeks after the war broke out, I'd already been deemed loyal to Ramsey and accepted into his new guard. I offered to stay and help take Ramsey down from the inside so we can set things right." He shrugged as if it were no big deal. "I've been working in Anluan ever since."

"Gage has saved countless lives from his position within the guard. Just by being in the Annex, he's given us the edge we need, now more than ever." Hayden looked at Gage with pride and fondness. "He's my brother in every way that matters."

I blinked, replaying every interaction I'd had with Gage since leaving medical. "Wait, so when you kept letting me leave my room at night, you knew I was coming here?"

"Not exactly." Gage chuckled, rubbing the back of his neck. "I hoped, at first. You have to understand, Khara, this"—he motioned between Hayden and himself—"doesn't happen often. Not since the first few months after the divide. I can't risk anyone getting suspicious. Once my cover's blown, game over."

I cringed, imagining what might happen if he were caught. I'd been nervous about him keeping my secrets. All this time, he'd been carrying his own that were just as dangerous.

"When it's important," he added, "I slip information to trusted runners within Anluan. They make sure the details make it back to the rebel camp. Sometimes I have to send people whispering and hope the right rumors make it to the right people on time. It can get messy. Things happen fast sometimes, and I have to wing it. I don't always know what I'm doing."

"You do the best you can," Hayden said, squeezing Gage's shoulder. "That's more than enough."

"Yeah, well ..." Gage shrugged. "Still feels like I should do more, you know?"

I did. The weight of responsibility pulled me down sometimes. And I wasn't even in the same high-stakes situations Gage had been dealing with for the last two years.

"So at first, with you," he continued, nodding to me, "I was just hoping you'd find your way to Hayden with some hints. I couldn't just tell you to go find him or sneak you out here myself. I had to try to nudge you in the right direction."

"The day at the market?" I asked as realization dawned. He'd *wanted* me to hear him talk to Cethin?

Gage laughed. "Yeah, I knew you were listening. Talking about one of the tunnels into the city was a risk, but I know Ceth. He'd never bring something like that to Ramsey's attention without checking it out first. And he's not about to look into something I brought up on a whim." A delighted grin swept over his face. "He thinks I'm an idiot."

Cethin wasn't the only one in Anluan who'd underestimated Gage. I'd failed to see how clever he was behind his mask of broad grins and never-ending jokes. Gage was far more than he seemed, even to me. And I owed him a lot.

"Thank you," I said, my throat tightening. "I wouldn't have made it here without you."

Gage's smile softened. "I don't believe that. You'd have found each other again somehow. I'm just not as patient as Hayden." He laughed as Hayden shoved him, making his upper body sway. "But you're welcome. I've been doing my best to look after you."

The easy way he said it, as if it were no more than to be expected, brought tears to my eyes.

His shoulders dropped, and he motioned toward me. "Can I?"

Though I wasn't sure what he was asking, I nodded. I'd managed to place a measure of trust in Gage when I couldn't trust anyone. That was enough for me, especially now that I'd seen how highly Hayden thought of him.

Gage swept me into a tight hug. I froze, surprise stilling my limbs. But his arms were gentle, cradling me with care, and I relaxed.

His voice was quiet when he spoke. "I've missed you so much."

I blinked rapidly, fighting back tears as I slowly brought my arms up to return the embrace. I could feel the truth in his words. Gage was someone to Hayden, but he was someone to me too. Someone I had yet to remember.

He swiped at his eyes as he pulled back, flashing me an embarrassed smile. "It's been hard, staying distant enough to do my job."

What could I say to that? I didn't remember what we were like before. Didn't know the true nature of our relationship. I glanced at Hayden. He leaned against the tree at his back, watching us with a pinch of sadness in his eyes.

"Ramsey knows we were friends before. It's part of why he chose me to be one of your guards—he knows I'll protect you. But he believes I'm absolutely loyal to him because of my family and what happened in Anluan when the war broke out." Gage sighed, folding his arms. "I can't give him any reason to suspect differently. I have to be careful, especially around you."

I squeezed Gage's arm, wishing I had words to comfort him and more memories to guide me. My mind replayed moments I'd shared with Gage since we'd met all those weeks ago.

I frowned as my mind latched onto a memory. Maybe it wasn't the time, but I had to ask. "What's the deal with the princess thing?"

Gage laughed outright, his chest shaking with mirth.

Hayden's lips twitched as he shook his head. "Seriously? You're still resurrecting old world titles?"

"What? I was trying to jog her memory!" Gage grinned wildly as he turned to me. "I used to call you that all the time during training. Drove you nuts."

"It still does," I said. "This might've been worse. I've been so confused!"

"Then it seems my plan was effective. Made you wonder, didn't I?"

I rolled my eyes, though I didn't bother hiding my smile. As I glanced up, the sky stole my attention again. I grimaced. "It's getting light."

Gage turned to Hayden. "What do we do?"

He looked at me. "Khara?"

I closed my eyes. It was easier to decide if I wasn't looking at Hayden. The more time I spent with him, the more I wanted to stay. But Ramsey had been so confident yesterday. He was planning something, and he seemed sure it would hurt the rebels. I didn't know his strategy, but I knew enough to be wary.

"Ramsey's up to something," I said, measuring each word as I finally looked at Hayden. "Something big. He's been talking for weeks about taking care of the rebels once and for all. Yesterday, he said it would be soon."

"He called the guard together to tell us to be ready, but he didn't go into detail about his plans," Gage said. "I'm trying to gather more information, but he's keeping it close. Inner circle only."

"You're not inner circle?"

"Not yet. I've been working my way up, but as you know, not everyone's fond of my attitude." Lifting his chin, he added, "Ramsey is, though. He likes that I don't take myself so seriously. But for now, I don't have a way to get more information about whatever he's up to. I have to wait until information is given to me."

Hayden frowned. "And that might be as it's happening, not before."

"That's what I'm afraid of."

I folded my arms, tuning out their conversation. There had to be another way. Hayden needed to be prepared for whatever Ramsey had in store. If he wasn't, it could be devastating. Gage couldn't get the information we needed, but maybe I could.

"What if I find out what he's up to?"

Hayden and Gage froze midconversation and turned to me.

Gage tilted his head. "What did you have in mind?"

"I'm not sure," I said. "But I have more access to Ramsey than anyone. The day I was attacked outside his office, he was meeting with his advisors. There were papers. Maybe they're what we need. I could try to grab them?"

Hayden went quiet. His lips pressed into a thin line as he clenched his hand into a fist. His tattoo held the faintest glow around the edges. I winced, remembering how he'd lost control of his powers before.

Gage followed my line of sight. He frowned, placing a careful hand on Hayden's shoulder. "You okay?"

Hayden released a long breath and shook out his hand. "Fine. Just haven't slept well lately." He searched my eyes. "Are you sure you can do this? Go back to Ramsey and act like nothing's wrong? Sneak around to find what we need?"

I wasn't sure, not really. Just yesterday I'd felt like I was unraveling in Ramsey's presence. Could I go back and pretend nothing had changed?

It would be difficult, but I had to try. Whatever his plans, they were too important to leave discovering them to chance. "I can do this."

Hayden stayed quiet, considering my words. All the while, he held my gaze.

"This could work," Gage said. "Hayden, if anyone could do it, it would be her."

There was an implication there that made me want to know more about the girl they remembered. I had a feeling she was braver than I was. That I could use more of her in me.

"I don't like it," Hayden said at last. "I've never liked you being in danger. But if you want to do this, we'll do what we can to help you."

"Absolutely," Gage said. "Whatever you need."

"Just—" Hayden ran a hand through his hair and looked away. His brows pinched together, and when he looked back at me, pain shone in his eyes. "Are you sure you'll be okay with Ramsey?"

My stomach dropped as my mind flashed to the night of the engagement party. Nausea swirled in my gut any time I thought of it. I swallowed thickly.

"I can handle him." My voice came out hoarse. I'd have to do better than that to reassure him. I cleared my throat. "He backed off last night."

It was the wrong thing to say. Hayden's eyes flashed with anger, a jagged bolt of lightning flaring across his iris as soon as the words registered. His anger wasn't directed at me, but it pierced my heart just the same. I spared a glance at Gage, but he looked just as upset.

"Hayden," I said firmly, "I can handle Ramsey. I know what I'm dealing with now."

He kept his eyes squeezed shut for a moment, then exhaled a long breath. Hand fisted against the tree to his left, he nodded. "Okay." He ran a rough palm down his face, gathering himself. "Gage."

Gage straightened at the command in Hayden's voice. It startled me to see such attentive posture from someone who appeared nonchalant all the time. My appreciation for his acting grew even more.

I assumed there would be an order of some kind to follow, but Gage nodded as if he'd heard everything he needed to in the way Hayden had said his name. He placed a closed fist directly over his heart.

"With my life."

Hayden covered Gage's fist with his hand. "From the ashes."

Gage echoed the words before Hayden pulled him into a tight hug. When they broke apart, they turned to me with watery eyes.

The dual observation didn't unnerve me the way I would've expected it to. Somehow, being near them only made me feel stronger, like I was coming back to myself.

When Hayden stepped toward me, Gage quietly backed away. "I'll wait for you in the clearing."

I nodded, but my eyes didn't stray from Hayden. He stood close, one of his hands rising to cradle my face. The other settled against the side of my neck and his fingers curled into my hair. He didn't speak for a moment, just stared into my eyes like a man desperate to keep what he treasured most.

"I know it's in your nature to risk. You're a fighter. That's all I can ask you to be." His lips pulled up at the corners. "Be who you are, but please, be careful."

His eyes held me in place, trying to tell me everything he didn't have the words to say. Those messages swirled in their depths, drawing me in though I could only translate a few of them into words. Love and concern. Belief and a desire to protect.

Hayden was fierce and gentle in his love for me, all at once. He believed in me, but was concerned for me too. He wanted me to be cautious, not just for himself, not even just for me—but for both of us, and for us all.

I couldn't promise to be safe, but I could give him my word to be careful.

"I will."

He pressed his lips to my forehead. Somehow, that kiss felt more intimate than any other.

77

GGAGE AND I MADE our way back to the city in silence. Rays of morning light peeked through gaps in the cloud cover, and my heart raced. I'd never been out during this time of the morning. Gage seemed tense as well, which only heightened my anxiety. Being caught beyond the gates now would be devastating.

We were almost to the edge of the forest when Gage gently set his hand on my arm. I stopped, looking around to see if I'd missed something, but there was no immediate danger. When I turned back to him, he wouldn't look at me.

I frowned. "Gage?"

Lifting his head, he finally met my eyes. His shone with tears. Beyond their sheen lurked an angry glint that made me want to step back. Seeing someone so full of joy holding that kind of anger unnerved me.

"I'm sorry, Khara." His voice broke as he released my arm. "I'm so sorry."

I'd grown used to being confused over the last several weeks. Still, this was one of the most confusing encounters I could remember. My heart plummeted. What if he was betraying me?

I could run. He might catch me, but—

"I, uh—" Gage shook his head, swiping his hand down his face. "I know what Ramsey did. The night of the engagement party."

The blood drained from my face. Memories of that night flashed in my mind, powerful and conflicting. I wanted to retch every time I thought of it. It all felt so wrong now.

"Are you okay?" Gage's eyes widened and he held up his hands. "I'm making a mess of this." He spoke in a rush, the words tumbling out like he couldn't stop them. "I'm so sorry. I didn't know he was going to do that, not until it was too late. I swear, I would've stopped him."

Guilt. I swallowed thickly, letting my heart slow. Guilt was an emotion I was familiar with—and not one I liked seeing on his face. It aged him. Took away his vibrancy. Gage should always look alive.

"It wasn't your fault." I grimaced at the thought of what might have happened had he known and tried to interfere in Ramsey's business. "Besides, you would've given up your place in the Annex if you'd tried anything. And that's only if you hadn't been killed in the process."

Gage scoffed, rubbing his free hand over his eyes and swiping traces of tears against his uniform pants. "Like that matters. I'd have done it anyway. I would've killed him or let him choke the life out of me trying before I'd have left you to him like that. Believe me."

His eyes were bright with emotion. He meant it. He'd lay his life down for me without hesitation. I saw it in his fiery anger toward Ramsey, in the love he had for me, in the respect he held for Hayden. He was on my side, irrevocably.

My throat tightened. "I believe you."

He nodded and sniffed, smiling slightly. "We better get back. If I'm going to get you to your suite without anyone noticing, we're going to have to hurry."

When we emerged onto the streets, Anluan was busier than I expected it to be. The sun had pushed its way out of the clouds, beating down on the pavement with unusual force for so early in the morning. Heat crept through the soles of my shoes as Gage led the way toward the Annex.

At times, we slunk through alleyways like fugitives. Others, Gage motioned for me to join him in brazenly walking down the road as if we had every right to be there. With him by my side, maybe I wasn't technically breaking any rules. Still, better to be safe than have our motives questioned.

The closer we got to the Annex, the louder the city became. My brow furrowed and I tilted my head, trying to make sense of the growing shouts. I looked to Gage, who wore the serious expression I was still getting used to.

"What's going on?" I asked quietly, stepping closer to him.

"Nothing good."

He glanced at me, then to the towering Annex. We were close now, and I could see Gage warring with himself. Deliver me safely to my room, or check out what was happening down the street?

I wanted to know as badly as he did. Maybe more. "Let's find out."

At his hesitation, I raised a brow and crossed my arms. I was going for intimidating, but must have missed the mark.

Gage scoffed. "Yeah, okay."

With a heavy sigh, he glanced around. A booth caught his eye, and he wandered over to the collection of scarves on display. The vendor was absent, but Gage grabbed a lightweight shawl and left a handful of bills in its place.

He hurried back and held it out to me. "We need to hide your face."

I frowned, but took the scarf and positioned it into a makeshift hood.

When I looked at Gage, he smiled faintly. "Perfect. Let's go."

Monusbé Circle sat in Anluan's city center, close enough to palace grounds that the Annex and its twin tower loomed over the surrounding buildings. One of the roads leading away from the circle created a clear view of the front of the palace. Past an iron fence with white stone pillars, collapsed columns and a half-shattered glass dome served as stark reminders of the war's outbreak.

In the center of the circle rose the remnants of a crumbled monument. As I looked up at the jagged stone, I failed to picture it whole. Ramsey hadn't bothered to restore it, despite the circle being in a high-traffic area. What had it looked like before it was destroyed?

The closer we came to the monument, the louder it became. Gage took my hand as we neared the crowd, and I squeezed his for reassurance. I had a feeling he'd figured out what was going on. I was still clueless as we skirted the edge of the crowd gathering around one side of the monument.

I could make out some of the cries as we moved closer. Taunts and jeering shouts of *traitor* resounded. Fists were thrown high in the air, shaking in time with the yells. People pressed together so tightly there was barely room to move. It was chaos.

Gage frowned as he surveyed the scene. He tugged on my arm and led me to the edge of a brick building the color of rusted blood. Behind us sat an alley, a perfect getaway should we need to make a fast exit.

"What's going on?" I whispered, pressing close to him.

"Execution," he said tightly. "They caught another rebel."

I inhaled sharply, whipping my head back to the circle as the crowd grew louder. Cethin and Commander North stood on either side of a man so bloodied and bruised he hurt to look at. He was barely on his feet, his head hung low as they moved to the center of the monument's base. When they reached it, Cethin forced the man to his knees with a single push on his shoulder.

The crowd quieted as Commander North raised her hands. I stood, transfixed and uneasy as the man lifted his head. Beside me, Gage breathed his name, and my heart sunk heavy like a stone.

The battered man kneeling on the platform was Jonah, the glassmaker from the market.

78

Ramsey sauntered up the stone steps of the monument to the echoing cheers of the people. In his pristine suit, he stood tall and collected, a picture-perfect Sovereign. Despite his deliberate calm, something dangerous simmered beneath the surface. It sent a shiver down my spine.

I inhaled shakily, wrapping my arm around Gage's waist as I leaned into him. He held me to his side with one arm in turn, tense and quiet.

When Ramsey raised his hand, the crowd went silent.

"People of Anluan," he called as he gestured to his prisoner. "The man before you is a traitor to each of us. He was caught attempting to reach the rebels beyond the city walls. Do we tolerate such betrayal?"

The crowd roared its denial.

Ramsey's dark smirk widened into a wicked grin. "No, we do not." He turned to the guards behind him and nodded. "Commander."

A grim-faced Commander North gestured to Cethin before stepping aside. Fisting a hand in Jonah's hair, Cethin wrenched his head back, forcing him to look up at Ramsey.

My heart hammered in my chest as I got a better look at Jonah's face. Once so full of warmth, it was now swollen, covered in dark bruises and splotches of dried blood. Dread filled me, as though my body knew what would happen before my mind could process it.

"Jonah Zalmon," Ramsey proclaimed, "you are guilty of the highest treason. I hereby judge you as a traitor to Anluan and its people. Your sentence is death."

A cheer rose from the crowd. I tightened my hand around Gage's shirt as nausea swelled. Were they all so convinced by Ramsey's lies that they couldn't see how wrong this was? I knew better than most how charming he was, how easy his lies were to believe. Even so, there had to be someone else who was as sickened by this as I was.

"Trinity Zalmon is also hereby marked as a traitor of Anluan. When we find her," he said, "she will face execution for her crimes, assuming she isn't already dead at the hands of the rebels."

I cast my eyes over the crowd, desperate to find a face that wasn't lined with hatred or excitement. A woman at the edge of the throng caught my attention. She clutched a hand to her chest, her face set in a deep frown as she took in the proceedings. As though she sensed my gaze, she turned and our eyes locked.

Despite my covering, her back stiffened and her eyes widened with recognition. Tears dripped down her cheeks as she made a fist and moved it to rest right over her heart. My throat tightened when she dipped her head in a solemn bow before slipping onto a side street and out of sight.

I turned my attention back to where Jonah knelt before Ramsey. He showed no signs of remorse and no inkling of fear for his wife. My shoulders lowered a fraction. Trinity must have escaped. She would be safe outside of Anluan.

Jonah glared at Ramsey, a fire in his eyes that I could see even from the far edge of the crowd. "I am not afraid of death," he said, voice hoarse but steady and loud enough to echo around the circle. "And I'm not afraid of the likes of you."

The crowd hushed, waiting with bated breath for a blow we all knew was coming.

"But you do fear," Ramsey said as he moved to stand directly behind Jonah. My breath caught at the dark edge in his words. "That's all I need."

Gage squeezed my hand, and I tensed. I seemed to be the only one in the crowd who didn't know what was coming. I held my breath, blinking back tears. I didn't want to see whatever came next, but I refused to dishonor Jonah by turning away.

"May your soul find forgiveness in its release," Ramsey said with a mocking edge. Then he pressed his hands roughly against both sides of Jonah's head.

Jonah seized up and screamed, his tormented bellow the worst sound I'd ever heard. I flinched into Gage's side, but kept my eyes fixed on Jonah. I would not—could not—look away. Not from the agonized lines of his face or his corded neck. Not from his eyes, clenched shut, or his arched back. My next breath came as a shuddering gasp, and Gage held me tighter, his body so stiff I could feel it tremor.

Ramsey removed his hands, but Jonah's screams continued. My vision blurred, and I blinked, letting the tears fall and placing a hand against my stomach as it roiled.

This was not an execution. It was public torture. A glaring warning of what would happen to those who stood against Ramsey's reign.

Ramsey raised his hands from behind Jonah, pressing them together, then slowly pulling them apart. A thick smoke formed between them, dark and foreboding. He watched it swirl to life with fondness in his eyes. When he stared at the man at his feet, his expression shifted to disgust. Jonah gasped for breath between cries, face pale and lined more with pain than age.

Ramsey had no mercy for him.

The smoke shifted from where it hovered in the air as Ramsey turned his hands. He directed it, showing it exactly where to go—straight down Jonah's throat.

Jonah began to choke, the sound somehow worse than his screams. Ramsey's lips twitched upward as he coaxed the smoke to expand until it blocked Jonah's face from view. With a sharp pulling motion from Ramsey, it covered Jonah's face entirely. He would suffocate in minutes.

The crowd cheered again. Ramsey reveled in it, unbothered that Jonah had fallen on his side and now spasmed at his feet. I bent at the waist and heaved.

Lifting my eyes, I caught wisps of smoke curling away from the spectacle on the raised platform. They hovered overhead, thin tendrils dipping to weave through the crowd. Foreboding settled over me like a heavy blanket as the smoke moved farther into the street.

As my attention locked back onto the scene in front of me, my hands trembled at my sides. My breath quickened. Fear. Wrapping around my throat, tightening my chest—this was *fear*. Of Ramsey. Of his power. Of moving against him only to end up right where Jonah was—broken and dying at his feet while a crowd watched.

This was fear. And as the smoke settled above my head but did nothing to impede my view of the proceedings, I realized it was born of manipulation. Ramsey's powers had blended together. Amplified fear slipped from the smoke, bleeding into the crowd. Making us uneasy. Afraid. Easier to exploit.

It registered in my mind, but I could do nothing about it as my heart beat faster in my chest.

"Come on," Gage said, his strong hands helping me straighten. "We should go."

We fled into the alley unnoticed. My breath came in short gasps I couldn't control, and I placed a hand against my chest, blinking through tears. It was too much. I slowed to a stop, leaning against the cool brick of the building beside me.

"We need to get out of here," Gage said, his voice tight as we heard another cheer echo from the circle.

I knew that. We were too close to Ramsey, too close to the crowd. If someone saw me falling to pieces out here, it wouldn't end well. But I couldn't stop the breakdown.

"How can they support him like this, cheer while he suffocates a man?" A sob burst from my lips, and I pressed a shaking hand against my mouth to smother more.

Gage pulled me from the wall and into his chest, holding me so tight I could feel the strain against my ribs. "Some have been convinced by his lies. Some believe the violence is necessary."

I shuddered, my mind flooding with the ways I had so easily believed Ramsey myself.

"Most have learned to fear him," Gage continued. "Any public disagreement with his rule is severely punished. But this is just one crowd. There are others in this city—more than you think—that don't approve and never will. There are still people fighting. *Your people*. Here in the city and in the rest of the kingdom. He doesn't have everyone under his thumb."

I managed a jerky nod against his chest.

"I'm sorry," he whispered. "I know how it feels, seeing it for the first time. And with all you've been through, I can't imagine ..."

I shook in his arms, my breaths hitching. He let me cry for a moment, holding me through my attempts to regain my composure. When I managed it, he released me and met my eyes.

"Jonah knew the risks of what he was doing. We'll find Trinity, make sure she's safe. We'll remember Jonah. We'll fight in honor of him and everyone else Ramsey's destroyed. He won't be forgotten, not by any of us."

I nodded, steadying myself with a deep breath as I held onto Gage's forearms. Even without remembering our relationship, I knew why I loved him. His strong, protective support was like a brother's.

"Thank you," I whispered.

"I'm always here for you," he said as if his support needed no thanks. "We need to move, though."

I glanced at the alley's opening. People milled around, moving away from the circle. The spectacle was over. They would return to their normal day as if the loss of Jonah's life didn't matter. I shuddered at the callousness, then turned away and followed Gage back toward the Annex.

More determination filled me with every step. I would find out what Ramsey was planning, and I would put an end to it. After what I'd just witnessed, there would be no stopping me.

79

I DIDN'T TRULY APPRECIATE how sneaky Gage was until we'd made it safely back inside the Annex. Once in the main halls, we were able to traipse around as if we hadn't just been trekking through the city after breaking the law. A law that—as I'd just witnessed firsthand—was punishable by death.

I tried to wipe the remnants of horror from my face before we made it inside, but I wasn't sure it worked. In my mind, Jonah's face shifted from screaming to smothered in dark smoke. Pushing it from my thoughts seemed impossible. Why did I remember the things I wanted to forget, while the memories I was so desperate for alluded me?

Gage followed me to my suite. He had to slip back into his role here—the jokester guard, friendly but kept at a careful distance. While I understood, I longed to spend more time with the warm friend he'd been to me beyond the gates.

The intricate design of my door came into view, and I sighed, pressing my palm flat against the wood. I could already imagine the relief of hot water against my skin. If only it could wash away what I'd witnessed.

As I cracked the door open, I turned to Gage, who offered me a sad smile. "I'll be right here. Shift change is in"—he glanced at his watch and grimaced—"twenty minutes now."

"I'll be fine." It probably would've been more convincing if I didn't sound so wrecked.

He shook his head but didn't get a chance to reply.

Emila burst through the door and pulled me into a fierce hug. "Where have you been? I was about to call for the guards! I've been so worried."

I blinked dully, trying to figure out what to say as she released me.

"We went for a walk," Gage said. "Don't worry, I was with her the whole time."

Emila arched her brow. It was hard to tell if she believed him or not.

"I was too restless to sleep," I said. "Gage was kind enough to escort me around the halls and garden for a while."

"Are you sure that's all it was? You look …" She winced at the same time I did. "Sorry, I didn't mean—"

I shook my head. "It's fine."

Behind me, Gage cleared his throat. "She *is* in need of rest. We left hours ago. There's no way she got enough sleep. Don't princesses need like twelve hours?"

I could hear the smirk in his voice and marveled at his skill. Even as this other version of himself, he kept protecting me, and it worked so well.

Emila rolled her eyes, but relented after scanning my face. "You do look like you could use more sleep. I'll let Ramsey know you weren't feeling well when he gets back."

Right. He would still be in the city. But this version of me shouldn't know where Ramsey was, wasn't supposed to know the horrifying thing he'd just done.

I frowned and tilted my head. "Back? Where is he?"

She flashed me a tense smile. Finding these cracks in her facade never hurt any less. "Nowhere interesting. He just had some business to attend to in the city. He should be back soon."

"Oh." I hoped she attributed the dullness in my voice to disappointment or exhaustion. Either way, she sensed the time for talking was over. She stepped closer and kissed my cheek.

"Rest well, Khara. I'll come by later today, if that's all right."

There was a hint of uncertainty in her words, like she was worried I'd say no. I hated that I cared, that I worried I'd hurt her feelings more than I'd realized when I pushed her away after learning the truth. Hated that I still instinctively reacted to her as if she were truly my friend.

"Of course it is," I said, forcing a tired smile. "A few hours of sleep and I'll be better company."

Emila's eyes brightened as her smile turned teasing. It made her seem more genuine. I hated that I could tell the difference now. "I'll look forward to it."

As she walked out, she pointed to Gage. "You'll watch out for her?"

"Until shift change."

"Good."

I moved to shut the door, catching Gage's eyes before it closed and mouthing a *thank you*.

He flashed a playful grin in return, bowing dramatically. "Of course, Princess."

I huffed a weary laugh and shook my head.

When he straightened, Gage motioned to my suite with his head. "Get some sleep."

Finally, an order I could get behind.

80

THE CROWD JEERED, THEIR words biting as they echoed around the circle. I cringed at every shout of *traitor* thrown my way. The concrete bit into my knees where I'd been forced to kneel. The hands against my upper arms felt more like iron bands than flesh. That was the least of my pain.

My ribs radiated it with every shallow inhale. My ring fingers were broken, twisted into angles that hurt to look at. Bruising around my neck made swallowing agony.

The crowd exploded into cheers as Ramsey strode up the steps to the monument. This time, he wasn't smiling, but the murderous rage filling his body from burning eyes to clenched fists was worse. He looked at me with such hatred, I couldn't help but flinch. His lips curved at the reaction.

Ramsey turned to the crowd, projecting his voice so it echoed throughout the circle. "Khara Laveya," he spat, "you have been found guilty of the highest treason. The penalty is death."

Defiance filled me as our gazes met. Though my heart pounded, I forced myself to show no signs of fear. If this were to be my end, I would face it with all the courage I had.

Ramsey moved behind me, and I jolted as he unleashed his powers against me. Harsh screams tore from my throat, blending with sobs. As brave as I wanted to be, I couldn't stop them. My heart thundered too fast, my breaths came too impaired. All I knew was overwhelming terror and pain unlike anything I'd ever felt.

"Khara, let me in!"

I cried out, shoving my hands up to force Ramsey's from my temples, but they were already gone. The first tendrils of heavy gray smoke formed in my peripheral vision.

"Khara, you're dreaming. Let me in!"

Hayden? Clarity rushed over me, and I sobbed in relief.

This was a dream. And if I was dreaming ...

I clenched my eyes shut to block out the smoke curling in front of me. Instead, I focused on Hayden. Him saying he loved me. His hands against my temples, pushing away pain. His voice, saying my name with reverence and hope and so much love that it overwhelmed me in an entirely different way.

As soon as I sensed his presence, I opened my eyes.

The dream had frozen. Smoke hovered inches from my face as Hayden knelt beside me, his gaze roving from me to the gathered crowd. His eyes flashed with fury.

When he spotted Ramsey behind us, arms raised to control the smoke, he jolted to his feet. Striding to Ramsey, he shoved, directing his power toward him. Light flared so brightly from his palms I had to shield my eyes. Everything disappeared. Only Hayden and I were left, standing in pure white.

He closed the distance between us, sweeping me into a fierce hug. "I will never let him do that to you." He pulled back, staring into my eyes as his hand cupped my face. "*Never.*"

I gave a jerky nod. I wanted to speak, to acknowledge his vow, but I had no words. The dream had left me too shaken.

I turned my hands over, expecting to find crooked fingers, but they were whole again. I took a deep breath and felt no pain.

Relief swept over me in a wave. I sagged under it, pressing my head into Hayden's chest, and cried.

When I regained control of myself, I didn't move from Hayden's chest. He held me steady, trailing one hand up and down my back in a soothing rhythm. I inhaled, deeply but shakily, before pushing myself back.

Hayden searched my face with stricken eyes. "I'm sorry you had to see that."

I scrubbed a hand down my face, then wiped under my eyes. "It's not your fault. At least I know what Ramsey's capable of now."

Hayden frowned. "I told you about his powers."

"But I didn't know they were like *that.*" I shuddered. "He's a monster."

"He wasn't always."

The grief in his voice softened me. I took his hand and squeezed. "In my dream," I said carefully, "when he touched me, I felt so terrified that it hurt."

Hayden grimaced. "He developed that power around the time he betrayed us. We're not sure how it formed. Our best guess is it's some sort of a manifestation of darkness within him." He let out a frustrated breath. "It allows him to fill anyone with immense fear. We're not sure how it works because as far as we know, no one he's used it on has survived."

My heart clenched. "Jonah."

Hayden shook his head, angry tears making his eyes shine. "Jonah was a good man. He didn't deserve that. No one does." He sighed heavily before pressing a kiss to my head. "Think of something good."

My mind was full of the morning's horrors and the intensity of my nightmare. It took a minute to think of anything pleasant. But with my eyes closed and Hayden's steady presence beside me, I shifted my thoughts to a sky full of stars and tall grass bent beneath my feet.

"Much better." I could hear the smile in Hayden's voice.

When I opened my eyes, we stood in the grove. A thousand stars glimmered overhead, and a gentle breeze moved through my hair. A trace of magic thrummed against my skin.

Hayden laced his fingers with mine as we stared up at the stars. It was exactly the kind of dream I could stay in forever.

81

Winding through the halls of the Annex with Cethin was a completely different experience than when I was with any of the other guards. Unlike with Gage, there was no teasing or laughter. Unlike with Charna, there was no reassuring presence at my back. As I struggled to keep up with Cethin's quick strides, the hem of my dress brushing my knees with every hurried step, there was only heavy silence and a simmering sense of unease in my gut.

There had always been something about Cethin that didn't sit right with me. His sharp edges had never cut me, but I'd shied away from them all the same. I'd thought it was just me being unfair, our personalities clashing. We'd never really made an effort to be friends to begin with. The guards had their duties to attend to, and I could appreciate setting boundaries between us. But after the way I'd seen him take part in Jonah's execution, being near him unnerved me in a new way.

I wasn't the only one uneasy around him. As Cethin charged toward Ramsey's office, people in the halls were quick to dart out of our path. While most usually steered clear of me in the Annex, this time, I didn't think it was because of me. More than once, I caught wary guards grimacing and exchanging glances behind his back. My attempts to give apologetic smiles didn't seem to do much good, but it gave me an excuse to trail farther behind.

I wasn't sure how much Cethin knew, but his loyalty to Ramsey was clear. He followed orders with cold precision and was one of the few guards assigned to escort me alone. Ramsey took great care in deciding who would guard me. Cethin had some measure of his trust ... but how much?

When he reached the elevator, Cethin held the door open and turned to me. Sunlight poured in from a side window, highlighting his blond hair and glinting against the steely blue of his eyes. It also accentuated the annoyed scowl on his face.

Despite his obvious impatience, I was in no hurry to catch up. The longer it took to reach our destination, the better. I'd only been to Ramsey's office once, the day I'd been thrown through the window by Lachlan. I winced, tracing the small scar forming at my hairline—another added to my collection from the war. I'd been terrified then. Today, fear sent my heart pounding for different reasons altogether.

Ramsey had called for me, just as Gage had said he would, and I had no idea what he wanted. After my nightmare and what I'd seen him do at the circle, the thought of being near him chilled me more than ever.

But I'd chosen to come back here. I had to see this through.

"Thank you," I murmured to Cethin as I slipped inside.

He grunted, but said nothing as he pressed the button for the office floor. He moved back a step, folding his arms, the flexing of his muscles visible through his uniform jacket. The glimpse of his strength while we shared an enclosed space sent my nerves buzzing.

I cleared my throat. "Do you know what Ramsey wants?"

He continued to stare straight ahead, not bothering to look at me. "Only that he wants to see you."

"I thought maybe he would've told you why."

"I don't need to know why." He shifted his weight as the elevator leveled. "It's none of my business."

The doors opened, and Cethin stepped out, keeping a hand in place to hold the door open for me. When he inclined his head, I followed him into the elevator bay and froze. The marble floor gleamed in the light, clean and polished. The windows had been restored. The only difference was the new painting hanging on the wall. They must not have been able to salvage the one I'd crashed into.

"It looks like nothing ever happened," I murmured, my hand gripping the sleeve of my thin sweater.

"Why wouldn't it?" Cethin scoffed, his brows rising. "It's not like we'd leave evidence of that rebel scum lying around."

Trepidation weighed down my chest. "What happened to him?"

Cethin's smirk was sharp as a blade. "He was taken care of."

"Was he sent to Kilhelm?"

He let out an annoyed breath and turned. "Why does it matter? He's not going to bother you again, that's all you need to know unless Sovereign Ramsey decides to tell you otherwise."

Without waiting for me, he moved to the access panel and pressed his palm to it.

"Let's go," he said as he swung the door open. "I won't keep him waiting."

Any desire I had to attempt further conversation vanished. Cethin's clipped answers and obvious disdain grated on my nerves. I swallowed back my frustration and stepped into the office wing.

With the door securely shut behind us, Cethin led me to a small lounge in the middle of the hall. The décor in the room was just as sleek and modern as Ramsey's office, but it seemed comfortable enough for casual gatherings. There was even a small patio accessible through a pair of arched glass doors. Under other circumstances, I might have rested well enough in this space.

Cethin motioned for me to sit on a black couch. "Wait here."

I bristled, crossing my arms as he moved to walk away. I hated that he expected me to do what he said. Then again, I'd been doing what I was told, following everyone else's lead since I'd woken up here.

"Oh, so I'm allowed to be alone now?" I asked, raising a brow when Cethin turned back to me.

His shock morphed into a sardonic glare. "For the moment, yes. This area is secure. You'll be safe and you won't be alone long." He smirked. "Enjoy it while it lasts."

I was supposed to be pretending we were on the same side, but as Cethin left the room, I couldn't help glaring at his back.

Not long turned out to be longer than I'd expected. It seemed a waste to sit obediently in the lounge when I could make an effort to find out what was going on.

I peeked around the doorway. The corridor was empty. Everything was quiet, save for a soft murmur of voices down the hall.

I crept toward Ramsey's office, where the muffled conversation came from. Many of the walls on this floor were mostly glass, preventing me from getting too close. I stopped just shy of his office suite and pressed my head as close to the glass as I could without being seen. The conversation remained muffled, but when I focused, I could make out the words.

"You're sure it will work?" Ramsey sounded cautiously excited.

"With Khara's test results, I have no doubt the adjusted version will perform just as well, if not better," Doctor Jensen said.

My breath caught. What test results?

"There were issues with the implementation in Khara."

"Those were unforeseen. But she's recovered well, and I've made the necessary adjustments to the process."

Whatever they'd done to me, they were going to do to more people. My stomach lurched and my breath quickened, too loud for the quiet hall. I shoved a fist in front of my mouth as I tried to stop my fear from shifting into sheer panic.

"We got what we needed out of Zalmon?" Ramsey asked.

"He wasn't well trained." Cethin sounded amused. "I got everything we needed. Three entry and exit points. We block those, the rebels are cut off from the city."

"Excellent." I could picture Ramsey's grin, the vengeful glint darkening his eyes. "We'll deal with them as soon as we enact the first phase. How soon can we make it happen?"

A voice I didn't recognize spoke. "A week, maybe less. The materials for the attack are ready. We just need to ensure that all evidence of the destruction points to the Shalémos and their rebels. Anyone who might have doubts about your rule will settle once they see the results."

"Risk of casualties?" Commander North asked.

"Minimal in the central regions. We'll plant the device near one of the rebels' exit points. The Eastern District will see the most loss."

Cethin snorted. "Not much of a loss."

Disgust surged in my chest at their disregard for our people. The Eastern District still struggled with the destruction caused by the initial outbreak of war. It was well known that some of Anluan's most vulnerable citizens lived there. Emila's mother's business was on the outskirts of the Eastern District.

"Every life lost is a loss to Anluan," Ramsey said. "But if this is the price required to turn the tides against the Shalémos, it's one worth paying. Commander?"

There was a pause before Ramsey moved on.

"Then we're in agreement—one week's time?" A beat. "Where's the device now?"

"Safely stored in my private lab," Doctor Jensen assured him. "Not even my assistants have access."

I'd heard enough. I couldn't allow this device—whatever it was—to be used. They would destroy the city to solidify Ramsey's control. People would die. Hayden would be blamed. And they wanted to invade someone else's mind like they had mine.

Fire ignited in my bones. I pushed off the wall and strode back to the lounge. This could not happen. And if I had anything to do with it, it never would.

82

Ramsey sauntered into the lounge with an ease that made me want to scream. He kissed my forehead in greeting. Despite the way my stomach churned, I did my best to smile back. I hoped my determination to ruin his plans would help me act as if all was well.

"Emila told me you were sleeping late," Ramsey said, voice warm as he settled beside me on the couch. His eyes held a possessive glint that filled me with unease. "You couldn't sleep last night?"

"I did for a while," I said. "But I woke up in the middle of the night and didn't want to toss and turn until the sun rose. Gage was kind enough to accompany me around the halls."

"I'm glad you were able to rest this morning, then." His hand brushed my thigh, where he drew lazy circles with his thumb. I forced my body not to tense. "How do you feel now?"

"Much better, now that I've slept." I paused and bit my lip, glancing at his hand before meeting his eyes. "Actually, I'm a little embarrassed."

He tilted his head. "Embarrassed? Why?"

"I didn't mean to be so ungrateful yesterday." I poured as much apology into my eyes as I could, covering his hand with mine. "I know you're only trying to protect me. I shouldn't have reacted the way I did. I was just tired and feeling cooped up and"—I flashed him a sheepish smile—"I took it out on you. I'm sorry, Ramsey."

Surprise flashed in his eyes before he blinked, shaking his head. "It's truly for your protection. I want to keep you with me, Khara. Losing you now would be unimaginable." He smirked as he caressed my cheek. "I think I'd lose my mind."

It was meant to be a joke, yet something in his eyes hinted at a level of truth. I worried Ramsey *could* become unhinged if he lost his hold on me. More so than he already was.

My heart clenched. The time was coming. No façade could last forever. What would happen then?

"Anyway," he said, shifting to interlace our fingers, "I wanted to see you. Make sure you were okay. I have a busy afternoon, but we could have dinner tonight. I'll cook."

That meant being in his suite. Alone. Bile rose in my throat. It would be too easy for him to expect more from me than I was willing to give—pretend or not.

I barely forced the lie through my teeth. "That sounds great."

"Good." Ramsey's eyes sparkled with pleasure. "I'll make sure you know when I'm ready for you."

He leaned forward. My body tensed and my heart raced, but I forced myself to relax as he kissed me. Leaning in, I cupped his face, and he smiled against my lips before deepening the kiss.

When he pulled away, I breathed raggedly as he moved his lips to my ear. "I love that you're mine." He played with my hair, running it between his fingers. "Having you here with me, like this—" He kissed the edge of my mouth before returning to my lips.

It was painful to respond in the way he expected me to. But I needed to sell this memoryless, devoted version of myself long enough to find the device. If I did, this would be worth it. At least, that's what I told myself as Ramsey's hands made possessive trails up and down my sides.

He shifted, lowering me on the couch, and my panic flared. If he could feel the way my heart jumped, I hoped he mistook it for excitement.

I didn't know what to do. The device was important, but I couldn't let this go any further. I hadn't wanted it to go this far to begin with. No device was worth this.

The kiss grew more intense, sending my mind flashing to the night of our engagement party. Tears stung my eyes, and I knew I'd have to do something to stop this. Now.

Before I could pull away with an excuse, a knock rang out. A throat cleared, drawing my eyes to where Commander North stood in the doorway, pointedly looking away. Heat flooded my cheeks.

Ramsey's lips left mine. He glared toward the door, but when he noticed the interruption came from Commander North, he relaxed.

"Commander," he said, voice rough. "Did you need something?"

She glanced at me before averting her eyes. "You're needed in your office, Sovereign. The advisors—"

Ramsey held up a hand as his eyes narrowed. "I'll be right there."

She nodded sharply. Her eyes flicked to me again before she turned and left the room.

Ramsey sighed, his disappointment almost tangible as he sat up. But then he smirked down at me, taking in my flushed cheeks and swollen lips. "You look good like this," he said, voice low as he leaned down to kiss me again. "We'll continue this later."

He left me lying on the couch, catching my breath and swallowing back tears.

I refused to let him do this again. If I had to steal the device tonight to stop Ramsey's advances, then that was exactly what I would do.

83

Dinnertime came and went with no word from Ramsey. Part of me was concerned. What could have come up in his meetings to make him cancel plans with me? Mostly, I was relieved. As the sun set with no sign of him, I could breathe again.

I spent the evening on the couch, bouncing my knees up and down. So much of my life felt like a waiting game these days. I needed night to fall so I could go where I needed to be. Tonight, that was the medical wing. Though I'd promised myself I'd never willingly set foot there again, finding this device was more important.

After hours of biding my time, I couldn't wait anymore. I strode to the door. It was still too early to leave, but I needed to know who was on guard duty. At least then, I'd have time to make a plan before sneaking out in the middle of the night.

Gage turned to the open door with a grin, dipping his head. "Princess."

I huffed, relaxing against the frame. "Hi, Gage."

"You look better. Beauty sleep did you good, huh?"

I ignored him, searching the hall for anyone else. "Are you here all night?"

His brows rose. He motioned toward my suite, and I moved so he could slip inside. "Planning a little rendezvous?"

"Something like that." I hesitated to tell him exactly what I was up to. I trusted him with the information. At this point, I trusted Gage with my life. I just wasn't sure I could trust him to let me do this. Attempting to steal the device would be a risk, one I wasn't sure his protective instincts would allow me to take.

My gut told me he would try to talk me out of it—or worse, try to help me. If he were to be caught snooping around medical when he was supposed to be here, watching over me ... I wouldn't be able to live with the consequences.

Gage's eyes narrowed. "What are you up to?"

It would have been so easy to tell him. He might've even been able to help me from a distance. But I couldn't. "It's better if you don't know."

"*Khara*—"

"Gage, this is important. Don't worry about me."

He scoffed, crossing his arms. "You realize that's pretty much my entire job at this point?" He glared at the floor for a moment, then sighed. "What do you need me to do?"

The tension left my body in a rush. "Thank you."

"Yeah, yeah." He waved his hand. "What do you need?"

"I need to get out of here tonight without anyone knowing."

Gage shifted closer, lowering his voice. "So you can meet Hayden?"

"Eventually."

He tossed his head back, making a noise of frustration before scrubbing a hand over his face. "Do you realize how hard it is for me to watch out for you here? And that's when I know what you're doing."

"Sorry?"

He rolled his eyes. "Not what I was after."

"I can't tell you."

"Why not?"

"I don't want you to get in trouble for what I'm going to do. Your place here is too important."

He threw his arms out, his voice ringing with exasperation. "And what do you think will happen if you're caught doing whatever it is you're planning when I'm supposed to be keeping an eye on you?"

I winced, deflating. It hadn't occurred to me he'd be in trouble either way.

Gage raised his brows, shrugging with a snarky smile. "Yeah, see? You might just need my help here."

Rubbing my temples, I began to pace. If trouble would find him either way …

"I won't stop you," he said, so seriously I stopped in my tracks. Our gazes locked. "If that's what you're worried about, I promise I won't try to stop you. You might not remember, but I do. You're one of the most capable people I've ever known. I won't stop you, Khara, but please, let me help."

With a heavy sigh, I caved and told him everything.

"You're insane."

Gage held his head in both hands, muttering more to the floor than to me. Sitting beside him on the couch, I still heard every word. He looked up, eyes full of incredulity. "Like completely, one-hundred percent *insane*."

I bumped his shoulder with mine before pointing to myself. "Capable, remember?"

He huffed an unamused laugh. "This is nowhere near what I had in mind." He sighed and pulled at his hair. "Okay." He blew out a deep breath and sat up straight. "So you're going to grab this device from the doctor's lab. Then what?"

"I take it to Hayden." Of course it wouldn't be that simple. But if I thought about the details too much, they would overwhelm me. I had to get this thing away from Doctor Jensen and Ramsey.

Gage flung his arms up. "That's it? That's your whole plan?"

I raised one shoulder, giving him a sheepish smile. "Pretty much."

He groaned, thunking his head against the back of the couch. "And you're not going to let me go with you?"

"I told you—"

"What I do here is too important. Yeah, yeah, I heard you the first four times." His voice turned more sarcastic as his frustration and worry grew. I found it oddly comforting.

"Okay, so say you get the device without setting off an alarm—*yay*—and you make it out of here. You go through the tunnel—which, according to your eavesdropping, they may know about—and reach Hayden. You give him the device. Then what, you sneak back here?"

I bit my lip. I hoped to not come back at all. Hayden loved me—I knew that now. I wasn't sure I could say the same, but I felt *something* toward him. I assumed he'd be okay with me staying with him, but I couldn't help the doubt swirling in my mind. It felt like a lot to ask.

"No," I said slowly. "I'm ... going to stay with Hayden."

Gage froze. Then a wide grin spread across his face. "Well, that's the least crazy thing I've heard you say all night."

I stared at my hands. "You think he'll be okay with it?"

"Are you kidding me? You saw him when we left the grove! He wanted you to stay *then*. I mean, come on, that was the saddest goodbye I've ever seen."

"You said you were giving us space."

"So I spied on you." He shrugged, completely unapologetic. "That's my job."

I rolled my eyes, but my stomach fluttered with nerves. "This will work, right? I can do this. Grab the device, get it to Hayden, and never come back."

Gage nodded, but his smile faded, and his voice betrayed his worry. "Yeah. Get in, get out, stay gone. Simple as that."

He took my hand and squeezed. I wasn't sure if it was meant to reassure me or himself.

<h1 style="text-align:center">84</h1>

THE SHARP ODOR OF disinfectant sent my heart racing before I even set foot inside the medical wing. My mind didn't recall what they'd done to me after the attack, but my body seemed to. Dread coiled thick in my belly as the large double doors creaked open.

It was quiet as I slipped inside, the lights dimmed for the late hour. As my eyes adjusted, I could make out the few private rooms that sat to the right. A soft glow spilled from the crack beneath a closed door. Whoever was inside, I hoped they stayed put. Being seen was the last thing I needed.

With bated breath, I tiptoed past the recovery rooms and toward Doctor Jensen's office. I'd only been inside a few times. A private exam room and the more expensive equipment were located in the same area. Beyond them stood the door to her office. And there, I'd find the device.

The wooden door thrummed with familiar magic as I neared it, but unlike the one to my suite, its center emitted a soft blue glow. While I'd never been restricted from a space guarded by Isiraden magic before, I couldn't be sure I'd have access here.

I placed my palm flat against the wood and magic kissed my skin in welcome. The blue light glowed bright around my hand before shifting to a pulsating red. I drew back in a panic. Something was wrong.

Something was *very* wrong.

A voice in my head—one that sounded remarkably like Gage—told me to run. But I was so close. This door was all that stood between me and stealing the device. I wasn't sure I could walk away. What if I never had another chance?

The door swung open, and Doctor Jensen stared out at me with narrowed eyes. My heart thundered in my chest as I forced a smile and an awkward wave.

"Khara, what are you doing here?"

I swallowed thickly, rubbing sweaty palms against my pants. "I wanted to talk. You weren't out in the bay, so I thought I'd try here."

"And you didn't think to knock?"

I let out a strained laugh. "I guess not."

She held the door open wider. "Come in, then. We can talk."

Smiling tightly, I stepped over the threshold. When the door shut behind me with a soft click, I flinched.

"What's on your mind?" Doctor Jensen asked, leading me to a small lounge area at the back of her office.

I took in the room as I followed. Her desk was covered in paperwork, files open and scattered across it. My eyes lingered on what looked like a blueprint before I turned, afraid she'd catch me staring at the wrong thing. Bookshelves lined the walls on two sides, filled to the brim with books and journals. A door stood at the far end, locked with another wooden access panel. A perfect place to secure the device.

I sat across from Doctor Jensen, trying to stay focused. "I just—haven't been to see you in a while."

"Is something wrong?" she asked, her brows dipping. "Are you experiencing hallucinations? Worsening migraines?"

"No, no," I assured her, resisting the urge to fidget under her heavy gaze. "Nothing like that. I've just been feeling run down over the last week. Ramsey and Emila have both tried to get me to come see you, but I keep putting it off."

Doctor Jensen raised a brow. "And you thought the middle of the night was the best time to come to me?"

"I'm sorry," I said, standing abruptly. "This was a bad idea."

"Sit down," she said sternly. "It's quite all right."

I lowered myself back into my seat, willing the panic coursing through me to fade. "I was just having trouble sleeping. And I thought if something *were* wrong with me, maybe I should be seen sooner than later."

Her tight smile unnerved me. "While I can understand you not wanting to spend any more time here after your lengthy recovery, it would be advisable to come to me as soon as you experience any problems. We're on the same side, Khara."

She patted my hand twice before she stood, moving to her desk. I pushed to my feet, ready to follow.

"I have something that will help you sleep. We can see how you do tonight and evaluate from there."

"Thank you."

"Of course." She dug around in the top drawer of her desk. "You're taking your pills, yes?"

"Every day," I lied. Each time the refills came, I flushed the dosage one day at a time. If anyone checked the bottle, it would look like I was taking the prescribed amount.

"Good," she said as she shut the drawer and straightened.

There was nothing in her hand.

"Doctor Jensen?"

"Khara," she said, infusing my name with an impressive amount of disappointment, "what's really going on here?"

My pulse sped, but I tried not to falter. "I'm not sure what you mean."

"I think you do," she countered, stepping closer to me. I took a step back. "What are you really after?"

She pressed forward and again, I shuffled back. I couldn't stop myself. Something about this woman terrified me. My heart hammered as though it were screaming *danger* with every beat.

I stumbled as the back of my legs hit against a side table, sending a coffee cup and remnants of a late dinner rattling on their tray. My eyes darted back to Doctor Jensen as she drew closer with her hand held out, palm open as if she were approaching a wounded animal. To her, maybe that's all I was.

She smiled and the sight made my stomach churn. "It's going to be okay, Khara. I can fix you."

"Fix me?" A cold tendril of fear snaked up my back and sent chills down my spine.

"I don't think it's the magic," she muttered to herself as she studied me. "The implant must be malfunctioning."

The way she looked at me was terrifying. Like I was an experiment rather than a person. Like it didn't matter what I heard anymore.

"We can fix that."

I dropped all pretense. "You're not going to touch me."

Doctor Jensen smirked, her eyes dark with amusement. "You said that the first time. It didn't do you much good then either."

Bile rose in my throat. The flashes of terror and pain in my dreams, the panic I felt on waking in the clearing with Hayden. She was responsible for all of it.

Anger and fear surged in my gut until I thought I'd be sick. I stumbled back another half-step. Desperate for anything to help me, my fingers latched onto her cup. It was still hot to the touch.

In one swift movement, I grabbed the handle and flung the coffee into Doctor Jensen's face. I winced as she screamed and bent over at the waist, her hands flying to her face. But I didn't let it distract me.

The plate of food crashed to the floor as I whipped the tray into my hands, wielding it like a weapon. While she was distracted, I slammed it over her head. She staggered, dazed, but lunged at me with an angry bellow. I sidestepped, my heart pounding, and she dropped to her knees.

Her eyes were wide, her face splotched with painful red burns. I swallowed my unease, steeled myself, and swung the tray at the side of her head. The blow connected so hard I felt the echo of it up my arms. She fell heavily to the floor.

My chest heaved as I waited, tray still raised, body shaking. When she didn't move, I let it slide from my fingers and clatter to the floor. She was out. I was safe, but not for long.

I glanced at the door to her private lab. If my touch couldn't unlock the outer door, I doubted it would unlock this one. From the way she'd spoken in Ramsey's office, Doctor Jensen was probably the only one who could open it.

Bracing myself, I reached under her arms, lifting her as best I could. Doctor Jensen was tall, and much heavier than she looked. Her feet dragged against the tiles as I shuffled back toward the door.

Hefting her body against my side, I grabbed her wrist and pushed her palm onto the panel. Glowing blue shifted to a single pulse of green light before the door unlatched. I closed my eyes in relief before kicking it open further.

Doing my best to be gentle, I propped Doctor Jensen's body against a bookshelf in the office. She slumped to the floor. I winced, but left her and stepped into her lab.

The lights flicked on automatically, revealing a large room with walls full of shelves and scattered worktables. White and steel blended throughout the room, so bright it almost hurt.

I wasn't sure where to start. I moved to my left and scanned the shelves. Doctor Jensen's attention to detail worked in my favor. Everything appeared well labeled. I skimmed the top shelf before moving to the one below.

Halfway through the room, I found a label that simply read *Eastern District*.

The device was smaller than I expected and strangely delicate. The sides were made of mirrored glass, held together by thin strips of gold that glinted in the light. I picked it up and brushed my fingers over the smooth sides. This was the device that could cause so much devastation?

I frowned, not seeing any hint of what it would do or how to activate it. There would be time to study it later. *After* I left the city.

I pulled off my thin sweater and wrapped the cube inside, just to be safe, before turning to the rest of the shelf. Unassembled pieces of additional cubes were laid out in tidy rows next to a set of three smooth cylinders. I gathered it all, nestling the pieces beside the cube before tying my sweater into a makeshift bag.

There might have been more to take or even destroy in the lab. But the room was large, and I could feel my time running out with every second I lingered. I had the device. The rest I needed to leave behind, at least for now. I strode to the door, ready to make my escape.

Two steps out of the room, I caught a flash of metal before something slammed into my face.

85

BLACK SPOTS DANCED IN front of my eyes. I'd fallen to my hands and knees, my sweater—and the device—abandoned at my side. Doctor Jensen towered over me, tray in hand and a fire blazing in her eyes. She swung again and I cried out as my head snapped to the side.

My vision wavered, strips of black overtaking everything as I desperately tried to blink them back. I had no time to move before she reached down and pulled me up by my hair. I clawed at her arms, but she didn't seem to notice. Her hold didn't loosen as she dragged me toward the couch.

My feet scrabbled against the floor as I tried to regain my footing, but it was useless. Between the splitting headache and vicious pull of my hair, I was drowning in pain. I cried out as she threw me onto the couch.

"You know," she fumed, panting heavily, "I've never liked you, Khara. If Ramsey weren't so obsessed with you, I'd kill you like he should have instead of bringing you here in the first place."

My head spun. I could barely focus on her words, disturbing as they were. For a moment, there were two doctors in front of me. I blinked rapidly until they slid back into one. A groan escaped my lips as my hand jerked in a failed attempt to grip my head.

"Pathetic," Doctor Jensen spat as she turned away.

Her hand darted out to steady her as she reached for my sweater. *The device.* I pushed myself up, and bursts of black and white filled my vision. Dizziness surged and I swallowed back bile as I blinked against the spots. I searched for something—anything—I could use to fight, but there was nothing. Only the heavy tray, which lay discarded near where Doctor Jensen knelt next to my sweater.

Still, I had to try.

Pain flared as I rose to my feet, and I bit down on my tongue to keep from crying out. There was no time to wait for the dizziness to fade. I had to move.

I staggered toward Doctor Jensen. She scoffed as she peered into the makeshift bag, wavering with the change in position as she stood. As if she sensed me, she turned and shoved at me. I saw it coming and pushed her hand aside before throwing my fist at her face. Her eyes widened as she tried to dodge, but the hit glanced off her cheek.

Rage shone in her eyes as she threw the device on the floor. She surged forward, reaching for my hair again. I moved just in time, kicking to sweep her legs out from under her. To my surprise, it actually worked. She landed hard on her knees.

I kicked again, knocking her the rest of the way down, and dove for the tray. It was my best hope of getting out of the room. But Doctor Jensen rallied too quickly. She charged, yelling in rage, and shoved me into the bookshelf. My breath left in a rush as my back connected with the shelves. They toppled, falling on us both.

Groaning, I grabbed a glass paperweight and lobbed it at her head. It impacted, dazing her, then thudded to the floor at her feet. I reached back with desperate hands until I found the ragged edge of a shelf. Gripping it tight, I rose shakily to my knees, then to my feet.

Doctor Jensen stirred. Her eyes flashed to me, blown wide. I winced but didn't stop. Lifting the shelf into both hands, I aimed for her chin, closed my eyes, and swung. The wood smacked against her jaw, snapping her head to the side. She crumpled to the floor.

When she didn't move, I sagged, the shelf dropping from my hands. My body threatened to collapse, but I braced myself, gathering my sweater and the device hidden inside before staggering to the office door. I wasn't sure how I was going to make it to the exit, let alone all the way to the grove to find Hayden.

I had no time to dwell on it. My only option was to keep moving.

I pushed myself forward and wrenched open the door. When I slipped back into the testing room, I froze.

Cethin and four other guards blocked the double doors of the medical wing, every eye trained on me.

86

THE GUARDS BLOCKED MY only way out. I had no choice but to walk toward them. They had already seen me—seemed to be waiting for me, like they'd known I was here when I shouldn't have been.

My heart sank. Doctor Jensen must have alerted them while she was rifling through her desk drawer.

Exhaustion weighed heavily on me. I wasn't sure how I'd be able to get out of this. What could I do against five trained guards? But I couldn't give up now.

"Let me pass," I said as I stepped farther into the room.

Cethin's sharp laughter echoed around us. "The only way you're leaving is in our custody. Personally, I don't care if I have to drag you."

My eyes darted over the guards. One shifted uncomfortably on the far left. It was too much to ask that he help me, but I couldn't stop the sliver of hope that rose at his hesitation. He opened his mouth to speak—I hoped in my defense—but the guard beside him shook her head, just barely, and he closed it again.

It was probably for the best. Cethin was unkind on a good day. I doubted he'd react well to any opposition.

"I'm not going with you." I took pride in the strength in my voice, though I doubted it fooled anyone. I was a wreck. My legs trembled beneath me, and I could feel the bruises forming on my face. A slow trickle of blood dripped from a cut along my hairline. But if nothing else, I would be brave.

Cethin snorted. "Wrong answer."

He motioned with his hand, and the guards spread out, ready to detain me.

I swallowed my fear and searched the room. A set of scalpels shone where they sat discarded by the sink to my right. I lunged for them, grabbed a handful, and turned to face the guards. The weight of the blades felt off, but they were all I had.

I turned my attention to the closest guard, and with a flick of my wrist, sent a scalpel flying. It barely grazed his cheek, but the guard hissed, staggering back as his hand shot up to cover the cut. I aimed for another guard and winced as my attempt missed. But the next blade landed, sticking out of his upper arm before I turned to throw another at the guard on the left.

I continued with varying degrees of success. The blades felt strange in my hands, but I kept trying. My supply dwindled fast. When the last guard—the one I thought might help me—inched toward me with wide eyes, I faltered.

Once again, my hesitation cost me.

Cethin stormed up and grabbed my wrist, twisting it sharply. I cried out as the last scalpel slipped from my fingers and clattered against the tiles. Cethin drove his fist into my stomach, and I dropped to my knees, fighting for air that wouldn't come.

I grasped at my chest, desperate to breathe. When I finally managed an inhale, I lost my breath again as an agonizing current of electricity surged in my head. My mouth opened, but I had no air to scream. My hands moved to reach for my head, but they froze against the burning pain. When it finally stopped, I sucked in air and collapsed onto my side.

Cethin crouched so I could see the small rectangular device he held. "You're not that special," he spat. "And you deserve this."

With the press of a button, the electric energy surged again. This time, I had the air to scream as my body tensed and writhed on the floor. The agony stopped for a moment, just long enough for me to manage a harsh sob, before Cethin turned my world to pain again.

Just as my awareness began to fade, a fierce command rang out.

"*Enough!*"

87

Ramsey marched into the room, his eyes blazing when he saw the way I trembled on the floor, my breaths hitching as I struggled to compose myself. His anger thickened the air, and I caught a swirl of dark smoke in his gaze before he turned away from me.

He strode to Cethin, who straightened into tense attention. Without a word, Ramsey backhanded him across the face, flinging his head to the side.

"Did I say you could hurt her?" Ramsey seethed, voice low and darker than I'd ever heard. He wasn't even speaking to me and I was unnerved.

Cethin gave a sharp shake of his head. "No, Sovereign."

"Then what made you think you could touch her, let alone harm her?" Tendrils of smoke curled off his arms as he snatched the weapon from Cethin's hands and pocketed it, turning to the other guards.

Still shivering on the ground, my body heavy on the floor, I observed them too. Two had scalpels sticking out of their limbs. One stood frozen, his eyes wide with fear, as the woman beside him held a bloody scalpel she'd removed from her body.

"You and you," Ramsey said, pointing to the latter guards. "Help her up. *Carefully.*"

They were quick to obey. The man knelt, gently pushing sweaty hair from my forehead to get a better look at my face. He turned to his partner, who nodded from my other side. Together, they lifted me from under my arms, holding my weight as I collapsed against them.

"You two," Ramsey turned toward the injured guards with disgust, "get cleaned up."

They nodded sharply. Ramsey's eyes flickered to me, then fell to my bunched-up sweater on the floor. He reached for it, holding my gaze. When he opened it and found the device, he stiffened and turned sharply to Cethin.

"Radnor, you will take this to my office. You will wait until I get there, and you will protect this like your life depends on it—because it very well might." His voice went soft, but didn't lose any of its dark edge. "Do you understand me?"

The danger in his tone filled the room. The guards beside me tensed, hands tightening under my arms. No one said a word. Cethin nodded sharply, taking the device still bundled in my sweater. He was out the door before Ramsey had dusted off his suit and stood.

The room grew so quiet, I could hear nothing but my wheezing breaths and the soft inhales of the guards behind me. Ramsey exuded a dark energy I'd be a fool to ignore. His words from earlier—*I think I'd lose my mind*—haunted me. The Ramsey before me was dangerous. Which had he lost first, his mind or his heart?

He stormed up to me, his eyes dark with fury. As he looked me over, he shook his head. "I wanted to believe you." He chuckled darkly, a bitter smile overtaking his face. "I wanted to believe you so badly I ignored the signs. Trusted the magic to keep you in your proper place. That's my fault."

He sniffed and ran a rough hand through his hair. There was something wild about him now, dark and predatory. I kept my eyes fixed on him. The air was too tense to look away, no matter how much I wanted to.

He surged forward without warning, gripping my cheeks in his hands. I hissed in surprise and jerked back. But with the guards' arms holding me in place like iron shackles, I couldn't do more than sway.

"Of course," Ramsey continued, his words a soft murmur against my ear, "it's your fault too." He gave another bitter laugh that sent chills down my spine. "And it's Hayden's fault most of all."

He shoved me away from him. I focused on breathing to beat down my panic, but didn't miss the agitated words he mumbled to himself as he stepped away. "Isn't it always?"

I braced myself, opening my mouth to speak as I watched him pace. My voice was barely a croak. "Ramsey—"

"No!" He slammed his fist on the nearest table of equipment, and I jumped at the echoing bang. "You don't get to speak my name. Not anymore. You don't have the right."

Fury built in Ramsey's eyes. That didn't bode well for me. I had little hope of escaping this, and I wasn't about to make matters worse. I shut my mouth and went back to watching him. He strode back to me, glancing at the guards with disdain before fixing his eyes on me. They were full of hurt and a hatred I wouldn't have been able to imagine coming from him a week ago.

"You can release her. She's not going anywhere. Are you, Khara?"

The guards slowly let go of my arms and stepped back. They seemed as nervous as I was in the face of Ramsey's wrath. I followed their movements from the corner of my eye, but Ramsey stood close enough to notice my shifting attention.

"No, no," he murmured, grabbing my chin with his hand. "Don't look at them; look at me. You will only look at *me*."

I met his gaze, swallowing my fear. Could he sense it? Could he see the pain and uncertainty I felt standing before him like this? Gathering all the courage I could muster, I let my own fire blaze in my eyes.

"That's better."

He dropped his hand from my face onto my shoulder, gripping too tight. I did my best not to grimace, but the press of his fingers would leave me bruised. If he let me live that long.

"Do you know how I discovered your betrayal?"

A hot rush of anger flared in my gut. *My* betrayal? I wanted to shove him, scream everything I'd come to learn about him and what he'd done to me. But the hostility simmering in his eyes halted the words in my throat. He held all the power here, and we both knew it. I stayed quiet, hoping the heat in my chest would overflow into the glare I leveled at him.

"You drew him," he said, his lips pressed against the shell of my ear. "You drew Hayden in the journal *I* gave to you."

He grabbed a fist full of my hair, and I cried out as he jerked my head to the side. My hands scrabbled at his to make him let go, but he gripped tighter.

"You drew him and wrote out your dreams. You cataloged everything, Khara!" He laughed and shook my head in his fist. "And then you left it sitting out. Tell me"—he pulled me flush against his chest, gripping my hip—"did you think you wouldn't be watched? That as soon as Emila realized what was happening, she wouldn't come to me? Or did you *want* to be caught?"

He released me, pushing me back so abruptly, I lost my balance and fell to my knees. I looked up at him, breathing heavily, and held my silence.

Ramsey squatted in front of me, tilting his head to the side as he regarded me. "No, you didn't consider any of it. Not nearly enough. I started shutting you out of our systems this afternoon, adjusting the magic, restricting your access. I'd hoped I was wrong." He scoffed and shook his head. "But of course I wasn't. You can't be trusted. I thought if you were here with me, if I gave you everything I could, we'd be okay. A fresh start. It might've worked too. It might've worked ..."

Ramsey stood, expelling a slow breath as he turned away. When he spun back to me, he extended his arms out wide. "Well, no more pretending. There's no need, is there? We can be honest now. There are no more secrets to keep."

He motioned to the guards behind me. They stepped forward and knelt, grabbing me by the arms and hoisting me from the floor. I might've imagined it, but their holds felt gentler this time. More careful.

"I'm disappointed, Khara," Ramsey said. Anger still simmered in his eyes and in the tense lines of his body, but it was more controlled, fading into the background. It didn't leave me feeling quite so afraid.

"Put her in a cell," he ordered the guards tiredly. He stared at me like he could peel me back in layers and see all my thoughts. "I'll deal with her in the morning."

The guards shuffled me toward the exit. I could barely lift my feet. My body was past the point of exhaustion.

"Wait."

Ramsey's call halted our steps. I lifted my head as he drew near. He stopped close enough to pull me into his arms, his eyes narrowing as he tilted his head. He leaned in, pressing his lips against my ear.

"My greatest fear has always been losing you," he murmured. "What are you afraid of?"

He placed a rough kiss to my temple, then thrust his hands against my head. I barely had time to register the rush of power that surged into me before my heart thundered and a scream wrenched itself from my chest.

Everything went black, and I was lost to my fears.

88

I stood in an empty wasteland. I called out into the darkness, but there was no answer. By the time I realized I was screaming, my throat was already raw.

Ramsey's body pressed against mine. His fingers trailed along my skin. I shivered as our fingers intertwined and he moved his lips to my neck.

The grove stood completely desolated around me. Trees were scorched. Burnt branches littered the ground. When I stepped across them, they disintegrated to ash beneath my feet.

The rough concrete of the circle's dais bit into my knees. Two sets of hands held me back, squeezing my forearms as Ramsey formed thick, black smoke between his hands. He turned and shoved it down my throat.
I can't breathe. I can't breathe.
I choked while trying to scream.

Hayden stood before me, his eyes lit with power. He shook his head in disgust as he walked away. He didn't turn back, even when I begged.

Soft earth squished beneath my bare feet. When I opened my eyes, I looked out over Anluan. It was whole again, restored. I smiled and glanced down at my feet.
A hand. I was standing on a hand.
I flailed backward and in my hurry to move, fell hard onto my back. As I turned and scrambled to stand, I was struck still by the lifeless eyes of Gage and Hayden. I flung my hands over my mouth, but couldn't stifle my screams.
Ramsey emerged from the shadows, gesturing to their corpses. "You did this to them."

"Take them off—*now*! I'm not going anywhere."

I barely heard the words. Barely registered the sudden cold seeping into my body. I was too busy screaming, the images in my mind unrelenting.

A man threw a glass at me, his face contorted with an anger I couldn't understand. I ducked, wincing as it shattered against the wall behind me. He yelled as I cowered on the floor, too small to fight back, too scared to run. He dragged me to my feet and shoved me out the front door.

"You're dead to me. You hear me? As good as dead! Don't ever come back here!"

I needed to wake up. The world had to be more than these nightmares filling my head. But if I was asleep, surely I'd have woken myself screaming by now.

"Khara."

It was the barest whisper, my name said on a desperate breath. I'd recognize that voice even in my darkest nightmare. But Hayden couldn't be here ... unless I *was* dreaming.

My attempt to say his name failed. A choked cry came out instead as visions of empty eyes, black smoke, and charred trees overlapped in my mind. I gripped the sides of my head as I let out a breathy yell.

Gentle hands covered mine.

"I need you to let go." His voice broke as he spoke. "Khara, please, let go for me."

It took all my strength, but I relaxed my grip. My hands fell heavy to the floor.

It was cold. Or maybe I was. Why was I so cold?

The hands moved to my temples, and with a rush of warmth, power seeped into my mind. The nightmarish images flickered, and I blinked, desperate to be rid of them. When they faded, I saw him through tired, blurry vision.

"Hayden."

I'd thought his voice was barely there, but it was loud compared to mine. I slid a hand to my neck, swallowing thickly. My throat felt as raw as I did.

"Are you okay?" he asked. One tender hand cupped my face and the other lowered to wipe my tears. I hadn't even realized I'd been crying.

I didn't say anything, too focused on slowing my heartbeat as I shivered on the ground. I was hollowed out. Whatever Ramsey had done, it left me feeling more drained than anything I could remember. I stared at the ceiling, content to breathe and blink.

"Khara?" Hayden shook my shoulder. His eyes grew panicked when I didn't speak. "I need you to answer me. Come on."

He lifted my limp body from the floor, pulling me against his chest. "Hey! Khara, come on—look at me!" He shifted me so he could pat my cheek. "*Khara*!"

It took monumental effort, but I managed to shift my head and focus. My eyes met his, and Hayden collapsed over me. His head rested against mine and he breathed in raggedly, pressing a kiss against my hair.

"Okay," he said. "You're okay. I've got you. I'm right here."

I felt disconnected from my body in a way that made me question how I could possibly be okay. But Hayden was here, holding me in his arms. That was close enough.

89

REALITY SANK IN SLOWLY. I noticed my bare feet first. Someone had taken my shoes. A chill seeped into my soles where they pressed against the concrete floor. The cold contrasted with the warmth of Hayden's body tucked against mine. I shivered, and he drew me closer.

In a daze, my eyes trailed around the room. Gray concrete walls matched the floor. A metal bed was mounted against the wall. Beside it sat a toilet and a small sink.

As I took in the glass door and the guards standing beyond it, I tried to think back to what had led me here. Ramsey had caught me trying to steal the device. From my journal, he'd found out I'd been seeing Hayden. He knew I'd been remembering. He'd used his power on me, forced me into my fears, and apparently, into a prison cell.

Hayden shouldn't be here.

The thought had come before, but now it evoked a fresh dose of panic. What was he doing here? How did he even—?

"You can't be here." Wincing as my voice cracked, I pushed against him. "Why are you here?"

Hayden pulled me back into his side and trailed a hand through my hair. "I'm here for you."

"I'm in a cell. Tell me Ramsey doesn't know you're here." He didn't respond, and dread pooled in my gut. "Hayden!"

"He knows." He sighed, rubbing his eyes with one hand. The other stayed wrapped around me. "He knows, but it's okay."

"*How?* How could this be okay? Hayden, what did you do?"

He shifted, helping me sit upright. While he kept one hand ready to catch me if I fell, I let my head fall into my hands. He shuffled us back until we sat side by side against the wall. With his help, I leaned partially against it and partially against the metal bed frame. It wasn't any more comfortable than lying in the middle of the floor, but at least this way, we could see each other.

Tears stung my eyes at the sight of him. Blood smeared the skin around a cut near his eyebrow. Mottled red and purple bruising surrounded his swollen right eye. Though I couldn't see the wound that caused it, blood dotted the lightning-like design shaved along the side of his head. Some of his curls were matted, his clothes disheveled. With the way pain tightened his eyes, there had to be more bruises hidden beneath his shirt, but he didn't seem to care. He was too fixated on me.

Carefully, Hayden took my hand. My breath hitched as he reverently laced his fingers with mine.

"Our mutual friend came to me," he said, voice low. "He probably started sending word as soon as you'd left your suite. He's good at anticipating trouble like that, though usually, it's trouble of his own making." His lips twitched before falling flat. "As soon as he heard they'd restricted your access, he came running to the grove. He knew he wouldn't be able to stop whatever was going to happen. I came as fast as I could."

Hayden shook his head and ran a hand through his hair, grimacing as it caught in a blood-matted curl. He glanced out the door toward the guards, who stood blatantly watching us. I glared, though I doubted it bothered them.

Squeezing Hayden's hand, I drew his attention back to me. "What did you do, Hayden?"

"It doesn't matter."

If it really didn't matter, he would tell me. The dread coiling in my gut was suffocating. "*What did you do?*"

He closed his eyes and covered his mouth with his hand. When he opened his eyes again, they were shiny, laced with apology. "I made a deal with Ramsey."

Hayden wouldn't make any deal that would endanger Anluan or its people, but I couldn't imagine Ramsey agreeing to let him see me for anything less. He'd demand a victory over us both.

I gritted my teeth. "What deal?"

"Your life," he said softly, "for mine."

His words sucked the air from my lungs. He couldn't trade our lives like that. My pulse thrummed painfully fast as nausea gripped me, and I pulled in an unsteady breath, shaking my head. "No. Hayden, why would you do this? You *can't* do this!"

"It's already done."

He leaned closer, trying to still me, but I pushed against him with trembling hands. I couldn't stop shaking my head, the movements sharp and jerky.

"No. You're not doing this. You're not going to do this for me!"

"Khara—"

"No! Did you even think about this?" My voice cracked, breaking into jagged pieces alongside my heart. My breathing grew harsh as panic bled into my words. "What this means for Anluan? For your people? Your father? Hayden, it won't work. You'll be giving everything to Ramsey when I'm as good as dead anyway!"

Hayden's eyes flashed as he pulled me into his side. "No, you're not. He gave me his word. You're to be released."

"What good is Ramsey's word? You're the one who told me he's a liar!"

"He's not lying about this."

I could feel his heart beating, quick but steady, and I knew he'd resigned himself to this. But I couldn't allow it.

"I can't let you do this, Hayden," I whispered, all my brokenness laid bare. I clutched the front of his shirt in a tight fist, as if it would keep him with me. "I won't."

Hayden kissed my forehead, tightening his arms around me. "It's not your choice, Khara. And it's already done."

The words rang with a finality I couldn't ignore. He was doing this. It had been decided before he'd set foot in this cell.

My throat tightened and sobs built in my chest alongside my resignation. A cool tear hit my neck and slid down my skin, but it wasn't mine. It was Hayden's—and that broke the fragile hold over my emotions.

Harsh cries burst from me, so strong that my whole body shook. Hayden pulled me even closer in his arms, his grip tightening as I collapsed into grief.

After everything we'd been through, how could it end this way? I'd barely found him again, but the thought of losing him—especially like *this*—seared through my heart. What was I supposed to do when he was gone? Sometimes it felt like his presence was the only thing holding me together. Our meetings in the grove had been a refuge, an overwhelming source of hope and safety, because *he* made me feel that way. Without him ...

"I can't," I choked through heaving sobs, clutching desperately at his shirt, his arms, whatever part of him I could grasp to keep him with me. "I can't. *I can't.*"

His chest shuddered, his arms contracting until his hold was almost bruising. I welcomed the pressure, the reminder that he was still here. He rested his head against mine, shifting until his lips hovered just above my ear.

"It's all right, Khara." His voice was too hoarse, too full of anguish to be believable. My head jerked in a desperate *no*, and he pressed a kiss to my hair. "It'll be all right."

It was the first lie he'd ever told me.

He was going to die. Nothing would ever be all right again.

90

"We don't have much time."

Hayden was right. I could feel our time together slipping away with every passing second.

I tried my best to pull myself together, but the last thing I wanted to do was release my grip on him. I let my hands linger—against his arm, gripping his shirt in a fist. I held him so tightly my hands whitened with strain. If it bothered him, he didn't say anything.

When I shifted to sit up, Hayden grasped my hand, lacing our fingers together again. It seemed he wanted to hold onto me as long as possible too.

I blinked back more tears. Words escaped me. There was so much I wanted to tell him, but I had no idea where to start.

Hayden took my other hand, squeezing gently as he met my eyes. "I never got to say this on our wedding day. I'd like to now, if you'll let me."

All I could do was nod. I'd listen to anything he wanted to say for as long as I could.

He leaned forward, smiling at me so softly I couldn't look away. "Khara Laveya, I willingly bind myself to you in mind, body, and soul. The power resting inside of me, now to live and rest inside of you." As he recited the words, he pressed his palm flat against my heart. A spark lit in his eyes. "Shared and accepted freely, as we have shared and accepted one another in love, I give this gift to you, now and enduring for all your days."

Hayden brought his free hand to cup my cheek. His eyes shone as he stared into mine. "Do you accept?"

"I do." My voice wavered with tears. His smile grew as he closed his eyes and let out a long breath.

"What is bound together in love and readiness, no power above or beneath may break."

I gasped as a rush of power burst to life inside of me. It was warm, like when Hayden healed me, but also different. Stronger and more powerful—like energy igniting in my bones. I blinked rapidly as the sensation settled into a soft buzz beneath my skin.

I looked at my hands, sensing something had changed, but unable to see what it was. A thousand questions filled my mind as I brought my eyes back to Hayden. The way he sat—shoulders relaxing, lips lifting at the corners as he swallowed thickly—silenced them all.

"It will protect you," he said. "Keeping you safe is all I care about."

Ramsey had told me the same thing once, but his protection had been twisted by his selfish desires. With the result of Hayden's vows still thrumming lightly beneath my skin, his soft-spoken words rang with undeniable veracity. This protection, born of love and sacrifice, was one I could trust.

He kissed my forehead, thumbing away more of my tears. His voice gentled when he asked, "Can I kiss you?"

My breath hitched, and all I could offer was a nod. Like everything else I'd given him since we met, it was enough. He wove his hand into my hair and stared deep into my eyes, searching to make sure I meant it—and I did.

A slow smile spread across his face before he leaned in. When his lips met mine, it felt like coming home.

"The binding will protect you," Hayden whispered. We stayed close, near enough our breaths mingled. "Ramsey won't be able to do this to you again. Darkness can't overcome light."

My head dipped in a nod, but it was hard to focus on his words. Hard to focus on anything other than how close his lips were to mine. Our eyes locked, and we moved as one for another kiss.

The door opened with a whoosh. I jumped and Hayden spun, planting himself in front of me.

Guards filed into the room, followed closely by Ramsey. Smugness seeped from him in waves.

"Don't hold back on my account. It's nothing I haven't seen before." He glanced from me to Hayden and smirked. "Nothing I haven't experienced before, either."

Anger twisted with lingering shame, but I said nothing, just clenched the back of Hayden's shirt in my fist.

"Leave it, Ramsey," Hayden ordered.

Ramsey chuckled. "What, you don't want to hear about how much Khara wanted me? The way she felt when we were tangled up in her bed?"

"*Stop*," I bit out. My hands shook. I was afraid I would be sick.

"Ah, she speaks!" Ramsey shifted so he could better see me. "Tell me, Khara, what did you see when I touched you with my power? You screamed quite loudly—faster than the others, even." He tilted his head, his dark eyes glinting. "You're the first I've used it on who hasn't died in the process. Of course, I wasn't trying to kill you, but even so ... I wonder how much longer you would've lasted had Hayden not interfered."

I cringed, instinctively shuffling into Hayden's side. He wrapped his arm around me and took my hand. When he gave it a gentle squeeze, I felt like I could breathe again.

"Isn't that touching?" Ramsey scoffed. "I think your time is up now, Hayden. Unless you've changed your mind."

"You know I haven't."

Ramsey's eyes were stony as he stared Hayden down. "Then let's go. I'm giving you too much consideration as it is."

I was already shaking my head before Hayden turned to me. He could be as sure as he wanted, but I hadn't made peace with this decision. I doubted I ever would.

Hayden smiled sadly as he brought my hand to his lips and pressed a kiss to my knuckles. At a gesture from Ramsey, the guards stepped forward to grab him.

"Hayden—" My voice broke as sobs threatened to overtake me again.

"I love you," he said as he surrendered himself to the guards.

My ears rang, my heart racing as a buzz grew beneath my skin. I didn't care if Hayden had made a deal. I didn't care that Ramsey could kill me. They wouldn't take him without a fight. If it wasn't going to come from Hayden, it would come from me.

I pushed forward, intent on taking out anyone I could, but it was over before it began. Two guards rushed me, pinning my arms as soon as I moved. Tears blurred my vision, and I yelled and thrashed in their arms, but it was no use. I was helpless as they shoved Hayden out the door.

"I love you, Khara," he said again, craning his neck to look back at me. "Remember how much I love you."

When they'd gone, Ramsey pushed himself off the wall. "If you'll excuse me, I have an execution to oversee."

Without another word, he strode out the door.

"Ramsey, don't do this." The words spilled from my lips in a desperate plea that made Ramsey flinch. He stopped in the hall but didn't turn around. "Please," I begged, my voice wavering with tears. "Please, don't do this."

His back stiffened, but still, he wouldn't look at me. "It's already done," he said. "I'll come back for you after."

He left, and the guards released my arms to follow. No longer held up, my legs buckled, and I fell to my knees, bending forward until my forehead touched the floor. The door shut, sealing me inside with a whoosh of air that echoed like a final breath.

91

Time passed in a haze of sorrow and disbelief. Tears streamed down my face in unrelenting waves that left the corners of my eyes stinging and raw. The tears might as well have carved their paths into my skin. I'd remember them forever. I'd remember this *grief* forever.

Hayden was gone. And it was all my fault.

By the time the guards returned, I felt completely hollowed out. Hunched over myself on the floor, I didn't bother looking up as they entered my cell. Whatever they did to me now didn't matter. Nothing did.

I didn't fight their hands as they grabbed me by the arms and hauled me to my feet. I didn't fight as they shoved me from the cell. What was there to fight for now? Ramsey had already won. Hayden was gone, and with him, my hope.

It was only when the guards pushed me through thick wooden doors that I blinked back to myself. I hadn't seen the path to the cells before, too lost in the fears Ramsey had trapped me in, but I knew the hallway we stepped into. When I glanced behind me at the dark door, I couldn't help the frantic burst of laughter that shook my shoulders. Emila's words from the day I left medical echoed in my head: *there's nothing scenic down there.*

The guards tensed, tightening their grips as they hurried me forward. My hoarse laughter died in my throat as I struggled to keep my feet beneath me. I let myself drift again, not paying attention to anything around me until the guards pushed me into the main hall. There, my attention was demanded.

Hayden's body lay crumpled on the floor.

There was no rise and fall of his chest. No signs of life.

Seeing him like that was the worst thing I could remember. My vision blurred as grief tightened around me like a too-small coat.

No one stopped me as I took halting steps toward him. I fell to my knees beside his body, and the horrible truth crashed over me. Hayden was dead. There was no mistaking it, and yet, I found myself reaching for him as if reality would bend with the action.

My hand shook as I touched him, and the chill of his skin met my fingers. With a sharp inhale, I jerked away and sobbed. I leaned over his body, pressing my hands against his shirt, careful not to touch his skin again.

"It's a shame it had to be this way."

Ramsey's voice cut through my sorrow like a knife.

I lifted my head and found him lounging on an ornate wooden throne at the front of the room as though a dead man at his feet didn't bother him. As though Hayden hadn't once been his friend.

The throne sat positioned on a dais that made sure all who approached would be forced to look up at him. I had no doubt Ramsey reveled in it every time he was in the room.

He regarded me with a dark glint in his eyes as he motioned to Hayden's body. "I'd say all this could've been avoided, but I think we both know that would be a lie. If it's any comfort, I gave him what he bargained for—it was just us, no witnesses."

He offered this detail to me as if the way Hayden had died in here, alone with him, was a gift. Some benevolent gesture on his part. What comfort could I find in that when Hayden was *gone*?

When I said nothing, Ramsey stood and made his way toward me. He crouched beside me, close enough I could feel his breath on my face.

"It's terrible," he said, voice low as he tucked a strand of hair behind my ear. "But it really is better this way. Where's his power now? What good did it do him in the end? He'd rather deal himself into death than fight for his family's throne. That's no Sovereign."

I clenched my eyes shut and focused on breathing past a hot rush of anger. Now wasn't the time to lose my temper. Hayden was dead. I was alone. I needed to keep a level head, not react from my pain. But as Ramsey's hand trailed up and down my back, my entire body stiffened.

"You could join me, you know," he murmured, standing and moving away.

Two guards replaced him at my side and yanked me to my feet. Ramsey motioned for them to bring me closer, and they pulled me away from Hayden.

"Give us the room."

"Sovereign—"

"I won't repeat myself."

The guards released me and filed out the door. They left it cracked, but the men turned their backs to us. It was the most privacy they could give without leaving Ramsey unprotected.

"I mean it, Khara." Ramsey's eyes were sincere, his voice soft. This was the Ramsey who'd sat by my bedside while I spent months recovering, the attentive fiancé who'd tricked me into trust. "You can join me now. Everything is out in the open. There'd be no more secrets between us. I love you. Don't get me wrong, I am *angry*. But even when I'm furious with you and Hayden and even myself, I can't seem to let you go. You're meant to be with me. I've always known that, ever since we were kids."

Tension thickened the air, making it hard to breathe as the buzzing under my skin intensified. It made focusing a challenge, even as Ramsey closed the distance between us.

His eyes searched mine while he caressed my cheek. "I can give you everything." His words rang with promise, slow and seductive in a way that made me shiver. He smiled. "Everything you've ever wanted, and everything you haven't realized you want yet. You and I, we'd be a force beyond what the Diamond Kingdoms have ever seen."

He brushed his lips against mine before moving them to my ear. "Together, we can make Anluan into everything it should be."

He pulled back and I forced myself not to look away as our eyes met. He clearly believed what he was saying. Despite everything, he wanted me by his side. But how could he think I would want to stay after everything he'd done? After everything I'd been through because of him?

Ramsey tilted his head, observing me closely in the silence. He slid his hands down to my arms, and his voice gentled even more. "Khara, what's left for you but me?"

I didn't have an answer. Even if I made it off palace grounds, I didn't have anywhere to go. I had no family. Hayden was gone. Gage couldn't come with me. I doubted I could find the rebel camp on my own. Even if I did, their reception of me couldn't be warm. Not when it was my fault the Sovereign Heir of Anluan was dead.

I was a traitor. Who would want someone like me after all I'd done? After all I'd lost?

My heart clenched. I didn't know what was left for me. I just knew I'd take whatever it was over remaining here with Ramsey.

"Stay with me, Khara," Ramsey crooned, his fingers playing with my hair. "All will be forgiven. Just say you'll be mine."

"No." The word left my lips as a hoarse whisper, pained but adamant.

He dropped his hands and took a half-step back. "No?"

"Ramsey, you just trapped me in my worst fears and threw me in a cell. I could have died if Hayden hadn't—" I cut myself off, shaking my head.

"That," Ramsey said carefully, "was an overreaction. It won't happen again. You just made me so angry, Khara. You *betrayed* me."

"You betrayed me first!" I yelled, shoving against his chest. He stumbled back, his eyes narrowing. My chest heaved as indignant anger melded with my grief. "You might be willing to forgive me for whatever sins you think I've committed, but I'm not ready to forgive you. What you've done—to me, to Hayden, this entire city—I can't just pretend it didn't happen!" Keeping my eyes up, I pointed to the ground. "Hayden's body is *right there*. You killed him. And you ask me to stay with you? He died so I could get away from you!"

Ramsey's lips pressed into a thin line. "He died because he was weak, a coward. He—"

"Dead or alive, he and I are connected." The words came without thought, but I recognized the truth of them as soon as they left my mouth. I could still feel Hayden with me, as close as the buzzing beneath my skin. With a renewed sense of surety, I met Ramsey's eyes. "I'll never belong to you, Ramsey. Never."

The air thickened as his anger flared. His fists clenched until they shook, and his eyes narrowed into dangerous slits. Still, I wasn't afraid of him. Not anymore.

"I'm taking Hayden's body, and I'm leaving. You made a deal, and I'm going to make sure you honor it." I glanced at Hayden, cold and still on the floor, and my voice dropped to an anguished whisper. "He won't die for nothing."

Straightening, I turned back to Ramsey. "I've seen you at your worst, but I've seen you at your best too. Part of you is still an honorable man, however small that part may be. Keep your word. Let us go."

92

"Let you go?" Ramsey laughed, running a hand through his hair as he paced away from me and spun back. "You do realize *I'm* the one in charge here. *I* hold your future in my hands. *I* am the most powerful man in this kingdom. You'd be hard-pressed to find one more powerful outside of it, either."

I raised my chin. "Galen Shalémo."

Ramsey's head snapped toward me. "What did you say?"

"*Galen Shalémo,*" I repeated, drawing my hands into fists. "I bet he's still more powerful than you."

"If Galen had any semblance of power, any desire to rule, why hasn't he come to take Anluan from me? Why hasn't he come for *you?*"

The snarled words gutted me, piercing deeper than any blade. I went dizzy as their weight settled over me. I would've had no answer to give, even if Ramsey had let me speak. He stalked toward me, grabbing my wrist.

"He's not who you think he is, Khara. None of them are! Galen isn't fit to be Sovereign. He'd hold us back like he always has, keeping our gifts and the magic of Isiraden so regulated we'd never make any advancements. He's not fit to rule. Not like I am."

"So you betrayed his family and stole the throne? How does that make you any more worthy to rule?"

"My family is just as renowned as his. My plans for this kingdom are well supported. If I weren't worthy, how did I manage to take Anluan? How did I convince others to join me against the Shalémos that night? How have I kept control of the kingdom all this time?"

"Using brute force and fear to control our people doesn't mean you deserve to rule."

He huffed a disbelieving laugh and pulled me against him. I tried to push away, but his hands gripped too tight.

"Let go of me." He scoffed in the face of my anger, and I pushed harder against him. "You made an agreement, Ramsey. Let me go."

"The terms were for your life, not your freedom. As it was never my intention to kill you, I saw no reason not to agree." Ramsey snorted. "Hayden always was a terrible negotiator."

He tangled his hand in my hair, using the leverage to tilt my head so I was forced to look at him. "You're out of options, and I'm out of patience." His grip tightened as he pulled my face to a stop, inches from his. Smoke swirled in the depths of his eyes. "I'm the only one you have left."

He captured my lips in a bruising kiss. My heart slammed against my chest as fear and indignation set my body on fire. This was all wrong—but I had no idea how to stop it. No way to make things right.

My body stiffened, and Ramsey pressed against me harder, as if his forcefulness would change my mind. As if it would erase the horrors he'd created for me and the city. As if I'd kiss him back.

I shoved against his chest, but all my strength barely moved him. Tears stung my eyes as outrage simmered beneath my skin. Though I wasn't sure what good would come from it, I relished the idea of letting it boil over. At least then, I'd feel like I could fight back.

But this wasn't just anger. The intensity of the strange buzzing beneath my skin began to rise. It pulsed and whirled inside me as if it were alive, aware of my feelings and reacting to them.

Ramsey bit my lip, and I flinched at the sharp sting. As the bitter tinge of copper touched my tongue, a dam burst open inside me. Fiery power shot from my gut, its sizzling energy darting up to my heart. Hot and cold flashed over me so quickly, I went dizzy with the rush of it.

In that moment, I knew I wasn't powerless. I wasn't alone.

I brought both of my hands to Ramsey's chest and shoved as hard as I could. He hurtled away from me in a burst of light.

This will protect you, Hayden had said.

As Ramsey rolled across the floor, I stared at my hands in wonder, then turned them over, searching for a sign of something different. But already the light had faded from my palms. Though there was nothing to see, I could feel it as surely as the wild thrumming of my heart.

What had Hayden done?

Grim satisfaction rose in me as Ramsey staggered to his feet. He thundered toward me, wisps of smoke rising from his shoulders, and I stepped back. A glance behind me revealed the guards had blocked me in. My display of power hadn't gone unnoticed. I wasn't trapped in Ramsey's arms anymore, but I was still trapped.

Unless ...

I looked at my hands, willing whatever power lived in me to rise. My pulse thundered in my ears. My breathing turned harsh and heavy.

A single spark jumped from my hand.

Ramsey stopped in his tracks. "What—?"

I closed my eyes and let myself feel everything. My grief over Hayden. My anger at what Ramsey had stolen. The pain of being so deeply violated and betrayed. The fear that I wouldn't survive this—or worse, that I would live but remain trapped with Ramsey forever. Energy crackled in my palms, erratic and hot, as flaring light turned everything red behind my eyelids.

Most of all, I let myself feel the love Hayden had given me. Every kindness. Every careful moment. The brush of his lips against mine, soft and unhurried, without expectation of anything more. I let myself feel what I'd been so afraid to before—the weight of being loved and the recognition that those feelings were reciprocated.

When I opened my eyes, everything seemed sharper. Crackling energy turned my attention to my hands. I watched in awe as flickers of light spiraled around them, dancing against my skin. I lifted my hands from my sides, mesmerized as the light spun into the air to join a trail already gathering above our heads.

My eyes darted to Ramsey. He stood stunned, mouth agape as he stared up at the light. The guards boxing me in shifted back several steps.

Releasing a pent-up breath, I followed the trail of light with my eyes and froze.

Light curled and flickered around Hayden's body. All the energy leaving me made its way toward him. The closer it came, the more it shifted into something lightning-like, jagged bolts that demanded attention.

In a daze, I moved beneath the trail. I needed to be near Hayden. Near the light. It called me forward, the pull as insistent as the buzzing beneath my skin.

When I was steps away, a burst of light sprang from Hayden's chest. The light above hurtled down, blending with it and careening to wrap around Hayden in a fast hold. His body lifted from the ground, the light flaring around him until it was blinding.

I flung my arm up, using the crook of my elbow to shield my eyes. As if he were far away, I heard Ramsey shouting but couldn't distinguish his words. The hair on the back of my neck rose as static built in the air. The buzz within me grew to a whirling hum, excited and so alive it brought tears to my eyes.

The light shifted, dimming just enough to chance uncovering my eyes. When I blinked them open, the only thing I could see—the only thing that mattered—was Hayden, suspended in the air as light twisted around his limbs and flickered in his open eyes.

93

Hayden was breathing.

It was the only thing I could focus on, watching his chest expand and contract as lightning flickered around him. He was breathing. Alive.

Hayden was alive.

I inhaled, my trembling fingers reaching toward where he hovered in the air. Everything about him was fierce, from his narrowed eyes flashing with streaks of lightning to the muscles tensing in his arms. The Shalémo symbol on the side of his wrist was lit up brighter than I'd ever seen.

But when Hayden looked at me, he softened. The light around him took on a warm glow and his lips twitched into a small smile.

"Hayden!"

Ramsey's shout shook me from my awe. I stumbled backward, closer to Hayden, then turned to face Ramsey. I flinched at the cold rage in his eyes and the plumes of gray smoke hovering around his body. He hadn't hesitated to call his own power. Thick smoke formed between his hands, darkening from wisps of white to deep gray as he strode toward us. The smoke snapped and curled around him, as harsh in its movements as Ramsey was in his.

"Khara, step back."

I did as Hayden said, my head still spinning with shock and relief.

"You shouldn't be worrying about her," Ramsey spat, thrusting his arms down and releasing more smoke. "You should be worrying about me."

He launched a burst of smoke toward us with a shove of his hands. I dove to the floor, sliding behind Hayden and landing harshly on my side. Hayden didn't hesitate. He blasted light toward the smoke. The two energies met with a harsh boom that shook the floor and rattled the walls.

Before the echo had faded, they threw their power toward each other again. Smoke and light collided, and the world turned to chaos.

94

Hayden shifted the fight with Ramsey to the far side of the room, putting more distance between us with every step. Swaths of dark smoke began to thicken, hiding their battle from view. Though Hayden's lightning dissipated some of it, I struggled to see past the blinding bursts.

Watching them wouldn't be an option, and I doubted my ability to help Hayden against Ramsey's power. But leaving him to handle Ramsey didn't mean I was out of the fight altogether.

A sharp crackle of light flared to life in my palms just before a burst of fire flew at my head. Yelping, I ducked, and a rush of heat brushed over my skin as I instinctively swept a guard's legs out from under him. He fell to the ground, the fire disappearing from his hand.

I spun toward another guard who wielded a knife. Lightning flickered in my hand, and I thrust it toward him, desperately hoping the power would work. It burst forward in a flash and connected with his chest. The force threw him to the ground, where he convulsed.

I blinked down at my hands. A small burst of pain flared behind my eyes. I winced, shaking my head, and the pain left as quickly as it had appeared.

The guards did not.

The first had regained his footing. Flames rose in his palms as anger drove him forward. Biting my lip, I took a half-step back and raised my hands to push him away like I had the other guard.

Before I could try, something caught my wrists and wrenched them back. I cried out, forced to move as the hands dragged me farther from where Hayden and Ramsey fought.

"Do you think Sovereign Ramsey will care if I hurt you now?" Cethin hissed in my ear as he jerked my wrists. I gasped and tried to pull away, but he tightened his grip. I could feel bruises forming where he touched.

I tried to direct the light, use it to help me, but it didn't work. My breath sped as I struggled against the pain and fear of Cethin dragging me away. I tried to think, but my mind spun with panic. I strained to see past the smoke and blinding flashes of light Hayden and Ramsey were producing. It was no use. I couldn't see anything beyond a dark band of smoke that hovered like a wall.

Then a burst of light broke through, and the smoke disintegrated as if it'd never existed.

"Khara!" Hayden bellowed, voice taut with worry as he searched for me. Our eyes met, and I fought to suppress my pain and fear.

It didn't work. Hayden saw it all.

His eyes narrowed at Cethin, and he hurled a bolt of lightning our way. It tore past my face, sending a crackling burst of heat over my skin as it struck its target. Cethin's grip loosened. He fell to the floor, gasping as his body jerked.

I glanced down at him, rubbing my wrists, before turning back to Hayden. He had already re-engaged with Ramsey. I let out a relieved breath. He needed to focus on his fight, not worry about mine.

A sharp gust of air slammed into my side, sending me to my knees. Gasping, I brought my hand to my ribs and looked toward the door. A contingent of guards stormed into the room, their arms and batons raised. One had his eyes fixed on me as he lowered his hand. He'd thrown the gust of wind that knocked me off my feet.

I took in my side of the room. The guard I'd struck with lightning started to rise to his knees. The other wasn't where I'd left him. He stood to the side of the fresh group of guards. He'd found reinforcements while I was occupied with Cethin.

Keeping one hand on my ribs, I raised the other so my palm stretched out in front of me. I inhaled deeply, cringing at the pain in my side, and tried to call on the power.

Please, please, please …

A crackle of warmth surged in my palm, and light shot out. It hit the guard who'd hurt me, flinging him into the wall. He slumped to the floor, unmoving, and I could have cried with relief. If there had been time, I might have.

Instead, I was thrown deep into the fight. The guards rushed me, wielding metal batons and thick blades. Those that had powers of their own raised their palms.

With energy crackling against my skin, I pushed to my feet and threw lightning as fast as I could. I couldn't call much power. When I did, it was unreliable, spluttering and jumping in my hand before fizzling out. I had no idea what I was doing, but I had no choice but to keep going.

Five guards made it too close for me to rely on the power alone. Two of them came at me with loud cries, throwing fists and feet my way. In my peripheral vision, I caught the others circling behind me. My heart thundered in my chest. If they managed that, I'd be trapped.

Their movement distracted me. A fist slammed into my face, sending me to the ground. As I tried to rise, a vicious kick to my ribs startled a cry from my lips. My breath hitched, and I curled against the debilitating pain. The kick had landed on the side that had been hit by the wind.

Light blinded me as a rush of power flickered overhead. I blinked rapidly, taking stock of myself. All I felt was the familiar warmth and pinpricks of Hayden's power, but around me, the guards were on the ground.

My head shot up in search of Hayden. He caught my eye and nodded sharply as he panted. I'd never seen him look so tired. Worry pricked my heart, but I didn't have time to dwell on it. Behind him, Ramsey raised his arms above his head and pushed.

My eyes widened in panic. "Hayden!"

He turned, but not fast enough. A burst of smoke shoved him off his feet, and Hayden slammed onto his face. His arms shook as he pushed himself up.

Without a second thought, I left the guards and ran toward him. I didn't care that my ribs screamed with every step. Hayden needed my help.

Ramsey saw me coming. Shaking his head, he flung smoke at me. I knew the light could destroy it, but I didn't know how to use it. I wanted to cry in frustration. If I couldn't figure this out, Hayden might die. *Again*. It would all be over.

I pushed as hard as I could. A small burst of light shot from my hands and collided with the smoke. Some dissolved on impact, but it wasn't enough. The remaining smoke knocked me off my feet, flinging me backward.

My head bounced off the floor, and everything went black.

95

WHEN I MANAGED TO blink back the spots bursting in my eyes, my head pounded in time with my pulse. Bile rose in my throat, and I groaned as I pushed myself to sit up. Dizziness flared, and I kept blinking, desperate to pull myself together. I had to protect myself and Hayden. We needed to escape.

As my eyes cleared, I took in the scene. Hayden had risen from the floor and engaged Ramsey in a ferocious battle, but I could tell he was tiring. He dodged and attacked slower than before. Still, he fought with more fire in his eyes and grace in his steps than anyone I'd ever seen. For the first time, I saw him as the warrior he clearly was, and the sight left me awestruck.

Hayden's movements and the lingering dizziness distracted me for too long. I spun as a whoosh of air sounded behind me. A guard had snuck up and swung his baton at me. My breath caught. It was too late to move. The blow would land.

My muscles tensed and I closed my eyes—only to fling them open at the resonance of clanging metal.

Gage stood over me, blocking the attack with his baton. He pushed against the guard's weapon and stalked after him. My heart pounded as my hope soared. Hayden wasn't the only warrior I knew.

Watching Gage attack the guards was almost as mesmerizing as watching Hayden. He moved as if the battle were a dance, and he knew every step. He fought with the baton like the metal was an extension of his arm.

On shaky hands, I pushed to my feet. Exhaustion seeped into my bones. Lightning crackled around my hands, but it was fainter now. Was it because I was hurt, or was I losing the ability altogether?

I shook off the question. There were too many guards for Gage to take on without help. Raising my hands, I stepped back into the fight.

I managed to incapacitate two more guards. My energy waned with each use of the power, leaving me swaying on my feet, but I couldn't stop. There were still guards in the room. The fight wasn't over yet.

Something whistled through the air, grazing my arm. I bit back a cry at the sharp sting and raised a hand to the wound. Blood seeped between my fingers as I turned to find the culprit. The world spun around me, and I staggered, landing harshly on one knee.

A glint of metal on the floor caught my eyes. A throwing knife. My blood glistened on its edge.

I gripped the handle tight, taking in the weight of the blade as my eyes roved, unsure of where my attention should go.

Cethin stood near the wall, smirking as he flipped a second knife in the air and caught it. I wasn't sure I would be able to dodge his next attack. I was running on fumes. He raised his knife and on instinct, I threw the blade in my hand at him.

It spun end over end and pierced his chest with a wet thunk that made my stomach turn.

My eyes widened as Cethin dropped to his knees. The blade in his hand clattered to the floor.

"I don't want to kill you, but I will." Gage's voice tore through my shock. "Stand down."

He'd overpowered the final guard. The man paused for a long moment before nodding once. He stayed on the ground, his arm gripping his side, and averted his eyes.

Satisfied, Gage dashed to my side. His eyes roamed over my body and his jaw tightened as he took in my injuries. "Come on," he said, reaching for my hand.

As he pulled me up, I looked to where Hayden and Ramsey were still locked in a vicious battle. The once pristine hall was destroyed—walls cracked, Ramsey's throne split in half, the floor broken up from where smoke and lightning had impacted. On our side of the room, guards were splayed out on the ground, most unmoving.

When Gage and I reached the door, I planted my feet.

"We have to go, Khara."

I shook my head. "Not without Hayden. He died. I'm not going to leave him."

"What? He's fine." Gage turned toward the battle raging on the opposite side of the room, brow furrowing as he watched Hayden fight. "Fine as any of us can be right now, anyway."

He shot a worried glance at me before peering out the door.

I flinched as I watched Ramsey land a hit on Hayden, trying not to panic. "Ramsey killed him, Gage. He was dead. I don't know what happened, but he came back."

"Came back," Gage said slowly, "from the dead."

"I know how it sounds." My heart sped faster. "But I swear that's what happened! I had his powers, and then there was this light, and he just—"

"Wait," Gage said, his eyes blown wide. "Wait, wait, wait! You were using his powers."

"Yes!"

"You two did a *binding ceremony*?"

"What? No!" I paused, considering. "Well, Hayden said some vows, but we didn't—"

Gage's jaw dropped as he blinked at me. Then he shook his head, running a rough hand over his face. "Later," he muttered, bouncing on his feet as his eyes darted around the room. "We're dealing with all of that later. Right now, we have to go."

He was right, but I couldn't walk away from Hayden. Not now.

Across the room, Hayden drew a pulsating ball of light between his hands and glanced at us. "Go!" he yelled, voice strained. "I'm right behind you!"

Gage nodded, wrapping his arm around my waist. "We gotta go."

"I told you, not without—"

A loud boom cut me off as Hayden threw the ball of lightning at the ceiling. The impact shook the room, and the ceiling began to crack and crumble.

"Yep, we're going! *Now*." Gage pulled me from the room faster than I could argue.

We sprinted down the corridor as another deafening boom rattled the walls. My ribs protested against every step, but I ran until Gage led us around the corner and slid to a stop before the main hallway. While he peered back to ensure the coast was clear, I took the opportunity to lean against the wall, holding my side as I took ragged breaths. He turned to me with a worried frown.

"I'm fine," I said, but I couldn't keep the pain from my voice or stop my shallow panting.

Gage's eyes darted from me to the hall. "I don't think we have time for me to look."

"I'll be fine. We need to get Hayden and get out of here."

He jerked a nod before wiping the sweat from his brow. "Let me know if you can't run. I mean it, Khara. I'll carry you out if I have to."

I gestured to the baton he clutched in his hand. "And probably still use that thing like it's part of you. Who taught you to fight like that?"

Gage huffed a laugh. "You did."

I blinked, sure the shock was written all over my face.

"Okay, so not just you." Gage smirked. "Most of it was my mother. She trained me growing up. I learned more in guard training. But some of the dirtier moves? Those I learned from you."

I gaped at him. There was so much about my life—about *myself*—I still didn't know. Despite the danger we were in and the exhaustion clinging to my body, curiosity bloomed bright in my chest. I wanted to know who I was more than ever. What other surprises would I find?

"I want to hear more about that when we're out of here," I said, my lips twitching into a smile. "And maybe learn some of those moves."

Gage grinned. "It'd be nice to teach you something for a change."

He poked his head back around the corner and stiffened.

"What?" I whispered, my own muscles tensing. I wasn't sure I'd be able to last in another fight. I wasn't even sure if I'd be able to run out of the Annex. Everything hurt and I was spent.

Gage didn't answer. He didn't have to.

Hayden bolted around the corner seconds later. His eyes flicked from me to Gage and back, searching for injuries as he sprinted toward us. His eyes tightened when he caught my gaze, but he said nothing about the blood staining my clothes. He barely paused to take my hand. "Let's go."

Without hesitation, the three of us turned and ran.

96

As we turned the next corner, the lights pulsed red above our heads. Someone had raised the alarm, signaling danger just like when Lachlan had escaped and attacked me. Only this time, I *was* the danger.

Even so, the halls were quiet. Only our panting breaths and the padding of our feet against the floor reached my ears as the three of us jogged down the corridor.

A shiver ran down my spine. Something was wrong, beyond the obvious. My eyes darted, watching for anyone who might step out and attack.

We paused at the end of the hall. Gage took the lead, craning his neck around the corner and searching for trouble in both directions. I leaned against the wall, my heart pounding as I tried to catch my breath. My bare feet burned, and I willed the chill of the floor to soothe them. I'd have to keep running. Our lives depended on it. It was the only thing keeping me going when I felt like I could pass out and sleep for a week.

Gage nodded to Hayden. When they turned to me and took in my shallow breathing, concern lined both of their faces. But for once, neither said anything. We all knew there was no choice but to keep moving.

"We're going left," Gage said, glancing at us before returning to watch for guards. "The closest exit's that way. I want to get the two of you out of here as fast as possible."

"The three of us," Hayden corrected. "You're done here, Gage. Your cover's blown."

He threw his hands up. "Yeah, sure. The three of us." He huffed a laugh, a snarky grin forming on his lips. "And my cover isn't just blown. I'd say it's been completely obliterated."

I snorted. I admired Gage's ability to find humor in any situation—or make some himself.

"It's clear," he murmured, shifting back to seriousness. "Let's move."

I pushed off from the wall, ready to run, when I remembered the device.

We couldn't leave without it. It was in Ramsey's office—and hopefully unguarded.

"Wait!" I hissed. "We can't leave yet."

The boys came to a quick halt and turned to look at me—Hayden with questioning eyes, Gage in utter disbelief.

"Uh, yes, we can. And we have to. Like, now." Gage hiked a thumb to the left.

Hayden ignored him. "What do you need?"

My heart swelled, and I nodded toward the right. "Ramsey has this device. I tried to steal it. That's how I got caught. Ramsey's planning to use it in the Eastern District. I'm not sure what it does, just that he didn't care that people would die. He'll blame whatever it does on the rebels, and then use the same device to try to take you out."

Hayden ran a hand through his hair, pursing his lips. "Okay. We'll get it."

Gage flapped his hands above his head. "Have you completely lost your minds?" He glanced down the hall again. "I need to get the two of you out of here. I'll come back for the device—"

"No. We need to do this now," I argued. "Ramsey will have it too well guarded once he recovers."

"Which could be any minute now. Which is why you need to get out!" Gage looked to Hayden, his arms out wide. "Well?"

"She's right. We need to make sure Ramsey can't use this device. It's too dangerous."

Gage scrubbed his hands over his face, groaning in frustration when they covered his mouth. He shook his head as he dropped his hands. "Fine. *Fine*. But if this ends badly, I will hold it over both of you for the rest of your sorry lives."

Hayden huffed, his lips twitching. "Deal. Go clear a path for us. Khara, you'll come with me to get the device."

Gage flailed. "Are you *serious*?"

Hayden held up a hand. "We don't have time for this. Clear a path. Make sure we can run straight to the exit."

"Do you even know where you're going?" he asked tightly.

"I can get us to Ramsey's office and back here." I stepped closer to Hayden. "What door are we going to?"

Gage sighed heavily and pinched the bridge of his nose. "The one you've been sneaking out of the last few weeks."

"Then we'll be fine."

Hayden nodded. "Go."

Gage stared at us for a beat, baring every ounce of his worry in the jittery movements of his hands and the glint of panic in his eyes. He obviously didn't like this plan. Still, he gave a jerky nod. "I'll meet you at the door. If you're not there in ten minutes—"

Hayden squeezed his shoulder. "We'll be there."

"You better be," Gage grumbled.

I nodded to Gage, determination filling me. We would get the device. We would come right to the exit door. We'd run out of this place. And this time, I wouldn't look back.

97

HAYDEN AND I MOVED down the hallway as fast as we could. My bare feet slapped against the floor and my ribs jarred with every step, forcing me to slow. Hayden kept pace with me, his eyes darting to where my hand gingerly held my side. He didn't say a word as he shifted closer.

The entryway to the offices was tinged in red. My eyes flicked to the restored window, and I brushed off my unease, striding to the door. My access had been restricted, but I hoped my handprint might still allow me to enter.

I pressed my hand against the panel. It glowed for a moment before flashing red. My heart sank, and I dropped my head against the wall. "I don't know how to get in."

Hayden placed a hand against my back. "We'll get in."

He said it in the same tone as every time he made me a promise. I believed him now without question.

Voices rang out down the hall. I startled, looking wide-eyed at Hayden. He pulled me against the opposite wall, tucking me behind him.

Two guards rushed toward the entry. The first pressed his hand against the panel as the second stood rigid at his side. He glanced behind him and froze as his eyes fixed on me.

He stumbled back a step, bumping into his partner. I winced. We'd have no choice now but to fight.

"Watch where you're tripping!" The guard turned to face him, and his eyes fell on us.

He reached for his weapon in one fluid movement, but Hayden was faster. He raised his palm and sent a pulse of light that caught both of their feet. They jolted, falling to their knees.

I dashed to the unlocked door, propping it open. Hayden hurried to follow, knocking out the first guard with a swift punch to the head, then turning to do the same to the second. Hayden took an elbow to his side but didn't falter. The second guard was unconscious seconds later.

Heart pounding, I pushed the door open fully and entered the office wing. Hayden followed closely behind.

The same eerie quiet from the other halls filled the space. Unease shuddered down my spine, but I did my best to shove it aside. All we had to do was grab the device and get out. It wouldn't be like the last time I tried to steal it. This time, I had help. I had Hayden.

When we reached Ramsey's office, the glass walls were opaque. I'd never seen them darkened before. It only fueled the pounding of my pulse and the nerves swirling in my gut.

There was a new wooden panel in front of the door, glowing a soft blue. My shoulders slumped and I rotated to face Hayden. "That wasn't here before."

He motioned me to the side. "Stay back."

Raising his arm, he pushed a streak of lightning at the panel. The wood cracked on impact, the blue glow brightening before it faded. He turned his attention to the door, hitting the handle so hard it burst off and clattered to the floor. Hayden followed, folding over at the waist and then dropping to one knee, breathing heavily.

"Hayden!" I slid to my knees at his side, barely stopping myself from hissing at the pain in my ribs. I cupped his face in my hands. "What's wrong?"

"I just need a minute."

We didn't have time to spare, and we both knew it.

"I'll be fine," he panted. "I just need to stop using my powers for a while."

That was only slightly better news. Whatever power was inside of me had fizzled down to a slight buzz beneath my skin. I'd have very little fight left in me if we were ambushed.

I didn't mention any of this, instead focusing on the task at hand. "Can you stand?"

Hayden nodded, bracing before pushing himself upright. I wanted to help, but I had to gingerly make my way back to my own feet. This time, I couldn't stop a hiss of pain from escaping. I bent forward, my hand hovering at my side. As I straightened, I caught Hayden's concerned gaze. I shook my head, panting shallowly as I motioned to the door.

I shuffled forward, Hayden close behind me, and pushed the door with my foot. It cracked, and I pressed harder until it opened fully. I stepped inside—only to freeze as a strange weapon leveled directly at my chest.

98

MY EYES FOCUSED ON the weapon—some sort of wide-barreled gun, not the legal kind used for hunting—but that didn't keep me from noticing who held it.

Emila's back was straight and her face flat as she aimed at me. In her other hand, she held my bundled-up sweater, the device still wrapped inside.

I waited for the anger to come. She'd pretended to be my friend only to help keep me prisoner. Invaded my privacy. Betrayed me to Ramsey. I should've been furious with her. But all I could feel was deep, aching grief and the fear that my best friend would be the one to kill us.

Hayden shifted beside me, raising his hand to disarm her with his magic, and my heart constricted. He couldn't use his power. I didn't know what it would do to him and hoped I wouldn't have to find out.

Besides, using them meant hurting Emila, and despite everything, I wasn't sure I could stomach that, either.

She aimed the gun directly at Hayden's chest. "Don't."

He lowered his hand slowly.

We were at a standstill, stuck at the mercy of a woman I wasn't sure I knew after all. The thought stung. We'd spent so much time together. She'd been one of the only constants in my life here. It couldn't have all been a lie. Was she that good of an actress?

If I was having such conflicted feelings about Emila and seeing her hurt, maybe she had them for me too. Maybe she cared despite her lies. However slim a possibility it was, I had to try to reach her.

"Emila," I said, my voice wavering, "you don't want to do this."

She met my eyes, hers brimming with turmoil as she shook her head. "You don't know me. How do you know what I want?"

I took a small step forward, ignoring the way Hayden reached for me. She was talking to me. That was a good sign. "Because despite everything that's happened,

I can't believe it was all a lie. I might not know everything about you, but I know you well enough to know you're not a killer."

She didn't relax her stance in the slightest. I gestured to the sweater in her hand.

"Do you know what that thing does? Ramsey's going to use it to destroy the Eastern District. I know you don't want that."

Pain flashed in her eyes, though her stance didn't waver. "You don't know that. He said—"

"Ramsey is a *liar*."

Did the reminder hold as much weight for her as it did for me? She knew how capable of deception he was. She'd been privy to one of his greatest lies. She'd helped keep it alive.

"You can't trust whatever he's told you. I heard him talking about destroying the Eastern District firsthand." I gestured to the sweater. "I found that in Dr. Jensen's lab, labeled for the Eastern District. You can go look for yourself if you want proof, but you have to know I wouldn't lie about this."

Desperation laced my voice. I'd lied to her before—we both knew that—but never about anything like this. I needed her to believe me, needed her to understand what was at stake for all of us.

"Ramsey doesn't care about the people there, people like your mother. All he cares about is power. You don't want this, Emila. I know you don't."

She glanced at the sweater in her hands. When her eyes flicked back to me, they held a glassy sheen. She blinked rapidly. Still, her weapon stayed trained on Hayden.

I waited with bated breath for her to choose.

As Emila stared at the device, her eyes narrowed. She slowly lowered the gun to her side. "This shouldn't exist."

She tossed the sweater toward me. It landed at my feet with a soft thump.

No one spoke until Hayden bent to open my sweater, revealing the device. He looked up at me. "Is this everything?"

I peered at the contents. "I think so."

He nodded, swiftly rewrapping it and tying the sweater back into a makeshift bag.

"I'm sorry." Emila's low voice brought my attention back to her. She stared at the floor, her arms crossed. "For my part in this ... Khara, I'm sorry."

She glanced from Hayden, standing at my side with the device in hand, to me. Sadness overtook her face, and part of me longed to pull her into a hug. Another part wanted to shove her, to shout and cry until I made her tell me what led her to do any of this. I stayed where I was, silent and serious and far sadder than I wanted to be.

"You didn't deserve this." Emila covered her mouth and looked out the window, fighting back tears.

My throat tightened. I hadn't expected an apology. Somehow, it made my heart ache even more.

"Take the device and go."

"Come with us." The words tumbled from my mouth before I'd thought them through. But as soon as I said them, they felt right. While she stared at me in disbelief, I took a step closer, reaching out to her. "Emila, I mean it. Come with us. You don't belong here."

Her eyes swirled with pain as she shook her head. "I belong here in ways you never have, Khara. You need to go. Now, before the guards find you."

"No. Emila, you—"

Noise in the hall stilled us. Hayden shifted to stand directly in front of me.

Emila glanced at the gun in her hand, biting her lip before raising it slightly. "Go. Now!"

But it was too late. Pounding footsteps sounded just outside the office.

99

THE DOOR CRASHED OPEN, and Gage flew into the room. His brows lifted when he saw Emila holding the weapon, but he didn't linger on her. Panting heavily, he turned to Hayden and flashed a cheeky grin.

"Pathway's clear. It's been over ten minutes. This is the part where I come and drag you out of here, ready or not. I saw Commander North in the hall, rallying the troops, and I don't know about you, but I really don't want to have that fight today. We need to go. Now. Like, *right now*."

He'd meant it before, but his tone was different now. More urgent. We had to get out of the Annex and leave the city, and we needed to do it fast.

Without hesitation, Hayden grabbed my hand and started to pull me toward the door.

"Wait."

We stopped in our tracks as Emila sighed. She barely glanced our way as she removed her sandals and held them out in front of her. "Take these."

"What?"

"You're leaving the city. You can hardly run barefoot. So, take them." She tossed the sandals at my feet. "They'll be small, but they're better than nothing."

Tears stung my eyes as Hayden hurried to help me into the shoes. "Emila—"

"Less talking, more walking. Wouldn't want Gage to have an aneurysm."

I snorted, my lips lifting in spite of myself as I glanced at my feet. Hayden tightened a strap around my ankle and gave my foot a gentle pat. I set it back on the floor, shifting my stance to accommodate the slight heels. My toes dangled off the front edges. I'd have to be careful moving in these.

I wanted to thank Emila, to say something meaningful in our last moments together. But I could only think of one thing she'd allow.

"These shoes are really impractical."

Though her eyes remained sad, her lips twitched. "Those shoes are designer, and I expect you to take good care of them."

My laugh was watery as I nodded.

"Now *go*."

Hayden took my hand in his and led me to the door. Walking in the sandals felt awkward and didn't help the pain in my ribs, but I would manage.

"What will you do?"

Gage's question stopped us at the door. We turned and found him staring intently at Emila. I held my breath, wanting to know the answer as badly as he did.

"Don't worry about me." Emila shook her head. "Ramsey and I have unfinished business. I'll be fine. You won't. You need to go."

Despite the tense set of his shoulders, Gage nodded. He turned from Emila and jogged to meet me and Hayden. My heart sank at the grieved look in his eyes. Neither of us wanted to leave her behind, but neither of us could spare a look back.

We raced through the halls as fast as we could, but Hayden and I both struggled. Gage noticed and took it upon himself to cover us both. He attacked any guards we came across with surprising precision and intensity. In the end, he was the reason we made it out of the Annex and onto the streets of Anluan.

No one bothered us as we wove through the city. Most of the people paid us no mind as we slipped in and out of side streets and alleyways. The ones who did seem to recognize Hayden quickly turned away. I couldn't tell if they were pretending not to see him, or were about to run and turn us in.

Either way, we didn't linger. We dashed through the streets until Gage stopped us at part of the southern wall and revealed the entrance to another tunnel.

"I did say there was more than one," Gage said with a tired smile as he gestured me forward. "Come on."

It was much the same as the other tunnel—tight, but passable. My ribs protested as I crawled through. By the time I emerged on the other side, I was gasping. Hayden reached to help me stand while Gage shimmied out behind me.

I squeezed my eyes shut and focused on taking shallow breaths. We weren't safe yet. We had to keep going.

Steeling myself, I stepped forward, and Hayden's hands slid from my arms. I could tell he wanted to reach for me again, but instead, he walked by my side. Close, but not touching.

The cover of the forest wasn't far from the wall, but with every step a struggle, it felt like it was. Though the boys didn't say anything, I knew I was slowing us down. Once we made it into the trees, Gage took the lead so Hayden could stay by my side. He led us into the brush and revealed a narrow path I couldn't imagine anyone stumbling upon without prior knowledge of it.

A few feet down the trail, my legs folded under me. The next thing I knew, I was on my back, blinking past pain as I stared up at the treetops. In a daze, I watched as the leaves danced in the breeze.

Hayden dropped to his knees at my side, his hands hovering over me.

Gage joined him, looking at Hayden with stricken eyes. "What happened?"

"I don't know," he said, a hint of panic bleeding into his words. "She just dropped."

I frowned. Why were they talking about me like I wasn't here?

"I'm fine."

My voice was barely a breath, but somehow they heard me. Two pairs of eyes bored into me incredulously.

"Yeah, you're fine." Gage scoffed as he fidgeted, his sharp eyes darting around the forest.

Hayden's hand wound around mine. "Can you sit up?"

It was a good question. Considering I didn't even remember hitting the ground, I wasn't sure. Still, I nodded and shifted forward. The movement sent a sharp stab through my side, and I fell back with a cry.

Hayden leaned over me and settled his hand against the side of my head. "Don't move." His words were soft, even giving orders. His other hand hovered at my side. "Can I look?"

I nodded. He had my trust, and it was hardly a time for modesty.

He carefully lifted the side of my shirt and inspected my ribs with a grimace. Gentle as he was, I couldn't help but whimper as his fingers glanced over my side. My breath hitched, tears escaping as I blinked through the pain.

Hayden sat back, lowering my shirt before he ran a hand over his face.

"I think your ribs are bruised, maybe broken. I can't tell." He turned to Gage, communicating something with his eyes I was too worn out to try to decipher. When he looked back at me, his face seemed even more pained than before. "Do you know what did this?"

"Wind power." I thought back to the moment I fell to the ground and cringed. "Guard kicked me after I fell. Before you knocked them all out."

He nodded, a spark of anger lighting his eyes. It was strange seeing him exude so much ferocity and power on my behalf. I wasn't sure I'd ever get used to it.

Bending low, Hayden reached to touch my face again. His eyes shone with frustration. "I can't heal you."

"I wouldn't ask you to," I said. "Not now."

His lips twitched, just barely. "I'm going to help you sit. Ready?"

I wasn't, but I nodded anyway. Hayden motioned to Gage, and he knelt on my other side, carefully placing his hands beneath my shoulders. Bracing myself, I grasped Hayden's hand, letting the two of them lift me.

My head swam with the movement, and my stomach churned. The twinge of pain in my side sharpened, but it was less overwhelming than when I'd tried to sit on my own. Gage's arm stayed secure around my shoulders, propping me up as Hayden knelt in front of me, holding my hands. It was quiet as I did my best to breathe through the pain.

When I opened my eyes, Hayden searched my face. I gave him a tired smile. "I'm okay."

This time, he seemed to believe me.

"Can you stand? I'll help you walk, but we need to keep moving. We're not far enough from the city to rest."

I moved my hands to push myself from the ground, but Hayden held them fast. He shook his head, and I relaxed again.

Right. That would end badly.

He squeezed my hands. "Let us do most of the work."

When I nodded, he moved to my injured side. He and Gage moved as one, helping me to my feet as carefully as they could. The shift filled my vision with black spots, but they held me up until the worst of it faded.

I blew out a shaky breath. "I can keep going."

"Take the lead, Gage. I'll help her walk," Hayden said, shifting as if to take more of my weight.

Gage scoffed. "No, you won't. You're going to focus on staying on your own two feet. I'll help her walk."

Of the three of us, Gage was in the best shape. He hadn't fought as long as we had, though he'd fought just as hard. He wouldn't back down, and he shouldn't. He was right.

"Hayden, let Gage help me."

Hayden sighed but slowly released me. Gage slid into place at my side, wrapping my arm over his shoulders. Letting him take more of my weight, we shuffled farther from the city.

100

Time dragged as we trekked through the forest. Narrow pathways of uneven ground meant every step sent a twinge of pain to my side. Hayden trailed behind me and Gage as we moved at the quickest pace I could handle. Though we saw no signs of being followed, we hurried to put more distance between us and Ramsey. The last thing we needed was another fight.

The longer we trudged forward, the more I could feel Gage's muscles tighten beneath my arm. The silence grew heavy.

"Are you okay?" I asked when I could no longer bear the tension.

He dipped his head, flashing me a strained smile. "Just thinking."

"About what?" Hayden asked.

Gage tensed even more, his smile growing sharp. "I am *so* glad you asked, Hayden."

I stiffened, the biting undertone of his words a warning if I'd ever heard one. Whatever was on his mind, it wasn't good. Still, his emotions didn't change the gentle way he held his arm around my waist.

"See, Khara mentioned something interesting back at the Annex. She said you died."

Hayden's steps faltered behind us. "Oh."

"Yeah, *oh*. You wanna tell me what you were thinking? Or should I just keep assuming you weren't?"

"It was a calculated risk," Hayden hedged. "I knew what I was doing."

Gage stopped walking abruptly, and I bit my lip against a spark of pain at the jostling. I peeked up at Gage and winced at the tight set of his jaw. "Are you kidding me?"

Hayden sighed. "I knew redamancy would give—"

"*Redamancy*?" Carefully, Gage propped me against a tree before rounding on Hayden. "You staked your life and everything else on *redamancy*?"

I frowned, confusion pulling me further into exhaustion. "What's redamancy?"

"A fairytale," Gage bit out. "A myth. Something you tell kids before bedtime."

Hayden shrugged, weariness lining the movement. "Apparently not."

"Apparently—!" Gage flung his hands up, his eyes flashing with anger. I sank further into the tree at my back. "No, you know what's it not, Hayden? *A plan.* Do you have any idea how done I am with you right now?"

"I have a feeling you're going to tell me," Hayden muttered, shoulders slumping as he rubbed his forehead.

Gage laughed bitterly. "No, you know what? I'm *not* going to tell you. I'm going to tell your father." He shoved a finger against Hayden's chest. "I'll let Galen deal with you. I deserve a break. A very long, relaxing break where I don't have to deal with any of this reckless stupidity!"

"Can I have one too?" I asked as I panted against the tree. My ribs ached, and though our pace had been slow, it still left me short of breath. Their argument wasn't helping. "I could use a break like that."

They both turned to face me. I imagined I made a sorry sight, leaning against a tree trunk with my hand cradled against my side. Hayden's face fell, and Gage's posture slackened. The two shared a glance, speaking without words again. Then Gage sighed, clapped his hand against Hayden's arm, and made his way back to me.

"You get the longest, most relaxing break of all," he said as he shifted to support me. "I'll even let you go first."

"Why don't we go together?" I offered, sparing a glance at Hayden. "I'm not thrilled with the way all that panned out, either."

Gage barked a laugh. "Sure, Princess." He gently led us forward again. "You know, he's lucky he's getting off so easy. Wait until you actually remember."

He blew out a long, slow whistle that made me huff. The movement jarred my ribs, and I hissed as my hand clenched the shoulder of Gage's shirt.

When I caught my breath enough to loosen my grip, I glanced from Gage to Hayden. "Maybe we could save the rest of this discussion for another time?"

The apology written across their faces was answer enough, but dual nods followed.

"Good," I said on a sigh. "Because I don't understand half of what you're saying, and I don't think I have the energy for an explanation."

Gage snorted, a tired smirk spreading across his face. "You don't even know how right you are."

Hayden winced. "When we're safe, Khara. I'll explain everything when we're safe."

101

AFTER MILES OF TRUDGING through the dense Lyaran Forest, we reached a break in the trees. Around the large clearing, grassy hills loomed in every direction. I cringed. No matter which way we went, the incline would be murderous on my ribs.

Gage slowed our pace, helping me take the climb one agonizing step at a time. Hayden followed closely behind, hands raised to catch me if I started to fall. Having him at my back comforted me as much as having Gage beside me. I knew they'd both protect me as best they could.

By the time we crested the hill, sweat pooled at the nape of my neck. My breath came in gasps that sent pain tearing through me. I staggered forward a few steps, near tears, and Gage gently helped me rest atop a large boulder.

"Breathe, Khara." He knelt at my side, catching my eyes as I bent forward slightly. "Just like that. Slowly."

A moment later, Hayden knelt in front of me. Gage moved away to give us some privacy. Lacing our fingers, Hayden ran his thumb along the back of my hand.

"How bad?" he asked.

I was afraid if I opened my mouth, the sob I'd been repressing would spill out. I let my pained eyes speak for me.

Hayden's face fell. "Maybe I could heal you, just enough to ease the pain."

"No." I shook my head. "You're not endangering yourself because of me."

I wouldn't allow it. Not now, and if I had any say, not ever again.

His eyes softened as if he could read my mind. "This is different."

"I know. And I'm still not going to let you do it."

We held each other's gaze for a long moment. Slowly, he nodded, though it looked like it pained him to agree. That was one thing I loved about Hayden—he gave me what I needed, even when he didn't like it.

I looked away, taking in our surroundings for the first time. From the top of the hill, we had a perfect view of Anluan. The angle let us see over the thick stone wall and into the heart of the city. The lines of narrow streets and curves of the outer road blended with rows of buildings and open spaces. The layers formed a stunning image. My eyes roamed over the rise and fall of buildings before they locked on a glimmer of evening light reflecting off the waters of the canal. I followed its winding path until a copse of trees blocked it from view.

My heart sped as I spotted the palace grounds. It was hard not to notice them. The Annex and its twin tower hovered as formidable sentinels on the far sides of the expansive palace. I flicked my eyes away, not wanting to spend any more time focused on that place than I had to. But my breath caught as I took in the sprawling view of the palace itself.

It was damaged, yes, but it still stood. The white stone palace stretched wide across the lawn. Though crumbled pieces remained visible even from this distance, they didn't account for as much of the building as I'd expected. Strips of gold still supported the half-shattered glass dome that gleamed in the evening sun. Somehow the palace had managed to retain a magnificent presence despite the devastation it had faced.

It looked strong enough to be rebuilt. That alone bolstered my spirit with hope. The palace could be restored and so could Anluan. We would make sure they were.

I glanced at Hayden, watching how intently he surveyed the city before I turned back to it myself.

Gage ambled over, wiping the sweat from his brow on the hem of his shirt. He cast his eyes over the city, searching for anything out of place. "Seems quiet."

Hayden nodded. "I think we can stop for the night."

My shoulders sagged, and I closed my eyes as my heart swelled with relief. Every part of me ached. I wasn't sure how much longer I could have stayed on my feet. Plus, sunset was approaching, and traversing the forest in the dark would've been a nightmare.

"It's too open here to make camp. I found a smaller incline that way." Gage motioned to a gentler path to the west. He frowned at me. "Do you think you can—?"

"Just give me a few minutes."

He turned to Hayden. "I can take the path a bit, make sure it's clear."

Hayden nodded, his worried eyes fixed on me. "I'll stay with Khara."

Gage flashed me a tired smile, then started back down the hill.

Hayden sat beside me, and the two of us breathed in the quiet of the day. I closed my eyes as a cool breeze blew over my skin. It was a welcome relief after working my body so hard.

When I looked back over the city, my heart ached for it. So many people were trapped under Ramsey's rule. Worse, too few of them realized the danger they were in. My eyes stung as I imagined the devastation Ramsey could have caused with the device in the sweater tied tight around Hayden's back.

Hayden squeezed my hand. "What's on your mind?"

"All those people," I said, my voice breaking. "They don't understand who Ramsey is, what he's capable of. What he's willing to do to them."

I looked away from the city, letting my eyes trail over the forests and barely visible patches of farmland before I met Hayden's eyes. They were soft with understanding. This pain was one we shared.

"We have to help them, Hayden. We have to stop him."

"We will," he promised, his eyes unwavering as they bored into mine. "Soon."

The weight of his words settled in my heart. Hayden would do everything in his power to restore Anluan, just like he did everything in his power to restore me to his side. I nodded, squeezing his hand. He squeezed back, then stood.

"First, we need to rest. We'll come up with a plan to stop Ramsey when we get back. Come on."

He gently helped me to my feet, shifting to take some of my weight.

"Where are we going?" I asked as we made our way to the edge of the path.

He smiled down at me. "Home."

After everything, there was nowhere I wanted to go more.

THE
AFTERMATH

EMILA

WELL, THIS DAY HAD turned into an unmitigated disaster.

I blew out a breath, the prototype of Ramsey's new weapon heavy in my arms as I tried to figure out what I was supposed to do now. Despite the continued glow of red light from the hall, it was quiet in Ramsey's office. That should have given me all the space I needed to think, but the only thing distinguishable in my mind was the thick cloud of doubt covering my most recent choices.

I shouldn't have let them go.

It had been an easy choice to make while staring into Khara's face. The only one, really. No matter how our friendship initially formed, the two of us had truly bonded these last few months. My motives for agreeing to Ramsey's plan had been selfish, but being Khara's friend was more than a job to me. Though I doubted the two of us would be much of anything after today, whether she and Hayden made it out of the city with Gage or not.

A shudder ran through me. I didn't want to see what Ramsey would do to any of them if they didn't.

I didn't want to see what Ramsey would do if they *did*.

With a heavy sigh, I turned and dropped the gun—a weapon that would never have been considered a few years ago—onto Ramsey's desk with a heavy thud. No matter what happened now, things were going to get ugly in the worst ways.

Tapping a finger against my lips, I paced the office, trying to let go of the doubt and fear. I needed to focus. I didn't have time to wallow. When Ramsey got here, I had to have an answer for what had happened. As it was, I had no excuses he would allow, even for me.

Boots fell on the tile in the hall, and my heart skipped a beat. I was out of time. Maybe out of luck, too, despite all I'd done to change my situation.

The door burst open, and Charna entered, stopping short just inside the room. She'd been prepared for a fight, something to step into. I could tell by the set of her jaw, the tense coiling of her muscles. She'd always been a force to be reckoned with. It was one of the things I admired most about her.

"Stand down, Commander," I said, dropping my arms to my sides. Though I went for teasing, my tone rang with weariness. "Just me in here."

Charna relaxed, but only just. Her eyes swept over the room, taking in more with a quick evaluation than I ever could. Her expression was unreadable when she turned her gaze on me. "You let them go."

My brows rose. That didn't take long. As I'd suspected, my luck had run out. Steeling myself, I gave a single, jerky nod. "Yes."

Charna stared, and I could see her mind at work. She'd always been brilliant in her own way. Strategic. Sharp. She was piecing something together. I held my breath as I waited to learn what.

"We need to set the scene," she said, breaking eye contact to look around the office. "And I need to punch you in the face."

A startled laugh burst from my lips. "I'm sorry, *what*?"

Charna strode to Ramsey's desk and gave a swift kick to the corner. I flinched as one side scraped across the floor, but as usual, Char wasn't fazed. She pushed a stack of papers to the floor.

"Your face." She gestured to it with her chin before knocking more of Ramsey's things to the hardwood. "You don't look like you've been in a fight."

"Because I wasn't in one."

"That's the point. You should have been." Charna paused in disrupting the papers on the floor with her boot. "What do you think Ramsey will do when he finds out what happened?"

My mind flashed to dark smoke, moving as if alive until it curled around my throat and pulled. I couldn't help but touch a hand to the base of my neck at the brutal image. Charna nodded, her face grim. Something sparked in her eyes, something I'd never noticed before.

Then it hit me.

"You called him Ramsey."

She never used his first name without the title. It was always *Sovereign Ramsey* or *Sovereign*. Even when off duty, Charna never lost the respectful decorum of Commander North.

Until now.

She ignored me. "You won't get a second chance. Not for this."

The words cut through my heart even as denial roared in my chest. After everything I'd done, all that I'd sacrificed, I refused to let it end like that. Not for me. Not for my mother.

But Charna's words didn't ring with condemnation. I wasn't sure what she was thinking, but I was willing to play along to find out.

"And you giving me a black eye solves all my problems?"

"Hardly. But if we act fast, it will stop some of the questions you won't be able to answer."

It's hard to lie to a man like Ramsey, one so adept at manipulation. I'd fallen for his lies, even while helping him perpetuate others. Charna was right—what happened here wasn't a question I could answer. Not with the truth and not with a lie. Not if I wanted to survive.

And I did. Long enough to gain the power and protection I'd been promised when I agreed to Ramsey's plan. Long enough to see things change. And maybe, if it were possible for someone like me, long enough to find a way to atone for some of my sins.

I eyed the prototype, now on the floor, then glanced at Charna. "Do these things really work?"

Her brow furrowed, her words hesitant as I bent to pick it up. "They do."

"Good. Let's make this truly believable."

I aimed the weapon at my stomach and fired.

"That was foolish."

A moan fell from my lips as I came to across the room with Charna's hand cupping my face. She stared with disapproval from where she crouched in front of me.

Breathing hurt.

I'd been attacked using air powers before, but not like this. The prototype gun Doctor Jensen created could change the way Ramsey waged war. With weapons like this, he could make the Tower Guard twice as powerful. Move on the rebels. Have whatever he wanted.

I reached a hand to my forehead, grimacing at the tacky feel of blood against my skin as much as at the pain.

Charna helped me sit, eyeing me carefully. "How do you feel?"

"Like a Corodenian punched through my stomach with a gust of wind." I swiped a hand over my forehead to stop a trail of blood from falling into my eyes. My face stung more than it should have. "Did you punch me?"

"A few times. Thought you'd appreciate being out for that."

I snorted. "You're a true friend, Char."

Her eyes bored into mine. "I am."

The solemn honesty was too much for me. I had to look away. Charna's friendship had always seemed surface-level. All my friendships did, really. Until Khara. And I wasn't sure that counted as friendship at all.

My eyes landed on the weapon, smashed to pieces on the floor. "What happened to the gun?"

"Rebels must have destroyed it."

She said it so simply that if I hadn't known better, I would've believed her. I knew she was lying and almost believed her anyway.

"Must have," I said after a beat, looking up to meet her gaze.

A promise filled her eyes, one I knew was mirrored in mine. Whatever this was, we were in it together. And we would take these secrets to our graves.

Acknowledgments

In many ways, releasing this book has felt like coming home. Writing has been part of my life since I was a kid, and young Kristin dreamed of publishing a book one day. I pursued other things for a time, but writing was always there. For this day to finally come—and with *Smoke and Light*, a story that's hovered over my heart for more than a decade—it's a homecoming and new adventure, all rolled into one.

This book wouldn't have happened without many people being in my corner, both now and way back when. I could spend pages listing everyone who's been part of this journey in some way. From teachers to family to friends, there were so many people who influenced, supported, and encouraged me over the years. To each of you, whether you know the impact you've had or not, thank you.

To Jesus, who continually reminds me of who I am when I forget and always welcomes me home. Thank you for using this book to encourage me, grow me, and give me something to put my heart into during a heavy season. It will always hold a special place in my heart. Forever grateful for this time together and the gift of co-creating with you!

To Renee, editor extraordinaire and *Smoke and Light*'s biggest champion—your friendship and support are the gifts God knew I needed in this season. Your insights, edits, and encouragement have been invaluable. *Smoke and Light* is a better book because of your time, energy, and enthusiastic care. I couldn't have done this without you, for so many reasons. Thankful for you always.

To Savannah, the first person to read this book, thank you for diving into draft two and for all your encouraging words and thoughtful suggestions!

To my incredible beta readers—Abigail, Danielle, Denise, Doodlebug, Lizz, Marije, Misty, and Sindy—who said yes to reading this book when all they knew was my love for it, thank you. Your comments helped me take this story deeper and your enthusiasm still brings me joy. Thank you, Abigail and Nicole, for helping me catch proofreading errors before going to print. Thank you, Michele, for answering the random editing question texts I sent your way.

To all of my Rulers and Rebels, the best street team an author could ask for—Abigail, Caroline, Danielle, Holly, Jacquie, Lizz, Misty, Nay, Taylor, and Tracy—thank you for showing up, supporting me, and making it your mission to get *Smoke and Light* in front of more readers!

A huge thank you to all of my Kickstarter backers for helping me launch this book into the world with love and celebration! You blew me away with your early support and excitement. You're amazing! A special thank you to Samantha M., Terry S., Leandra Wallace, Danielle R., Amanda Balter, Corinne Brucks, Shannon Davidson, Chloe Hey, Caitlyn Price, Rinna, N.A. Carlson, Amanda Eschmeyer, Mariah Hatley, Karah, Abigail McGovern, Makenzie A., Xyvah M. Okoye, E.A. Hendryx, Ashley H., Beth F., Caroline R., Cindy F., Erin D., Alyssa, Rachel R., Hannah U., Christina, Hannah A., Kristen Tesoro Lumsden, Kathleen Clipper, Jonathan S., Davin G., Teresa Beasley, Kasey S., Aimee Eliason, Julie H., Holly Davis, The Tademy Family, Felicia, Monica Kim, Shanon M. Brown, Kristy Van Wyhe, S.D. Huston, Danielle Cage, Dru K., Joseph M., Angela Morse, Tahirah, Denise C., Bethany B., Rosa B., Ashley K., Zee, Nicole H., Kristina A. S., Kelsey Stenberg, Andie Vargas, Will, Misty Danielles, Savannah G., Anne S., Emily C., Billye Herndon, Jacquie Engbrecht, Sarah C., Justine, Chris-André Pedersen, Nay, Ashton Smith, Julia S., Melanie, Lizz and Cody, Rebecca and Elisabeth Pierce, and Tim.

To Mom and Dad, thank you for encouraging a love for reading since I was a kid and supporting whatever creative endeavors I embark on. To Jess, for the notebook passing co-writing days of high school. To Nicole, for staying up to read this book and saying it would make a good movie. To Hannah, for supporting and sharing this book. To Matt, for letting me borrow your headphones years ago and not asking for them back yet. To V, for saying, "that's really cool!" when I told you I was writing a book, and for the days you sat in the loft with me to "work on our nobels." To S, for inspiring a name in this book and giving me the best reaction when you first saw my author photo on the hardcover.

To Alicia, Annie, Mackenzie, Michele, Rachelle, and Savannah—thank you for the laughter at book launches and birthday parties, for the supportive gifs and exclamatory text messages, and for pursuing your dreams and encouraging me to pursue mine. You're part of why I started dreaming bigger for my writing again. I love and appreciate each of you for that and more!

To Lizz, for being one of my best friends and most enthusiastic supporters throughout this process. Thank you for the first art piece inspired by this book! To Megan, for inspiring me to pursue my God-given passions with courage and for all the adventures over the years. To Rebecca, for your support and encouragement in this and so many other endeavors.

To Grant and Melissa, for the supportive smiles every time you came home to find teenage me writing in your living room on the nights I babysat your girls. To Ms. Bedford, for telling middle school me that you thought I could be a professional writer; here I am. Thank you for submitting *Ralph* for an award instead of sending me to the guidance counselor. To Ms. King, for seeing my potential and teaching me advanced English beyond our curriculum. I am happy to report I now understand passive voice, even if I still use it sometimes. And for being willing to read the fanfiction of my early teen years, God bless you.

And to you, reader, for diving into *Smoke and Light* with me. It means the world to me that you're here reading Khara's story. I hope it stirs your heart to remember who you are when you've forgotten and serves as a reminder that no matter where you are, you can always come home.

About the Author

KRISTIN ARDIS writes emotional YA/NA fantasy books for those who believe in hopeful endings and the enduring power of love. Her stories take place in magical worlds where resilient characters must grapple with who they are and find their way home to themselves. When she's not immersed in twisting tropes or curating a playlist for her next book, she's probably enjoying her second cup of tea, living her best aunt life, or hiking the wooded trails at her favorite park. She'll be the one staring at trees, taking photos, and typing story notes on her phone whenever inspiration strikes.

Sign up for her emails at kristinardisbooks.com to receive exclusive bonus content, sneak peeks, and the kind of conversations you'd have over a cup of tea.

Connect with her on social media @kristinardisbooks.